Erin

& Oliver

By Marjorie Joseph

Higher Ground Books & Media

Springfield, Ohio.

http://highergroundbooksandmedia.com

Printed in the United States of America 2020

CHAPTER ONE

The pulse of the District Attorney's office was bustling and energetic. The Assistant to the DA, David Reed, the prosecutors, the deputy attorneys and legal reps were in top form. All were immersed in work, talking on the phone to potential clients, drawing up documents, and bragging about their cases as they often did. Erin Brasfield stalled outside Oliver Wright's office. Oliver was Silver County's new DA. Her heart thrashed nervously in her chest, she felt flustered, and butterflies were in the pit of her stomach.

It should not have been this difficult to approach Oliver, but for Erin it was gut-wrenching. Oliver Baron Wright had been appointed the District Attorney for all of Silver County, encompassing the districts of Silver Water, Georgia. He'd only held the office for a short while. However, Oliver was such a natural at his new job, it was almost as if he'd been born to enforce the law and prosecute heinous felons.

The thirty-four-year-old District Attorney was not only brilliant, but he was licentiously good-looking-one of Silver Water's most coveted bachelors. Standing at 6'3", coffee skin, dark wavy hair, light brown eyes and the perfect body, Oliver was a dream man. Notwithstanding, he was the complete package. Aside from his good looks and success, he was an amazing person. It was impossible to ignore how thoughtful, caring, faithful, generous and even philanthropic he was. Moreover, no one argued more convincingly in the courtroom and was tougher on crime.

So, with all of Oliver's wonderful attributes, it should not have been such a challenge for Erin to walk into his office to have a word with him. She and Oliver had been friends for years. They were also a part of the same church family. Both attended *Deliverance Tabernacle*. Given their history, it should have been a cakewalk to address him. However, Erin's heart twisted in knots over the thought of facing Oliver again. Prior to the election, Erin had cut back her hours working as a Paralegal for a law firm in downtown Silver Ledge in order to volunteer her services for Oliver's campaign.

Shortly after his appointment as DA, Oliver had hired her to

work through the DA's office. However, on that Friday afternoon in
December, Erin had paperwork to hand in to her boss regarding a
domestic violence case. The DA's office was seeking prosecution
for the offender, and none of the attorneys involved were leaving any
stone unturned. In addition to law documents, she also had written
out her letter of resignation, which she planned to tender to her boss
and *friend* that afternoon.

With Christmas about two weeks away, Erin was still nursing
a broken heart. She'd opened up her heart to Oliver and had
admitted to having feelings for him. Erin closed her eyes and
cringed in embarrassment to recall the night they'd gone out to
dinner. In a gentlemanly manner, Oliver had walked her to her front
door. Erin had taken a chance and had pressed a kiss to his
tantalizing mouth. However, when she'd leaned in for a deeper kiss,
Oliver had respectfully pulled away. At the time Erin had felt
hopeful that he'd been ready to turn a corner from his breakup with
Kennedy Proctor-Bohm in the spring. Kennedy had married
Billionaire Mogul Kayden Bohm. Erin knew Oliver's history with
Kennedy. He'd been in love with her for a very long time prior to
the breakup.

Erin had stepped in and had offered Oliver a shoulder to lean
on in the aftermath of the failed relationship with Kennedy. Erin
had gone out with Oliver a few times during his campaign bid. In
fact, they had even attended a few socials and black-tie events
together. For all intents and purposes, it seemed as if Oliver had
been ready to move on, but Erin was wrong.

The memories of Oliver's kind rejection still resonated in her
thoughts. *"Erin, you have no idea how flattered I am that you feel
that way about me. A man should be so lucky…"* Oliver had kept a
firm grasp on Erin's shoulders, as he'd delved meaningfully into her
eyes. *"Believe me when I say that it means a great deal that you feel
so strongly about me."* His face had creased in hurt, and he'd
shaken his head in the negative. *"But, honestly, my heart isn't at a
very good place right now. I can't offer you the kind of commitment
you're looking for."*

Erin had tried to counter, *"I'm not necessarily looking for a
commitment, Ollie. I just want to spend more time together, and see*

where our friendship goes," she had established. Telling Oliver she wasn't looking for a steady relationship had gone against her core beliefs. Erin had been compromising, because she'd wanted to be with him so badly. As a Christian woman, a *commitment* was the *only* thing she was looking for.

"Erin, you're beautiful, smart, funny and so much more. You deserve a lot more than half a heart. And, you certainly shouldn't be anyone's alternative," Oliver had argued. His perfect face had contorted, pertained. Nevertheless, he'd been firm in his resolve.

"You're still in love with Kennedy, aren't you?" Erin had decried, feeling defeated. Things weren't supposed to pan out this way. She had prayed and had waited for God to work in and through her circumstances with Oliver. She had even submitted to fasting.

Erin's former best friend Anika had advised her to engage in witchcraft in order to *snag* Oliver. However, Erin had chosen to denounce her friendship with Anika, and had repudiated her ungodly advice. Rather, Erin had chosen to press in and to pray on the matter, because she was totally in love. Still, on the night in question, Oliver had made it clear that friendship was the only thing he was interested in.

"There will always be a special place in my heart for Kennedy," he'd told Erin. *"However, I have accepted the fact that she isn't in the will of God for my life. It wouldn't matter if I was still in love with her or not. That ship has sailed,"* Oliver had explained. *"The sad part is that I was so sure about our connection. Erin, things being what they are, I'm not looking to jump into another relationship."* Tears had gleamed in Oliver's eyes. *"I am trusting God to bring the right person into my life, but it isn't something that I'm actively looking for. I've just jumped out of the frying pan...."* Oliver had expounded, stroking fondly on Erin's cheek.

"Not all risks pan out the same. It sounds to me as if you're ready to give up," Erin had assessed with tears in *her* eyes. Despite the arguments, Erin had longed to feel Oliver's arms around her. She was still praying, but wasn't sure what God was telling her at that point. God had not shown her that Oliver *wasn't* in His will.

Regardless, Oliver had made it clear. *She* wasn't the one who would help piece the broken pieces of his heart in the aftermath of the failed relationship with Kennedy Proctor-Bohm.

"Erin, you're wrong. I'm not giving up. I'm just taking a little time to mend after... well after that experience," Oliver had been totally honest. He'd hunched down and had pressed a kiss to Erin's cheek. *"I'm carrying so much baggage, and I don't want to burden you,"* he'd said.

"Nothing about our relationship is a burden to me. But I can't make you see things my way, neither can I... I understand your reluctance to try again so soon," Erin had submitted, blinking back tears. That night, Erin had waited for Oliver to dismount the steps of her house out in *Silver Leaf Falls*. She'd watched him hop into his car and drive away. The moment he'd driven away, Erin had shut her front door, pressed up to it, and had crumbled in dejection.

Since *that* night she and Oliver hadn't really spent any *real* time alone. Erin had seen him around the office but had kept it low key. The truth was that being around Oliver had become awkward to say the least. Erin couldn't deny the fact that she loved him. And even if she hadn't given up hope, it was sheer torture seeing him every day, while contending with such strong feelings. Nevertheless, Erin would continue praying for God's will and His plan in respect to Oliver. She trusted God for the answers, even they weren't the ones she wanted.

Erin wanted Oliver in every way a woman could want a man. In the wake of the epiphany they'd had on the night in question, Oliver had also pulled away. Their constant talking and texting had all but abated. Erin struggled not to connect to Oliver whenever she saw him around the office. It also didn't help that most of the women in Silver County were virtually throwing themselves at him. It was difficult enough having to attend church together. However, for Erin, seeing Oliver strut into the DA's office in all of his glory on a regular basis, only added to her misery.

That afternoon, in spite of the inner conflict, Erin said a prayer, and courageously took steps towards Oliver's office.

Hammering heart and all, she deliberated before diffidently knocking on the door.

"Come in," she heard Oliver's muffled tone through the door.

Erin cautiously opened the office door and popped her head through.

Oliver was preoccupied on the phone. However, he smiled and gestured for Erin to come in.

Erin reluctantly stepped foot inside of Oliver's lavish office. Offering a faint smile, she watched him pace around his desk. Erin's heart raced all the more, noticing how incredible Oliver looked in his tan-colored business suit with matching accents. For all intents and purposes, he was modeling business attire, as he traipsed busily over the plush rust-colored carpeting. His stalwart arms flexed involuntarily with every motion of his graceful body.

Erin gulped nervously doing all she could not to stare. It was truly an exercise in self-control. She slipped into the leather armchair across from Oliver's desk. Every time their eyes met, Oliver smiled warmly at her. Malaise, Erin smiled back, as heat rose to the pores of her skin and tingled. Her heart kept skipping a beat, and the butterflies were in the hollow of her stomach.

"You're absolutely right, Will. I'll have my top prosecutor on the case today. For me, it's personal. It's an offense of the worst kind," Oliver said passionately over the phone. "We're seeking the maximum sentence for the homicide." Oliver's face creased in criticalness. "Of course. My assistant, David Reed, will also be coming out to your office first thing Monday morning. Absolutely..." Oliver gave an affirming nod. "You have my word. Will do... You have a great weekend as well. Bye," Oliver finalized.

"I'm sorry I didn't mean to interrupt," Erin began to say. Suddenly having Oliver's undivided attention was a little unnerving for Erin. His eyes were already delving hers.

"Not at all," Oliver reassured with an open smile. "I'm never too busy for *you*." He walked over, taking his place behind the desk in his armchair. "How are you? It's been a minute since we've actually seen each other," he said amiable.

Erin's smile was plastic, as she forced herself to maintain eye contact. "I guess it *has* been a while since we've seen each other, but that's to be expected. It goes with the territory. You're responsible for everything that goes wrong in Silver County. That's a pretty heavy load," Erin rationalized.

"You're certainly right about that. Still, I am so grateful to God for opening up this door for me," Oliver assessed. "It's a privilege to serve the good people of Silver County," he said confidently.

"Listen to *you* sounding like the proverbial Boys Scout," Erin teased.

Oliver chuckled. "Believe me it isn't intentional. I might add that I couldn't have gotten here without you," he said kindly. "Thank you for your hard work and unfailing support." His face warped in gratitude.

"You're welcome," Erin said graciously. "Your record pretty much spoke for itself. There wasn't anyone better suited for this office. I'm also discovering that you're no joke when it comes to upholding the law."

"Oh, that...?" Oliver razzed, "I'm as harmless as a lamb." He smiled curiously.

"Right... Okay, if you say so," Erin quipped, but the moment was fleeting. She kept reminding herself that she was there to regain some of the power she'd lost because she was totally lost in love with him. Pulling back at all costs was her goal.

"You have paperwork for me?" Oliver asked noticing the file in Erin's hand.

"Yes, this is from Roland Laurie who will be working on the Shaw Case," Erin informed trying to remain professional. She extended the folder over to Oliver.

"Thank you," Oliver told her. Taking the file, he immediately began perusing what was inside. He frowned in urgency as he reviewed the document. "So far it looks good. Of course, I'll have to go over the details with Roland first thing Monday, but this is a great start!" Oliver looked up and gave Erin an affirming smile.

"There is something else…," Erin said hesitantly, avidly searching Oliver's amber eyes. Feeling so disconnected from him was unnatural when they'd been so close in months past. Oliver had taken her out to lunch, dinner, and had even danced with her at a few socials leading up to the election. And now, it seemed as if none of it had ever happened-at least that's the way it seemed on Oliver's end. Erin, on the other hand, couldn't get her heart to stop skipping a beat, her body to stop sweltering, and the butterflies to stop just because they were in the same room.

"Is there something wrong, Erin?" Oliver's face wrinkled in concern.

"Not really. I just wanted to give you this." Erin shakily extended her letter of resignation over to her boss.

Perturbed, Oliver took the letter Erin tendered. His face fell in disappointment and hurt. "What…? You don't want to work here anymore?" he questioned, bewildered.

"I'm sorry if it seems as if I'm bailing on you so soon. You just took office a little while ago," Erin reasoned.

Oliver's face warped in despondency as he set the letter on his desk. Pulling out of the armchair, he walked around the desk in order to connect to Erin.

Daunted, Erin immediately stood to her feet as he drew closer. At that point they were only inches away and facing each other. Their eyes locked intently. "I realize that a two-week notice for this office isn't much notice at all…," she stammered, gulping. Erin stared up into Oliver's face and marveled. Being that close to him again felt overwhelming. Moreover, his clean, musky scent was enticing.

"Erin, are you leaving because of me?" Oliver asked straightforwardly, as his eyes searched hers.

"Oh, no. Not at all," Erin said, eyes wandering away from his intent stare.

"Erin," Oliver prompted her to look at him, "if you've come to this decision based on what happened that night, I'm asking you to please reconsider. You're such an asset to this office. The truth is that we'd be lost without you around here," he admitted. Taking a moment of pause he sighed. "Regardless, the last thing I would want is for you to feel uncomfortable working here. *Are* you uncomfortable around me?" he asked, probing her eyes.

Erin nodded in earnest. "I would be lying if I said that I wasn't." Her head slumped, and she played nervously with her fingers. "I told you how I feel that night. I totally respect your decision, but it isn't easy seeing you every day, being around you...," Erin admitted. She finally allowed her eyes to explore Oliver's heavenly face.

"Erin, I'm so sorry," Oliver said in earnest. "You're a very dear friend, and I apologize that my drama has caused you pain. You didn't do *anything* wrong. You're perfect." He placed his hand caringly to the side of her face and stroked warmly on her cheek.

"The truth is that under different circumstances, a beautiful woman telling me she cares about me, would be a dream come true. Wanting to distance yourself is something I understand completely. I can't say that I blame you for wanting to move on. Nonetheless, *I* would be less than truthful if I said that I hadn't hoped you'd stick around. Our friendship means a great deal to me."

The feel of Oliver's gentle hand brushing her cheek was too much for Erin. So, she gently shied away from his addictive touch. "I'd like to stay friends too, Ollie, but I think it's best if we stayed friends from a distance," Erin's voice undulated, and tears gleamed in her eyes. Irrespective of the inner turmoil, she realized that it was only by God's strength that she'd been able to tell Oliver the truth. Everything in her cried out for him. However, none of it mattered if *he* didn't feel the same way.

Oliver nodded sadly and acquiesced. "If that's what you want... However, would you be willing to work through another office downtown?" he quizzed, hopefully.

Erin shook her head in the negative. "I'll be fine, Ollie. I'm sure God will order my steps, and direct me to where he wants me to be." She continued to ogle covetously at Oliver, but Erin grasped that she would *truly* need to let go, so that God could have His way.

"Okay," Oliver ceded, disappointed. He and Erin had been good friends, and the thought of not having her around affected him a lot more than he was even willing to admit. "Erin, if there's anything I can do for you-anything at all-don't hesitate." His eyes explored hers sensitively.

Erin nodded. "I won't hesitate, but I *will* be around for the next two weeks or so. So, we'll probably see each other from time to time," she reminded him.

"Erin, could you do something for me?" Oliver impressed weightily.

"Of course," Erin affirmed.

"Can you promise not to leave until after Christmas? It would break my heart not having you around for Christmas," he appealed.

Erin forced a smile and nodded compliantly. "Okay. Does that mean you accept my letter of resignation, DA Wright?" Erin asked on a lighter note. Inwardly, she was faltering. The thought of having to pull away from Oliver for *any* reason was tearing her apart.

"Do I have a choice?" Oliver asked, thwarted.

"I'm afraid the choice is pretty clear in this matter."

Oliver nodded silently. "Again, if you need me…"

"I'll be fine, Ollie," Erin reassured. "Thanks for sitting with me this afternoon." She issued a dejected smile and continued to pull away. It took all of the restraint she had not to reach up and bridge her lips to Oliver's, but Erin staunchly resisted.

Starting for the door, Erin felt Oliver hot on her heels. When she twisted the knob and opened up the door, she turned towards him again. He was standing in very close proximity again. "Thank you for understanding," Erin said again.

"Of course," Oliver told her. "Thank you for being upfront with me."

"That's the one thing I've always admired about our friendship-that we can be completely transparent."

"I agree." Oliver stared longingly at Erin.

Erin turned to leave. She needed to get away from him. Having him so close, and not be able to touch him was cruel. "Have a nice weekend, Ollie."

Oliver lingered at the door watching Erin walk away. "You too," he said. For a moment he stood there feeling totally conflicted.

Erin could feel the weight of Oliver's gape, as she sauntered down the hallway, drifting out to the busy office area. It was nice that he cared, but the last thing she wanted or needed was his pity. That Friday afternoon Erin avoided seeing Oliver around the office at all costs. Luckily, Oliver left not even half an hour after their talk. He had a meeting with a local congressman.

Fortunately, the coast was clear by the time Erin hopped into her SUV early Friday evening. She needed to get home. Once there, she would slip out of her work clothes, change into comfortable house clothes and surrender to her knees. In the presence of her heavenly father, she could interpret her heartache, as He was the only One who *truly* understood. She had no clue how to stop loving and wanting Oliver. However, she trusted that God had a plan and a solution for her excruciating set of circumstances.

***

Oliver got in from work early Friday evening feeling totally exhausted. His work as the new DA of Silver County had taken its toll. Between attending hearings, filing brief memorandums and writing out recommendations for potential prison parolees, it was difficult to find a moment. However, immersing himself in work was exactly what he needed. It meant less time to think about other things. Moreover, it left very little time to contemplate the fact that the woman he'd loved for over seven years had chosen *to do life* with another man. Kennedy had chosen Kayden Bohm, and they were now married. And, in light of everything in social media, the couple seemed to be ridiculously happy.

As Oliver loosened his tie and stepped into his bedroom, thoughts of being with Kennedy overwhelmed him. It was challenging not to tear up every time he thought about losing her. Remembering how it felt to be close to Kennedy, the sound of her voice, how it felt to hold her in his arms and kiss her, always brought tears to his eyes. Oliver had honestly believed that he was over Kennedy. They'd split amicably. Kennedy had been his date and had supported him for one of the biggest fundraisers of his campaign last spring.

Moreover, Oliver had attended her wedding. In fact, Erin Brasfield had not only agreed to be his date for the wedding, they'd had a blast dancing the night away at the reception. Notwithstanding, he and Erin had also attended several other black tie, campaign-related events. Oliver had tried wholeheartedly to move on since Kennedy had chosen Kayden.

On some level Oliver had always sensed that he would not have had Kennedy in his life for very long. However, he'd been hopeful. Erin had been such a great friend during that difficult chapter of his life. Oliver cared about Erin a great deal. He cared far too much to offer her anything less than his entire heart. The half-broken heart he was still nursing wasn't something he could extend.

Now that he had a moment to process, it bothered him that Erin wanted to quit her job at the office. Still, he had to allow her to do what she thought was best. If he couldn't offer her anything more than friendship, he needed to let her go. And yet, having made peace with that concept, the thought of not having Erin around at the turn of the New Year, rattled Oliver a great deal. Nevertheless, he would have to find a way to deal.

Oliver peeled off his work clothes and changed into a pair of black sweats and a burgundy T-shirt he'd had since law school. He'd ordered a pizza on his way home that night. Having pizza would be his only meal since having had breakfast earlier on. Hopefully, it would only be a few minutes before his *Uber Eats* deliver arrived. Crossing over into the kitchen, he opened up the fridge, and pulled out a bottle of water. Thirstier than he realized, it took less than a minute to down the entire bottle. He opened up the trash bin and placed the bottle into the recycle bag. As he did, the doorbell rang.

Thinking it was his pizza delivery, Oliver rushed out to the front door, opening it up eagerly. However, the messenger beyond it just wasn't who he thought it would be. His face stretched in a cordial smile when he saw Lilianna Pederson. She was the beautiful, over-forty, recently separated neighbor, whose apartment was down the hall from his. "Hello, Lilly," Oliver greeted temperately.

Oliver knew that Lilianna was romantically interested in him. Since separating from her husband, Lilly had hinted that she wanted him to take her out. Lilly was nice, but Oliver had mixed feelings about their connection. "What's going on?" he asked spiritedly. Being anything less than affable wasn't something Oliver was terribly keen at. Besides, his parents had taught him to be kind in every situation.

"Hello, Ollie," Lilly said, eying Oliver as one would dessert inside of a display case. "Sorry to bother you, but I'm not really that handy. My husband Jack used to handle all of these little annoyances."

"What's going on?" Oliver asked concerned. "Is everything alright?"

"Sure," Lilly said, "my entire living room curtain just fell." There was a pleading yet ambiguous expression on her face. "Can you come over and help me put it back up?" Lilly explored the contours of Oliver's rugged body, virtually X-raying every aspect of him.

Oliver chuckled and shook his head nonsensically. "Of course I can." His face wrinkled in uncertainty. "I have pizza coming…," he began to explain.

"Oh, I'm sorry. Silly me, here I am interrupting your evening," Lilly said only half-apologetic.

"No, don't be silly. It's fine. As soon as my delivery gets here…" Oliver didn't get to finish his statement. He saw the elevator doors part just down the hallway, and a young guy stepped off carrying a pizza box. "And there he is," Oliver said.

"Great," Lilly cheered, seeing the pizza delivery guy only feet away. Before long she watched Oliver sign the receipt, and tip the delivery guy. "I really didn't mean to be a nuisance," Lilly said following behind Oliver inside of his place.

Oliver drifted into the kitchen and rested the pizza on his eclectic and spacious Island counter. "Not at all, Lilly," he turned and told the woman with a smile.

Lilly took in Oliver's state-of-the-art and pristine living space. It was the first time she'd been inside of his apartment, and she was beyond impressed. His place was *almost* as beautiful as *he* was, and she hoped it wouldn't be the last time she would get to visit. "Your place is really nice, Oliver! We've been neighbors for years, and this is the first time I'm actually in here."

Oliver smiled and shook his head nonsensically. "Thank you. Are you all set? We can go get a look at that curtain…"

"Well, if you're hungry I should really let you eat first. *Are* you hungry?" she asked, crossing over to where Oliver was standing.

"Actually, I *am*. With my schedule it's kind of difficult to find the time," he explained.

"I can only imagine what your desk must look like as the new DA of Silver County," Lilly's voice was silken as she inched in closer to him.

Oliver took cautious steps back in retreat. "Would you like to join me?" he extended staring down at his pizza box. Inwardly, he felt conflicted, because he didn't want to get into any compromising situations with Lilly, and yet Oliver sensed that it was exactly what *she* wanted.

"Oh, that's awful sweet of you. I would love a slice of pizza." Lilianna made herself completely at home. She found plates in the cupboard. She then set slices of pizza on a plate for Oliver and set one on a plate for herself.

Oliver stood back and watched this beautiful woman-who must have been at least ten to twelve years his senior-move about in his kitchen as if she lived there. Inwardly, Oliver prayed and asked God for wisdom in the situation. *How was it that he always found himself in these types of situations?* Oliver realized that he was just way too nice and welcoming. He chided himself for being much too friendly and resolved to do better. *How had he gone from anticipating a quiet night alone to entertaining Lilly?*

"So, I told him to pack up his stuff and leave. I refused to allow him to continue making a fool of me-flaunting his affair in my face," Lilly explained why she finally separated from her husband Jack, while she and Oliver finished up their pizzas and sodas.

"Well, I can't say I blame you for making such a tough decision. Having someone to share your life with is great, but love and respect go hand in hand," Oliver upheld.

"That's right. Just because you love someone doesn't mean they get to abuse you," Lilly added.

Oliver nodded in agreement. He sat there with his balled fists supporting his chin at the counter and smiling until his face hurt. All the while he kept trying to find a way to redirect Lilly to the reason why she'd come over in the first place. The sooner he could help her put the downed curtain back in its place, the sooner he'd be able to regain his solitude. "I'm truly sorry your husband behaved that way,

Lilly. In my opinion, some men just don't *deserve* to be married."
Oliver offered an encouraging smile.

"What about you, Ollie?" Lilly reached over and grasped
Oliver's hand in hers. She stroked on it fondly. Opening up
Oliver's right palm, she began delineating the lines with her fingers.
"Why aren't *you* married?" She stared dreamily into his eyes.

Oliver unobtrusively reclaimed his hand. "I guess I haven't
found the right person yet," he said generically. Hopping off of the
stool, he collected their plates, and placed them into the kitchen sink.
Oliver made a sudden turn, and found Lilly standing virtually on top
of him.

"I'm *sure* you *will* meet the right person soon." She smiled,
standing so close to Oliver she could discern the beating of his heart.
"You forgot the glasses." She held up their empty soda glasses.

"Oh… Thanks." Oliver stepped aside and allowed Lilly to
place the glasses into the sink. "I know that I will, but things are a
bit hectic for me now," Oliver said, taking respectable steps away
from Lilly. "My schedule was exacting before, but things are even
more complicated now that I've taken office," he expounded.

"I can only imagine." Lilly followed behind Oliver. She
grabbed the soda bottle from off of the counter and put it back into
the refrigerator.

Oliver sighed, relieved for a bit of breathing space.

Lilly shut the fridge but turned to face him and offered an
alluring smile.

"Are you all set? I can go and see about that curtain now,"
Oliver reminded with an amiable expression on his face.

"Yes, of course…" Lilly laughed awkwardly. "After all, that
is the reason I came over in the first place. Thank you for dinner,"
she said. Lilly gaped at Oliver like someone who'd been living on
the moon for years, and he was the first person she'd encountered in
the aftermath of total isolation.

"You're welcome! Thank you for joining me. You saved me

from eating alone." Oliver marched out of the kitchen and took his time to cross over to the front door.

"It was my pleasure," Lilly said, taking in the apartment one last time. Passing through the living room, she noticed that he hadn't yet put up a Christmas tree. Lilly followed behind Oliver to the front door. Before they walked out, she queried, "No Christmas tree yet?"

"Unfortunately, I haven't had the time," Oliver admitted. Opening up the door, he stepped out into the hallway. He waited for Lilly to step out of his place before he shut the door closed.

Lilly fell into step with him, as they trudged over to her place. "If you need someone to help you put up the tree, it would be my pleasure." She gave Oliver a meaningful sidelong look.

"That's a very kind offer. And if I happen to find the time, I just might take you up on it." Oliver looked down at the pretty woman and smiled. He couldn't say that he wasn't stirred that she was going out of her way to connect to him. What Lilly and *all* other women who'd tried to get close weren't aware of was that his heart was splintered. It had shattered on the night Kennedy told him that she wanted to be with someone else.

Oliver cautiously dismounted the step ladder after straightening out Lilly's curtain rod, and properly positioning the curtains. He'd helped her push back her sofa in order to make the repair. He'd just stepped foot on the carpeting, when he felt the warmth of her body near him again-in the same way he'd experienced it in his kitchen a while ago. Oliver made an instinctive turn, but found himself enveloped in Lilly's arms. "I don't think the curtain will fall again," he reassured her. Oliver felt malaise, and his cheeks reddened in embarrassment.

"Uh-huh," Lilly said mesmerized. She draped her arms around Oliver's neck. "You're absolutely perfect," she said entranced. "Thank you for coming over and helping," she said looking as if she'd just been placed under hypnosis.

Oliver laughed. "You're welcome!"

"I like you a lot, Oliver."

Oliver tried to handle the matter delicately. She was a nice woman, and he didn't want to make matters worse in the wake of her recent separation. "I like *you*, Lilly, but-

"I've been so lonely since Jack left. Don't *you* get lonely sometimes?" Her face wrinkled in jeopardy.

Oliver gently removed her arms from about his neck. "Yes, I do get lonely at times. Still," he shook his head in the negative, "I'm really not looking to get into a relationship right now." He subtly moved away. "I'm sorry, Lilly. It has *nothing* to do with you. I think you're beautiful! The truth is that I think your ex-husband is a total idiot, but-"

"I used to see you with that pretty woman not too long ago. Ken-" Lilly remarked with a face creased in uncertainty.

"Her name was *Kennedy*," Oliver corrected.

"I know she married that billionaire guy. They're on social media all the time. She hurt your heart, didn't she?" Lilly pursued Oliver to the front door and stood there facing him.

"I've got to get going, Lilly. I'm glad I could help with the curtains."

Lilly nodded with a sad expression on her face. Realizing that Oliver's head was in a totally different space, she opened up the front door.

"Goodnight," Oliver told her.

"Oliver…?" Lilly called after him as he began to drift away.

Oliver turned. "Yes…?"

"You said that you think Jack is an idiot. Well, I think Kennedy made a big mistake by letting you go." Lilly offered an encouraging smile.

"I appreciate you saying that," Oliver's voice was gravelly. He gave Lilly a faint smile and continued down the hallway to his place.

***

Later back at his place, Oliver had devotions. Pouring out his heart to God, he waited in the stillness to hear from his Heavenly Father. Opening up the word of God, Oliver was led to a passage of scripture. It was from the book of Philippians 3:13, "Brethren, I count not myself to have apprehended: but this one thing I do, forgetting those things which are behind, and reaching forth unto those things which are before…" (KJV) The Spirit of God highlighted the part in respect to *forgetting the past*. Isaiah 43:18-19 was also brought to mind. "Remember not the former things neither consider the things of old. Behold, I will do a new thing, now it shall spring forth; shall you not know it?"

Oliver questioned in what regard he was to forget about the past. The impression he received just then was that he was to forget about his past relationship. It was imperative that he let Kennedy go. Oliver argued that he *had*, because she'd married someone else. However, the message resonated that even if Kennedy belonged to someone else, he was still holding on. Tearfully, Oliver submitted to the conviction of God's Spirit, and cried out for God's help.

Loving Kennedy had been the one immutable factor in his life for close to eight years. Now that she was gone, moving forward seemed too difficult a task for him to face. However, Oliver resolved to be obedient to God even if it was hard. Notwithstanding, the Lord highlighted how unwise it had been to entertain Lilly at his place.

The message resonated that Lilly Pederson wasn't in the will of God for his life. The obvious reason being that she was still a married woman. Even if Oliver had no idea *how* to move forward, he trusted that God would guide him every step of the way. He deemed that if he was willing to be obedient, maybe God would do a brand-new work in his life and heal his broken heart.

As Oliver slipped into bed that Friday night, he did his best to push away all business-related matters. There was so much he had to do, including scheduling a meeting with the Attorney General in the upcoming week. However, the one factor he couldn't lock away to a corner of his mind was Erin. Oliver had checked his phone all night in the hopes that she'd called or texted, but neither had happened. Oliver tussled with the emptiness of not hearing from her. Once upon a time they'd chatted and texted all the time. He acquiesced to the fact that he missed her.

Suddenly, it dawned on Oliver that maybe getting a Christmas tree was one sure way of dispelling the melancholy in his life. Christmas was a little over two weeks away, and he'd gotten so caught up with work that he'd neglected to do anything fun. That seemed to be the story of his life. The idea picked up momentum when he contemplated going out to one of his favorite tree lots in the area. They had the most beautiful spruces! Oliver also considered throwing a Christmas bash for the staff down at the DA's office.

Still, the thought of not having Erin to help him pick out a tree, or to help plan the party, took the wind right out of Oliver's sails. With the lights dimmed in his bedroom, he cradled his phone and deliberated about calling or texting Erin. She had been his right-hand person all throughout the campaign. Erin was a fantastic organizer. Notwithstanding, her spirited personality was absolutely infectious! And, up until that very moment, Oliver had not realized just how much he'd come to depend on her.

Thus, her decision to leave the DA's office had affected him a lot more than he realized. Conversely, he wasn't a selfish man. He was in no place to offer Erin what she needed. So, Oliver refused to lead her on just because *he* had a broken heart and was extremely lonely. Because he *genuinely* cared about Erin, his *desires* had to take a backseat to her *needs*. Oliver sighed with a sense of resignation. Silencing the ringer on his phone, he closed his eyes, and allowed himself to drift off to sleep. Perhaps, in the morning, he would find the motivation to go out to the tree lot.

CHAPTER TWO

"DA Wright, you've got to promise me that you're going get justice for Noel. I know my boy wasn't perfect, but to be gunned down like some animal out in the street..." Roberta Warner's face warped in misery, and she surrendered to tears.

Tears shone in Oliver's eyes, as he collected her into his arms in comfort. "I'm so sorry, Mrs. Warner, so deeply sorry for your loss," Oliver mitigated. "I promise to do everything in my power to ensure that the ones responsible for Noel's death, don't get away with it." He pulled back to stare into Mrs. Warner's eyes and set his hands caringly on her shoulders.

"Do you promise me?" she exacted. "They have no idea what they've taken away from me. I can't believe how evil the kids of this generation are...," she muttered as tears teemed over her eyelids.

"Look at me," Oliver stated urgently, "I will exact justice for Noel. His murderers will stand trial and be prosecuted for what they've done." Oliver's eyes lowered into hers critically. "Now, I need for you to be strong while I work this out," he told her. "I am working *personally* on the case, so you've got to hang tough for me for just a little longer." Oliver cradled the side of her face.

"I wish that I could go back in time. I would keep Noel from going to that party, but I can't," she said reflectively.

"I'm sorry that I *can't* give your son back to you, Mrs. Warner. But I can do the next best thing. I can make sure that those who are responsible for murdering him won't be able to hurt anyone else. When you lay your head on your pillow at night, you'll sleep soundly knowing that the streets of Silver County are a little bit safer," Oliver explained.

Mrs. Warner nodded and wiped the tears away from her eyes. "Thank you, DA Wright. Thank you for fighting this battle alongside me. I know that you've made bringing Noel's murderers to justice a top priority."

"Exacting justice for Noel *is* a top priority," Oliver affirmed. "And I'm glad you came in today. Feel free to call me anytime you need to," he extended sincerely. Mrs. Warner had been through hell ever since her son was murdered weeks ago. As the DA for Silver County, Oliver was dedicated to ensuring that the members of the community remained safe. So, in that regard, he couldn't help feeling as if he'd in some way failed Mrs. Warner. Regardless of the tragedy, he was doing everything he could to alleviate her burden and to help her through the ordeal.

"So, you *will* keep me informed on the progress you're making every step of the way?" she asked, apprehensive.

"That is my promise to you. I will keep you abreast of everything that's happening every step of the way," Oliver avowed.

"Thank you so much for everything you're doing, DA Wright," she emphasized, exploring his eyes. "You're a good man and the right one for the job!" She offered a faint smile.

"You can thank me when Noel's murderers are behind bars," Oliver upheld.

Mrs. Warner smiled a bit more openly. "I will thank you then too." She wrapped her arms around Oliver and squeezed him in gratitude.

Oliver crushed her in his arms. "You've got our total support-anything you need," he consoled.

Oliver walked her over to his office door. "You should never apologize for needing to come here. We're here for you," Oliver told her.

"I know that. It means a lot more than you know." Mrs. Warner stood in the doorway facing him.

"I will give you a call next week to fill you in on the details. I have to meet with the judge on Tuesday morning," Oliver told her.

"Okay." She smiled. "Thank you."

"No worries." Oliver smiled in return.

"Bye," Mrs. Warner told him just before she veered, and began heading down the hallway.

Oliver's heart went out to the woman. He'd been called into the office early Saturday to handle two separate cases. One case had to do with the murder of a teenage boy shot by a local gang out in Silver City. The other had to do with a teenage boy who'd stolen a car and had gone on a drunken joyride with friends. Mrs. Warner's son Noel had been murdered by a group of boys, while he was walking home from a party a few weeks ago.

Darren Dockery had gone on a drunken joyride with his friends. His mom had stopped by pleading for her son not to be arraigned. Oliver was working on it and trying to offer up alternate ways in which Darren could repay his debt to society-as he had no past history of criminal behaviors.

Oliver checked his phone as he worked on a number of law documents. It was almost two in the afternoon. He guffawed and shook his head nonsensically, because his plans for an uneventful Saturday had gone straight out the window. He'd been working since about eight that morning-mandated to handle a few pressing matters. Weekends were unpredictable, as he was beginning to realize. Only a handful of staff had come into work through the office on that day. Apparently, there were quite a few loose ends to tie up.

As Oliver worked, he looked across the room over at the window, and noticed the onset of snowfall. It was just a couple of weeks before Christmas, so the snow seemed fitting. Georgia weather was often capricious, but it seldom snowed in December. However, this was one of those rare days where the temperature had dipped below thirty degrees Fahrenheit, and the skies were overcast.

Oddly enough, Oliver had remarked sunny skies on his drive over to the office. He smiled thoughtfully seeing the arrival of snow. Despite the wispy and fluttery quality of the snowflakes, they seemed to be accumulating. It was then that Oliver remembered hearing snow forecasted over the news the day before. It was such an infrequent occurrence that the matter had slipped his mind.

Oliver wrapped up his work and set the documents into

folders. Standing to his feet, he drifted over to the window in order to get a better look. The snow was definitely beginning to come down. Through the window, the quiet locale with a few pedestrians sprinkled throughout, the surrounding office buildings, landmarks and trees, felt like looking into a snow globe.

He was definitely one of those sappy types who prayed for snow during the Christmas season. Crisp weather made Oliver yearn to be in front of a crackling fire. It was nostalgic and reminiscent of drinking hot chocolate with marshmallows on a snowy day when he was growing up in Michigan. He'd make snowmen with his friends, and then come in from the cold. Oliver was sentimental for simpler days. Those reflections evoked a hailstorm of memories about Kennedy.

It was difficult not to think about her, because he'd loved her for such a long time. In fact, he'd loved her a lot longer than their short-lived relationship. However, he was forced to remember that she no longer belonged to him. Notwithstanding, God had asked him to put the past behind him. Furthermore, it was sinful to entertain thoughts about Kennedy-as she was now a married woman. So, as much as he'd loved her, Oliver needed to let go.

Working through his tangled emotions, Oliver shut down his laptop, grabbed his coat and scarf and turned off the office lights. He shut the door and began treading down the hallway. Turning a corner in the direction of the general office, he froze in his tracks when he saw Erin using the copier. Oliver wasn't certain why he felt so overjoyed to see her. In her cream-colored sweater, gray dress slacks and stylish floral-print scarf, she looked absolutely breathtaking.

Oliver had seen Erin more than a dozen times. He'd even seen her dressed to the nines in ballroom attire. And yet, there was something very delicate about the way she looked that afternoon. With her lengthy hair out bouncing in curls framing her sweet face, she looked positively angelic. Erin had the face of a movie star. With skin the color of butterscotch and honey eyes, it was difficult not to notice her. Her tiny waist, long legs and curvy hips were the epitome of womanhood. In that instance, Oliver felt as if he were seeing her for the first time.

Smiling musingly, Oliver subtly closed in on Erin, and came to stand close to where she was using the machine. For one reason or another she was oblivious to his presence there. Oliver assessed that the main office's copier was a bit on the noisy side. "Hey there, stranger," he said, inching in even closer.

"Ollie!" Erin made a startled turn, totally shocked to see him. "I didn't know you'd be here this afternoon," she said still clutching her heart from shock. And there it was again, Erin's heart was thrashing, and the butterflies had returned with a vengeance, as she caught sight of Oliver's dreamy face. He looked positively ethereal in his cinnamon-colored sweater, black jeans and comfortable shoes. As *hot* and desirable as he was, there was a sense of conservatism about Oliver which was endearing.

Oliver shook his head contrarily, smiling. "*I* didn't even know that I would be here this afternoon. Sorry that I startled you," he said considerately, searching her glossy brown eyes. They shone like quartz stones. "I certainly didn't expect to see *you* around here so soon," he pointed out.

"Well, David asked me to go over the Grant motion, make copies, and fax the original document over to Silver City. I wanted to make sure that the party gets the paperwork first thing Monday morning," Erin explained. Standing in such close proximity to Oliver again was totally unnerving. Heat rose to the pores of Erin's skin, and made her feel flustered.

Erin was virtually melting again, as she stared longingly into his face. She was frazzled and had no idea what to make of this chance encounter. Just yesterday she had vowed to remain as far away from Oliver Wright as humanly possible. She had cried out to God for help so that she could put her friendship with Oliver behind her. But there he was again wreaking havoc on her heart and sparking the flame she'd willed to die over and again.

"Well, aren't *you* the dedicated one," Oliver uplifted. "I guess that's why it's going to be so hard to see you leave." His eyes lowered intuitively into Erin's.

"Oliver…" Erin stared reticently into his eyes, "we've already been through this."

"I *know*. Still, you can't blame a guy for trying." He smiled hopefully. "Will you be hanging around here for a little while longer?" he asked pertained.

"Actually, I was about to leave for the day," Erin said matter-of-factly, timidly giving Oliver the once, twice and thrice over.

"Oh, I was about to leave as well."

"Did you handle the things you need to?" Erin asked nervously. Her heart was whipping so loudly it resonated in her eardrums. She wondered if Oliver could hear it.

"I did…at least for today. I had a very productive meeting with Roberta Warner…"

"Oh, I *did* see her a while ago-poor woman." Erin shook her head in commiseration. "What happened to her son is beyond sad." Her face warped in melancholy.

"I know. It's such a tragedy. Noel had his entire life ahead of him, and now…" Oliver shook his head in empathy. "Well, that's why I'm doing my best to ensure that the perpetrators are prosecuted. It feels personal when a young person is gunned down in his or her prime," he said passionately.

Erin smiled seeing Oliver all fired up. His earnest concern for the wellbeing of others was only *one* of the many reasons why she loved him so much. "And I know that you're committed to giving nothing less than two hundred percent," she said softly, smiling into his eyes. "It's what you always do."

Oliver realized that he was in superhero mode again. He smiled quietly back at Erin. "You know me so well," he remarked, with cardinal cheeks.

Erin nodded. "You're a good person to know," she uplifted searching his eyes wonderingly. Realizing she was losing herself, Erin quickly gathered up the paperwork.

"And so are you," Oliver hunched, and connected to her eyes, as she picked up the copies to the side of the copier.

Erin's heart skipped a beat hearing Oliver's resonant voice so close to her ear. Regaining full stature again, she stared nervously into his eyes. "Any plans on this beautiful, snowy afternoon?" Erin felt like kicking herself for asking, but she'd blurted it out-feeling totally inept around the incredibly good-looking DA.

Oliver smiled and quietly explored her face and eyes. "Honestly, I had planned on going by *Blue Spruce Land* and picking up a Christmas tree. I know it's late in the game, but with everything going on, getting a tree has been really low on my list of priorities."

"Oh...?" Erin said surprised. "You haven't put up your tree yet?"

"Nope," Oliver verified, happy to be in Erin's presence. Oliver was beaming that afternoon. He loved that Silver Water was experiencing a rare snowfall in December, and that he'd inadvertently bumped into Erin. In his assessment, it didn't get any better than that! He couldn't help thinking that God had read his *email* so to speak the night before. He'd truly missed hanging out with Erin and having her there sparked some hope in his heart.

"Well, would you like some help in trimming it?" Erin found herself asking in a commonplace manner.

Oliver's smile was wider than the state of Texas. "Erin Emily Brasfield, I would love that!" His heart raced in his chest, as their eyes locked furtively for a moment.

Erin gaped at Oliver as one would admire a shooting star darting out from the sky. "I'm going to put this paperwork away, and I'll meet you out front in a few."

"I'm not going anywhere. I'll wait for you." Oliver followed behind Erin as she crossed over to her office.

Erin moved around self-consciously, as she set things in order inside her office. The door was ajar, and Oliver was waiting beyond it. Recurrently, their eyes would meet as she closed up shop, and they smiled at each other. Erin wasn't sure what she was doing. *Willing* herself to stay away from Oliver and *actually* doing it, were two different things. Seeing him unexpectedly that afternoon had weakened her resolve. Erin acceded to the fact that only God could help her overcome her fixation to this man. Erin was counting on God's strength to move forward if Oliver wasn't in His will or plan.

"I'm all set," Erin said, stepping out of the office. She was holding her coat and pocketbook.

"Allow me…" Oliver chivalrously took the coat out of Erin's hand, and gently helped her slip it on.

The feel of Oliver's gentle hands brushing her arms sent chills throughout Erin's body. Moreover, there was a sinking feeling in the hollow of her stomach. "Thank you," she said, gulping.

"You're welcome!" Oliver's eyes linked softly to Erin's, and he smiled. "Shall we go?" he established.

"Absolutely," Erin told him. Things only got worse as Oliver led Erin away from the office. He kept his hand on the small of her back the entire time.

Oliver wasn't sure why he was suddenly so protective of Erin. He shielded her from the falling snow, brushed snow from off of her windshield, and secured her inside of her car. "So, I will follow behind you. Drive slowly, okay. The flurries have slowed down a bit, but it's still pretty slippery out, so you can't be too careful," Oliver cautioned.

They would first go by Erin's and park her car. Then, the two planned on going out to the lot together. Regardless, Oliver was reluctant to even budge one inch away from her. There was a sense that she'd disappear if he let her out of his sight.

"I'll be careful, Ollie, but you've got to promise to do the same," Erin said sweetly. It felt good to hear Oliver express concern for her.

"I promise to be careful." He winked. "So, I will be right behind you."

"Okay," Erin ceded. "See you in a bit."

"Bye."

"Bye, Ollie."

Erin watched Oliver walk away, leaving footprints in the dusting of snow on the ground. He hopped into his steel gray BMW SUV. Her gape connected to his from across the lot. Erin nodded in indication that she was on the move.

Oliver gestured he was all set with a thumb's up. He watched Erin roll away from the parking lot and into the street. Cautiously, he pulled out following behind her.

***

Oliver and Erin made it over to the Christmas tree lot a little before three in the afternoon. *Blue Spruce Land* wasn't as busy as they'd expected-with Christmas being only two weeks away. It wasn't *terrible* out, but because the sun had slipped into a bed of ashen clouds for a nap, many potential customers had remained at home. There were just a few patrons spread throughout the lot trying to find their perfect tree. It was brisk, but luckily there were very little gusts of wind. The impressive, full evergreens were sprinkled in snow. Oliver was holding Erin's hand as they tread the narrow alleyways looking for the perfect tree.

Being out in the cold weather with Erin, holding her gloved hand as they shopped for the right tree, was Oliver's idea of happiness. With his family still out in Virginia and with the kind of work schedule he kept, the holidays were often very lonely. Oliver smiled down at Erin and gave her a sappy sidelong look.

"What…?" Erin asked, smiling up at Oliver. The feeling she had being with him that afternoon was indescribable. Even if it was only for *one* day, she wanted to relish every second they spent together. Oliver's personality was very addictive. Not only was he ridiculously good-looking, but he was also the nicest person on the planet. Even when Oliver had been breaking her heart, he'd done so with such compassion that she couldn't be angry with him.

"Nothing…," Oliver's cheeks turned ever ruddier. "I was just thinking that it's nice being out here with you. I've really missed hanging out with you." Oliver smiled in earnest at Erin upon saying those words.

"I've missed being with you too, Ollie…" Erin pursed her lips and set out to include a conjunction but desisted. She didn't want to ruin the moment. If Oliver wanted to be friends, even if it was gut-wrenching, she wouldn't waver. "Oh, Ollie, look at this one!" Erin said evadingly but had also stumbled across the most beautiful spruce. It was taller than Oliver-and Oliver was 6'3", the color was a vivid green, and it was full and lush.

Oliver examined the tree. They'd been walking through the

tiny trenches surrounded by spruces, but this one actually stood out. He surrendered to a slow nod. I could definitely work with this one," Oliver agreed.

"It's perfect, Ollie," Erin raved. "*We* can definitely work with this one." She met his smiling eyes with a sense of expectation.

"Thank you, Erin." Oliver connected to Erin's excited expression with anticipation of his own.

"Stop thanking me. Let's go back up front and tell one of the guys we want *this* guy right here." Erin pointed to the perfect spruce. She reached into her coat pocket, and removed the tiny red bow given to her by one of the employees. They were to use it as a marker for the tree they'd selected. She gave Oliver a knowing look, and he nodded. Erin happily placed the bow on the tree they'd agreed on.

"Well, let's go tell them this is the one." Oliver tugged playfully on Erin's arm, and they rushed back through the tiny troughs littered with Christmas trees of all shapes and sizes, back up to the storefront.

"Okay, then… You're *not* bossy at all," she razzed on him.

Oliver turned and tugged even more on her arm. "No, not even a little…" They laughed as they sprinted over to the store area.

The snow's momentum seemed to be picking up again by the time Oliver helped the guys haul the tree over to his SUV. They set the tree on top of the automobile and roped it around until it was secure enough. Oliver kept checking in on Erin who was sitting in the car waiting for him. Even if she'd argued that she'd wanted to help, he'd pleaded for her to remain safe and warm inside of the car.

After Oliver tipped the guys who'd helped him with the tree, he took his place behind the wheel. Staring pleasantly over at Erin, he noticed the farcical expression on her pretty face, and that her arms were crossed in defiance. "Can you tell me what I did wrong,

Ms. Brasfield?" he quipped.

"So, is *that* what I'm to expect of you, DA Wright? You wouldn't let me lift a finger," Erin badgered.

Oliver felt satisfied being in the driver's seat next to Erin. He gave her a crooked smile. "What are you implying, Ms. Brasfield?"

"I'm just saying that in *this* day and age, if a woman wants to help haul a tree and secure it to the roof of a car, they should be allowed to…just saying," she teased, trying to keep a straight face. She looked over at Oliver, and he was already laughing before she burst into laughter.

"I will keep that in mind for future reference," Oliver said, in between spurts of laughter.

"You'd *better* keep that in mind." Erin pointed a finger at him in feigned accusation. When the laughter died down, she looked over at Oliver, and their eyes locked again. Whenever their eyes met, it had made Erin's heart sink to the floor. "But I forgive you this time. Just don't let it happen again," Erin said self-consciously, trying to sound confident.

"Yes, Ma'am," Oliver ceded. "I promise never to do it again." He winked at Erin and shook his head comically. "Are you all set to help me trim the tree?" he asked before he started to pull away from the tree lot and nursery.

"I am all set. Oh, by the way, Ollie, do you have all of your ornaments?"

"I have quite of few things locked away in a closet over at my place. A couple of years ago I found an antique store and picked up some really nice pieces," Oliver said, slowly rolling out to the main road.

"I can't wait to see them," Erin said, excited. "Are you a Christmas Angel or a star Christmas tree topper?" she asked in anticipation.

"Oh, I'm definitely an angel guy," Oliver told her proudly. "The look on your face right now…" Oliver turned to look at Erin as they stopped at a red light.

"What *about* the look on my face?" Erin asked puzzled.

"Well, you look like a little girl opening up her presents on Christmas morning. I love that you're so excited about trimming the tree."

"I am… It's so much fun."

"Can I tell you something?" Oliver's eyes veered away from the road for a minute.

"You can tell me anything." Erin's eyes connected furtively to his again, causing her heart to dip.

"If for some reason you'd said that you couldn't help me trim the tree today, I don't think I would have bothered." Sadness masked his handsome face for a moment.

Erin's face warped in empathy and commiseration. She realized how much Oliver was probably still hurting over losing Kennedy. Moreover, the two would have been spending Christmas together. Rather than bringing up the debilitating hurtful past, Erin strove to encourage him. "You would have had a tree-less Christmas. My goodness! That's totally unheard of," she punned, making Oliver laugh. "It's a good thing I said yes then, huh?" She gave him a sidelong quirky look.

Oliver turned and gave her a hopeful smile. "It's *such* a good thing. You totally saved me," he emphasized and issued a quiet smile.

For a moment, the sound of the SUV's motor, and the whipping blade of the windshield wipers brushing snow off of the windshield were the only discernable noises. "I don't think either of us have had lunch. Are you hungry?" Oliver brought up.

"I am, but the weather isn't the best right now, so maybe we should just get the tree over to your place," Erin assessed. Her heart was racing again, because she was going over to Oliver's place. She had never been to his place. Notwithstanding, they were going to be alone for a while. Being alone with Oliver to any capacity always took her breath away. Erin prayed inwardly that she'd be able to contain the heat of her desire for him. There was a very real sense that even if *she* couldn't, Oliver was a true man of faith, and a total gentleman, and that would definitely quell the flame.

"I was thinking we could order something back over at my place," Oliver countered. "Let's just do our best to get off of these messy streets first." Oliver turned to ask Erin properly, "Are you sure you want to hang out with me today?" There was a well-meaning expression on his face. "I'm not the best company when the weather's inclement."

"District Attorney, Oliver Wright, there isn't anyone I would rather hang out with today!" Erin uplifted with a confident smile.

"You are too kind, Ms. Brasfield," he praised.

"Well, it's the truth. Come rain, snow, sleet or sunshine…"

"Yeah, that's exactly why I asked…" Oliver's smile was irrepressible.

***

It took about half an hour to get to Oliver's place, but having Erin beside him made it feel like five. Oliver pulled into his usual spot in the parking lot of his complex. Opening up the car door, he stepped out then went to get the door for Erin. The winds were howling, and the snowflakes were still coming down, but nothing too terrible. Silver Water seldom got more than a couple of inches. "Are you okay?" Oliver asked extending his hand out to Erin.

"I'm fine." Erin stepped out of the car, and looked up at the quartz-colored sky, as the wind seared like a blade. "I like snow just as much as the next person. But, it's freezing, and the sky isn't very pretty right now," Erin assessed.

"I don't know if I agree with that," Oliver countered. "I like it. Reminds me of snowy days back in Michigan when I was a kid."

Erin studied him quietly but didn't say a word. Rather, she smiled thinking that Oliver was a little sentimental.

"I'm just a cornball, huh?" His cheeks turned cardinal.

"Not at all," Erin countered, smiling musingly.

"So, come with me," Oliver said. "If it's alright, I'd like for you to wait inside while I haul this thing up," Oliver looked up at the tree on the rooftop of his car.

"Ollie, I want to help...," Erin argued.

"Erin," Oliver's face was pleading, "just this once. Allow me to bring the tree inside. We can do the rest together," he goaded.

"Okay," Erin acquiesced, "I will wait for you inside. At least you *asked* this time." She smiled.

"Of course," Oliver took Erin's hand. Guiding her over to the complex, he delivered her into the warm toasty lobby. "I'll be right back," he assured. Before going through the set of doors, Oliver looked over at Erin again. He felt extremely protective of her. There was an indescribably sense of gratification that she was safe and warm. Now, he needed to brave the winds, and find a way to haul the sizable blue spruce into the building.

"I can't believe you managed to bring the tree up here all by yourself," Erin said, standing next to Oliver at his front door.

"It wasn't as heavy as I thought it would be. What I *am* grateful for was not making a huge mess with the pine needles, and leaving a cluttered trail," Oliver said. He then opened up the door to his place and allowed Erin to step inside first. Following behind her, Oliver insisted, "Allow me." He helped her off with her coat.

First impressions were everything, and Erin was totally blown away by Oliver's lavish place. Everything from the décor, to his furniture and artwork on the walls, indicated he had the best tastes. She'd been busy sizing up the place, when she felt the warmth and electricity of Oliver's touch again. His gentle, caring hands brushed over her arms, as he helped her off with her coat. "Thank you," she said, startled.

"You're welcome," Oliver said, staring curiously at her.

"Ollie, I love your place!" Erin finally managed to say. Her heart dipped to the floor because he was standing inches away again. Trying her best not to become adrift, she evaded, "I love everything in this room!"

"Thank you," Oliver said encouraged by Erin's reaction. For a moment he towered over her, examining just how pretty she looked in the soft lighting at his place. "I'm finally beginning to actually like it here," he commented looking around.

"I like it here too," Erin said, breathlessly exploring his eyes.

"I'm glad you do." Oliver reached over and brushed his fingers through her silken hair.

Erin flinched in shock over his fingers brushing through her hair and grazing her earlobe.

"You had a few snowflakes there," Oliver said, losing himself in her jewel eyes.

"Thanks." Erin suddenly felt flustered. She imagined how florid her face had turned, because she had virtually jumped because Oliver had touched her.

"Time to drag in this big old tree," Oliver said, cutting through the intensity in the air. For a minute it seemed he'd been slipping into a trance.

"Now, I can help you haul it in here," Erin offered.

"Okay, you can pull while I push." Oliver smiled and winked.

Oliver and Erin hauled the tree over to the living room. Before long, Oliver drifted over to the guest bedroom. There, he found his Christmas paraphernalia. The items had been kept in a couple of bins and crates at the bottom of one of the closets. He removed the tree stand, while Erin sorted through the boxes containing the ornaments. "How are you doing over there?" Oliver asked.

"I found some really cute things. You even have nutcrackers. They're adorable! The crystal stuff is amazing..." Erin's voice trailed, and her heart nearly stopped, because Oliver had wandered over. He was on his knees pressed up close to her right side.

"Some of the crystal ornaments are *my* favorites. Most of them I got at that antique store," Oliver said, huddled only inches away from Erin. Oliver examined just how beautiful Erin's mouth was. He'd seen her in so many different ways, but it seemed as if he was taking in every contour of her symmetrical face for the very first time. Her lips were absolutely perfect-well-formed, as if an artist had drawn them.

"I like the gingerbread men and the cabins...," Erin said adrift... The butterflies were somersaulting in her stomach at that point.

"My personal favorites are the reindeers." Oliver shook off his disorientation. Sifting through the box, he pulled out a crystal reindeer. "Like this one." He explored Erin's eyes.

"That's so pretty," Erin delighted trying to remain in control.

"It *really* is...," Oliver said staring right into Erin's face.

Erin smiled timidly, and nervously continued rummaging through the box.

"Are we ready to order?" Oliver redirected.

"Order...?" Erin asked confused.

"Yeah... Are we doing Chinese, Thai, Indian Food, pizza?" Oliver chuckled.

"Oh…?" Erin's cheeks turned scarlet, embarrassed. Just then, Erin picked up on Oliver's musky yet floral scent. He smelled positively divine! Heat radiated from every pore of her body. She wanted to move away but wanted to savor the moment of having him this close. "I was thinking we could do something easy," she said awkwardly.

"Like…?"

"We could do Mc. Donald's through *Door Dash*," she suggested with a racing heart. Erin forced herself to maintain eye contact.

"Oh, okay…," Oliver said surprised.

"If you don't want to that's fine…"

"Erin," Oliver set his hand on her shoulder, "we can do whatever you want. If we do Mc. Donald's right now, then I *owe* you a proper dinner one of these nights. I don't do *cheap*," Oliver razzed.

"Well, I'm kind of in the mood for their apple pie. It's my *thing*," Erin admitted reticently. "I will however hold you to that *proper dinner* though."

"Absolutely… So, Mc. Donald's it is, my lady," Oliver said pleasantly. "I'm not sure that I have the *Door Dash* app on my phone."

"I'll order for us," Erin offered, smiling. "What would you like?" she met Oliver's eyes wonderingly. It felt so nice being with him.

"Uh, I guess I'll have a *Big Mac Meal*. I haven't had Mc. Donald's in forever," he admitted.

"Leave it to me to ruin your perfectly healthy diet," Erin razzed.

"You're the *only* one I would abandon my diet for," Oliver affirmed farcically.

"Wow! I feel so special."

"You *are*," Oliver delved her eyes more urgently, "you *truly* are."

There was another contemplative moment between the pair. They stared silently but satisfyingly into each other's eyes. Breaking the spell, the two continued sorting through the boxes and crates of Christmas effects.

CHAPTER THREE

"We need to get the angel just a little higher up." Erin tilted her head to the far right in order to examine what Oliver was doing. "And it's a little crooked." She was gaping at him while he stood on the step ladder.

"Should I move it a little bit more to the right?" Oliver tested doing all he could to adjust the sizable crystal angel ornament on top of the incredible looking tree. He and Erin had been working on it for the past hour and a half, and it looked absolutely amazing-if he *did* say so himself.

"A little bit to the left, Ollie, so that it can look straight," Erin directed, standing close by. "There! I think you've got it!" she cheered and clapped her hands in celebration. "It looks so good!" She marveled.

Smiling hopelessly, Oliver inched back for a moment in order to get a look. "You're right. This is perfect!" He beamed. Stepping cautiously off of the ladder, Oliver took the hand Erin extended in order to help him down. Setting his feet on the floor, he kept a firm grasp on her hand. It felt great to be linked to her in that way. "I love it!" he told her, searching her eyes with a sense of novelty and anticipation. "Oh…," Oliver remarked seeing the Mistletoe above their heads. He hunched down and pressed a kiss to her cheek.

"What was that for?" Erin asked, pleasantly surprised but nonplused.

Oliver pointed up at the Mistletoe hovering above them. "It's a tradition," he reminded pleasantly

Erin blushed, and her palms were getting sweaty. So, she gently reclaimed her hand from Oliver's heavenly grasp. "Uh-huh…," she razzed. "Likely story. So, okay, you get a pass this time," she joked.

"The truth is that I just wanted to kiss you," Oliver confessed with crimson cheeks.

"I figured as much," Erin countered feigning suspicion. She wished that Oliver had *really* kissed her. He'd told her that he wasn't at a very good space emotionally, because he'd been hurt. Erin knew Oliver well enough to know that he seldom changed his mind. There was no doubting that he cared about her. However, Erin wasn't fooling herself. She doubted that Oliver felt for *her* the kind of love and passion he'd felt for Kennedy.

Erin subtly inched away and admired their handiwork. Oliver was indeed irresistible. And yet, Erin had to *try* to resist him anyway, because she didn't want to go on breaking her own heart. "Oliver, this is amazing!" She turned towards him and smiled in earnest.

"It is *spectacular*! The tree at Rockefeller Center in New York City can't hold a candle to this one. Are we ready to light it up?" Oliver asked, excited.

"We're as ready as we'll ever be," Erin said, pumped. Her face felt hot where Oliver had planted his kiss. Then, there was a sense of coldness, as wistfulness to experience it again waved over her in cadences. Erin prayed through it, reminded of 1 Corinthians 10:13. God would not allow her to be tempted beyond her limits. So, she smiled until her face hurt, watching Oliver access the main power cord for the tree lights. He issued a command to Alexa to dim the living room lights.

"Are you ready?" Oliver asked, staring at Erin as if he were a child seeing Mickey Mouse at Disney World for the first time.

Erin nodded. "Light it up, Ollie!" She clapped in anticipation.

Oliver plugged in the cord and transposed the entire living room. He stood back, found Erin and slipped his arm around her waist endearingly.

Startled by Oliver's sudden move, Erin tried to keep her wits about her. Between the exquisite work they'd done on the Christmas tree and Oliver's addictive touch, she *was* overwhelmed.

"What's the matter?" Oliver asked, keeping Erin close to his side. "We did an amazing job!" he praised, staring down at her agreeably.

"I think we did too. It's breathtaking, Ollie! I think we really work well together," she added, swallowing hard. Oliver's beautiful hand rubbed rhythmically and caringly to the side of her waist. She could tell that it was his way of being affectionate, but it affected her a great deal.

"I think so too." Oliver stared down at Erin with so much appreciation. "Thank you."

"Why are you thanking me?" Erin asked mislaid and absolutely mesmerized.

"Thank you for coming here today and helping me trim this amazing tree! I could not have done it without you," Oliver said in earnest.

"I'm having the best time with you, Ollie. So, it's my pleasure," Erin's voice undulated, as she slipped deeper into trouble. Luckily, the doorbell rang at that moment.

"Food's here!" Oliver announced, removing his arm from about Erin's waist.

Erin sighed in relief when Oliver let go. Although she could tell that he liked her-as a friend, she knew for *sure* that she was in love with him. She found a moment to collect herself when Oliver went to get the door.

"So, where would you like to eat this fine cuisine, my dear lady?" Oliver asked facetiously holding the large brown Mc. Donald's paper bag in hand. "We could eat in here if you'd like." His face creased in concern as he examined Erin. "Are you cold?"

"Just a little," Erin said, floating over to him.

"So, I will turn on the automatic fireplace." Oliver issued another order to Alexa, and instantly the synthetic logs in his faux fireplace began to redden inside of the mantle.

"I love that, Oliver," Erin praised. "This is awesome. I feel warmer already."

Oliver rubbed her arm affectionately. "Good. I *want* you to feel comfortable here." His eyes explored hers.

"I *am* comfortable here." Erin's eyes fastened to his.

"Good… So, give me a moment. I will get us a couple of plates, napkins and ketchup for our French fries, because as you might well know…"

"They *never* send napkins or ketchup with the order," Erin said laughing.

"That's right. So, make yourself at home, enjoy the beautiful scenery, the fireplace, and…" There was a playful expression on Oliver's face as he glided over to his entertainment center. He pressed a few dials and Nat King Cole's, *The Christmas Song* instantly filled the air

"Chestnuts roasting on an open fire, Jack Frost nipping at your nose…," Oliver crooned parodying Nat King Cole.

Erin shook her head comically and laughed as he sang. Oliver gestured dramatically as he performed. He didn't stop until he disappeared out into the kitchen for a moment. Erin couldn't hold back her laughter. "You're a total nut," she called out.

Oliver's head popped to the side of the dining room entryway. "Thank you for saying that. I pride myself in being a total nut…" he quipped, winking at her.

"And, *this* is the man Silver Water has elected to be our new DA?" she razzed, giggling.

"Yep, I warned everyone that it was at their own risk," Oliver called out.

"I guess it was a risk they were willing to take." Erin kept laughing.

"Erin, you're right. These apple pies are bomb!" Oliver admitted munching on his pie. He and Erin had eaten their meal, and now they were sipping Sprite through their straws and enjoying dessert. The two were seated on the plush carpeting out in the living room. They'd used the coffee table to set up the food. Christmas music played softly in the background, and the air was nice and toasty.

"Right…? They *are* the best," Erin agreed. "Although I have a problem…" Her face creased in waggishness.

"What might that problem be?" Oliver rose to the occasion.

"It's just weird hearing the DA say that anything is *bomb*," Erin jested.

"Hey, the new DA of Silver County is allowed to say *bomb*," Oliver argued, feigning hurt feelings.

Erin shook her head contrarily and had a farcical look on her face. "I wouldn't…" she joked.

Oliver picked up one of his French fries and tossed it at Erin's nose.

Shocked, Erin's mouth gaped, and she gave Oliver an idiosyncratic look. "Did you *really* just do that?" she asked impishly.

Oliver smiled mischievously and threw another fry in her direction.

"Oh, it's on right now," Erin determined. She picked up a few of her fries and flung them at Oliver.

"This is war," Oliver declared.

"You started it," Erin tossed more of them at Oliver's face. There was back and forth for a while. The two were laughing uproariously. Erin jumped to her feet and moved away in order to dodge the ones Oliver were throwing at her.

Oliver drifted over near the window. His eyes lowered playfully into Erin's. "What do you have there, little lady?" he asked, noticing that Erin had her hands concealed behind her.

"Do you *really* want to know?" Erin's eyes lowered into his just as menacingly.

"I don't think I do," Oliver razzed. He gently took hold of Erin's hands and restrained them. The only problem with that was that he was practically holding her in his arms. Magnetized, Oliver was frozen in the moment. *Why did it feel so right to have her close? Why was it taking him such a long time to let her go?"*

"No fair, DA, Wright," Erin said quietly, totally spellbound. If Erin's heart had been racing before, it felt as if it would beat right out of her chest. Oliver kept a gentle grasp about her waist while softly restraining her hands from throwing anymore fries in his face. In the soft dim lighting in his living room, Oliver looked positively otherworldly.

However, remembering their talk just the day before-how Oliver had not rescinded his stance in respect to being anything more than friends-Erin unobtrusively began pulling away. Evadingly, she pushed back the curtains and got a look outside. "Look, Ollie, it looks like the snow is ebbing away," Erin remarked, eluding the moment.

Oliver respectfully retreated. His entire body rippled in coldness because Erin had pulled back. He had to keep reminding himself that being attracted to Erin wasn't the issue. The issue was giving her a broken and dilapidated heart, ruined in the aftermath of putting it all out there for Kennedy. Oliver sensed that Erin's withdrawal was to protect her own heart, and he estimated that she had every right to do so.

He and Erin were great friends, and he didn't want to mess that up. Oliver stood behind Erin and perused what was going on outside. "Yeah, it looks that way. I think they were just passing flurries anyway." He took a moment to examine Erin's face. She wouldn't look at him, and Oliver wasn't sure why it hurt so much. "It's almost seven. What would you like to do?" Oliver brought up-working past his tangled emotions.

Erin suddenly turned towards Oliver, connecting to his eyes. "Do *you* have anything in mind?" she asked cautiously. She had moved away from Oliver, because now more than ever she was drawn to him.

"Well, as my guest, I *am* leaving the choice up to you. Is there anything you'd like to do?" Oliver asked politely.

"Would you like to watch a movie?" Erin suggested. She figured that if their attention was directed elsewhere, it would alleviate some of the intensity *she* was grappling with. Although, she couldn't say for sure how Oliver was feeling.

"Okay…," Oliver smiled walking over to one of the end tables. He accessed the remote controls for his expansive flat-screen and his cable box. "Is there anything you'd like to see? We can order a movie on demand?" Oliver turned and looked over at Erin.

"Sounds good," Erin agreed.

Oliver drifted over to the sofa. He turned the television on and perused the channel guide.

Erin watched every move he made but remained frozen to a corner of the living room. She looked over at Oliver, and he was staring back at her baffled. "What's the matter?" she queried, bewildered.

Oliver offered her a reassuring smile. "Will you come and sit with me so that we can decide…together?"

Erin laughed nervously-not realizing that she was unconsciously keeping her distance. "Sure," she told him, sauntering over and bridging the gap between them.

Oliver picked up the loose fries scattered all over and set them into the Mc Donald's paper bag. He then turned towards Erin. "Have a seat," he encouraged, shaking his head nonsensically. "I promise not to bite."

"Are you teasing me?" Erin asked timidly as she set down next to him.

"Oh no, not at all," Oliver razzed. "Erin, it's alright." His eyes inspected hers intuitively. "I know I'm not the most exciting guy on the planet, however I *am* working on it," he said humorously.

"You are such a mess, Oliver Wright. Now, will you hand me that remote so that we can choose which movie we want to see?" She met Oliver's roguish grin with a semi-confident one of her own.

Oliver laughed lightly and handed her the remote. "I'd be a fool to argue with that." There was an irrepressible smile on Oliver's face, as he watched Erin browse the list of movies on demand. The sense of satisfaction he'd had since he'd run into her at the office earlier only intensified.

"You'd better recognize," Erin said trying to sound intimidating. Her goal was to remain as focused on *anything* else but on Oliver. So, she looked straight on as she inspected movie choices.

"Oh, I do-I *totally* recognize," Oliver said teasingly and chuckled. It was difficult to define the sense of contentment he felt, because Erin was with him. Maybe it was because he'd been so lonely and broken since losing Kennedy but having Erin with him on that lonely Saturday night made all the difference in the world.

"Just saying…," Erin got a sassy expression on her face. Turning to take a peek at Oliver, she found him staring curiously at her. Unable to keep a straight face, they simultaneously burst into laughter.

"I thought we were choosing a movie, but you sound like a mafia lord." Oliver laughed heartily shaking his head comically over Erin's quirkiness.

"I do not."

"I'm afraid you do, Ms. Brasfield." Oliver's eyes met Erin's again in laughter. "Although, I have to say that I'm *so* glad you're here!" he told her in earnest.

Erin's heart melted just then, and her face warped in sappiness. "Oh, Ollie, I'm glad to be here with you! You're so sweet," she gushed, staring fondly at him.

"Yeah, yeah, yeah…," he razzed on her. "Can you please stop it with the sappy?" He winked. "Let's pick out this movie already," Oliver baited.

But Erin's smile was unstifled. Even as she browsed the movie selections, she kept looking intermittently over at Oliver, and it was the same with him. Every time their eyes met, at least on Erin's end, it was intense and totally overwhelming. He'd made her entire night by telling her that her presence in his home made him happy.

"I can't believe how this thing ends," Erin complained after having watched the suspense/thriller *Look behind You* with Oliver. "It's such a tease," she assessed. By that time, she and Oliver were sitting on the sofa, and he'd just shut off the T.V. It was fifteen after nine p.m.

"What…? Are you kidding me? You couldn't tell that her uncle was the murderer throughout this entire movie? They always try to downplay the culprit," Oliver argued.

"You *couldn't* have guessed that from the beginning," Erin told him-standing to her feet and staring skeptically at him. She needed to pull back, because it had been torture trying to keep her focus on the movie, while she and Oliver had sat side by side in such close proximity.

"I knew it from the first time they introduced the uncle that he was the one behind the murders." Oliver shook his head in the negative, smiling.

"I guess you have one of those minds. I thought it was the main character all along."

"That's what they wanted you to think."

"I will pay closer attention next time," Erin ceded.

"Erin, this isn't a test," Oliver razzed on her.

"I get that, Mr. Hot Shot, DA-with the criminal mind." She rolled her eyes.

"I'm sorry, that's just who I am." Oliver rubbed his knuckles on his chest boastfully.

"Whatever…" Erin shook her head in skepticism.

"Don't hate…" Oliver jived and made a quirky face. "By the way, are you hungry?" Oliver stood to his feet.

"As a matter of fact, I am. I thought I'd be full for a while," Erin said facing him.

"Oh, yeah, having Mc Donald's *always* leaves a person feeling totally full," he pestered and winked at Erin again.

"Yeah, as a matter of fact it *always* does," Erin said farcically.

"Come with me," Oliver invited.

Erin followed Oliver out into the kitchen. She'd only been in the kitchen once since she'd been at his place that day. Taking in his broad kitchen with state-of-the art, brand new amenities and high-end appliances, blew her away again. "Did I tell you how much I love your place?"

"Yeah, but I don't mind hearing it again," Oliver said while rummaging through his modern fridge. He looked up from the task and met Erin's eyes from across the countertop. "I have some cold cuts and cheese. We could make sandwiches," he suggested.

Erin bravely walked across the room and stood close beside him to get a look inside of the fridge. She hunched down and browsed the selections. Her shoulders brushed up to Oliver's at that point, making Erin's heart dip to the floor again. "You have leftover cake?" Erin delighted, delirious of their close physical connection just then.

Oliver chortled over her reaction. "Sorry, I didn't mention it. Yeah, I went to a function earlier in the week, and they served Carrot

Cake. I didn't know you were a fan." He smiled quietly watching Erin peruse what was in the fridge.

"Well, I *am* a huge fan!" Erin looked up at him. "I think we should make frozen pizzas," Erin decided.

Oliver nodded in satisfaction. "I didn't think about having those, but whatever you want."

"We should also have carrot cake," she added, smiling up into his eyes.

"Your wish is my command. I will make hot chocolate." Oliver remained locked in that moment gazing into Erin's eyes.

"Do you have marshmallows?" Erin asked, trying to move away, but completely frozen.

"I do," Oliver said leaning into her, uncertain as to why. Oliver was temporarily awestruck. However, in the back of his mind he was reminded that he needed to respect the boundaries of their friendship.

"Well, *Wright*, what are you waiting for? Let's get this party started," Erin told him. For a moment Erin could have sworn that Oliver was leaning in to kiss her, but she had to remember that his heart was still tied into Kennedy. And, as much as she loved and wanted him, Erin couldn't be his second choice or an afterthought.

"Oh, okay…," Oliver said shaking himself free from the trance. "Are we microwaving our pizzas or baking them?" He tried to remain focused.

"Definitely baking them," Erin said drifting over to another part of the kitchen. "They're too mushy when they're microwaved."

"Okay," Oliver ceded, laughing.

"I will get the hot chocolate and marshmallows. She met Oliver's eyes from across the kitchen. "Are they in any one of these cabinets?" she asked.

"In that one over on the left," Oliver told her. "I'll put our pizzas into the oven and cut us up a couple of pieces of carrot cake."

Oliver watched Erin turn and open up the cupboard in order to find what she was looking for. Staring wistfully after her, he felt conflicted. There was no doubting his attraction to Erin, because she was extremely beautiful. However, was he at the place where he could offer her what she needed? Because he was uncertain, he would tread cautiously. What he *did* know nonetheless was that he was glad she was there, and he didn't want for her to leave.

It was a quarter to ten when Oliver and Erin sat cross-legged on his living room floor with their backs pressed up to the base of the sofa. Christmas music hummed lowly in the background. Warm and toasty, they were in front of the faux logs, admiring their handiwork with the Christmas tree. They'd both had pizza, carrot cake and hot chocolate.

"So, are we pulling out all the stops for this Christmas party?" Erin asked, excited.

"Look at *you* all excited about the Christmas party!" Oliver teased. "Your energy is exactly what this party needs. That's why I wanted to ask for your help in putting it together," he goaded.

"Of course, … I would love to help you, Ollie!" Erin affirmed, but frowned.

"What's the matter?" Oliver asked perplexed.

"I was just thinking that the party will probably be the last time I will get to hang out with you guys."

Oliver's face changed at that point, and sadness overwhelmed him like rainwater fills a lake. "That's right," he forced a smile, "I was trying to forget all about that. I *did* ask if you would stay on until Christmas." Jeopardy strained his winsome face. "But I totally understand if you're preoccupied with other things until then." Oliver searched Erin's face with a frayed expression on his.

"I have a few engagements up until Christmas, but I always have time to help out a friend." Erin explored Oliver's eyes in quiet reassurance and offered a candid smile.

Oliver's face radiated hope as he gazed meaningfully into her eyes. "It would mean a great deal to me, but if it gets to be too much just let me know. Although…"

Erin's face twisted in culpability. "What, Ollie?" she asked softly.

"Nothing…," Oliver evaded.

"Ollie, what is it?" Erin prodded.

"It's going to be tough not seeing you around the office. You're the best at your job. Not to mention the fact that you've been one of my biggest supporters from the start." His eyes shone affectively.

"Ollie, I will *always* be one of you biggest fans. It doesn't matter where I'm working," Erin encouraged.

Oliver issued a sad smile. "I know that, and it means a great deal. Erin, I'm sorry," he said throatily.

"Why are you sorry, Ollie?" Erin questioned, surprised.

"I'm sorry if I've caused you any pain. Maybe, I leaned on you a little too heavily after things fell apart with Kennedy. That wasn't very fair." Tears shone in Oliver's eyes.

Erin's expression paralleled Oliver's. "Oliver, you can *always* lean on me if you need to," her voice undulated. "I *get* that you feel incapable of opening up your heart right *now*, because of how deeply you were hurt. Still, I know that it's only a matter of time before you *do* open up to someone, even if that someone isn't *me*. You have such a strong and loving heart. Some lucky girl's going to be smiling every single day."

"That's very sweet, but I seriously doubt it."

"And why is that?" Erin confronted.

"Well, it's because I would never want to give her the shards left of my broken heart."

"Can I tell you something?" Erin asked quietly.

"Of course," Oliver allowed with a well-meaning look.

"*She* would be lucky to have *any* version of you-broken or otherwise." Erin explored his face and eyes emphatically.

Oliver flinched back, surprised by Erin's response. He offered her a thoughtful smile. "Wow! Hearing you say those words have left me floored," he admitted. "*Now* do you see why I need for my friend to stick around?" He winked at her. "However, I do understand why you've decided to leave.

"Erin, I want you to know that I would *want* for *you* to be that person...*my* person," he said straightforwardly. "But I care way too much about you to offer anything less than what you deserve." He lowered pointedly into her eyes.

Erin was shocked to hear those words come out of Oliver's mouth. Hope sparked in the ashes of her discouragement. It was the first time he'd openly admitted to how much he cared about her. Even if she wanted so much more, she was heartened that given time, he would open up his heart again. Perhaps, she would be instrumental in helping him to heal. She remained silent as Oliver shared his heart.

"You deserve so much more than just a piece of an already shattered heart," his voice broke.

"And so do you, Ollie," Erin said insightfully with tears gleaming in her eyes. "But, I understand. Some wounds run so deep that only God and time can heal them. But they *do* eventually heal. And you *will* be happy again..." Tears escaped the corners of her eyes, but she brushed them away.

"I know that things will get better in time. Still, I wouldn't want for you to miss out on anything. And I certainly don't want you working in an environment where you feel stifled for one reason or another. I want you to be happy, fulfilled, free and confident wherever life takes you," Oliver expressed croakily.

Erin nodded quiescently. "I know you do, Ollie. I think we

both need a little time right now. I get that," she agreed.

"Can you promise me something?" Oliver's sad eyes bridged to hers.

Erin nodded again in compliance.

"Promise that you won't slip out of my life completely."

Erin issued a hopeful smile. "I promise not to slip out of your life at all."

Oliver nodded, encouraged. "That's very comforting."

"I'm glad…" Erin smiled through the tears. "Now, about this party…?" she eluded. "Are we working on a tight budget?"

Oliver shook his head contrarily and chuckled. "We can work out a budget together, but we're not limited by any means. I trust your judgement. Oh, and we've got to do the *Secret Santa* thing. Everyone down at the office should have something really nice-nothing cheap…"

"I know, I know…," Erin razzed on him, "you *don't* do cheap."

"Ah…" Oliver baited and pointed at her, "you're beginning to know me so well."

"Speaking of which, *you*, Mr. Wright, owe me a proper dinner," Erin heckled.

"Oh, yeah, after having Mc Donald's tonight, you can definitely hold me to that." Oliver laughed.

"So, we're decking out the entire office, putting a tree out in the lobby, even if we already have one in the main office area. We're also doing the white icicle lighting in some parts of the office. Oh, for the food, we're hiring *Delish Confection Caterers*…

"Oh, we can also play Christmas charades. That's when everyone has to write out anything Christmas-themed and put the ideas into a stocking. The guests will randomly pick out what the idea or concept is and act it out," Erin contrived.

"Wow, you're on a roll. Everything you've said sounds amazing so far," Oliver told her with a pleasant expression on his face. Seeing Erin so fired up about helping him throw the party was inexpressibly gratifying.

At one point Erin stopped brainstorming, and caught Oliver just staring at her with an undeniable smile. "What...? Why are you looking at me like that?" Her cheeks suffused.

"It's just nice to see you so fired up about the party. I knew you were the right person to ask."

"Whatever, Oliver..." Erin rolled her eyes playfully. "Are you taking notes?" she deflected.

"Of course," Oliver took notes on his phone.

The two worked out tentative plans in respect to the Christmas social. Discussing the upcoming event was a lot more fun than Oliver had even imagined. Both Oliver and Erin toyed with a few ideas and suggested a number of games and activities they believed could lighten things up for the party. The pair also took notes.

For a while the conversation remained upbeat, light and easy. It had veered away from the heaviness Oliver and Erin had just shared. Still, the duo individually mulled over their previous exchanges, and wondered if they'd said the right things. When talk of the Christmas party wrapped, the conversation took another turn.

"How are things looking for Taren Cook?" Erin asked on a serious note. She and Oliver had talked about some of the cases the DA's office had recently taken on. The two were sitting across from each other with the points of their knees touching.

Taren Cook had been Kennedy Proctor-Bohm's former bestie. Taren had plotted against Kennedy in order to win Kayden Bohm's heart. Her fixation with Kayden had so spiraled out of control that she'd snuck into Kennedy's home, and had threatened her at gunpoint. She had subsequently submitted to care at a psychiatric facility, but was nonetheless deemed coherent enough to be arraigned and to face sentencing.

"Because Taren pleaded guilty and has no prior record, Mitch and I have been working diligently in appeal for leniency in her upcoming sentencing. Taren has expressed sincere remorse and has also continued with outpatient care through the psychiatric hospital.

"Whatever the case, she will be sentenced in a couple of weeks." Oliver sighed. "Mitch and I are doing everything in our power to keep her from having to face any real jail time. We're hoping she receives the minimum sentence of a year's probation," Oliver Clarified, frowning.

Erin shook her head in the negative, saddened by the circumstances. "It's sad how all of that played out. I truly hope it works out for her. I pray that Taren gets the help she needs without having to go to prison," Erin said compassionately.

"You and me both… Mitch and I are definitely working on that, but only God knows how the matter is going to play out," Oliver established.

"I'm so sorry for the way things turned out with Kennedy. I know you'd loved her for a long time," Erin stated bravely. When Kennedy had initially broken Oliver's heart, Erin had tried to sweep the matter under the rug-hoping that her presence in Oliver's life would have been consolation enough. However, she now realized just how wrong she'd been in handling the matter.

Oliver smiled sadly and guffawed. "Erin, you've got nothing to apologize for." He explored her eyes caringly. "The truth is that if *you* hadn't been there for me during that time…" He shook his head in the negative. "I doubt I would have survived it." Oliver reached over and took Erin's hand in his. "You kept me alive," his voice broke and tears shone in his eyes

"Oh, Ollie…" Erin's heart fluttered over his touch, and tears glimmered in her eyes to see him so vulnerable. "You didn't deserve to have your heart shattered that way," her voice undulated. "I'm so sorry that it happened. And from the look on Kennedy's face when she saw you at the wedding, it was clear just how much she regretted hurting you."

"Kennedy is truly a wonderful person! So, I couldn't even bring myself to be angry with her. It just wasn't in the will of God, and I've come to accept that," Oliver affirmed, stroking fondly on Erin's hand.

"Even if what happened was painful, I choose to trust that God knows what's best. Sometimes, we have our own agenda. We think we know how the story is supposed to play out. However, God always steps in, and shows us just how much we *don't* have things figured out," Oliver expressed wisely, pushing back tears.

"You're certainly right about that. We don't even have the *little* details figured out, but I'm grateful that God does," Erin concurred. Oliver's strong and gentle hand brushing over hers felt like home. In fact, spending the day with him had felt like embracing warmth, safety and security. Erin was hopeful that Oliver did care. It was a lot more than she'd expected.

Oliver smiled and nodded in agreement. "You're right. God's ways are past finding out, but I adhere to Romans 8:28. God uses all things for our good," Oliver affirmed.

"I believe that too," Erin agreed. "So, you've got to know that God only has the very best for you, Oliver Wright, because I think you're pretty wonderful!"

Stirred, Oliver reached over and pressed a fond kiss to Erin's cheek. "Hearing you say that means more to me than you even know." Tears were in his eyes. "I think you're pretty wonderful yourself, Ms. Brasfield," he said gutturally. Oliver pulled back and stared meaningfully into Erin's eyes.

"Thank you," Erin said softly, admiring him. Inwardly, she was falling apart. Now more than ever she was in love with Oliver. It hardly seemed fair that they'd shared such a special day together, when she was doing all she could to distance herself and to move on.

"So, are you ready to call it a night?" Oliver asked, moving past the intensity of the moment.

"Wow, I didn't realize how late it was," Erin said looking up at the time indicator on Oliver's cable box.

"Half past ten," Oliver affirmed, releasing his hold on Erin's hand and standing to his feet. He then extended his hand out to help Erin up. "I'm so sorry. I didn't mean to keep you out so late." His face creased in remorse.

"Ollie, you didn't keep me. I *wanted* to stay. I'm so excited about our upcoming Christmas bash! Besides, it was totally nice hanging out with you today." Erin grasped the hand he'd offered.

"It was *really* nice hanging out with *you*," Oliver said with a gravelly tone, as he intuitively searched her eyes. Oliver tightened his grasp on Erin's hand, realizing that on some level he wanted to keep her there. Working past his fascination, he finally let go. "I'll go get our coats." He issued a quiet smile.

"Okay. I'll be right here." Erin watched Oliver drift away for a moment.

She sighed and her face flushed in frustration and uncertainty. There was a sense that she'd made a total fool of herself and had put it all out there for Oliver. He'd told her how much he cared, but still made it clear that friendship was what he wanted. Saying that he *wanted* her to be his person, and actually taking steps to *make* it happen, were two different things. Erin found comfort in his words, but at the end of the day, she loved him and wanted a lot more. Still, she could tell that Oliver was terrified to try again. His heart had been shattered after things had fallen apart with Kennedy.

"Hey, are you ready?" Oliver returned suddenly.

"I'm all set," Erin said staring into his maple brown eyes.

Oliver deliberately helped Erin on with her coat. The realization that she was actually leaving created such an emptiness on the inside. Up until that very moment they'd both been talkative and playful, but as they set out to leave his place, the two were extremely quiet.

Moments later, Oliver led Erin out to his SUV and secured her inside. It was brisk out but nothing too terrible. The snow flurries had completely evanesced. Oliver had started his car automatically from the apartment, so it was already nice and toasty.

He walked around and took his place behind the wheel. However, before he pulled out of the lot, he looked over at the pretty woman sitting next to him. "I'm sorry for monopolizing your *entire* day," he offered sincerely. "I didn't mean to take you away from your important Saturday tasks."

Erin stared over at Oliver in total skepticism. Shaking her head in denial, she countered, "I don't know what you're talking about, Oliver Baron Wright. You actually *made* my Saturday!" Erin acclaimed, with reddened cheeks.

Oliver smiled warmly at her, reached for her hand, and gave it an affectionate squeeze. "You made my day too," his voice resonated.

That said, Oliver pulled out of the parking space, and rolled away from the apartment complex. Erin lived a few towns over, about half an hour away, and the goal was to get her home before midnight. Oliver wanted to enjoy the last few minutes they had left together. Hence, he'd have to go home, and face the loneliness again.

***

"Thanks for taking me up on a whim today," Oliver said standing in front of Erin's house. "It was an unbelievable day!" He stared down at her with warmth and appreciation.

"I agree." Erin stared into Oliver's eyes, completely mesmerized. There were moments where she could better handle being in that hypnotized state than others. Oliver's fresh wind-kissed face took her breath away again, as he stood only inches away from her at the door. He towered over her, and his stalwart arms rippled just underneath his navy-blue wool coat. "I think we needed this day. It might be a while before we get to hang out again," Erin reasoned.

"Don't say that," Oliver countered with an urgent expression on his face. "Even if you won't be working through the DA's office, we will make time for each other." Oliver took in Erin's beautiful face. Having spent most of the day with her, it was difficult to let her go. Nonetheless, he had to. They both had church in the morning. More importantly, he refused to jerk her heart around. He'd already delineated that they were going to be friends. So, he had to give her the space to find someone who could offer her the kind of love she deserved.

Erin nodded. "Of course, … We'll always be the best of *friends*." She smiled. "Oh, by the way, you're going to need some presents under that tree."

"Right… Hopefully, I will be gifted with a few this year." Sadness blanketed Oliver's face, and an indescribable sense of emptiness on the inside.

Erin turned and accessed her house key. When she managed to open up her front door, she turned back towards Oliver. "I'm sure *you*, Mr. DA, will have lots of presents under the tree." She winked. "Anything special you want this year?" She cocked her head back and stared curiously at him.

Oliver stood gaping at Erin in utter captivation. He hadn't even realized she'd posed a question, because he'd been so swept away by how strikingly beautiful she was. "Did you say something?" He asked, trying to shake free from his trance.

Erin laughed lightly. "I asked if there was anything special you wanted this Christmas?" She stared into his eyes optimistically.

"Uh-huh," Oliver said, dazed.

"Goodnight, Ollie." Erin cautiously set her arms about his neck and squeezed lovingly.

"Goodnight, Erin." Oliver automatically slipped his arms around her waist and crushed her to himself. For a moment he just held her contemplatively. Again, as it had been a little while ago over at his place, he was finding it difficult to let go.

Erin relished the moment of being in Oliver's arms-if only for a short while. She'd almost forgotten what a wonderful and safe place it was to be enfolded by them. However, the realization that Oliver had solidified their *friendship* compelled her to pull away. "Get home safe," she said softly looking up into his eyes.

"Thanks." Oliver hesitantly removed his arms from about her waist. "Thanks again for everything," he emphasized-taking steps backward. "Bye."

"Bye, Ollie." Erin watched Oliver dismount the steps. He'd parked in her driveway, so she stood by as he slipped into his SUV. Oliver waved at her again before he pulled out of the driveway. Erin waved back, as the automobile rolled out. So much had taken place on that day, so Erin needed to pray through, and process the events with her Heavenly Father.

Just the other day she'd resolved to forget all about Oliver. However, after spending the day together, she was more in love than ever. *What on earth was she going to do, what was God's will in the matter, and would she ever stop hurting this much?* Those were questions only God could answer. And Erin was confident that He would light her way one step at a time.

CHAPTER FOUR

"In light of the heinous nature of the crimes committed, I recommend that bail be set for two million dollars, Your Honor. The defendant also poses a flight risk," Oliver argued in criminal court on Monday morning at an arraignment hearing. "The forensics report also gleaned that the defendant's deceased spouse was brutally beaten before she was shot," he added.

Oliver was seeking prosecution in the homicide case. John Morgan had killed his wife and his two children. He'd suspected that his wife had been having an affair. However, in the aftermath of the murders, he'd discovered that she had remained faithful. John had murdered his children under the premise that his two boys, 6 and 9, would never be raised by a stepfather.

"That is extremely unreasonable, your honor," the defense attorney disputed.

However, after a while, Judge Jeannine Landry tendered her response. "I will take the DA's counsel under advisement," she settled. She then directed her attention over to John Morgan, who was standing next to his attorney with a frayed expression on his face. "Bail is hereby set for two million dollars," she determined.

Oliver sighed, relieved, despite the fact that the defense was grumbling in respect to the judge's decision. Oliver thanked God that the judge had seen things his way. He listened in as the judge informed the defense of subsequent court dates, and on other impending hearings. However, Oliver was preoccupied making notes in his planner and in his journal. He had a few ideas about key evidence needed to ensure that John Morgan was prosecuted. The DA's office was seeking life in prison without the possibility of parole in the first-degree triple homicide.

Stepping out of the courtroom, Oliver traipsed quickly through the carpeted hallway. Before long, he was on the elevator going down to the ground floor of the building. Erin had pressed on his mind for the past two days. Called in for an emergency meeting with the authorities in respect to the Morgan case on Sunday, Oliver had missed church.

So, he had not seen or heard from Erin since he'd said goodnight on Saturday. Oliver just couldn't thank her enough for hanging out at his place. They'd shared a very unique and special day. Oliver had beamed each time he'd caught a glimpse of the Christmas tree in his living room. But he was smart enough to know that the tree wasn't what brought a smile to his face. Being with Erin had made him extraordinarily happy, and he missed her.

As Oliver dismounted the courthouse steps, he fiddled with his phone. Whether or not to call Erin was the internal conflict. The desire to connect to her was daunting, even if it was just to ask how the party-planning was coming along. Oliver was almost to his car when he heard someone calling him.

"DA Wright… DA Wright…," came within earshot. Oliver made a sudden turn and saw *her* at that moment. He instantly halted, and an open smile stretched across his face. Tucking the phone into the inner pocket of his dress suit, Oliver shook his head in skepticism. "Rain McGrath," he said, beaming.

Rain was an old friend from law school. There had been a time when he and Rain had been very close. The two had studied for the Bar Exam together, and both had graduated with high honors in law school. Oliver assessed how beautiful Rain was. She hadn't changed very much in the past decade. In fact, it seemed the years had been very kind. Her long, curly, honey blonde hair bounced gracefully over her shoulders and back. Her slender yet shapely body could not be concealed by the deep forest green skirt suit she was wearing, and her blue eyes gleamed in the morning sunlight.

"Should I call you *Oliver* or *Mr. DA*?" Rain asked, sauntering over to Oliver. She instinctively threw her arms around him and squeezed affectionately.

"You can call me whatever you'd like." Oliver crushed her to himself. "Rain," he pulled away but kept a grasp on her shoulders, "how long has it been?" Oliver marveled, smiling openly.

"It must be at least eleven years since the last time we saw each other. "Rain shook her head provocatively as she took Oliver in. "I can't believe that you're even *better* looking than you were back then." She eyed him in total fascination.

"Stop…," Oliver deflected with cardinal cheeks. "You look absolutely amazing! I was just thinking how great *you* look. What have you been up to?" Oliver took his hands from off of her shoulders.

"Oh, everything…and nothing," Rain said cryptically. "I'm here this morning for the arraignment of a client of mine. He raped and brutally beat a local woman," she said openly.

"Yeah, just fun all around," Oliver said caustically.

"I've recently moved back to Silver Water, and I'd *heard* that the DA *might* be here this morning. I tried to catch up with you earlier on, but I was tied up handling my case. I can't believe my old friend is the new DA of Silver County," Rain said wonderingly, eyeing Oliver like someone watching a fireworks display on the Fourth of July.

"Welcome back, Rain!"

"Thank, Ollie."

"The truth is that I wanted to switch up a bit. Trust me when I say that being DA isn't all it's cracked up to be," Oliver explained.

"Tired of the grind of arguing cases?" Rain inquired, intrigued.

"Something like that… I wanted a greater level of control. Too many perps get to walk when they should be jailed.

"Wow, a prosecutor… If anyone would have told me…" She shook her head nonsensically. "Then again, you've always had that superhero complex thing going on," she teased.

Oliver shook his head comically. "That's me-always trying to save the world," he acceded. "What about you?"

"Nothing too radical… I've partnered with Brice, Stratton and Pierce," she informed.

"That's fantastic, Rain! I'm happy for you."

"Are you married, Ollie?" Rain asked without mincing words, virtually X-raying Oliver.

"No, I'm not..."

"I'm surprised to hear that," Rain said inwardly jumping for joy. "You always struck me as the committing type." She issued a playful wink.

Oliver chuckled. "You're right, but I guess things haven't worked out in the way I had hoped or planned. What about you?" he evaded.

"Never married," she gladly announced. "I've been too busy with my career. It's kind of hard to make time for anything when you have such a demanding schedule," she admitted.

"I know what you mean." Oliver nodded and smiled.

"So, Ollie, have you had breakfast?" Rain introduced. Her cheeks flushed as she stared hopefully into his eyes.

"I had coffee," Oliver related.

"That's *not* breakfast." Rain took hold of Oliver's strong and broad shoulders. "Our new DA has got to keep his strength up."

Oliver chortled. "Okay..."

"So, will you have breakfast with me-that is unless you're not in a rush?"

Oliver found himself surrendering to a slow nod. "Sure. Why not?" It had been forever since he'd seen his old friend, and that warranted at least breakfast together. "But only on one condition..." Oliver began to haul over to his SUV, and Rain fell into step with him.

"Anything..." She gave him a beguiling sidelong look.

"That you let me pick up the tab." Oliver stared down at her smiling. He'd truly missed Rain and was glad that they'd bumped into each other.

Rain put both hands up in surrender mode. "You won't get any arguments from me." She looped her arm possessively through Oliver's, as he led her over to his car. "Is this *you*?" Rain asked perusing his steel gray BMW SUV.

"It is…" Oliver opened up the passenger's side door for Rain.

"Nice ride," she said, winking at him once he took his place behind the wheel. For Rain, she could not have planned it any better. She'd been looking to reconnect to Oliver for a while, and now that she had, she would never let go. He was the best person on the planet. Notwithstanding, he was insanely hot, good-looking and successful.

How on earth had he evaded getting married all these years? Rain had heard through the grapevine that he'd dated the wife billionaire mogul Kayden Bohm for a short while. Even if Rain was certain Oliver's heart had been broken by the failed relationship, she couldn't help thinking that Kennedy Proctor-Bohm's loss would be *her* gain.

"Thanks, Rain." Oliver beamed. "I can't believe how long it's been since we've seen each other! I'm so glad you're here!" Oliver considered, while pulling out of the parking lot.

"I'm glad I'm here too. And as they say, everything happens for a reason," Rain assessed.

"Well, what do *you* make of our chance encounter out here after over a decade?" Oliver had a quirky expression on his face.

"I call it a divine appointment. We *both* had appointments. Seeing each other again is absolutely *divine*!" she razzed, laughing.

Oliver chuckled and shook his head comically. "I see you haven't changed a bit, Rain."

"Is that a good or bad thing?" she trifled.

"It's definitely a *good* thing." Oliver caught her eye at another light.

***

"So, they cuffed him and read him his Miranda Rights," Rain shared a joke with Oliver. They'd just finished up breakfast and were sipping on coffee.

"Rain, that's terrible. I know that guy was asking for trouble, but I was hoping for a better ending," Oliver countered, shaking his head in denial.

"Oh, *you*, with your happy endings…" Rain stared sensitively into Oliver's eyes. "Thanks for buying me breakfast. This is the first time I've been in here." Rain perused the *Peach Pit Restaurant* in downtown Silver Water. "It's really nice."

"You're welcome, Rain! It was my pleasure!" Oliver acclaimed. "Whenever I'm in the area I sometimes stop in here. They make the best French Toast," he shared.

"They make the best *everything*!" Rain stared down at her three-quarter eaten vegetable omelet. "Oh, Ollie," she reached across the table, and covered Oliver's hand with hers, "being with you like this feels like old times."

"Yeah, I agree. We always had the best time whenever we hung out. I really missed you, Rain," he said in earnest. "It's a treat to get to spend a little time."

"I feel like a celebrity sitting here with the DA of Silver County. Everyone's been staring at us ever since we walked in."

"Stop… I'm just Ollie-the same guy who studied for the Bar with you."

"*Are* you the same guy?" Rain stroked fondly on his hand.

"The very same one…," Oliver reassured. "The only difference is some of the experiences I've had in the past decade. There are things I could have definitely done without." He shook his head musingly. "Even so, I think those experiences have made me a better person…stronger." He smiled thoughtfully. Oliver placed his hand over the one Rain had on his and searched her eyes.

"I don't doubt that. I'm so glad we ran into each other today," Rain applauded. "Being around you makes everything so much brighter! You're *that* person who brings out the sunshine." Rain's eyes wandered away timidly for a moment.

"Would you stop already?" Oliver's cheeks turned cardinal. He pushed back in his seat, unobtrusively reclaiming his hand. "Making the hearing this morning wasn't something I was looking forward to, but seeing you made it all worth it. I'm genuinely glad to be with you this morning!"

"I'm glad we've reconnected too, Ollie. Any plans for Christmas?" Rain asked hopefully.

"I would ordinarily be headed back to Michigan to see my family. However, things being what they are, I doubt I can get away this year," Oliver assessed. He sighed and smiled into Rain's eyes.

"Things are *that* crazy down at the DA's office huh?" Rain examined.

"Things are always a little bit crazy. Granted, my staff is amazing, but there are always pressing matters. More often than not, that usually means I have to lend time and attention to every crisis which might arise." Oliver was suddenly pensive.

"Well, how would you like an extra set of hands?" Rain brought up, enthusiastically.

"We *could* sure use another prosecutor on our trial team. Are *you* offering?" Oliver flinched in shock.

"Yes of course. That sounds right up my alley," she assessed. Inwardly, Rain hoped against hope that Oliver would say yes. Now that she had him within her grasp, there was no way she was going to allow him to slip through her fingers again. Oliver was a total prize, and she was grateful that he was still unattached.

"Having you on our team would be amazing, but what about

your law firm?" Oliver asked, still nonplused over Rain's offer.

"I can still work independently on some of the cases already in motion, but it certainly wouldn't hurt my career to work with *you* through the DA's office," Rain contrived.

Oliver smiled hopefully. "So, you're not looking to work through the DA's office because of my charming personality and winning smile?" He winked.

"Nope, it's strictly for the advancement of my career," Rain sassed. "Okay, so it's *also* because of your charming personality and winning smile."

"Uh-huh, flatter me why don't you?" Oliver razzed. "Rain, I wouldn't want for you to compromise your current position." Oliver frowned, pertained.

"Ollie, trust me when I say that if you hire me, it will only propel my career. Now, what do you say, Mr. District Attorney?" Rain sensitively explored Oliver's amber eyes. She found herself slipping easily into them. What she wanted more than anything else was to lose herself in *him*. Rain couldn't fathom why on earth she had not gone after him years ago. She could only attribute that error to temporary insanity.

"I say, welcome to our team, Attorney McGrath!" Oliver issued a welcoming smile.

"You will not regret bringing me onboard," Rain celebrated, taking Oliver's hand in hers again. "I can't believe my old friend is in a position to hire me," she marveled, shaking her head nonsensically. "It's hard to wrap my head around how much things have changed," she contemplated.

"And, yet they're still the same," Oliver reassured. "Don't thank me yet, Rain. The DA's office is a round-the-clock operation. So, you should know it requires making lots of sacrifices when you would otherwise want to bail. Most of the cases we handle are tough to say the least...," he explained more urgently.

"And I am totally up to the task. Over at the law firm, we're confronted with tough cases all the time. Ollie, I am not the least bit intimidated."

Oliver nodded quiescently. "Alright then… When can you come by?"

"How about I come by later on today?"

"You want to come by this afternoon? *I* might not be around, but my Assistant, David Reed or the Deputy to the DA Jason Press should be." Oliver quickly pulled out his phone in order to check his schedule. He knew he had at least three appointments for later. However, when he perused his lock screen, there was a notification that Erin had texted.

"I went out to the Pottery Barn yesterday to look for Christmas ornaments needed for the office. I can't wait to show you some of my awesome finds for the party. I've been at the office for the past couple of hours, and I haven't seen you. Hopefully, you can squeeze in a few minutes for me later on. That is if you ever make it into the office today. Lol. Don't work too hard." Erin had texted the *laugh out loud* and smiling emoji's.

Oliver's face flushed in joy and expectation over Erin's text. Remembering their time together over the weekend, filled his heart with joy and anticipation. He couldn't wait to see her later on.

"Is later on this afternoon okay?" Rain prodded, seeing that Oliver had suddenly become elusive. There was an unmistakable smile on his face. Rain was worried that maybe he had a girlfriend. So, she was determined to find out right away if he did. Once she had her answer, she would know how to proceed.

To Rain, it didn't matter one way or another if Oliver *did* have a girlfriend. She had no respect for girlfriends. *Wives* were a totally different story, but as long as Oliver didn't have a ring on his finger, all was fair in love and war. However, if he *did* have a girlfriend, Rain needed to work out a strategy in order to snag him away. "Ollie…?" Rain tried to rouse him from profound reflection.

"Oh, I'm sorry, Rain," Oliver offered with a sincere smile. "You might want to come after four. That's about the time things start winding down," he informed.

"I will be there," Rain said with a curious expression on her face. "Oliver, can I ask you something?" she brought up brazenly.

"Of course," he encouraged.

"Do you have a girlfriend?" she asked plainly, invading his eyes with her own.

Oliver laughed lightly. *"You're* a straight shooter," he commented.

"Then again, you already know that about me," she quipped.

Oliver sighed, and his face changed remembering his short-lived romance with Kennedy. He was also reminded of the night he'd told Erin that he couldn't offer her anything more than friendship. Oliver was overwhelmed with regret, because he acknowledged that Erin had decided to the leave the DA's office, because he'd rejected her. "No, I don't currently...and the truth is that I'm not looking to-"

"Oliver Wright, what *are* you talking about? You are one of the most eligible bachelors in Georgia. You can't just close yourself up to the possibility of having a relationship. I also know how staunchly you adhere to your religious beliefs. Even if things didn't work out in a past relationship, you can't give up," Rain delineated. "I doubt you were born to be a monk or a hermit," she quipped.

Oliver laughed. "Rain, you're too much. And yet, I doubt that I was cut out to be a monk or a hermit for that matter, but when your heart has been through the grinder..."

"You pick yourself up, brush off the hurt and press on to the future," she said exploring his eyes more urgently.

Just then, Oliver was reminded of the impression he'd received from God not too long ago. God had conveyed that he should leave the past behind and to press forward. Even if Rain didn't know it, God had just used her to *reaffirm* that he needed to move past his failed relationship. Oliver wanted to move on, but *actually* doing it was a difficult process. In spite of his misgivings, he prayed inwardly for God's strength to be able to do just that. "Yeah, I guess that's what you do," Oliver acceded, smiling.

"It's *definitely* what you do," Rain affirmed, sizing up everything about him. She judged that Oliver had absolutely no idea that *she* was going to be the one to help him get over the hurdles. There was no way she was going to ever let Oliver Baron Wright, Silver County's new DA, out of her sight. "So, I will swing by the office at around four," she reminded staring dreamily into his face.

Oliver nodded. "You can tell David or Jason that I'm expecting you. I should be back from *Silver Rose Point* by then," he affirmed. "I'm so sorry to have to cut our breakfast date short, but I have to be in *Silver Main* in about half an hour. I have a meeting at the State Attorney General's office. The John Morgan case is giving us all a run for our money."

"And yet, I have no doubt that John Morgan will be prosecuted. I know *you*, Ollie. You're like the kindest and most sensitive person on the planet. However, when it comes to justice and upholding the law... Well, let's just say that I know that any case *you* undertake, warranting justice, that perpetrator will be prosecuted to the fullest extent." She winked at him.

"For me, it gets really personal at times, especially when the innocent are victimized."

"I know that. That's one of the things I admire most about you. You've always been that way, even when we were both starting out."

Oliver smiled, revealing his straight set of white teeth and shallow dimples. "That's me. I'm your proverbial..."

"Superhero...," Rain filled in, while Oliver helped her out of her chair.

"No..." Oliver's eyes met hers playfully. "Just a guy who believes in standing up for what's right." Oliver left a bill on the table. He drifted out to the front door and opened it up for Rain. His SUV was parked only feet away from the restaurant's main entrance. Oliver Immediately got the door for Rain.

However, before Rain slipped inside of the automobile, her eyes connected furtively to his. "Isn't that what superheroes do?" Her heart trounced like jungle drums having Oliver stand so close. His hand on her arm helping her into the SUV felt like a dream, and he smelled like heaven.

Oliver smiled quietly over Rain's compliment. He walked around, hopped into the automobile, and took his place behind the wheel. Before driving back over to the courthouse, he looked over at Rain. "Thank you for saying that-and thank you for brightening up this incredibly drab and dismal morning."

"No, I should actually be thanking *you*."

"What for?" Oliver asked at a stop sign.

"Thank *you* for breakfast, for the wonderful company and for a new job." Rain's cheeks turned scarlet, and heat permeated through every pore of her body, because she was in such close proximity to Oliver. She felt flustered, even bordering feverish, as it resonated that she would be around him on a regular basis.

"You're welcome!" Oliver said, delving her blue eyes.

"Would you mind if I cracked the window a bit?" Rain asked as Oliver drove. She was fervid by then and had to talk herself down. Moreover, she had to find a way not to act on her impulse to make a romantic advance. The last thing she wanted was to scare away her old friend by coming on too strong. So, Rain resolved to cool the flames of her fire for Oliver, until she found a way to invite him into the blaze, and to overtake him in the conflagration.

"Not at all, are you alright?" Oliver asked, concerned, as he pressed the automatic down button for the front right-side passenger window for Rain.

"Fine, just a little warm," Rain told Oliver with an awkward smile.

***

Erin wasn't sure why she felt sad and empty, as she pulled into the parking lot of the *Dollar Dream* convenience store during her lunch hour. She had gotten to work at nine as usual and had worked until one. During the course of her day, she had hoped to see Oliver, but he'd been out on the field all day. Erin didn't want to feel out of sorts, because Oliver had been MIA. She understood that his new title carried tremendous responsibility.

Erin should have gotten used to his exacting schedule by now. Oliver spent very little time around the office. The man was called to handle one crisis after the next. She had texted him earlier on to let him know that she'd already started planning the upcoming Christmas party. Oliver had texted back, telling her that he would find a moment to connect. He'd also told her how happy he was that she was so on top of her game.

Yet and still, getting a text message in no way appeased her desire to see him. Since Oliver had walked her to her door early Sunday morning, Erin had felt some form of separation anxiety. For all intents and purposes, she was an alcoholic, and Oliver was a beautiful bottle of Cognac. That was to the extent in which she'd missed him.

However, she couldn't help feeling as if she were fooling herself. Oliver's heart was still tied into his past relationship with Kennedy. Erin ascertained just how deeply he'd loved Kennedy. And, even if Erin grasped that Oliver *did* care about her-that he even thought she was beautiful. In her heart of hearts, Erin acknowledged that Oliver would probably never feel for her as strongly as he had for Kennedy. That realization tore her apart, because she knew *she'd* never feel stronger for anyone else.

"Lord, I am trusting you to help me in this situation," Erin prayed as she sat in the car. "I don't know what I'm doing. All I know is that I love Oliver. You're the one who told me to pray on the matter. Well, Lord, I *have* been praying consistently and even fasting.

"When Oliver told me that he just wanted to be friends, my hopes were dashed," she admitted fighting back tears. "That's why I had to give him my two-week notice. It's so hard being around him feeling the way I do. But, after spending the day together on Saturday, I don't want to *not* be around him. Lord, I have no idea how to proceed. So, I am asking for your help, your strength and guidance." Tears escaped the corners of Erin's eyes.

While sitting there, she was reminded of Hebrews 11:6 "But without faith, it is impossible to please him: for he that cometh to God must believe that he is, and that he is a rewarder of them that diligently seek him (KJV)."

Erin humbly worshipped and acquiesced to the prompting of the Spirit of God. She looked heavenward and attested, "I will have faith in you, Lord. I know that nothing is too hard for you. So, I trust you to have your way in this situation, because it's breaking my heart."

That said, Erin stepped out of the car, and hiked over to the entranceway of the huge store outlet. She had heard that she could find Christmas items in bulk and for a reasonable price. She quickly checked her phone and realized she had already used up twenty minutes of her hour-long break. She'd had a late breakfast at her desk, so that she'd be free to come out to the strip mall. There were lots of things on the list she and Oliver had made, and the party was less than two weeks away.

Mostly, Erin was looking for varying items for the games which were to be played at the party. Then, there was the matter of finding white icicle lights to deck out the office and building lobby. The DA's office had a huge meeting hall which was perfect for the function. Erin had an idea of the decorations needed to set the right backdrop for the event. Stepping inside of the store, she grabbed a rolling cart.

Erin couldn't help smiling as she perused the exaggerated Christmas displays. By far, Christmas was the best time of year in her opinion. It seemed that some of the items she needed could be found in aisle seven. So, bypassing all of the Christmas hoopla and paraphernalia, she drifted into that aisle in order to browse through the types of Christmas lights they had to offer. She was so engrossed in looking through the Christmas light bin, that she didn't notice that someone else had rolled up into the very same aisle. "This one is 25 feet long…," Erin examined one of the packages.

"Well, don't act like you don't see me," the individual who'd rolled into the aisle said with an attitude. Her cart had stalled only a few feet away from Erin's.

Startled, Erin looked up, and saw her former best friend Anika standing there. Their shopping carts were all that separated them. Erin's heart fell in dread to see Anika. In spite of the malaise she felt, she remarked how beautiful Anika looked in a stylish black coat with a furry hood, designer jeans and black leather boots. Her peanut butter skin radiated with life and vitality, and her hair was out in bangs. Erin hadn't been this close to Anika in months. In fact, she had stopped talking to Anika altogether. Anika had not only *suggested* that Erin dabble in witchcraft in order to win Oliver's heart, she had *insisted* on it. "Hi, Anika," Erin said plainly-keeping her distance.

"So, that's the way it is, Erin?" Anika's face warped in mistrust and vexation. "We were the best of friends, and all of the sudden you stop talking to me?" She placed her hands cheekily on her hips.

"I've just been really busy," Erin said evadingly. "I've had a lot on my plate in the past few months," Erin said truthfully.

"Yeah, I know all about the *things* on your plate," Anika said caustically. "I know all about your volunteer work at campaign central to help Oliver win the DA's office. I also happen to know that you went out with him a few times after Kennedy Proctor-Bohm broke his heart." Anika's fair skin reddened in irritation. "How did all of *that* work out for you?" she asked acerbically.

"It worked out just fine," Erin said plainly, malaise. "Listen, it was really nice running into you, Anika, but I'm on my lunchbreak. I've only got a few minutes to pick up the things I need…"

Anika laughed derisively. "I know that you've been working through the DA's office. Again, I will ask you, Erin, how is *that* working out? I'll bet you're no closer to calling Oliver Wright your boyfriend than you were around this same time last year. You haven't gotten *any* closer to him, have you?"

Tears stung Erin's eyes to hear the mocking tone in Anika's voice. She had done her best to avoid her former bestie. Anika still attended Deliverance Tabernacle on Sundays, but Erin usually cut out right after service ended, so that she didn't have to connect to her. What hurt the most in that instance was that Anika was right. It seemed no matter how hard she tried Oliver was always just beyond her reach.

"You don't have anything to say, do you? The look on your face tells me everything I need to know. You and Oliver are great *friends*, but nothing more." There was a daunting and scornful expression on Anika's face. "I told you what to do last year to win Oliver's heart, but you didn't listen to me. And now that Oliver Wright is the new DA, you can best believe that scores of women who didn't know him before will be looking to get close to him." Calculation veiled Anika's pretty face.

"Okay, thanks for the overview. It's been good seeing you again, Anika. If we don't get the chance to see each other before Christmas, I wish you and your family a Merry Christmas!" Erin's voice undulated. She was crumbling on the inside as she considered Anika's words. Moreover, she sensed that Anika was absolutely right. Women were constantly throwing themselves at Oliver.

Besides, because he'd delineated that they were to remain friends, what was to stop him from being with someone else? Regardless of what he'd said, Erin knew that Oliver would open up his heart to love again. However, the thought of not being the one he opened up his heart to, seemed a bit more than Erin could handle.

"It isn't too late, Erin. If you *really* want Oliver, there are *steps* you can take to ensure that he's yours. Otherwise, play at your own risk," Anika disparaged. "I can't push you to do anything you don't want to. So, please let me know when Oliver meets his *new* girlfriend." She shook her head contrarily. "I can't believe you *really* think you're too good to be friends with me."

"I don't' think that I'm too good to be friends with you, Anika. I just don't think that our core values and beliefs are the same anymore."

"What? Are you judging me now?" She frowned, offended. "We both go to church."

"Yeah, we *do* both go to church, but the Christian life is a lot more than just going to church, Anika. It's about walking it out on a daily basis-no matter how hard it gets..." Erin's eyes momentarily drifted away from Anika's intent stare. She then looked up and boldly attested, "And, witchcraft has no place in the life of a follower of Jesus."

"So, you *are* judging me...?" Anika evaluated upset. "You're no better than me, Erin. You might think you are, but you're not. I also happen to know that you're in love with Oliver, and that you're going to have a heck of a time landing him with your passivity. Soon, it will be in all the papers how Oliver Wright is getting married-and it *won't* be to you."

"It's because of my love for God *and* for Oliver that I could never do what you've asked. And, as for Oliver finding someone else, as much as that would hurt, God's will be done in both of our lives," Erin's voice broke, and tears meandered down her cheeks.

"*Whatever* you have to say to make yourself feel better..." Anika rolled her eyes.

Erin shook her head in remorse. "You can't be on the fence with God, Anika. If you are, you truly don't belong to Him. And, if that's the case, I feel sorry for you. Satan never has anything good to offer. Death, destruction and misery are what you can expect, which will follow unto eternity. Get it right. Being in church doesn't make you a Christian. Following the word of God does."

"So, you *do* think you're better than me," Anika affirmed, exasperated.

"No, but I am doing all I can to follow the word of God."

"Good luck getting Oliver Wright, but if *your* way doesn't work, you have my number."

Erin issued a sad smile. "Take care of yourself, Anika. I will keep you in my prayers."

"I don't need your prayers, Erin. In fact, I don't need *you*," she hissed. Anika propelled her cart forward, brushed past Erin, and proceeded down the aisle.

Erin stood there for a moment completely frozen and dazed over what had just occurred. Affected by Anika's words, she prayed in her heart, fighting back the tears of hopelessness stinging her eyes. The Holy Spirit emphasized Hebrews 11:6 again reminding her to have faith, no matter how the circumstances appeared. The Spirit also affirmed that she should *definitely* pray for Anika. Erin swallowed the chunk lodged in her throat, and bravely continued to shop for the supplies needed for the party.

By the time Erin made it up to the register to pay for her items, Anika was standing at the register across from hers. As Erin stood there and watched the cashier itemize her purchases, she could feel Anika's contentious stare hot on her face. Luckily, Erin's cashier moved a lot faster. After Erin tendered her credit card and got the receipt, she rushed out of *Dollar Dream* like a woman on a mission. Making her way back out to the parking lot, she hauled her bags to the trunk of her car, hopped into the automobile, and drove away as quickly as she could.

***

"Erin, did you finish with the Gundry motion for me?" David Reed, the Assistant DA asked Erin over the phone later in the afternoon.

"I'm printing it out right now," she informed him. "Sure, I will also edit the Goodwin affidavit," Erin told him over the line.

She'd been sequestered in her office all afternoon long. Moreover, she was still nursing her wounds from the unexpected encounter with Anika during her lunchbreak. However, there was a gnawing on the inside-almost like the sensation of a pebble in her shoe. Erin knew that it was because she had not seen Oliver for the entire day.

She'd known that Oliver had a lot on his plate, but she had no idea he'd be gone the entire day. There had been no text messages exchanged since that morning. Erin had not initiated anymore messages, because she had not wanted to come off as too needy, and overly excited to be helping him plan the party. Now, it was almost four, and she'd be going home in an hour.

Working past feelings of jeopardy, Erin quickly browsed over the affidavit, and made the necessary corrections. In addition, she pieced together the motion for David Reed. There was no time to sulk over not seeing Oliver at that point in time. Erin rushed out of her office and headed over to the main office area with the paperwork in hand, but stopped short. Feet away, she caught sight of Oliver. He and David were engaged in conversation with a beautiful Caucasian woman with blonde hair and blue eyes.

Erin's heart thudded in her chest seeing Oliver again. There was an irrepressible smile on her face because he was back. He looked totally princely in his burgundy-colored dress suit and accents. The wine color highlighted his coffee skin and amber eyes. For a moment Erin stood back and took him in. Oliver always dressed to the nines. More often than not, he looked as if he was modeling men's apparel for a catalog of some sort. Erin wasn't sure why she always had the same reaction whenever she saw him. She felt flustered all over, her skin tingled, her heart thrashed, and the butterflies were dancing a jig in the hollow of her stomach again. Initially, she had not heard Oliver's voice. Only the woman's and David's voices had been discernable.

Oliver had just stepped into the office after being out most of the day. There were a number of cases for which he had to collaborate with the authorities in piecing together evidence. He'd thought that he'd make it back to the office before Rain got there, but she'd preceded him. Rain had already been waiting on him for a while. "So, Rain and I ran into each other this morning at the courthouse. She is my old law school friend. She's the newest prosecutor on our team!" Oliver told David.

"That's amazing! Welcome to the DA's office, Rain!" David

extended his hand in greeting to the young woman. "You *do* know what a whirlwind experience it is to work around here, don't you?" David tested.

"Oliver and I talked extensively on the matter earlier," Rain informed. "I'm not the least bit intimidated."

While David and Rain engaged in conversation, Oliver looked past them. From feet away, he saw Erin standing by with paperwork. Seeing Erin again immediately made Oliver smile. His heart began hammering in total anticipation. "Rain, David, will you excuse me for a moment?" Oliver asked the pair politely.

"Sure," David and Rain said in concert.

However, Rain's gape followed Oliver over across the office to the gorgeous, African American young lady whom he was going to connect to. Rain couldn't help noticing the irrepressible smile on Oliver's face. She wondered if this pretty black woman was going to pose a threat to her goal of making Oliver Wright completely hers.

Oliver went over to have a word with Erin. "Hey, there, stranger," he teased as he usually did. "I got your text earlier. And can I say just how impressed I am?" he praised exploring Erin's garnet eyes with a sense of novelty. "You're certainly more on top of your game than I am." He smiled warmly.

"Well, not everyone can attest to running the DA's office," Erin said totally elated to see him. "I've got so many awesome things to show you. I found the prettiest items over at the *Pottery Barn*. I also went out to *Dollar Dream* on my lunchbreak. I made a total killing with the white icicle lights for the office, the lobby and the meeting hall," Erin informed shakily, hypnotized.

"That sounds amazing! I can't wait to see-"

"Excuse me, Ollie," Rain said, floating over to stand next to Oliver, "I wanted to get started right away on the case you, David and I just talked about."

"Right…," Oliver said turning to look over at Rain.

He then redirected towards Erin again. "Erin, I'd like for you to meet a very dear old friend of mine, Rain McGrath. We went to law school together," Oliver told Erin. He'd never been the objectifying type, but he found himself taking in Erin's curves in her sage-green dress. The color did something to her gingerbread-colored skin and brought out her beautiful eyes.

With her lengthy light brown tresses shimmering over her shoulders and back, Erin looked like an angel. Oliver found himself taking in every inch of her. Swallowing hard, he explored her sweet features, and his gaze temporarily settled on her well-formed mouth.

Erin looked into the face of Oliver's gorgeous law school friend. Her heart twisted in uneasiness, because she sensed that this Rain McGrath was territorial. Just from her body language, Erin grasped that Rain was *into* Oliver. Anika's words resonated just then that women would be coming out in droves for Oliver. Despite feelings of malaise and insecurity, Erin offered Rain a genial smile, and extended her hand. "It's nice to meet you, Rain," she said as a matter of protocol.

"*Karen*, is it?" Rain tested, sizing up the competition. She took Erin in, appraising that the young woman had the potential to be a hindrance to her plan, but she refused to allow anyone or anything to get in the way.

"No, it's *Erin*," Erin clarified warily. Oliver hadn't stuttered or said her name unclearly. So, Erin gathered that this was Rain's first snub. "And, welcome to the DA's office!" Erin's smile felt elastic.

"Rain's our new prosecutor. I've already familiarized her with some of our cases going forward," Oliver said, unable to take his eyes off of Erin.

"That sounds great! We sure could use the help," Erin tried to sound upbeat and positive. Rain's lower was beginning to burn a hole through her. So, as much as she wanted to maintain eye contact with the woman, Erin's gape kept wandering back over to Oliver every time.

"Yeah, I know. Rain has no idea what she's getting herself into," Oliver razzed.

"Sure she does." Rain examined Erin curiously. "I told Oliver that I'm a lot tougher than I look," she said trying to sound humble. "*Erin*, what is it that you do around here?" Rain jumped right in, giving Erin the once over condescendingly.

"I'm a Paralegal," Erin said without flinching. She couldn't say for sure, but she sensed that Rain was trying to berate her. Notwithstanding, the woman was leaning closely into Oliver. It lacerated Erin's heart to consider that Oliver had no idea that his *dear old friend* had designs on him.

"Oh, that's nice," Rain said glibly. "Are we ready to look over the case?" Rain tugged on Oliver's arm, because he seemed completely absorbed in Erin. Erin's eyes were fastened to him as well, and they were exchanging quiet smiles. Rain had to kill that noise and fast. "Ollie, you wanted to go over that paperwork with me?"

"Oh, right… I have the documents in my office." Oliver's face creased in regret.

Erin's heart fell in disappointment. She had waited all day to connect to Oliver and had thought they'd have at least a minute to catch up, but she'd been wrong. Notwithstanding, this *Rain woman* couldn't seem to keep her hands off of him. Thus, because they were old friends, Oliver probably couldn't see Rain's angle. Before things got too carried away, Erin spoke up, "That's alright, Ollie. We can catch up in the morning."

Oliver's expression was that of discontent. "I'm so sorry. My day has been crazy, but we *will* catch up." Oliver searched Erin's eyes sensitively. "Thank you so much for taking this project to heart. It really means a lot to me!"

"You're welcome," Erin heartened, fighting back tears. "You go on and do what you need to." She forced a smile. "It really isn't that important."

"Hey, it's *very* important," Oliver countered, delving her eyes. "We'll talk later." He nodded affirmatively.

"Sure," Erin said offering a faint smile. *Why was it that her feelings for Oliver were growing every second?* Erin then directed towards Rain. The woman had been dissecting every exchange she and Oliver had. "It's nice to meet you, and welcome aboard!" Erin said with as much enthusiasm she could muster-which was very little.

"Yeah, sure, it's nice meeting you too, Erin!" Rain gave Erin a superficial smile. She then looped her arm through Oliver's and stared up into his eyes. "Are you all set?" she tested, icing Erin out.

"I'm all set." Oliver smiled. He and Rain began to walk away, but he turned back and gave Erin a pining look.

Erin stared wistfully back at Oliver, but inwardly she sensed trouble stirring. There was no doubt in her mind that *Rain* on their trial team, meant a brewing storm in her already overcast horizon with Oliver. She kept reminding herself that she needed to have faith and to trust God right now. God had promised to help her in one way or another. So, Erin would continue to anticipate his deliverance.

"Hey, are those for me?" David had crossed over to ask Erin. "Earth to Erin," he razzed.

"Oh, I'm sorry, David. These are definitely for you." Erin smiled and offered him the folder which included the motion and the affidavit.

"Are you okay?" David asked concerned.

Forcing a smile, Erin met his pertained expression. "I'm okay. I'm going to work on finishing up that deed for Mr. Gillis before I leave tonight."

"Have I told you lately how much I'm going to miss you around here?" David smiled.

"You might have told me a few times," Erin said graciously. David Reed was an awesome person and an amazing Assistant to the DA!

"You always know what I'm going to ask before I even open up my mouth." He shook his head contrarily. "Oliver won't be able to find *anyone* as good!" David affirmed and patted Erin's arm.

"Thanks, David." Erin smiled genuinely, feeling encouraged by David's words. In her heart and mind, she perceived that God had used David's words to relate a double meaning.

"It's the truth. Keep up the good work, kid." He winked and turned away.

Erin smiled and watched him float back to the bustling office area. David walked through the congested area in order to go to his private office.

Erin wrapped things up at about twenty past five. She shut down her office equipment, grabbed her coat and pocketbook, and shut the office door closed. In spite of the encouraging words she'd received from the Lord, there was an undeniable sense of sadness. As she walked through the hallway leading up to the main office area, her heart dipped in discouragement. She had been so excited over the thought of connecting to Oliver all day, but things had gone terribly awry.

Furthermore, her run in with Anika at the strip mall had only added insult to injury. Erin was willing to admit that the *worst* part of the day was finally seeing Oliver, but Rain McGrath's grubby hands were all over him. Erin turned a corner but stopped short when she saw Oliver and Rain standing outside of his office. Her heart thumped with a sense of dread, as she pulled back and examined their exchanges.

"I'm so comfortable around here, Ollie. It feels like coming home!" Rain told him, all wired up.

Oliver laughed lightly. "I'm glad you're acclimating. Trust me when I say that you might not be smiling in the days ahead."

"Oh, yes I will," Rain said, delving meaningfully into Oliver's eyes.

"And why is that?" Oliver asked pleasantly.

"Well, it's because my life has changed for the better in just *one* day." Rain impulsively threw her arms around Oliver and crushed him to herself. "Thank you so much! Thank you for everything!" She celebrated.

Oliver laughed and gasped, having gotten the wind knocked out of him. He slipped his arms about Rain's waist and hugged her back. "You're welcome!" He kept shaking his head humorously. Oliver pulled back and looked into her eyes. "Rain, you might want to check back with me in a week or two before you start thanking me."

"I won't need to wait a couple of weeks. I'm just happy that we've found each other again." She gazed fondly into his eyes.

Oliver nodded. "I'm glad too. It's really something that *today* of all days we should happen to bump into each other," he said marveling.

"I'm a firm believer that everything happens for a reason," Rain avowed. "So, there are no coincidences. We were *meant* to see each other again."

Oliver smiled musingly but didn't comment on Rain's observation.

Erin's heart throbbed in hurt, as she anticipated what Oliver would say next. She could tell that he was also very pleased to have reconnected to Rain. Moreover, Erin could see that Rain was chomping at the bit to connect to Oliver romantically. She was staring at him with a ravenous expression on her face. Erin could only describe Rain's gape as a wolf who'd just ensnared a small animal. It killed Erin to consider that maybe Rain was the *one* Oliver would finally open up his heart to.

She went on to listen to the two talk and laugh about old times. The fact that Oliver seemed happy around Rain was a stab wound to Erin's heart. Unable to take one more moment, Erin walked away in the opposite direction, and let herself out towards the back end of the building. She hiked over to her car and hopped in. Rushing away from the area, she did all she could not to fall apart.

CHAPTER FIVE

The police had already barricaded the crime scene with yellow tape in and surrounding the Wilson house in the early morning. It was just after six a.m., but Oliver had been called in by the authorities. The DA's office had to work in collaboration on this special case. Another young woman had been brutally beaten and murdered. Antonia Wilson had been found stabbed to death in her home. She was the fourth victim in the town of *Silver Commons* found in the same condition in the past month. So, the authorities were convinced they had a serial killer on their hands.

Oliver winced, stirred by sadness and empathy stepping onto the scene, as police and detectives inspected the area. Drifting cautiously into the bedroom, he saw blood everywhere. The body of the young woman had already been placed inside of a body bag.

Now, investigators were creating a forensics file. It seemed as if the coroners had just made it over to the crime scene. Oliver's heartstrings unraveled to consider what Antonia had suffered at the hands of her murderer. For that very reason he had to do everything in his power to help the authorities figure out who was behind the killings. Furthermore, he had to ensure that the killer was prosecuted to the fullest extent of the law.

"What are we looking at, Hal?" Oliver asked the head detective.

"It's not pretty, Ollie. Antonia Wilson was only twenty-six years old. From the amount of stab wounds, I would say that it was personal. There was also swelling to the base of her head, indicating that she was brutally beaten before she was stabbed in excess of thirty times," Hal Dayton explained.

"Man, I can't believe this. Something's got to be done about this dirt bag," Oliver groused, outraged that another young person's life had been cut short."

"We definitely need your help with this case. We suspect serial killings. All four victims were stabbed repeatedly, as if it was

a personal vendetta for the murderer. It could possibly be some
angry guy who has an axe to grind with women of a certain age."

"All four victims were of a certain age?" Oliver questioned,
making notes.

"All four were in their twenties, slender, of a certain height...
The perpetrator didn't seem to make any differentiation in respect to
hair or eye color as means of selection."

"That's curious," Oliver examined. "They usually go for the
same type."

"Well, this one isn't discriminating. He's an equal
opportunity sleaze," Hal disclosed, miffed.

"You can definitely count on us. Our office will work closely
with you in order to piece together the evidence needed to bring this
dirt bag out of hiding," Oliver affirmed, grieved by the
circumstances. "We're going to figure this one out. *Silver
Commons* is the very heart of Silver County, so that means no one is
safe. This miscreant has been terrorizing the good people of Silver
Water, but not on my watch." Veins pulsed at Oliver's temples.

"The last thing this county needs is the threat of a serial killer
loose. Ollie, just to be on the safe side, you might want to appeal to
the powers that be to set a curfew in the area. No young woman is
safe until that monster is captured," Hal affirmed. Just then, a police
officer came up, and handed him a sealed bag of particles found in
and around the murder scene.

Oliver nodded in agreement. "We'll get right on it. Thanks
for calling me in this morning. At least I have a better idea of what
we're dealing with." Tears shone in Oliver's eyes as he took in
everything happening around him. Another young woman's life had
been prematurely snuffed out by a depraved assailant, and the DA's
office wasn't going to take that sitting down.

As he perused the crime scene, Oliver spoke to the
investigators. Having firsthand knowledge of the atrocious murders
made the matter very personal for him. Right then and there he
determined to follow through until the killer was prosecuted and

brought to justice. The deputy attorneys who worked through the DA's office would do their part in assisting the authorities. However, Oliver vowed to leave no stone unturned until this serial demon was put behind bars. The safety of the good people of Silver County rested on their shoulders, and Oliver resolved not to fail them.

***

From the murder scene out in Silver Commons, Oliver returned home. He had to shower, dress and go into the work. Oliver was dress and all set to leave, but before stepping out of the apartment, he checked his phone, hoping for a text or a voicemail from Erin. Oliver sighed in disappointment because there were none. He'd meant to call Erin last night, but so many business-related matters had gotten in the way. There had also been a late-night call from a deputy attorney who was helping him on an urgent case.

In fact, Oliver had meant to swing by Erin's after leaving the office last night. It was important for him to express just how much he appreciated all of her hard work. Even if Erin was a dynamo, Oliver didn't want her singlehandedly planning the Christmas party. What he wanted was to ensure he *made* time to work alongside her. They'd tentatively planned the event together. And, despite his impossible schedule, he didn't want for Erin to think he'd left her hanging.

Oliver smiled as he wandered into the living room and perused the Christmas tree. It was still just as storybook perfect as it had been on the day he and Erin had set it up. He issued a command to Alexa to turn on the lights. Oliver wanted the lights on for when he got home later.

Between the gifts his family had sent via post, those offered by coworkers and members of the community, there were quite a few presents under the tree. Oliver smiled openly thinking about Erin. Whenever he found a free moment from the burden of his responsibilities, Erin always came to mind. Oliver realized that the only *other* person who'd so consumed his thoughts had been

Kennedy.

Oliver was still bewildered by the emptiness he'd grappled with since driving Erin home on Saturday night. He wasn't sure what it meant. *Was he ready to open up his heart again? Was he at the place where he could offer up more than just the shattered pieces?* Because he wasn't sure, he had to be careful. What Oliver *did* know was that he wanted to see and be around Erin all the time.

Oliver grabbed his satchel but stalled in front of the door. With a contemplative smile on his face, he decided to shoot Erin a quick text message. He realized that Erin would probably get his text when she got to the office, but that didn't matter. At some point she would, and hopefully she'd text him back. He wasn't certain how the day would go, but he *was* sure that wherever he found himself, receiving a text message from Erin would totally brighten things up.

"So, I'm about to leave for the office. I was called in to review a murder investigation by the authorities before seven this morning. It already feels as if I've fulfilled an entire workday of duties. LOL! Allow me to apologize for not giving you my undivided attention yesterday afternoon. I know how diligently you've been working through the office, while party-planning. I promise to do better. If you need to assign any duties to me while I'm out on the field, please don't hesitate. Whatever you need... Erin, I truly appreciate your hard work and devotion." Oliver added a smiling face emoji.

Oliver was beaming after sending the text. *Maybe, she'll forgive me for yesterday,* he considered before letting himself out of his place. However, the moment he opened up the door, he was totally taken aback. "Rain!" he declared, both surprised and nonplused. Rain was standing right outside his front door holding a bag from Dunkin Donuts.

"Good morning, Oliver!" Rain said with an alluring smile. Rain had been up at the crack of dawn trying to figure out some way in which she could connect to Oliver. She was determined to make use of every possible opportunity. Rain sensed that Erin Brasfield was also vying for Oliver's attention. Rain had also remarked that

Oliver was quite taken by Erin. However, that was where *she* would come into the picture. Rain felt it to be her solemn duty to veer Oliver's attention away from Erin.

But just then, she sized Oliver up in his steel gray dress suit. The suit fit his perfect body like a glove. Oliver's wavy dark hair with baby curls around the temples, framed his winsome face. His amber eyes glistened in the early morning light like liquid gold, and his musky scent was enough to make her lose her mind.

"Rain, what are you doing here?" Oliver asked, smiling but still puzzled.

"Well, I thought you could use a little breakfast and a fresh cup of coffee." She held the bag up in display.

Oliver laughed and shook his head nonsensically. "Rain, you *really* didn't have to drive all the way over here. I usually grab a coffee just a few blocks away from the office." Oliver's eyes lowered pleasantly into her eyes.

"It wasn't that big a deal. I wanted to surprise you!" Rain closed the small space between them and stared adoringly at Oliver. "I was hoping we could drive into work together," she anticipated.

"Okay, but *you* didn't drive over did you?" Oliver asked quizzically, searching her eyes.

"No, I took a Lyft over. If I learned anything from yesterday is that I *like* driving with you." Rain scrutinized every inch of Oliver, and her eyes rested on his perfect mouth. All of the sudden she was thirsty for a long satisfying drink from its source.

"Okay, I guess…," Oliver said uncertainly. "Thank you so much. Bringing breakfast by for me this morning is very thoughtful and sweet," Oliver praised, delving her pretty blue eyes.

"Well, *sweet* is my middle name," Rain said, beguilingly doting on him.

"Is that so…?" Oliver razzed. "I guess there are things that I *don't* know about you." He smiled earnestly.

"Well then, it's my *responsibility* to ensure that you learn *everything* there is to know about me," Rain said with a come hither expression, as she sized up Oliver's stalwart arms and broad shoulders, emphasizing how much she thought he was *working* that suit.

Oliver nodded quiescently. "Okay, I'm always up for learning new things." He winked. "Now, let me see what you have there?" He gestured to the bag in Rain's hand.

Rain happily handed the bag over to Oliver, and her face lit up to see his reaction the contents.

"Oh, Boston Creams and Hazelnut coffee…? How did you know they were my favorites?" he delighted.

"Just a lucky guess… Actually, I'm not being entirely truthful. I remember when we used to have those early morning exams."

"That's right," Oliver beamed, "we would sometimes stop in for coffee and donuts." His face radiated with new life to recall the events of his past with Rain. "Thanks for remembering." His eyes connected reminiscently to Rain's.

"You're welcome, Mr. DA!" Rain was all smiles. She considered that at some point she was going to have to *show* Oliver just how serious she was about taking their friendship to the next level. Furthermore, she refused to allow some *paralegal* who worked through the DA's office with an unmistakable crush on him to thwart her plans.

"Mm…" Oliver took a sip of his coffee. "I don't think it gets any better than that."

"I'm glad you like it, Ollie."

"I love it, Rain! Thanks again." Oliver shut his front door, and drifted out into the hallway, falling into step with Rain. They tread down the hallway over to the elevator. "You wouldn't believe the kind of morning I've had so far…," Oliver began to say.

However, before he could say another word, the elevator

doors opened, and his neighbor Lilly was inside. Lilly looked professional in a navy-blue skirt suit. Her dark hair fell over her shoulders and back with the same vitality of her olive skin. Oliver wondered where she'd gone so early in the morning. Lilly worked through Grandview University Hospital as an X-Ray Technician in the evening. Oliver wondered if she'd had a court date, because she was still in process of finalizing her divorce.

Lilly froze in her steps seeing Oliver with the beautiful young blonde. It felt like a knife to the heart after what had transpired last weekend. She'd asked Oliver out. He'd rejected her and had stated that he wasn't looking to be in a relationship. Of course, his snub had been kind. Lilly seriously doubted that Oliver Wright knew how to be anything but. Still, it hurt to see him with this beauty who was about ten to fifteen years her junior.

"Good morning, Lilly!" Oliver greeted with an open smile.

"Good morning, Oliver," Lilly said plainly, with a taut expression on her pretty face. That said, she brushed past him, and continued down the hall. Lilly hadn't bothered acknowledging Rain who was standing right beside him. Oliver followed Lilly's gait, pertained and perplexed over her slight. "What was that about...?" he asked mystified.

"Even the *older* women find you absolutely irresistible," Rain commented, watching Lilly power down the hallway like a machine. Rain couldn't help thinking she had her work cut out for her. She deemed that lots of women were vying for Oliver's attention. She couldn't say she blamed them, because Oliver was a dream man and totally worth it. However, at the end of the day, Rain determined to be the *one* Oliver came home to every night.

"I seriously doubt that," Oliver countered.

"You can't tell she's in love with you?" Rain asked, as she and Oliver slipped inside of the elevator.

"She's a very nice lady, and a sweet neighbor," Oliver evaded, protective of Lilly. He was concerned that he'd hurt her in some way. Oliver whispered a prayer that God would make everything okay. It bothered him to consider that he'd offended Lilly in one way or another.

"Okay… if you say so…" There was a mistrustful expression on Rain's face. She grasped that Oliver didn't want to expound on his relationship or lack thereof with this *Lilly* woman. So, Rain dropped the subject altogether. "You were saying how your morning started out…?" Rain asked as she and Oliver walked out to the parking lot.

"Right…," Oliver said passively. His thoughts were a million miles away. The murder scene from earlier on pressed on his mind. Oliver obsessed about the investigation. There was also the sense that he'd hurt Lilly's feeling in some way, and he wanted her to be alright. Besides, he kept wondering if Erin had read his text. Amidst the inner conflict, he imagined being able to talk things through with Erin. Oliver wanted her to know how much he appreciated her hard work. But, more importantly, he wanted to convey how much he *valued* their friendship.

Oliver helped Rain into his SUV, then walked around to take his place behind the wheel. "So, since you're going to be working through our office, you need to know the latest…" There was an urgent expression on his face, as he disclosed the details of the serial killings which had taken place out in Silver Commons. Thus, the deputy attorneys working through the DA's office would be working closely with investigators. Rain *had* to know it all, because she was now a member of their trial team.

Oliver expounded on the intricacies of the case, and what the DA's role would be in helping to solve it. For one reason or another, it always helped to talk about some of the ghastly things he came across in his line of work. That way he didn't have to solitarily internalize atrocities of the inhumanity inflicted upon innocent victims.

***

Erin was elated that Oliver had texted her in the early morning. She'd gotten into work at around 7:30 a.m. in order to get started on transforming the DA's Meeting Hall into a Christmas fantasy. She had brought in a few decorators on the project, and they'd helped with the white and silver themed backdrop. The crew had brought in giant silver and white iced ball ornaments, snowflakes, starbursts, crystal discs, ball box pieces and diamond patterned balls. The decorations were carefully placed in various corners of the extensive room. Moreover, the hires had helped Erin with the white icicle lighting inside of the main office. Furthermore, they'd decked out the Christmas tree in the building lobby.

Inside of the party hall were giant boxes, which looked like presents wrapped in white, silver, red, green and gold. The decorators had also draped feet of silver and white garland throughout, enmeshed with white LED lights. There were a few more details to handle in order to make the hall party-ready, but Erin was excited to see how beautifully things were falling into place.

As was her MO, she took on every project wholeheartedly. The endeavor had even more meaning, because it was something she and Oliver had planned together. Erin acknowledged that she was ready to go to any length to impress him. Additionally, she wanted to ensure that he came out on top in all of his undertakings.

Still, as excited as Erin was about the party, she was all the more thrilled over receiving a text message from Oliver. It was ten minutes to nine, and Erin had taken a break long enough to check her phone. She couldn't help smiling. It felt good knowing that he'd taken a moment away from his crazy schedule in order to send her such an encouraging message.

Remembering how things had played out the day before with Rain McGrath, Erin cringed in dread. However, she kept reminding herself that God had a plan. There was such so much love in her heart for Oliver, and it refused to go away no matter how much she'd willed it to. Thus, Erin was convinced that God would work it out. He would either remove the debilitating feelings or make a way for her to have the desire of her heart. Erin prayed for the latter.

"You're welcome, Ollie! It's a total pleasure to be working on such a fun project! I know how swamped you are being pulled in so many directions. So, don't worry, I've got your back. It's what friends do. And, if I do think of anything you can do while you're away from the office, I will definitely let you know. Guess what? I came in a little earlier to work on the building lobby, and on the

meeting hall. Ollie, you should see how beautiful it looks, especially the meeting hall. I hope you get a chance to stop in to get a look. Hope to see you soon," Erin texted.

Erin stood back and excitedly admired her handiwork. She couldn't wait for Oliver to come into the office. However, at that point, she had to take off her party-planner hat and submit to her job. It was almost nine, and there were a gazillion high priority case documents waiting on her desk. Several defense attorneys were looking to have their client's cases dismissed, while the DA's office was fighting for conviction and prosecution. And she *was* their communications mediator.

It was exactly nine when Erin drifted into the busy office area. She greeted some of her coworkers affably as she made her way across. However, her eyes were everywhere searching for Oliver. Erin was in good spirits and felt upbeat. Turning a corner down the hallway, she saw Oliver consulting with some of the deputy prosecutors. There was a critical expression on his winsome face, as he delegated responsibilities.

However, seeing Rain standing so close to Oliver with her shoulder pressed up to his arm, made Erin's heart crash to the floor. Rain also caught sight of Erin, and their eyes momentarily locked. Erin immediately picked up on Rain's antipathy. Whereas Erin was staring at *her* because she could clearly see that her MO was to win Oliver's heart at all costs, there were darts shooting out from Rain's eyes. Rain's face stretched into an artificial smile, as Erin made her way through the group.

Oliver was in the middle of explaining the way he wanted his staff to aid the authorities in the suspected serial killer investigation, when he saw Erin breeze past him. "Gary, I need for you to go out to the precinct today…," Oliver's words trailed, as he followed Erin's gait.

"You were saying, Sir?" Gary Britt, one of the attorneys tried to redirect.

Oliver shook himself free from the trance and tried to remain focused. "Work closely with the authorities. Starting today, I need for you to go out to the precinct," Oliver delineated, still following

Erin's stride as she headed over to her office.

"Will do," Gary returned.

"There will be a brief meeting this afternoon to discuss our strategies moving forward with the serial murders case," Oliver told the staff-all the while totally distracted. Having a moment to himself to go find Erin was all he could think about. Oliver felt like a child who couldn't wait to go outside and play with friends.

"About the motion to dismiss the charges against Angela Moss?" one of the staff members asked.

"I will review the matter again, and talk it over with the appointed judge," Oliver said. "So, I will see you all later this afternoon. If there's a crisis of any kind, page or text me," he told them.

Rain remained glued to Oliver's side during his impromptu meeting with staff. They'd driven into work together that morning and had shared a short breakfast in his private office. However, Rain had seen Oliver's reaction when Erin had come in. Notwithstanding, she could read his mind, and knew that his next move would be to go to Erin Brasfield's office.

"So, Rain, I trust that you'll help David to establish ironclad evidence on some of the more prominent existing cases," Oliver told Rain the moment the group had disbanded.

"Of course, you can count on me," Rain said, smiling and hanging on his every word. "I'm familiar with the drill."

"Are you sure you want to do this, Rain?" Oliver tested.

"Positive...," Rain affirmed, fawning over him.

"So, I will see you in a bit." Oliver's eyes wandered in the direction of Erin's office.

"Oliver, I *do* have a number of questions for you in respect to the Tanner case," Rain halted, noticing that Oliver was about to go and seek Erin out. "Can we go over the details in *your* office for a minute?" Rain smiled up into Oliver's eyes.

Oliver hesitated for a moment, but then offered Rain a clement smile. "Sure, I would be happy to go over the details with you." He placed his hand on the small of her back and guided her back into his office. Rain shut the door after them.

Drifting back over to his desk, Oliver set down in his comfortable armchair. Clasping his hands together, he listened to Rain's concerns and tried to address them. The only thing pressed on his mind was the moment he'd be free to go and see Erin. *Why was it so urgent for him to see her, look into her eyes and see her smile?* For one reason or another those things were paramount.

"So, that's generally all you have to do. David will guide you through the process," Oliver found himself telling Rain about twenty minutes later. He was bewildered as to why Rain kept asking him elementary questions. She was a prominent attorney and was only moonlighting through the DA's office as a matter of serving the community. Oliver wondered what was *really* going on. It almost felt as if Rain was detaining him on purpose.

At one point, Oliver halted her with a genial smile on his face, "Rain, what's going on here? You already know the answers to those question-probably better than I do."

"I guess I'm feeling a little bit out of sorts. The work around here is a lot more challenging than at the law firm," she fabricated.

"You'll be just fine, Rain. I trust you. In fact, I *know* you're an awesome addition to our team." He nodded in encouragement. "And I'm an *awesome* judge of character." He winked at her. Just then, his phone rang. Oliver pulled it out of the inner pocket of his suit and checked the number. "Will you excuse me, while I take this?" he asked Rain.

"Of course," Rain told him. She sat across from Oliver and examined just how gorgeous he really was. Inwardly, she felt conflicted. She had asked to work through the DA's office in order to stay close to him, not to actually *work*. But there was a sense of possessiveness on her part. She feared that the moment she let him out of her sight, he would go and find Erin. Rain had known she would have to submit to the *work* part, but the main goal was to get Oliver. Rain refused to lose him to anyone else. Nonetheless, she couldn't follow him around. Oliver was overwhelmed with the demands of his office.

"Of course, I'm still working on ensuring that Mark has adequate housing and a job once he's paroled," Oliver explained over the phone. "The social worker has already made several contacts, and it shouldn't be too much longer." His face creased in uncertainty. "No, that won't be necessary… You want to meet today?" he quizzed. "I'll have to check my schedule," he said perusing his phone. Oliver's face lit up with an encouraging smile when he saw that Erin had texted him back a while ago.

Rain examined the look on Oliver's face. It was obvious that something he'd just seen had made him smile. She wondered what it was. The thought of Oliver having a girlfriend made her burn feverishly with jealousy. Rain made a mental note to find out if he did, and how she could make that individual a nonissue.

"Alright, I will meet with you at around one," Oliver said over the phone. "Okay, will do. Bye." Oliver tuned into Rain again. With an affable smile on his face, he reassured, "You'll do just fine." Just then, Oliver got a call on the office's landline. He shook his head ironically at Rain. "You already know that I have to take this."

"I know." Rain nodded and flashed him a magnetic smile.

There was a knock to the door as Oliver answered the phone again. Oliver gestured that Rain answer the door while he got the phone.

Rain stood to her feet and went over to get the door.

David Reed was standing beyond it. "Hey, you're just the person I was looking for. I could use your expertise on a particular case," David told Rain.

While on the phone, Oliver gestured that Rain should go along with David.

Rain offered David an awkward smile. However, her eyes were glued to Oliver, who was totally engaged in his phone conversation. Hesitant to leave the office, Rain stared yearningly at him as she set out to leave. She stepped out of the office, closed the door, and followed David out into the hallway. She was nervous that Oliver would find a moment to go see Erin. For Rain, losing her old friend to Erin Brasfield or anyone else just wasn't an option.

Oliver finally managed to get off the phone with Shelley Rogers. Her daughter Shannon had been sexually assaulted while on a date with a young man on her college campus. Oliver had promised to fight for the prosecution of the offender. Moreover, he'd promised to allow Shannon to share an impact statement on the day the verdict was read. Oliver was confident that the DA's office had amassed enough evidence to put Darryl Ayers away beyond a reasonable doubt.

Oliver sighed over other matters but beamed when he read over Erin's text message. Overwhelmed with pride and gratitude over all of her work, he quickly pushed out of his armchair. Finding Erin in order to thank her personally was his sole mission. In the past couple of days, it had been a real challenge to find a moment. Recounting their uninterrupted time together last weekend made him want even more time together.

He reasoned that God had probably allotted Erin and himself that little chunk of time, because their moments from that point on would be few and far between. It killed Oliver to consider that in less than two weeks Erin would no longer be working there. She would be gone before they celebrated New Year's. Realizing that they were running out of time, motivated him to spend as much time with her as possible.

Hence, he would start by stopping into her office to say hello. She needed to know how grateful he was for everything that she'd done. Moreover, he didn't want to drift out into the meeting hall by himself to see how wonderful it looked. He *wanted* Erin to show it to him. Oliver knew that it would be considerably more rewarding to see the decked-out party hall through Erin's eyes. He floated out of his office and crossed over into the main office area. Erin's office could be found away from the bustle.

Erin immersed herself in work. There were law motions and recommendation letters to prepare before lunchtime. With her face practically buried in the desktop monitor, she fought back tears. In her heart and mind, she was fighting a losing battle. It was beginning to dawn on her that a man like Oliver Wright had a slew of women fighting to gain his affection.

Notwithstanding, there was *one* in particular who'd just happened on the scene-dead set on winning his heart. Oliver had told Erin that he wanted to stay friends. However, the one thing Rain McGrath had that Erin didn't was history with Oliver. They'd been friends and colleagues for a long time. Erin had seen Oliver with other women whom he had no interest in. He was always cordial and kind, while simultaneously remaining detached. In light of his and Rain's exchanges yesterday afternoon, Erin could tell that Oliver liked Rain…a lot.

Just then, the Holy Spirit of God reminded Erin of certain passages of scripture. 1 Samuel 16:7: "But the Lord said unto Samuel, 'Do not look at his appearance or at his physical stature, because I have refused him. For the Lord does not see as man sees; for man looks at the outward appearance, but the Lord looks at the heart (NKJV).'" The last portion of that verse resonated in for Erin.

Hebrews chapter 11, called *The Great Faith Chapter* also came to mind. Erin was reminded that she could not please God without faith. Wiping away her tears, Erin acceded to the Spirit's prompting. She said a prayer, asking God to keep her from getting discouraged and to strengthen her faith.

Moments later, there was a gentle knock on her office door. Erin jumped immediately out of her chair, thinking that it was David or Jason, a deputy to the DA, asking for paperwork. Thoughtlessly, she opened up the door, not even looking to see who it was. "I have the brief and the motion you asked for, David…," Erin's voice trailed when her eyes connected to Oliver's. Right then and there her heart began drubbing, pounding into her eardrum. "Ollie," she said surprised.

"Well, I'm glad to know you have the paperwork I've asked for," he teased with a crooked smile, winking at Erin.

"I'm sorry," Erin said awkwardly, "I thought you were David or Jason." Erin allowed herself to take in how surreal and amazing Oliver looked in his smoke-gray colored dress suit. Erin could only imagine how naïve and wide-eyed she looked, fawning over and gaping at him.

"So, I gathered," Oliver said, exploring Erin's jewel brown eyes. He was completely blown away by how resplendent she looked in her stylish red dress, and totally electrified just looking into her eyes again. Oliver swallowed the chunk lodged in his throat. "How are you?" he asked throatily.

"I'm fine, thank you," Erin said, entranced. "I guess I don't have to ask how *you* are. You're a really hard person to get a hold of," she added, doing all she could to break the intensity between them.

"I'm *so* sorry. Things *have* been very hectic lately. I wish I had a little more time on my hands," Oliver said, delving Erin's pretty eyes.

"Me too, but I guess it's what we signed up for when we were fighting to win the DA's office," Erin said.

Oliver smiled and shook his head humorously. "Yeah, that's right. But the one thing I don't regret is having *you* on my team," he said fondly exploring her eyes.

"I don't regret that part either." Erin gave him a quirky look. She was so overjoyed to have a moment alone with Oliver she wanted to burst. "Did you get my text?" Erin brought up, totally ecstatic. It was a balancing act not to allow the powerful undercurrents between them to overwhelm.

"Yes, I did, and I just wanted to say thank you," Oliver said in earnest. "Thanks for taking this project to heart. I can't wait to see what you've done to the meeting hall. I *did* however get to check out the lobby décor." He shook his head amazed. "You, Erin Brasfield, are a force to be reckoned with," he praised. "The backdrop is beautiful-even more so than I imagined."

"I'm glad you like it, Ollie," Erin said reticently. "It's been a lot of fun creating the right ambiance. Of course, it would have been a lot more fun working on it with *you*, but…" Erin stared yearningly at him.

"I know. I wanted to work on this project with you as well. I promise to do better. Why don't you leave the rest of the details to me?"

Erin shook her head contrarily. "Ollie, it's fine, you don't have to worry about the party. I've got it all under control. Besides, I've gotten wind of some of the new cases the DA's office has taken on. So, I *know* you have your hands full. There *are* very few details left. I've already gotten in touch with the caterers, found some really cute stockings at the *Dollar Dream*. So, the only thing left is to shop for the stocking stuffers and planning the party games."

"I *want* to be a part of this with you," Oliver said with his eyes lowering intuitively into her eyes. "Can you leave *some* of the tasks for me?" His face wrinkled in involvement.

"Okay," Erin acceded. For a moment she and Oliver stood there staring silently at each other. Erin wondered if he felt just as adrift around her as she did with him.

Completely hypnotized, Oliver found himself taking in how the red dress accentuated Erin's small waist and her curves. He gulped nervously for a moment, as he tried to conceal his self-consciousness. "So, do you have a moment to show me how you've transformed the meeting hall?" Oliver asked, subconsciously leaning into Erin.

"Sure." Erin smiled timidly, totally captivated. She began inching in closer to Oliver, but then broke the spell. "I'll just run this paperwork by Jason first. Then, I would *love* to show it to you," her voice was velvety as she gazed into Oliver's eyes.

"That sounds great," Oliver told Erin, completely spellbound.

"I'm just about done with the files for Jason." Erin gulped nervously and drifted away from Oliver. Her heart was racing again, and she felt flustered.

"I'm not going anywhere." Oliver smiled and watched Erin move about. *Was he dreaming? Were they really going to have this little chunk of time all to themselves?* Oliver celebrated inwardly.

"I'm just about done, Ollie," Erin looked up, but David had come over, and was having word with Oliver.

"Ollie, Mitch Channing just called. He says that he needs to see you right away," David told Oliver with an alarmed expression on his face.

"Did he say why?" Oliver asked pressingly, with a face creased in angst.

"He said it's about Taren Cook's case," David informed.

Oliver closed his eyes meditatively for moment. He then looked over at Erin with an apologetic expression on his face. "I'm so sorry, Erin. Maybe, you can show me later," he acceded

"Of course, Ollie, don't even worry about it," Erin acquiesced, disappointed. For a fleeting second, she had thought she'd have a little time with Oliver. However, once again he was being pulled away.

"*So* sorry…" His face warped in remorse.

"No worries. We'll catch up later," Erin mitigated.

"Bye," Oliver said reluctantly.

"See you later," Erin said standing at the opened office door. Oliver turned and looked at her just before he and David crossed away from that area of the office.

***

It was almost seven in the evening when Erin made her way out of the Super Walmart in *Silver Cottage*, a few miles away from where she lived. There she was again, hauling packages of the items she'd just purchased. To say she felt totally disillusioned was an understatement. Since her brief connection to Oliver back at the officer that morning, she had not seen or heard from him.

Being pulled in a hundred different directions was the nature of Oliver's job as a public servant. Moreover, he'd been called to address a very personal case. Taren Cook's case was complicated to say the least. Both Oliver and Mitch Channing-Taren's boyfriend-were working collaboratively to ensure she had a chance on the day of her sentencing.

Erin grasped the exacting demands of Oliver's work. However, it still hurt that they couldn't seem to find a moment to connect. It also didn't help that Rain McGrath had designs on Oliver. Moreover, it was crystal clear that the woman hated Erin. Granted, Erin was resolved to trust God to navigate the affairs of her life. Thus, God was more than aware how much she wanted for Oliver to be a part of her life. Therefore, Erin was convinced that if God wanted Oliver in her life, there was very little anyone-let alone *Rain*-could do to hinder His plan.

As Erin trudged through the spacious lot carrying a ton of bags, she was unaware that one of the bags had torn. So, before she even made it to the car, some of the cute items she'd found near the Walmart nursery crashed to the ground. The miniature snow globes she'd found and planned to use as stocking stuffers for the party were shattered. "Oh, no," Erin cried out frustrated. She dropped the other bags to the ground as well, feeling defeated.

"Are you alright, Ma'am?" A gentleman asked, genuflecting to the ground, and picking up some of the items which had fallen.

"I'm fine," Erin said, gasping in shock, because this man seemed to have materialized out of nowhere. Embarrassed that a stranger was picking up her items, Erin hunched down in order to finish gathering up her dropped purchases. It was then that she could see the stranger's face, and she was taken aback by how handsome he was. The gentleman stood at about 6 feet, he had dark curly hair, hazel eyes and a muscular build.

"You *know* you can always go back inside of the store, and they will replace the broken items," he told Erin, contemplating how pretty she was.

"But, it's *my* fault they're broken," Erin admitted, perplexed. The weight of the stranger's stare was extremely heavy, and Erin wasn't sure what to make of it.

"It doesn't matter. All you have to do is to show them your receipt." He smiled.

"Really…?" Erin questioned, staring curiously at the man.

"Sure. *I* could go back with you if you'd like," he offered genially, standing upright and smiling into Erin's eyes.

"No, that's okay. That won't be necessary. Thanks for letting me know," Erin said uneasily, because the guy's eyes were virtually burning a hole through her.

"I can carry the rest over to your car," he insisted with a friendly smile.

"That would be nice," Erin acceded.

"Don't worry about the broken items. I'll go inside and tell one of the employees that there's broken glass out here." The gentleman followed behind Erin.

Erin crossed over to her SUV and activated the car alarm. She popped the trunk door and turned towards the man. "You can put the items in here," she said reticently, eyes wandering away from his penetrating stare.

"I'm Grayson Andrews!" He extended his hand in greeting to Erin.

"Oh….," Erin said caught off guard, "Erin Brasfield." Erin shut the trunk of the car, turning to face Grayson completely, and hesitantly shook his hand. Now that she was getting to see him standing upright and up close, Erin assessed he was *very* handsome. Notwithstanding, even if he was dressed in jeans, a sand-colored sports shirt and comfortable shoes, she could tell he had expensive tastes. There was also no ring on his finger. Still, Erin didn't want to be unfriendly to the stranger, so she offered a faint smile.

"Thanks for taking the time to help me out just now."

"You're welcome, *Erin*. It's my pleasure. I knew your smile would be amazing!" Grayson said, taking in Erin's beautiful features.

Erin's cheeks turned scarlet. "Thanks again…I think." Uncertainty masked her sweet face.

"Of course," Grayson offered an earnest smile of his own. "I'm sorry for the trouble. Don't forget to go back inside and have them replace your items." Grayson took a moment to size Erin up. Even if he wasn't being overtly objectifying, he was ravenously eyeing every inch of her.

"I…I won't forget," Erin told him, feeling totally awkward under his intent scrutiny.

"Are you doing some late minute Christmas shopping?" Grayson pried, delving boldly into Erin's eyes.

Erin laughed lightly. "Not really. There's this Christmas party that I'm helping to plan for work," she shared openly.

"Oh, that sounds nice." There was a piqued expression on his face. "Would you happen to have a *date* for this Christmas event?" Grayson asked openly, but his cheeks reddened upon saying the words.

Erin laughed a bit more openly at that point. "Actually, I *was* hoping to attend with someone…a friend," she disclosed, shaking her head humorously. "You don't mince words, do you, Grayson?"

"No, I don't believe in mincing words, and please call me *Gray*, Erin." He smiled openly. "Now, what do you mean you were hoping to attend with someone? So, you *aren't* sure that you will?" His face creased in introspection.

"Well, it's complicated," Erin acquiesced. There was no way she was going to get into her friendship with Oliver with this man.

"I don't think it's complicated at all. You're *very* beautiful!" Gray said straightforwardly. "If this guy hasn't asked you to be his date to this party, then maybe he isn't worth your time."

"It isn't that way. We're *very* good friends," Erin found herself sounding defensive. She couldn't stand to hear anyone say one negative word about Oliver.

Gray nodded with a quiescent smile. "Okay, I get it. It's *complicated.* I won't push to attend this Christmas party, only if you agree to have dinner with me tonight," he said directly, smiling into Erin's eyes.

Erin chuckled and shook her head humorously. "Not a believer in beating around the bush…," she assessed.

"Not when I see something that I like." Gray contemplated Erin in fascination from head to toe.

"Oh, is that right?" Erin asked, marveling.

"Absolutely…"

"I'm afraid I can't," Erin said decidedly.

"And why is that? Is there a jealous boyfriend I should know about?" Gray invaded dauntlessly.

"Gray, are you *serious*?" Erin laughed. "It was nice meeting you tonight." Erin drifted around to the driver's side of her car.

However, Gray was hot on her heels. "Erin, it was nice meeting *you*. So, that's it? I'm supposed to walk away, and pretend as if we never met this evening?" Gray asked dramatically, making Erin laugh.

"We both knew that it wouldn't be a lifelong commitment," Erin razzed. "Thanks for helping me with my things." She opened up the driver's side door and hopped into the car.

"You're welcome, Erin! But, aren't you going back to exchange the broken items?" Gray asked quizzically.

"I will-maybe after work tomorrow. Right now, I'm too exhausted to go back for a few broken snow globes," Erin settled.

"I understand." Gray smiled but rested his hand on the frame of Erin's opened car window. Staring up at her wonderingly, he asked again, "So, that's it?"

"*That's it*," Erin said, laughing. "Merry Christmas, Gray," she said, shrugging nonsensically.

"Merry Christmas, beautiful Erin!" Gray said good-naturedly. "I hope to see you again…" He gave Erin a provocative look.

"Take care," Erin said, and began pulling out of the parking lot of the local strip mall.

"Bye, Erin," Gray ceded and watched the beautiful woman drive off.

He hesitated out in the lot for a moment and memorized her license plate number. Moreover, he knew her name was Erin Brasfield, so he would definitely look into who she was, and where she worked. There was something very special about the young lady, and Gray resolved to find a way to connect to her again in one way or another.

Gray trudged across the lot in order to find his black Audi SUV, unable to get the young lady off of his mind. He'd pulled into the strip mall in order to purchase a fruit smoothie, but changed his mind. Rather, he would get an iced coffee from down the road. As he pulled out of the lot, Gray shook his head and smiled humorously. "No, that's *not* it, Erin… This isn't over by a longshot…" There was a cunning expression on his face, as he strategized a way to see Erin again.

CHAPTER SIX

Erin dumped her packages onto the living room sofa the moment she got home from the mini- mall. What an exhausting day it had been! She smiled musingly when she recalled her chance meeting with Grayson Andrews out in *Silver Cottage. What a character,"* Erin evaluated. However, before crossing over to her bedroom to change out of her work clothes, she pulled her phone from out of her bag for the umpteenth time, checking for a message from Oliver. This time around she *wasn't* disappointed.

"Hey, Erin, just wanted you to know that I did get a moment to peek into the meeting hall when I got back to the office after six. It looks incredible! I love the white and silver theme! Then again, I didn't expect anything less from you. You are absolutely amazing! I'm in love with the décor, and now I'm actually excited about the party! I had hoped that we would come together again sometime today, but I guess it wasn't meant to be. I had to wait with Mitch at the courthouse to talk to a judge for a recommendation regarding Taren's appeal.

"So far nothing has been determined. I did the very best I could. Now, it's all in God's hands. By the way, it was nice seeing you this morning, even if it was only for a hot minute." Oliver added a smiley face emoji. *"And I thought you might be up to having dinner right about now. So, I took the liberty of ordering your favorites-McDonald's quarter pounder with an extra apple pie. So, while I was downtown, I found some cute stocking stuffer gifts for the party, and I wanted to come by your place tonight to show you. So, in case you're wondering who the extra food is for, it's for me. And, by the way, now that's a count of two decent dinners I owe you, LOL."*

Erin couldn't stop smiling, and her eyes twinkled with tears of joy reading over Oliver's text message. She was in process of crossing over to the bedroom to change, when the doorbell rang. Excited, she turned and headed for the front door.

"I have an order for Ms. Brasfield," the *Uber Eats* guy stood at the door holding a large Mc. Donald's paper bag with handles.

"Thank you," Erin said elated, "I will sign for it. Can I leave you a tip?" she asked the young, slender, dark-haired Caucasian kid.

"It's already taken care of. Enjoy your meal." He smiled, then turned and walked away.

"Oh, Oliver, what am I going to do with you?" Erin drifted into the kitchen and set the bag on her counter. Ensuing, she rushed into her bedroom in order to change. Oliver had said he'd stop by to drop off some of the party things, and she couldn't wait to see him. The thought of seeing him again made her heart hammer in her chest. Notwithstanding, Erin hoped that they could spend at least an hour together. She didn't think that was asking for too much.

So, she changed out of her work clothes, threw on a pair of jeans and a pretty cream-colored sweater. Erin's hair had been worn out in curls that day, but she took a moment to comb through the tresses and fluffed her curls. Erin preened and freshened up in anticipation of seeing Oliver. Moreover, she lit a few votive candles in the living room, turned her Christmas tree lights on and played Mariah Carey's *Merry Christmas* album on her phone. "All I want for Christmas is you…," Erin hummed around the house as she set up to receive a *very* special friend.

***

Oliver was on cloud nine. He'd gotten home after seven but had showered and changed before going by Erin's. Despite the fact that he and Erin had been pulled apart earlier that morning, he'd texted her, praising all of the work she'd already put in for the impending Christmas party. Saying he was proud of her was a gross understatement. Oliver was beyond impressed to see how easily Erin had balanced her work through the office, and had still found the time to set up such an amazing and extravagant décor.

Because he'd spent most of the day away from his desk, Oliver had texted Erin a message not only to applaud her talents, but had ordered her favorites from McDonald's. He'd learned over the past weekend that Erin liked McDonald's. She especially enjoyed their baked apple pie. In addition, he said he'd stopped by her place so that she could see some of the stocking stuffers *he'd* found at a specialty shop a few miles away from the courthouse earlier on. And now, it was time to take the drive over to Erin's.

Brushing his hair back, Oliver couldn't contain the smile on his face. Neither could he stop his heart from racing in anticipation over seeing Erin again. He had absolutely no idea how addicted he would have gotten to Erin after spending last Saturday with her. Oliver dressed down from his usual suit and tie, into black jeans and a wine-colored sweater and Timberland Boots. Being *this* excited about spending time with anyone was a foreign concept for him. For the longest, the only other woman who'd consumed his thoughts in this way had been Kennedy.

And yet, Oliver didn't know if he was ready to risk his heart again. He was skeptical about being able to offer Erin the kind of heart she deserved. The sting of his failed relationship with Kennedy still lingered, even if Oliver was doing the best he could to move forward. Still, there was undeniable attraction and chemistry with Erin. It was so powerful at times it almost felt tangible.

Erin was the entire package-beautiful, kind, smart, desirable, creative, quirky, funny and so much more. Most importantly, they shared faith in Jesus Christ. Finding Erin ridiculously attractive and appealing wasn't the matter at hand. It was that he cared for and respected her too much to shortchange her. Erin deserved the best, and Oliver couldn't say that he was at the place where he could offer her what she needed.

Once again, as had been the case every single time, Oliver was taken aback when he drifted out into the living room and admired the Christmas tree. It dazzled like jewels and sparked joy in the ashes of his tenebrous world. It warmed his heart to see it, and to remember how diligently he and Erin had worked to put it together. Oliver honestly considered that if Erin hadn't helped him pick out the tree and had helped him to trim it, he probably wouldn't have bothered.

Erin had brightened up his world. He'd been totally shattered when Kennedy had told him that *he* wasn't the person she saw herself spending a lifetime with. Oliver readily acknowledged that if Erin hadn't been a part of his life during that awful time, he would not have made it. So, for a number of reasons he both valued and cherished their growing friendship. Nevertheless, he refused to give her fifty percent of himself when she deserved two hundred percent.

Oliver was humming as he set out to leave his place. However, when he opened up the front door, Rain was standing beyond it poised to ring his doorbell. Startled, Oliver clutched his heart. "Rain, you've got to stop doing that." He shook his head with a nonsensical smile on his face.

"I'm sorry, Ollie. I just thought you might want to go out for dinner or something," Rain said, eyeing Oliver as if he were a piece of candy, and she needed a sugar fix. "I figured that you probably haven't gotten the chance to do anything about dinner tonight. My goodness, you've been out the entire day," Rain evaluated.

"Aw…," Oliver's face warped sentimentally. "*Were* you worried about me?" He offered a sincere smile.

"I *was*," Rain admitted with a sappy expression on her face. "You look like you're heading out." Rain sized Oliver up in his jeans, boots and dapper short gray wool coat. His face looked fresh and clean, and soft curly hair slicked around his temples, making him even easier on the eyes. Rain burned to connect to Oliver on a more meaningful level. That night she resolved to take the gloves off, and to come out fighting.

"Well, actually, I *am* headed out. I'm so sorry, Rain. You should have called me," Oliver said, frowning in remorse because Rain had made the sacrifice. Oliver took a moment to examine her olive-green denim dress, stylish black leather jacket and boots. Her blonde hair had been done in an upswept style, but there were loose strands cascading over her shoulders and back. "You look so nice," Oliver complimented.

"Thanks, but you're right. I *should* have called." Rain met Oliver's eyes, unable to conceal her disappointment. "I realize how busy you are, but it's kind of strange working together."

"Are you having second thoughts?" Oliver's face wrinkled in concern. "David tells me you're doing an awesome job," he denoted.

"Oh, no, I'm not having second thoughts at all." Rain stared intuitively into Oliver's eyes. "It's just that it's hard to be around you, and not actually be able to spend any time together. I've been on cloud nine ever since we've reconnected."

Oliver smiled reassuringly. "There *are* quieter days down at the DA's office-I promise. So, we'll have plenty of time to catch up." He sighed. "But part of being a public servant means being accessible to the people," Oliver explained.

"I get that. It's just hard having to *share* you with everyone," she admitted, searching his eyes.

"Oh, *so* now you're possessive of your old friend, huh?" Oliver teased.

"You have no idea just how possessive I am of him. He's truly something special. I feel like telling everybody *I knew him first...*," Rain said only half-joking.

"Rain, there's no need to feel that way. Everyone knows *we're* great friends," Oliver uplifted.

"Friends...right," Rain said. *Not for long*, she devised.

"Rain, it was thoughtful of you to come by, but *maybe* we can do a raincheck?" Oliver's face wrinkled in awkwardness. He didn't want to blow off his old friend, but he wanted to see Erin so badly.

"You're right, Ollie," Rain acquiesced with a quiet smile, "I should have called first. Sorry." Inwardly, Rain assessed the matter. In light of how Oliver was dressed, she gathered that he wasn't headed over to a business-related matter. Rain couldn't help thinking that he was going off to meet with Erin Brasfield. At that very moment, Rain decided that she was going to find a way to overturn Oliver's friendship with the *Miss-goody-two-shoes* paralegal who was crushing on him. "I'm sorry to have come over unannounced," Rain said again, endeavoring to sound sincere.

"It's alright. No worries." Oliver stepped out of his place, and shut the door closed. "And I promise we'll do a raincheck." He offered an understanding smile.

"That sounds good," Rain said. All of the sudden, her face warped in pain, and she immediately placed her right hand on her lower abdomen.

"Rain…?" Oliver examined her, concerned. "What's wrong?" He moved in closer in order to examine her.

"Oh, my goodness, Oliver," Rain's face contorted in pain, "I don't know. It's my stomach." She looked up at him with a face strained in agony and jeopardy.

"Rain, is there anything you need for *me* to do?" Oliver's heart whipped anxiously in his chest.

Rain continued to writhe in anguish. "I don't know. I just need to…" She kept shaking her head and groaning in discomfort.

"I'm calling an ambulance," Oliver settled. He stood there, keeping his arms supportively around Rain, as she winced and flinched in agony.

"We'll be outside of my apartment," Oliver repeated to the ambulatory switchboard.

"I'm so sorry," Rain heaved and gasped, holding on to Oliver for dear life. She cried out in discomfort as Oliver held her soothingly in his arms. She breathed heavily into his chest, pretending to be in pain, as she pressed covetously into his arms, relishing the feel of such a warm and tender enclosure.

Oliver stood outside of his place holding Rain comfortingly in his arms. Inwardly, he felt conflicted. The last thing he'd expected was for Rain to come over, and then to have her fall ill. He hated the thought of disappointing Erin again. However, he knew he couldn't just walk away from Rain when she was clearly suffering. He would have driven her over to the hospital himself, but he didn't think it was wise to have her ambulating and in such pain.

Moments later, Oliver found himself holding Rain's hand in the back of the ambulance. "You're going to be alright," he affirmed with a reassuring smile.

"Thank you for acting so quickly, Ollie. I don't know what I would have done if you weren't with me." Rain stroked fondly on Oliver's hand.

"You're going to be okay. I'm glad I was with you too, because I couldn't imagine you succumbing to that kind of pain while you were alone." He stared hopefully into her eyes.

"And I'm grateful that you're riding over to the hospital with me. I'm really sorry for ruining your plans tonight."

"That's alright," Oliver smiled wistfully, "it couldn't be helped. Besides, what are friends for?"

"Well, I'm certainly glad you're *my* friend." Rain continued to move nervously about in discomfort.

Oliver smiled but didn't say a word. All he kept thinking about was finding a moment in order to call Erin to let her know that something had come up. The level of frustration he felt just then was incomparable. As much as he was grateful to fill in the gap for Rain in her crisis, Oliver was equally grieved to be disappointing Erin...again.

***

Oliver waited with Rain in one of the rooms down in the ER of Grandview University Hospital. Because of his status as the town's DA, Rain was taken in almost immediately. A Doctor Jennings was overseeing Rain's care, and several tests had been run. Currently, Rain had been put on an IV drip in the event she'd inadvertently suffered food poisoning.

The second Oliver had gotten a moment to himself, he'd texted Erin, and had relayed that he had to be at the hospital with a sick friend. As always, Erin was understanding and sweet, but Oliver hated canceling plans with her. Not only did he hate having to disappoint her, but he hated that they were losing precious time.

Quite soon, Erin would be gone, and he wouldn't get to see her around the DA's office. Oliver wasn't sure why the thought of Erin's impending departure grieved him to such an extent, but it was the way he felt. He was doing everything in his power to make the most of the time they *did* have left. However, it was becoming increasingly more difficult to make that happen.

"How are you feeling?" Oliver stared down at Rain with involvement, while they waited inside of the hospital room.

Rain secured her grasp on Oliver's hand and stared dreamily up at him. "I'm feeling a lot better. Between the Prilosec and the IV, the pain has subsided." She smiled at him. "Thanks again for being here with me. I truly appreciate it."

"Sure. I'm so glad you're feeling better." Oliver slipped into the armchair across from Rain's hospital bed, gently reclaiming his hand. "You really had me worried for a minute there," he said in earnest.

"I'm so sorry, Ollie, I didn't mean to scare you." Rain shook her head in skepticism. "Ollie, I don't know what I would have done if you hadn't acted so quickly."

"Well, I'm just glad I was there. The worst thing would have been for that episode to have taken place while you were alone." He delved sensitively into her eyes.

"Yeah, that would have been the worst. Being alone sucks," Rain said with her eyes fastened to Oliver's. "Don't you think so?" she queried.

"It isn't easy being alone-I have to agree with you on that. But you know what's worse than being alone?" Oliver reversed.

"What could possibly be worse?" Rain granted.

"It's being with someone who doesn't feel as strongly for you as you do for them." Shadows played on Oliver's face upon saying those words.

"Sounds as if you know a little bit about how that feels," Rain said empathetically.

"I might know." Oliver issued a sad smile.

"It also sounds as if you've gotten involved with the wrong people. I can't possibly see how anyone could *not* love you with their whole heart!" Rain's caring gape caressed the contours of Oliver's face.

"Rain…," Oliver said surprised. "That's one of the nicest things anyone has ever said to me," his voice broke, and tears shone in his eyes.

"It's the truth, Ollie. I can't see how anyone could *ever* let you go."

"You'd be surprised," Oliver countered.

"Well, like I just said, you've been opening up your heart to the wrong women. Not all women are created equal, you know." She issued a fond smile as she explored Oliver's sad eyes.

Oliver laughed lightly and nodded. "I guess that's something I'm beginning to grasp." He winked at Rain, and his stare lingered on her. "Thanks for encouraging me."

"Oliver Wright, you are *everything*, and you deserve only the very best," Rain uplifted.

Oliver reached over and pressed a kiss to her cheek. "Thank you for saying that," his voice was gravelly, and he fought back the tears stinging his eyes. He was about to say something else, but Dr. Jennings breezed back into the hospital room just then.

At that moment, both Rain and Oliver directed their attention over to the doctor.

"Rain, we've run a number of tests, and I can't seem to find a source for your distress tonight. You don't have gall or kidney stones. We can only conclude that it was some kind of food poisoning. It isn't unusual to feel both nauseous and gassy after such an episode. So, I'm prescribing a few over-the-counter products in the event you struggle with extreme gassiness or nausea. Otherwise, you're fine. I'll have the nurse take you off of the IV, and I'll get started working on discharge papers," Dr. Roland Jennings said with a smile.

"Thanks, Dr. Jennings," both Oliver and Rain said in unison, watching the doctor step out of the room.

"See? I told you that you had nothing to worry about." Oliver guffawed with an open smile.

Rain smiled as well and opened her arms up-indicating she wanted a hug.

Oliver surrendered to her opened arms and sat with her on the bed. He rubbed her back supportively. "You're going to be just fine," he reassured.

"I'm so glad you came with me tonight." Rain held on to Oliver for dear life, savoring the nirvana of being in his arms. "Thank you. Thank you so much."

"You're welcome," Oliver mitigated.

"You're such a great friend." Rain buried her face in his chest.

"Well, it takes one to know one," Oliver pacified, grateful that things hadn't turned out worse for Rain.

***

"Thanks for walking me to my door, Ollie," Rain told him. Oliver was seeing Rain to her door after she'd gotten home from the hospital.

"Anytime," Oliver said kindly. "Now, remember what Dr. Jennings said. You should take the anti-nausea meds at bedtime." There was a pertained expression on his face. "And, if you're not feeling well in the morning, you don't have to come in-"

"Are you kidding me? Of course, I'm coming in." Rain stared admiringly up at Oliver. She'd been inching in closer to him by the second. "I'm treating this job just like I would any other. And there are no sick days yet."

"Oh, alright, I can totally respect that." Oliver chuckled. "Are you going to be alright?" he tested, searching her eyes.

Rain nodded. "I should be fine." She set her arms on Oliver's shoulders, and stared entrancingly up into his eyes. Rain's arms maneuvered around his neck. Before long, her hands were clasped about his neck, and she was fondly stroking his thick, wavy hair.

Oliver was taken aback by Rain's sudden gesture, but he didn't make any sudden moves. It felt awkward, but he didn't want to embarrass her. "Goodnight," he said hoarsely.

"Goodnight, Ollie," Rain said, completely dazed. She reached up and bridged her lips to Oliver's. The moment felt surreal to Rain; however, she nimbly teased the corners of his delectable mouth with hers. In cadences, she progressed to covering every inch with tender kisses.

For a moment, Oliver felt displaced, uncertain as to what was happening. He was baffled by how subtly Rain had made her move. Still, he found himself gently pulling away from her embrace. It was strange being kissed by his old friend. The last thing Oliver wanted was to hurt Rain in any way. "Rain, I think I need to say goodnight." Oliver's eyes bridged furtively to hers.

Rain stole one last kiss, pressing her lips to Oliver's again. "Goodnight, Ollie," she said, totally transfixed. "Thanks for everything."

Oliver smiled reticently before drifting away. "You're welcome. Feel better." Oliver turned away and walked down the hall from Rain's apartment. He hopped on the elevator feeling totally conflicted and bewildered. *What on earth had just happened?* Maybe, he was just too trusting for his own good, but he had *not* seen that coming. As Oliver stepped outside of the building complex and slipped into the Lyft waiting for him, the incident still pressed on his mind. God had asked him to forget the things of the past, and to move forward. However, Oliver couldn't see *Rain* being the person he moved forward with.

His heart was already vested in Erin. What he'd told Erin on Saturday was completely true. Moving forward romantically could *only* be with her. Oliver *wanted* for her to be his person. He wanted to offer Erin his entire heart once he was able to find it again. As far as he was concerned, there was no one else worth opening it up for. And in light of the kind of day he and Erin had shared last Saturday, despite the fact that he'd told her that he wanted to remain friends, Oliver acquiesced that he wanted more…much more. Nevertheless, he had no idea how to convey that message to her.

It felt as if he was in recovery from a prolonged illness. Now that his heart was beginning to come together again, Oliver considered that the cure had come much too late. Erin had already decided to leave the DA's office. There was also the possibility that she had someone else in her life. The very concept that Erin had met someone new maimed Oliver with debilitating feelings of jealousy.

***

The moment Oliver got home, he changed for bed and surrendered to his knees. God was always there to offer wisdom and guidance. Oliver opened up his heart to the Lord and prayed for God's direction in respect to his feelings for Erin. As he waited in the presence of the Lord, he was reminded of Psalms 32:8-9, "I will instruct thee and teach thee in the way which thou shalt go: I will guide thee with mine eye. 9. "Be ye not as the horse, *or* as the mule, *which* have no understanding: whose mouth must be held in with bit and bridle, lest they come near unto thee." (KJV)

Again, Oliver submitted to that passage of scripture. "I want for you to guide me, Father. More than anything else I want to be obedient to you," Oliver ceded-trusting God for clarity in his circumstances. Slipping into bed, he checked his phone for any messages from Erin, but came up empty. It was twenty after ten, and Oliver tussled with the idea of giving her a call. He wanted to properly apologize for standing her up so to speak. Because he was a man of his word, going back on plans was in his opinion a shame. Making excuses was something he detested, and he hoped that it would never happen again-especially with Erin.

***

Erin slipped quietly into bed after having had devotions. She fought back tears as she lay there imaging how things had fared for Oliver and *Rain* over at the hospital. Even if Oliver hadn't told her that he'd gone with Rain, Erin knew that was the case. Erin also doubted that there was anything *really physically* wrong with the woman. Rain's only ailment was being lovesick over Oliver. In that respect, Erin assessed she was suffering from the same malady. Oliver had texted her earlier on to say he couldn't make it over to her place. Erin had anticipated seeing him that night. She had also refused to eat dinner without Oliver being there. Regardless, she'd lost her appetite after he'd canceled.

Standing on the word of God was the key at that juncture. So, Erin tried to remember all of the encouragement God had given her through His word. She needed to have faith that God had an answer for her heartache. It seemed the more she prayed and fasted on the matter, the stronger her feelings grew for Oliver. And yet, Oliver had said that he wanted to be friends-and nothing more.

Erin's face warped in misery to remember their talk, but she refused to cry. She had shed so many tears that night that she'd given herself a headache. Being sick wasn't something she could afford at that point in time, because the DA's office had been a total madhouse of late. So, forcing herself to be numbed, Erin turned on the bed, and gently rested her head on her pillow.

However, just then, she noticed her phone ringing. She'd silenced the ringtone, but she could clearly see Oliver's name and his number flashing on the lock screen. Erin immediately sat up and answered, "Hey, Ollie." She blinked back the tears which had threatened to roll down her cheeks.

"Hey, stranger," Oliver's voice was gravelly. "I just wanted to say how sorry I am about tonight." Oliver frowned in jeopardy.

Erin guffawed and laughed-totally infused with new hope. "Don't worry about it. It wasn't a big deal," she tried to sound nonchalant.

"Erin, I'm *really* sorry-and it *is* a big deal. I don't like going back on my word," Oliver countered.

"Ollie, I *know* you." Erin was genuinely smiling. "I know that if things could have gone differently, they would have. I also know that you have the biggest heart. So, you would never turn away *anyone* who needed your help," Erin appraised, stirred by his gesture.

Oliver smiled in the shadowy backdrop of his room. "You know me so well," he said, marveling.

"Uh-huh. That's why I know that you would *never* go out of your way to hurt me," Erin said softly. "So, no worries, okay?" she pacified.

"You're certainly right about that. I would *never* do anything to hurt you, Erin."

"I *know* that, Ollie, so I don't want for you to worry about it."

"Did you save an apple pie for me?" Oliver quipped.

"Nope, I ate all three," Erin razzed.

"Really…?" Oliver asked, skeptically.

"Uh-huh, I didn't leave not even *one* for you."

"Wow, that's really cold."

"That's me-cold as a glacier."

"No, you're not," Oliver refuted with joy bubbling up on the inside.

"And how do *you* know?" Erin vamped. She couldn't believe they were actually flirting.

"Well, the Erin Emily Brasfield *I* know is totally kind and selfless. She's always thinking about how to make life better for everyone else. She would *never* eat my pie," he teased. "And that's just *one* of the wonderful qualities I love about her," Oliver revealed, surprising himself.

Tears shone in Erin's eyes to hear Oliver say those things about her. This time they were sentimental tears-ones of joy-rather than the sorrowful ones she'd shed all night. "Ollie, that's so sweet," Erin's voice undulated.

"Are you getting all sappy on me again?" Oliver asked farcically.

"Well, *you* started it," Erin badgered.

"I guess I did start…" Oliver hesitated for a moment. He wanted to tell her not to leave the DA's office, but the words weren't coming easily. They were at the tip of this tongue, but he couldn't seem to verbalize them.

"Ollie, are you okay? You're awfully quiet," Erin evaluated, as silence hummed over the line.

"I'm fine. Erin, did you finalize your decision to work for the *Grant, Morgan and Edmonson*?" Oliver asked in respect to the new law firm Erin had applied to work for.

"I'm considering it. I have to meet with them again sometime next week," Erin disclosed, nonplused. "Why?"

"Nothing…," Oliver said, grieved. His heart dipped down to his knees, because he'd hoped she'd say something else. "Just want to make sure you end up in good hands."

"They're one of the best law firms in Silver Water," Erin said, disappointed. She had hoped that Oliver would reemphasize how much he wanted for her to stay on at the DA's office.

"So, I hear," Oliver said with tears forming in his eyes. "You're going to do great over there. I can just feel it," he praised.

"It will certainly be a change of pace, but it's a challenge I'm looking forward to," she tried to sound positive.

"They will be lucky to have you," Oliver encouraged. "It will be *our* loss, because we're going to miss you a great deal."

"Ollie, I'm going to miss you too."

"Do you see why I'm upset about all of these distractions and near misses? I can't help thinking that things are about to change for us-like we won't be seeing very much of each other," Oliver's tone was glum.

"I promise to find a way to maintain our friendship if *you* will?" Erin was unsure what to say at that moment. Even talking about walking away from her current job was excruciating. *How on earth could she ever submit to not seeing Oliver as often?* Erin trusted God to guide her along in these complicated set of circumstances, because she was falling harder for him every minute. "Do you promise?" she tested.

"I promise," Oliver affirmed. There were so many impressions on the inside. Inwardly, the heart he'd thought would have forever remained shattered screamed, *fight for her*. However, fear kept him from showing her the heart, which she'd helped piece back together again.

"Okay, as long as we continue to be friends," Erin acceded.

"Just try and shake me off, lady," Oliver beleaguered. "Hopefully, I can show you some of my stocking stuffers sometime this week. Notice that I didn't indicate a time or place."

Erin laughed. "I'm sure you'll manage to squeeze me in sometime *after* the Christmas party," Erin joked.

"The way things have been going, I wouldn't be surprised."

"Thanks for trying anyway, and I appreciate that you called tonight," Erin said graciously.

"You're welcome...my pleasure."

"Goodnight, Ollie," Erin said, reluctant to get off the phone. However, she had to acquiesce to the fact that they both had very early mornings.

"Night, Erin," Oliver said, and gently shut down his cell.

Erin tossed and turned dissecting every aspect of her phone conversation with Oliver. There were so many aspects of their talk for her to pick apart, but she submitted her fears, concerns and insecurities to the Lord, and managed to fall asleep sometime after.

***

The sun was shining in full force, but the brisk December winds struck the faces of those gathered around the casket of Antonia Wilson at *Silver Grounds Cemetery*. Silver Water's Police Commissioner-along with the County's finest joined Antonia's family and friends in order to pay their final respects to the victimized young woman. Mrs. Lena Wilson wailed in anguish, while Oliver supported her as the casket was lowered into the ground. "She didn't have to die that way. God why did my baby have to die that way?" she lamented.

Oliver's heart twisted in his chest, as he kept his arms securely around her. Tears were in his eyes as he internalized her pain. Her youngest daughter had been latest victim of the suspected serial killer. Mrs. Wilson pulled away, but clawed Oliver's chest. "DA Wright, you've got to bring my daughter's murderer to justice. Promise me…," she groaned.

Oliver stared into her sad and lifeless eyes and nodded in compliance. "I promise to do everything in my power to bring her murderer to justice." Tears rolled down his cheeks. "I'm so sorry… I'm so sorry…" Oliver collected her into his arms again and allowed her to weep.

"She didn't have to go that way," Mrs. Wilson kept saying. "My baby did not deserve to go that way."

Oliver stared heavenward and whispered a prayer for the distraught mother of the County's latest victim. He crushed her in his arms and tried to mitigate her agony. Moreover, he took turns encouraging the late young woman's other family members and friends. He'd promised to support the Wilsons in their darkest hour, and Oliver was trying to remain true to his word. Grieving the loss along with the family made the matter even more personal for him. At that point, he was more resolved than ever to find the degenerate responsible for the murders.

As the group disbanded and drifted away from the cemetery grounds, Oliver talked to the authorities regarding the case. He needed to know if there were any new developments.

"The FBI has been profiling two different men who reside in the Silver Commons area, and we've also been analyzing the forensics data. So far, there has been no DNA found in any of their databases. However, both men *were* in town when the murders took place. One, Lloyd Barnett who works through the DMV, and the other Keith Norton, a cafeteria worker for *Silver Water High School*," Lieutenant Garrett explained.

"Both are civil workers," Oliver evaluated. "So, as it stands, there is nothing concrete-no DNA found on either at the murder scenes?" he pressed.

"No, nothing we can substantiate. Still, they are persons of interest, and we're watching them very closely. The FBI is following their every move. Lloyd Barnett was brought in for questioning. He claims to have been at home on the night of two of the murders, and with friends on the night Antonia Wilson was murdered. He doesn't have a substantial alibi for the night of the other murder," Lieutenant Garrett told Oliver.

"I'm going to need for your agency to broaden its field of suspects. The truth is that it could be anyone. That person may very well be a white-collar worker who blends in. As we've seen in the past, this person may not fit the usual profile," Oliver explicated.

"We're aware of that, DA, Wright. Believe me when I say that we're leaving no stone unturned when it comes to this killer. Things have been quiet these past few days, but we're guessing that this dirt bag is probably biding his time."

"I don't want to have to attend another one of these funerals." Tears shone in Oliver's eyes. "I couldn't even really look Antonia Wilson's family in the eyes. We've got to do whatever it takes to get that monster off of the streets. Now, the DA's office is *in* one hundred percent, so I need to know that we're making progress," Oliver denoted in frustration.

"Absolutely… DA Wright, come by the precinct later, and we can examine the evidence we've pieced together through our forensics teams so far."

Oliver nodded compliantly. "I will be there." His face wrinkled in remorse. "I'm really not trying to give you a hard time-"

"No, DA Wright, we get it. I'm confident that we're getting closer to bringing this miscreant to justice."

Oliver was miffed as he set out to leave the cemetery. "Lord, *you* know who's behind these murders. Please bring this felon to the light."

Whenever things were out of Oliver's control, he knew to surrender the circumstances to God. He was the new DA of Silver County. So, he had to prove to the community that he not only cared, but that he was actively working on their behalf. Therefore, Oliver knew the only way he could do anything was through the power of the Holy Spirit who resided within him. As Jesus had said in the gospel of John chapter 15:5, "I am the vine, you are the branches. He who abides in me, and I in him, bears much fruit; *for without me you can do nothing.*"

***

Oliver had been waiting at a table inside of the upscale *Bagel Box Restaurant* since about half past nine. He'd called Kennedy and her husband Kayden Bohm and had asked to meet with them personally. Oliver wanted to get a feel for where Kennedy and Kayden stood in as far as possibly helping Taren. He, along with Mitch Channing were looking for a reduced sentence for Taren, in light of the fact that she'd already pled guilty to the charges brought against her.

At best, they were seeking to have Taren put on probation. At worst, she would face a year or two in prison. Subsequent to the felony, Taren had voluntarily submitted to psychiatric care. She had pled guilty at her arraignment. However, while awaiting sentencing, she had continued with outpatient counseling sessions through the hospital.

Mitch Channing, Taren's love interest, had vouched for her character. In his estimation, she'd come a long way, had learned from her mistakes, and was ready to move on with her life. In short, Taren was prepared to accept full responsibility for her poor choices, no matter what the penalties entailed. Oliver wanted to meet with Kennedy and Kayden in order to ask if they were willing to say a few kind words on Taren's behalf. Oliver had no idea how Kennedy or her husband would feel about his crusade. Nevertheless, he was hopeful that an impact statement, even in the form of a letter, had the potential to sway the judge's opinion in Taren's favor.

It had been quite some time since Oliver had seen Kennedy. In fact, he dared say that the last time he'd seen Kennedy or Kayden had been at their wedding reception. Aside from that, he'd gotten glimpses of their lavish life together through the tabloids and social media. Oliver kept reminding himself that this meeting was strictly professional.

He refused to allow his heartstrings to be pulled in every which way when he saw Kennedy again. As much as he'd loved Kennedy, Oliver had made peace with her decision to marry Kayden Bohm. Kennedy was indeed a part of his past. Oliver smiled musingly as he recounted his conversation with Erin late last night. Inwardly, he affirmed that he wanted for Erin to be his future. Of course, he still had no clue how to convey that to her. Maybe, he considered, he would do a lot less talking, and a lot more showing Erin how much he'd come to value their friendship.

An instant smile spread across Oliver's face when he saw Kennedy come through the restaurant's set of doors. He instantly stood to his feet and crossed over to connect to her. "Well, hello there, Miss Kennedy!" Oliver said cheerily.

"Ollie!" Kennedy opened up her arms in greeting. Oliver surrendered to them, and they hugged. "I'm so happy to see you!"

Kennedy crushed him in her arms, and the two swayed together in celebration.

"I'm happy to see you too!" They pulled away mutually but took a moment to contemplate each other. "You look amazing!" Oliver praised, taking in the woman he'd loved for such a long time. Kennedy looked like an angel in a stylish black and salmon pink butterfly-styled dress and fashionable short-styled black boots. With her lengthy hair upswept, she looked like a supermodel. Her wind-kissed caramel skin radiated with life and vitality. Oliver also couldn't help noticing how thin Kennedy had gotten. For the longest she had struggled with her weight. However, it seemed she was finally where she'd said she wanted to be.

"*I* look amazing? Oliver, you're as handsome as ever!" she complimented, delving his eyes.

"Oh, stop...," Oliver's cheeks turned cardinal.

"Well, it's the truth, Mr. District Attorney," Kennedy said with cajolery. "I can't tell you how proud I am of everything you're doing to ensure that the citizens of Silver County remain safe." Kennedy looped her arm through Oliver's and allowed him to guide her over to their table.

"Listen to *you* sounding like a walking endorsement," Oliver quipped, as he pulled out her chair.

"Oh, that wasn't my intention, but I've got to give credit where credit is due," Kennedy said smiling. At that point she and Oliver were sitting across from each other. "Kayden sends his apologies for not being able to make it. Something came up last minute," Kennedy said regretfully.

"No worries," Oliver reassured. He clasped his hands together and stared over at Kennedy with a curious expression on his face. "I guess I don't have to ask how you've been. You're glowing, so I guess you've been really happy." Oliver's eyes shone in affect, because he acquiesced to the fact that he championed her happiness and would always care about her.

Kennedy's smile was irrepressible, and her cheeks turned

scarlet. "I *am* very happy, Ollie. God has been awesome to us!" She met his eyes intuitively. "How have *you* been? I mean, you look wonderful, but I know that life has been a little different, demanding even…"

Oliver nodded in agreement. "To say the least… It often feels as if I have the weight of the entire world on my shoulders," he admitted, searching her eyes. "There are times I doubt that I am cut out for the job, because my heart gets pulled in so many different directions." Shadows hung over his face just then.

Kennedy frowned in commiseration. "I can only imagine. I know that your duties far exceed anything you've seen in the courtroom, because there are times where you have to be in the thick of things."

"Tell me about it. I'm actually just coming from attending the funeral of a young woman who was murdered…"

"I know. I've been following the story on the news." Kennedy shook her head in empathy. "There's a suspected serial killer on the loose," she verified.

"It's definitely beginning to look that way," Oliver said broodingly. "Her mother was totally inconsolable at the cemetery." He shook his head in commiseration. "When something like this happens, I feel personally-"

Kennedy held her hand up haltingly. "Ollie, you can't. You can't carry the weight of the world on your shoulders. I've seen you try to do that in the past. You're like this invincible superhero fighting for the justice of all, while *you're* falling apart inwardly. Look, I have the utmost respect for your office, but you can't be that hard on yourself," Kennedy said softly. "God has placed you in the DA's office to make a difference, Ollie, but you can't take the entire load to heart." She issued an understanding smile. "I hope you get that and stop being so hard on yourself."

Oliver smiled and guffawed. "I'm really trying not to internalize it all." He swallowed the lump in his throat.

"Well, that's good to know, because I want you to focus on

yourself too. Ollie, ever since I've known you, it's been about helping everyone else. When do you get to focus on *you* and be happy?" Kennedy challenged. Even if Oliver had not been in the will of God for her life, Kennedy cared a great deal about him, and wanted him to have the very best. Notwithstanding, Oliver was such a wonderful person with a huge heart, he deserved to find love-just as God had blessed her.

Oliver chuckled nonsensically over Kennedy's observation. "All work and zero life…story of *my* life," he acceded.

"Ollie, I know your heart. You have so much to give. I want you to be as happy as Kay and I are. Speaking of which, how is *Erin*?" Kennedy asked with a mischievous grin.

Oliver laughed and shook his head humorously. "Thanks, Kennedy. Believe me, I want to get there too." His eyes reticently met Kennedy's. "And Erin is fine." His cheeks flushed.

"Will you tell her that Kayden and I send our best?" Kennedy encouraged.

"I will absolutely do that," Oliver said timidly, and shook his head again in the negative. "Thank you for agreeing to meet with me today," he evaded, still with reddened cheeks.

"Are you kidding me? Kayden and I were both looking forward to having breakfast with the new DA."

"No, Kennedy, just *Oliver*," he countered good-naturedly. "I'm the DA with everyone else except for with my *friends*." He winked at her.

"I understand." Kennedy smiled contemplatively at him.

"Sir…, Ma'am, are you ready to place your orders?" the waiter breezed over and asked the pair.

"Are you ready to order, Kennedy?" Oliver asked politely.

"We can start with fruit, coffee and croissants," she told the waiter. "Is that alright, Ollie?" Kennedy then redirected.

"Sounds good to me," Oliver concurred.

"The reason why I asked to see you today isn't the easiest subject to bring up," Oliver said as he stirred creamer into his coffee. He and Kennedy were just finishing up breakfast.

"What is it, Ollie?" Kennedy's face creased in apprehension. "You can tell me anything," she prodded.

Oliver took a moment to explicate the intricate details of Taren Cook's case. Kennedy's face changed the moment he'd brought up Taren's name, so Oliver wasn't very hopeful by the time he finished presenting his argument. "I'm so sorry to even bring it up." His face warped in penitence. "It's just that Mitch and I are trying to help her. As you know, Taren's sentencing is next week. So, we're advocating a reduced sentence, in light of the fact that she has no prior record. She's been extremely cooperative and has shown sincere remorse."

"Wow, that's a heavy one, Ollie," Kennedy said with a strained, yet faraway expression on her face. "You want me to write an impact statement letter in order to help Taren," Kennedy mulled over. Jeopardy changed her usually easygoing mien.

Oliver remained silent, seeing the brooding expression on Kennedy's face. He'd gone over the argument in his head a hundred times. However, it hadn't resonated well presenting the matter to Kennedy. She'd been the one whom Taren had victimized. "Kennedy, I'm sorry. I didn't mean to offend you." Oliver's head slumped.

"No, Oliver, you haven't offended me. It's just a difficult subject. When you said Taren's name just now all of those memories came rushing back," she admitted. "It was an awful time. Honestly, I can't say that I recognized her as that person who attacked me just days before the wedding. She *certainly* wasn't herself, and definitely not the best friend I'd come to know and love."

"That must have been unspeakably difficult for you," Oliver empathized. "You didn't deserve to have anyone treat you that way."

"It *was* heartbreaking to fall out with my bestie right before my wedding. Still, Ollie, even if what happened was painful, if *you* tell me that Taren has changed, I believe you." She looked into Oliver's eyes conclusively. "However, I would still have to discuss the matter with Kayden before I make such a life-altering decision," she said wisely.

Oliver nodded hopefully. "That's understandable and totally fair."

"Maybe, I should talk to Mitch. After all, he's the one who's been spending the most time with Taren," Kennedy evaluated. "Have *you* seen her?" she asked Oliver, with a frayed expression on her face.

"I have…and I've spoken to her. I can't decipher what's in anyone's heart. However, the times in which I've spoken with her, she has expressed genuine regret. She's continued outpatient treatment at the hospital and is prepared to deal with the penalties of her actions," Oliver clarified.

"Look, Kennedy, this isn't the DA speaking to you right now. It's just *me*. I understand just how deeply Taren hurt you. It was the worst kind of betrayal. Still, because she's someone we know and care about, we're doing all we can to keep her from having to spend close to a decade behind bars for her mistakes."

Kennedy nodded, stirred by the matter at hand. "It's like I said before, Ollie. I don't want to make a snap decision without first speaking to Kayden and to Mitch. I'm only asking for a little time," she conceded.

Oliver smiled, reached across the table, and covered her hand with his. "I understand, and you're absolutely right. Take all the time you need in deciding. I'm grateful you decided to meet with me today."

Kennedy's face lit up with a brand-new smile. "It's been

great seeing you too, Ollie. I'm so proud of all of your accomplishments, and I'm eager to help in any way I can." Tears gleamed in Kennedy's eyes. She had not expected to discuss such a touchy subject matter. Taren had taken a hatchet to her heart not too long ago, and Kennedy felt conflicted.

"I know that, Kennedy. I know that I can always count on my friends whenever I need them." Oliver offered a clement smile, truly heartened that Kennedy had even taken the time.

Sometime later, Oliver walked Kennedy over to her waiting limo. "Will you give Kayden my regards?" Oliver asked just before Kennedy slipped into the automobile.

"Absolutely…" Kennedy wrapped her arms around Oliver and squeezed him affectionately. "Please take care of yourself."

Oliver fondly crushed her in his arms. "I will. So, we'll be in touch?" They pulled back mutually.

"Definitely," Kennedy reassured. "Say hello to Erin," she reminded with a reticent smile. "Ollie, you should really take the time to smell the roses. Merry Christmas!" she cheered.

Oliver laughed lightly. "I will take your advice to heart. Merry Christmas, Kennedy!"

CHAPTER SEVEN

"Erin, there's someone here to see you," David told Erin, looking perplexed as he stood in the doorway of her office. "I didn't know who it was, so I asked him to take a seat out in the lobby." His face creased in uncertainty.

"Well, did you ask for a name?" Erin asked, confused.

"*Wayne* something…," David said glibly.

Erin sighed, but offered David an encouraging smile, nonetheless. "Okay, thanks for letting me know." She drifted over to her desk and minimized the appeal letter she'd been editing for the past hour on her desktop. Erin grabbed her phone and shut her office door closed.

Crossing over to the general office area, Erin's eyes skimmed over the entire space looking for Oliver. She and Oliver had talked on the phone late last night, and Erin was still on a cloud from the conversation they'd had. However, she had not seen him at all that day. Oliver also hadn't called or texted her. Erin had deliberated about texting him but had desisted-not wanting for him to think that she was clingy.

Oliver was a key player in overseeing the security of everyone in Silver County. So, it wasn't unusual if he didn't show up at the office until the middle of the afternoon. There were times where he showed up in the early evening. Erin's only regret was that David had not come out to her office to announce that *Oliver* was back, and that he needed her help to perform one task or another.

As Erin plodded out of the main office and wandered out into the lobby, she froze in her tracks to see Grayson Andrews standing there. *What on earth?* Erin's eyes widened in shock, and she gasped. "Gray…?" Erin questioned, flabbergasted.

"Hello, Erin," Gray said with a mischievous grin, advancing towards the young lady. Gray contemplated every inch of Erin in her gray and burgundy colored spade-designed dress.

"Gray, what are you doing here?" Erin asked, bewildered, searching his piercing hazel eyes. She couldn't help thinking how nicely Gray cleaned up. He had on a navy-blue dress suit and looked quite professional. "How on earth did you find me?" There was a needling expression on her face.

Gray held up both hands disarmingly, as he eliminated the small gap between them. He offered Erin his winning smile. "Before you get mad, I need for you to know that I didn't break any rules in finding you."

"How *reassuring*," Erin said caustically, staring at Gray in total incredulity. She sighed, setting her hands sassily on her hips. "*Why* are you here?" She shook her head in utter denial.

"Well, I was at the office, and I realized I hadn't had lunch yet," Gray said with a straight face.

"So, okay, *what* does *that* have to do with me? I'm sure you've been having lunch for a number of years now without having to consider me." Erin's eyes knifed through Gray's.

Gray nodded in agreement, but held his right pointer finger up as a philosopher would. "You're right, but since meeting *you* the other night, I haven't been able to get the idea of having lunch with you out of my head."

"Are you serious?" Erin's face creased in skepticism.

"Oh, Erin, you have *no* idea how serious I am." Gray's expression softened as he searched her eyes. "I haven't been able to stop thinking about you. So, I *had* to find you."

"Gray, you know what they call what you've done around *here*?" Erin gestured to the building. "They call it *stalking*. I'm grateful that you helped me with my shopping bags the other night, but…"

"Ah, speaking of which…," Gray said cryptically. "Wait here, and don't move." He crossed over to where he'd been sitting out on a bench and picked up a very expensive looking shopping bag.

Erin waited in the center of the lobby, tapping her right foot, with hands still defiantly on her hips. Not knowing quite what to make of what was happening, Erin looked heavenward and said a prayer, "God, help me. I don't even *know* this guy." *Ollie, where are you?*

"So," Gray returned holding the designer Christmas bag, "these are for you," he said, handing the bag over to Erin.

Erin gave him a suspicious look and shook her head in the negative.

"Just take a look before you say no," Gray prodded.

Erin sighed and took the bag from him. She opened it up and found that he'd gotten her a gazillion miniature snow globes-more attractive than the ones she'd broken outside of the Super Walmart shopping center on Wednesday night. Erin gasped in shock, and a slow smile curved over her lips. "They're actually beautiful, Gray-prettier than the other ones-but I can't…"

"Yes, you can," Gray insisted. "There is this holiday specialty store not too far from me. I saw them, and they screamed out to me. They said, 'please buy us for Erin, Gray. She really needs us as stocking stuffers,'" Gray said facetiously while making a quirky face.

"So, you talk to Christmas ornaments now?" Erin softened, smiling over Gray's silly humor.

"Don't tell anyone, because they will have me committed for sure. Seriously, it was my pleasure to get them for you." He smiled warmly into Erin's eyes.

"They *are* beautiful!" Erin examined the globes. There must have been at least thirty of them.

"Yes, they really are…," Gray moved in closer, and stared at Erin, mesmerized.

As charming, handsome and funny as Gray was, Oliver was the only one pressed on Erin's mind. She had hoped to connect to him sometime that day. It was Friday afternoon, and the Christmas party was a little over one week away. Before long, she would no longer be working through the DA's office. Erin started rethinking the decision she'd made to quit her job. However, it was difficult to focus when Gray was all up in her face.

"So, will you have lunch with me, Ms. Erin Brasfield, who works through the DA's office-very impressive by the way and also *scary...*," he razzed.

Erin laughed openly over his silliness. "Gray..." She gave him a nonsensical look.

"Are you free right now?"

"It *is* my lunch hour," Erin admitted.

"Perfect, so let's go out to lunch?"

"Gray, I don't know anything about you," Erin complained.

However, Gray gently set his hand on her arm, and began to guide her away from the lobby.

"Wait... I need to go back to my office. I have to put the snow globes away, and I have to grab my pocketbook."

"Okay, but I refuse to move from this post until you come out and have lunch with me today. If you don't come back, I might still be here when the office closes later on."

Erin looked over at the handsome stranger, shaking her head humorously. "No need for that. I'll be right back."

"I'll be waiting, beautiful!" Gray watched Erin drift away. He couldn't believe how incredibly beautiful she was. Furthermore, he anticipated having lunch with such a rare beauty on his arm. She looked incredible in her form-fitting gray and burgundy dress. The dress highlighted her tiny waste and curvy hips. Gray assessed that Erin had a great body and amazing legs. He didn't know whether or not she had a boyfriend, but it didn't matter one way or another. As far as he was concerned, he was ready to pull out all the stops to claim her as his own, and to assure that the striking young woman would fall in love with him.

***

Oliver returned to the DA's office in the middle of the afternoon on Friday. He'd attended Antonia Wilson's funeral, had breakfast with Kennedy Proctor-Bohm in order to discuss a recommendation letter to help in Taren Cook's case. In addition, he'd had a short meeting with the State Attorney General in respect to the ongoing serial killer investigation. Oliver stepped into his office and immediately checked the phone. He also perused the handwritten messages from his receptionist Betty. Powering through the demands of his day had in no way stopped him from obsessing about Erin. Oliver couldn't wait to see her.

Settling down at his desk, Oliver obligatorily returned a few urgent phone messages. He also took time to answer a few emails. Furthermore, he finally checked his cellphone for any additional messages or missed calls, as the phone had remained on silent mode for most of the day. Oliver's heart crashed to the floor in disappointment, because there were no calls or text messages from Erin. He wasn't sure why he expected to hear from her all the time, because he'd delineated that they were to be *just* friends. Therefore, they did not have that *kind* of relationship. And yet, Oliver found himself wanting to share the ins and outs of *everything* with Erin.

The thought of Erin being his last call of the day made Oliver smile. He'd certainly enjoyed kicking back and hearing her lilting voice over the phone the other night. Also, he was reminded of the talk he and Kennedy had earlier on. Life was much too short not to grab of hold of happiness in any way shape or form in which it could be found. Even if helping others was indeed a vocation, Oliver had to consider what *he* wanted. The more he thought on it, the more he realized that Erin was what he wanted.

The moment he got done talking on the phone with a social worker, who was helping a parolee, Oliver pushed out of his armchair, and stepped out of the office. It was a little after two in the afternoon, and he hoped against hope that Erin would be in her office. Perhaps, if she hadn't taken lunch, they could grab a bite together. Making his way across the general office area was never easy, as he was stopped by the members of his staff, who always had a gazillion questions.

It was always like crossing the Red Sea trying to make it through the congested area, but Oliver knew that it came with the territory. It took some doing, but he finally managed to make it over to Erin's office. Standing at the door, he knocked lightly.

"Ollie, don't even bother. Erin's out to lunch," David addressed, seeing Oliver knocking on her office door.

"Oh…okay. I guess I missed her." Oliver turned to speak to David. Discontentment inundated his heart that he'd missed Erin again.

"Yeah, it was the strangest thing. Some guy came over to the office a little while ago asking for her," David informed, with a mystified expression on his face.

"A guy…?" Oliver asked, affected. His heart had already dipped to the floor. "What guy?" His eyes lowered urgently into David's.

"I don't know, Ollie. I've never seen him before. He was white, dark hair, hazel eyes about 6'1" or 6'2", early thirties… In any case, he waited out in the lobby for her for a while. I can't be sure, but I think Erin went out to lunch with him," David told Oliver, in a cavalier tone.

"She went out to lunch with his man?" Oliver prodded, with his heartstrings unraveling. "Is there any chance it could have been business-related?" Oliver asked, conflicted, heart pulsing in hurt.

"It *could* have been, but I doubt it," David said glibly. He then gave Oliver a curious look. "Oliver Wright, are you *into* Erin?" His face wrinkled in mischief.

"I…," Oliver's words trailed. At that very moment, he saw Erin coming up the hallway with someone he'd never seen before fitting the description David had just detailed.

"Thank you for agreeing to have lunch with me this afternoon, Erin." Gray inched in close to Erin, exploring her eyes. "I hope you will let me take you out again."

"Gray, lunch was nice, but I really didn't expect…," Erin's words lagged when she looked down the hallway, and saw Oliver standing in front of her office door. *Oh no, this is the worst timing,* she assessed. Erin's face warped in remorse, and her heart immediately knotted up. It was difficult to read Oliver's expression. Was it disillusionment, disappointment or bewilderment? Perhaps it was all three.

"Erin, what's the matter?" Gray asked, following her gape over to the gentlemen standing down the hallway from them.

"Gray, come with me," Erin said bravely, decisively looping her arm through his. Nonetheless, her eyes were fastened to Oliver. There was nothing to hide. Gray was someone she'd *just* met-a stranger for all intents and purposes. During their lunch excursion, Erin had learned that Gray was an investor. He was single and didn't have any children.

"Hey, Ollie, David…," Erin greeted both men properly, with Gray standing to her left-hand side.

"Hey, stranger," Oliver said with feigned enthusiasm. Tears were stinging his eyes. Overhearing Erin's exchanges with the other guy had answered his question. They'd had lunch together, and it was totally non-business related. In fact, Oliver could tell that this man was completely *into* Erin.

"Gray, this is Oliver Wright…," Erin introduced delving sensitively into Oliver's eyes.

"You're the new District Attorney!" Gray said excited and extended his hand. "It's awesome to meet you! You certainly had my vote! I'm Gray Andrews!"

Oliver worked through tangled feelings, offered a genial smile, and shook the gentleman's hand. "Thank you! It's nice to meet you, Gray!"

"This is the Assistant to the DA, David Reed," Erin introduced properly.

"It's nice to meet you as well, David," Gray said cordially, and extended his hand out to David. The two shook hands.

"Gray and I met at the strip mall a few days ago. He helped me when I dropped my purchases from the Super Walmart," Erin said nervously, unable to keep her eyes off of Oliver. "I was such a klutz and wound up breaking some of the items."

"Well, you're the *prettiest* klutz I've ever seen! I'm just glad I was there to help," Gray said, totally dazzled by *everything* Erin.

"Sorry about your accident, Stranger. I guess I'm glad Gray was there to help," Oliver attested, staring from Erin to Gray. His eyes settled on Gray in a lackluster manner.

"It was my good deed for the day." Gray smiled, slipping his arm around Erin's waist. Staring from Erin to Oliver Wright, Gray picked up on the strong undercurrents between the two. The intensity was undeniable.

Startled by Gray's sudden move, Erin flinched and shrugged away from his touch. "Gray and I were just saying goodbye," she said and gave him an incredulous look. "Ollie, did you need something?" Erin redirected towards Oliver.

"It wasn't that important. David and I were just talking," Oliver eluded.

"Right...," David said picking up on Oliver's disappointment. "I'll see you later, Ollie," he said and turned away. "It was nice meeting you, Gray." David veered and looked at Gray once more.

Gray held up his hand in a cordial gesture. "Nice meeting you too, David."

"So, I will see you later, Gray," Erin said with eyes lowering meaningfully into his.

"Can we go out again over the weekend?" Gray asked with a sense of impropriety, searching her eyes.

"Thanks again for lunch-and for the snow globes, Gray. I really appreciate it," Erin emphasized. She was beyond mortified that Oliver had gotten wind of this impromptu date. She couldn't help thinking that she'd made the worst mistake by agreeing to go out with Gray. Erin's heart ached because all she wanted was to be completely alone with Oliver. It was crucial for him to understand that she loved *him*-and no one else.

"I will call you," Gray insisted.

"Bye, Gray, I will see you later," Erin said definitively, trying to distance herself. And yet, it was clear that Gray had other ideas.

"Okay," Gray conceded, "thanks for agreeing to have lunch with me this afternoon, Erin. I look forward to seeing you again." Gray's penetrating eyes drifted over to connect to Oliver's just then. "Mr. Wright, it was a pleasure to meet you!" he correctly acknowledged.

"Likewise," Oliver said, smiling until his face hurt.

Oliver was frozen to his post. The hurt he grappled with had left him maimed. He willed his legs to move, but they refused to comply. He smiled musingly as he watched Erin interact with her new friend. *Why did it feel as if his heart was about to stop?* It was clear that Erin was struggling with feelings of uneasiness over the matter. Oliver wondered if Erin actually liked Gray. Gray was definitely the suave and good-looking type. *Was it too late?* Oliver examined. *Had he made the worst mistake of his life by telling Erin he wanted to be friends, when his heart was screaming that she was the one?*

It was gut-wrenching to watch Erin walk Gray out of the office area, while he stood by with a bleeding heart. And there was no way Oliver could blame Erin for moving on. It was *his* fault that someone else had gotten the chance to step in. At that moment Oliver regretted not making Erin his to begin with. He'd hesitated, and now it was quite possible that he'd lost her.

Oliver couldn't help feeling that this was déjà vu. He'd stalled with Kennedy for years, and by the time he'd made his move, her heart was already vested in someone else. The thought of losing Erin in the same way seemed too bitter a pill to swallow.

"That was a little awkward," Erin said in a muddled tone, staring intently into Oliver's eyes. She had crossed back over to her office in order to have word with him.

"*He* seems nice," Oliver said trying to sound nonchalant. Inwardly, it killed him that Erin had gone out with anyone else.

"Ollie, he's just some guy I met over at the mall. I didn't even give him my number or-"

"Hey, you don't need to explain anything to me," Oliver feigned total aplomb." Covetously taking in every inch of Erin, he added, "I guess *Gray* knows a good thing when he sees it. He really seems to like you."

"Do you want to come inside and talk for a minute?" Erin indicated her office.

"I was just coming by to ask if you wanted to grab a bite, but I guess…"

"Oh, *you* haven't had lunch yet?" Erin asked, pertained.

"Actually, I had a late breakfast, but things got a little bit hectic from that point on."

"Nothing too demanding I hope," Erin's voice undulated, and tears pricked her eyes.

"Well, you *know* the drill. It's *always* demanding." Oliver smiled through the pain. Inwardly, it felt as if someone had just taken a hammer to his heart.

"Do you think you'll have a moment later? I would *really* like to update you on how things are coming along with the party planning."

"Right…the party. I guess you found a few stocking stuffers," Oliver affirmed, trying to sound upbeat. The truth was that he wanted to take Erin in his arms, so that he could tell her that he needed her so badly he could barely function.

"I would love to show them to you a little later if that's

alright?" Erin was leaning into Oliver. He looked so good in his black dress suit. It had been a while since she'd seen him in black. Oliver was an enigma and the *definition* of sleek in *anything* black. Everything about him appealed to her, from his perfect muscular body, to his well-formed mouth, to his golden-brown eyes. Even hearing his voice gave Erin chills. Sharing such an intimate moment together, his voice was making her totally insane. Oliver's throaty voice was enough to put a late-night radio announcer's to shame!

"Sure… I will swing by before leaving later," Oliver stated. His intention had been to pull away. Seeing Erin with another man had so affected him, but he couldn't seem to.

"Can we do a raincheck on lunch? I'm so sorry that I missed out on having lunch with the DA of Silver County!" Erin smiled in earnest, as their eyes momentarily locked.

"The DA of Silver County missed out on having lunch with *you*," Oliver emphasized. "So, how many rainchecks are we working with here?"

"Oh, *numerous* rainchecks. Hopefully, we get a chance to make up each and every one." Erin instinctively reached for Oliver's hand, and grasped it firmly in her own. It was her way of conveying that *he* was the person her heart wanted.

Startled by the tenderness of Erin's touch, Oliver stared fondly into her eyes. "If you'll give me a chance, I promise only *sunny checks*." He winked. The sensation of Erin stroking his hand was indescribably wonderful. Oliver had been completely surprised by Erin's sudden gesture, but it offered hope.

"I'm *all* for *sunny checks*." Erin squeezed Oliver's strong hand. "Enjoy your lunch." Their eyes locked once more.

"I'll be back soon," he said huskily. Oliver took Erin's dainty hand, brought it up to his lips and pressed a kiss to it. "So, I will see you in a bit." His eyes lowered sensitively into hers.

Erin gulped nervously, totally spellbound. "Okay… Bye, Ollie," she said swooning.

Oliver smiled a bit more openly. He turned and headed down the hallway away from Erin's office. However, he turned again in order to connect to her stare. Oliver smiled quietly and forced himself to walk away.

Erin stepped into her office and pressed her back up to the closed door. She sighed and allowed herself to breathe as her thoughts raced. There was internal conflict in respect to what had just occurred. She hoped that Oliver would not view her in a negative light, because she'd gone out to lunch with Gray.

Looking heavenward, Erin appealed to God for help. The last thing she wanted was to give Oliver the wrong idea. She wasn't *into* anyone else but him. Furthermore, she hoped that she had unequivocally conveyed to him that *he* was the one who held her heart. Erin couldn't say for sure, but she suspected that Oliver's heart might *finally* be turning toward her. The conceptualization of this epiphany inundated her heart with joy and infused her spirit with hope.

***

"Ollie, will you please stay with me?" Rain entreated on Friday evening. Oliver had come over right after Rain had gotten horrible news from her mom out on Rhode Island. "I really don't think I can be alone right now." Rain's red, melancholic eyes had connected direly to his.

Oliver nodded affirmatively. "Whatever you need," he said, crushing Rain in his arms in consolation. Rain had texted him, stating a personal crisis. When Oliver had made it out to the office earlier that afternoon, David had told him that Rain had called about a family emergency. And now, Oliver knew what that family emergency was. Her father had suffered a heart attack and had died. Edward McGrath, the seventy-five-year-old judge, had taken his last breath that morning.

Rain had barely spoken a word since Oliver had come over. In fact, it was clear to him that she had shut down. She'd been in a different world since talking on the phone with her mother. So,

Oliver had left the DA's office, and had rushed over to be by her side. His heart was broken over the matter. It was only a week before Christmas, and Rain had lost her dad. "Are you up to eating anything?" Oliver pulled away in order to look into Rain's sad eyes.

"Not hungry…" Rain shook her head in the negative. "My brothers are already headed out to Rhode Island. I feel as if *I* was the last one to know," she groused with fresh tears shimmering in her eyes.

"Oh, honey, you really shouldn't look at it that way. It seems as if they were trying to protect you. They know how close you were to your dad," Oliver placated.

Rain felt as if her siblings had hesitated in telling her about her dad. Oliver could only conclude that they had waited in order to spare her. "You really can't look at it that way. I doubt that your family would deliberately choose *not* to tell you." His face twisted in commiseration, as he tenderly brushed tears away from her eyes. "I know that it's hard for you to wrap your head around it right now, but I'm sure you'll feel differently once you're with them," he uplifted.

Too grief-stricken to say very much, Rain slipped her arms about Oliver's waist, and held on for dear life. It was too difficult to verbalize the pain, so she sobbed into his chest. "Why is this happening now?" she wailed. "My dad was supposed to walk me down the aisle when I got married. He was supposed to be there for when I had my children," she mourned. "And now…" Rain faltered and surrendered to the floor.

Oliver broke her fall. Catching her up in his arms, he sat on the living room floor along with her. For some time, Rain cried inconsolably as he held her in comfort. There was nothing he could say in that moment. Losing a loved-one was one of the bitterest pills a person could swallow on this earth. So, Oliver refused to pretend as if he held any of the answers. The only thing he *could* do was to be there for his friend.

Sometime later, Oliver stood outside of Rain's bedroom door, and knocked softly. He was carrying a tray of food. He'd made her a grilled cheese sandwich and had warmed up a bowl of cream of broccoli soup. Furthermore, he had a bottle of water and a couple of Ibuprofen pills. Rain had cried incessantly since he'd been there in the early evening. She'd been so distraught that he had to make traveling reservations for them.

In the morning they would catch a flight out to Providence, Rhode Island. Oliver had made the staunch decision to stand with Rain when she faced the ultimate reality of losing her dad. With all of the craziness taking place in Silver County-even with a possible serial killer on the loose-Rain needed him in that dark hour, and he couldn't turn his back on her. There were still arrangements to be made, but Oliver had already taken care of most of the technicalities. If everything worked according to plan, they would be on Rhode Island sometime after nine a.m. the next morning.

"Come in," Rain said with a muffled tone of voice. She lay in bed clutching her pillow. She had cried herself into a short nap. However, she was up and alert at that point. Notwithstanding, she realized that Oliver's presence there hadn't been in her imagination. Knowing he was there was the one mitigating factor. His kindness and support buffered the unspeakable anguish she felt over the loss of her beloved father.

"Hey," Oliver said with a faint smile, drifting into the room, "I really think that you should eat something." He rested the tray of food on Rain's nightstand.

Rain offered a weak smile through the sadness. Her eyes were sunken in at that point. "Thank you, Ollie." She reached for Oliver's hand, and he sat down on the bed across from her. "I don't know how I would be able to handle any of this if you weren't with me right now." Rain grimaced in cheerlessness.

Oliver covered her hand with his. "Oh, sweetheart, I'm *so* sorry. I wish I knew how to make things better." He shook his head in remorse and stared empathetically into her eyes.

"You *are* making things better for me just by being here." Fresh tears looped over Rain's eyelids. "This is the last thing I expected." She shook her head in skepticism. "Life...? You can never predict what's going to happen. One-minute things could be fine and then..."

Oliver's stared at her with compassion and understanding. "Change and unpredictability are the only things guaranteed in this life." He brushed over her hand in support. "Rain, I need for you to eat something."

"Ollie, I can't-"

"Yes, you have to. I wouldn't want you getting sick on top of everything else." His eyes searched hers intuitively. "Do it for me?" he implored.

Rain hesitantly nodded and offered him a feeble smile. "Thank you."

Oliver gently set the tray in front of her and encouraged her to eat a few bites of her sandwich. Rain had had stomach issues earlier on in the week, and he didn't want for her to take pills on an empty stomach. "Our flight leaves at 6:45 am from Silver Water International," he told her.

"You *are* coming with me?" Rain confirmed, setting a full spoon of soup back into the bowl.

"Of course, … I wouldn't want you traveling alone right now."

"Ollie, you've got so many responsibilities," she argued.

"I've already had word with David and Jason. They will be handling the ins and outs around the office. They will also handle any crisis which should arise in my absence," Oliver said with a bleeding heart. Despite the fact that he was utterly dedicated to work, what worried him most was being pulled away from Erin again.

"Ollie, are you sure? As much as I want you with me, I wouldn't want to get in the way of all of your responsibilities. The entire county looks to you," she reminded.

Oliver offered a hopeful smile. "I know. Trust me when I say that it's all under control. I don't want you worrying about anything right now, okay?" His eyes lowered into hers meaningfully. "There's already so much on your plate." Tears gleamed in his eyes.

"I feel guilty for having even asked."

"Well, don't. I'm sure it isn't anything *you* wouldn't do for me-if *I'd* asked." He gave her a well-meaning look.

"Ollie, there isn't *anything* I wouldn't do for you." Tears brimmed over in Rain's eyes, as she guided Oliver into her arms.

"I know that, Rain." Oliver held her in comfort. Regardless of his temperate and easygoing front, Oliver felt totally conflicted. As devoted as he was to the people of Silver County, the *one* thing that troubled him was being away from Erin. Notwithstanding, Gray Andrews was standing in the wings-ready, willing and able to offer her everything Oliver had told her he couldn't.

Now that Oliver was ready to tell Erin the truth, there was *yet* another distraction. In all fairness, as he and Rain had just determined, life *was* unpredictable. Neither of them could have foreseen her father's sudden death. She was indeed an old friend, and direly needed his support. Oliver hoped and prayed that Erin wouldn't give her heart to someone else, while he tried to work out the intricacies of his complex life. He submitted to the fact that losing Erin would undoubtedly destroy what was left of his already fractured heart.

Oliver ensured that Rain ate a bit of her dinner and stayed with her until she fell asleep. He'd already gone back to his place and had packed a bag. He'd prayed on the matter, and despite the unconventional set of circumstances, going out to Rhode Island with Rain was the right thing. The bible teaches that believers are to grieve to those who grieve (Romans 12:15). Regardless, Oliver wasn't going into the situation with his eyes closed. Rain had kissed him the other night. So, even if *his* intention was to offer support at a very dark time in her life, it was likely that Rain had other ideas. Furthermore, she was quite possibly on a totally different page.

Oliver crossed over to the bedroom one last time to confirm that Rain was asleep. Soon after, he went into the spare bedroom. Changing out of his work clothes, he washed up. After brushing his teeth, he said his prayers. Detailing the circumstances to God, Oliver shared his insecurities in respect to losing Erin. Opening up the word of God, the Holy Spirit highlighted 1 John 4:18, "There is no fear in love; but perfect love casts out fear, because fear involves torment. But, he who fears has not been made perfect in love (NKJV)."

It was almost ten when Oliver slipped into bed, mulling over that passage of scripture. Refusing to fear, Oliver would do his best to hold on to his faith. If God wanted things to work out with Erin, nothing and no one would be able thwart His plans. Having spent most of the day with Rain since she'd received the tragic news, Oliver had been waiting for the right moment to connect to Erin. He'd promised to touch base before leaving the office for the day. However, once again their plan had gone terribly awry.

***

"Thank you for acting so quickly, Erin," Stanley Crane, Violet Crane's eldest son told Erin late Friday night. Erin had just called an ambulance for his mom who'd taken a nasty fall. The Sixty-eight-year-old woman who lived a couple of houses down, had slipped while getting into the shower. She'd been in the house with her eleven-year old granddaughter. Violet had asked her granddaughter to go over to Erin's to ask for help.

Erin had called for an ambulance and had rushed over to the house to make sure the woman was alright. All the same, she'd phoned Violet's son and his wife. The couple had gone out for dinner and a movie. "You're welcome, Mr. Crane," Erin said graciously.

"If you hadn't come over and stayed with Angelica and my mom until we got home, I don't know what we would have done." The gentleman stared earnestly into Erin's eyes. "We owe you a debt of gratitude," he affirmed.

Deborah Crane, Stanley's wife, wrapped her arms fondly around Erin, and pressed a kiss to her cheek. "Thank you so much! We *do* owe you everything for what you did for our family tonight." She pulled away and stared endearingly into Erin's eyes.

Angelica, the Crane's eleven-year-old threw her arms around

Erin. "Thanks for helping my grandma," she declared, squeezing her. "You saved her life."

Erin shook her head nonsensically, staring devotedly down at the little girl. "*You* actually saved your grandmother's life, Angelica. *You* were so brave to come get me," Erin countered-contemplating the youngster with compassion.

"Grandma told me how nice you are and said that you would come out to help us right away." Angelica smiled. "And you were like Super Girl or something."

Erin smiled. "I don't think so but thanks for saying that anyway."

"It's time for *you* to go to bed, young lady," Deborah Crane reminded her daughter. Your father is going with your grandmother over to the hospital.

"Okay, mom," Angelica complied. She stood close to her mom as they watched the rescue workers set Violet Crane up inside of the ambulance.

Erin looked on as well, pertained by the matter. She sighed with a sense of gratitude that she was able to help the family. Once Stanley and his mom were secure in the back of the ambulance, Deborah Crane and Angelica said goodnight and thanked Erin again.

Erin hesitated for a moment staring out into the luminous Georgia sky. The panorama was deluged with stars. Wrapping her arms about her cold shoulders, she hiked back over to her house. Stepping back into the house, missing Oliver washed over her like mighty ocean breakers.

Once again, she and Oliver had made tentative plans. Nevertheless, since having word with Oliver back at the office in the early afternoon, Erin had not heard from him at all. She had hoped that he would have returned to the office after lunch. However, she had been grossly disappointed. It was now half past ten p.m. Erin drifted into the kitchen for a cup of tea. As she sipped on chamomile tea, her thoughts were going. There was an inkling that she'd messed things up with Oliver, because she'd gone out with Gray.

Maybe, Oliver was under the impression that she was *into* Gray. Erin had thought she'd made it clear that she and Gray were practically strangers. However, it was difficult to know how Oliver had perceived the incident. In her assessment, it seemed as if he was ready to explore the possibility of being more than friends. Still, Erin knew better. If Oliver hadn't *pronounced* the words, things were still pretty much up in the air. Erin knew him well enough to know that he was very direct.

She plodded back into her bedroom and rested the cup of tea on her nightstand. She'd just finished up devotions when Angelica had rung her doorbell. Erin was exhausted from the demands of her day. Nevertheless, she was fighting back the tears. There was nothing she wanted more than to be able to *solidify* a relationship with Oliver. It was pointless trying to deny that she was head-over-heels in love with him. Having such strong feelings made it impossible to feign a cavalier attitude. Her heart was totally vested, and she needed to know that his was too. Therefore, the source of her unbearable pain was a direct result of the uncertainty.

All the same, she resolved to put her faith in God. Erin couldn't imagine that He would allow her heart to go on breaking in this way. Dimming the lights, she thoughtlessly grabbed her phone as she slipped into bed. She hadn't even looked at it for the past couple of hours. She had not seen her notifications, but she gasped in shock when she did. *2 missed calls and a voicemail from Oliver-one hour ago,*" Erin saw the green and white notification icon on the lock screen of her iPhone.

"Oh, my goodness," she gasped, "Ollie called, and I missed it." Her face wrinkled in bewilderment and frustration. Erin immediately accessed the voicemail Oliver had left her.

"Hey, Erin, it's me. I thought you should know that I had to leave the office right away. Rain had called in today as a result of a family emergency. She received word from Rhode Island that her dad passed away. She's totally distraught, so I've been with her ever since. I apologize for not being able to touch base earlier on. I'm so sorry we keep missing each other for one reason or another.

"You should know that I'm going to be out of town for the

next few days. I'll be out on Rhode Island with Rain and her family. She truly needs a friend right now. Just to reiterate how proud I am of all of the work you've done for the party. Sorry that I've been a complete no show in helping out. It was supposed to be our project-go figure. Please promise that you will allow me to finalize the last few details in the upcoming week? Thanks again for everything, Erin. Will be in touch. Bye."

Erin listened to Oliver's voicemail a few times. She decided to redial his number, but it went straight to *his* voicemail. She figured he was probably asleep, or already on a plane headed for Rhode Island. There were mixed feelings about his message. On the one hand, she was totally stirred that he'd finally called her. Besides, she was totally enamored hearing his resonant voice.

And yet, on the other hand, she was grieved to hear that he was going to be spending the next few days out of town-and with Rain McGrath. Even if Erin was saddened to hear that Rain's dad had passed away, she didn't trust the woman as far as she could throw her. Rain had immersed herself in a campaign of obliterating anyone who tried to get in the way of her plans of winning Oliver's heart.

Erin lay in bed with racing thoughts. *What if Oliver was developing feelings for Rain? What if being together for the next few days was a total game-changer? What if being around Rain and her family made Oliver want to be more engaged in Rain's life?*

Rain was beautiful, and she and Oliver had a history. A long history was something Erin *didn't* have with Oliver. She had only been attending Deliverance Tabernacle for a couple of years. During those years she'd endured watching Oliver be in love with Kennedy Proctor-Bohm. Oliver had told Erin that his heart was shattered, and that he couldn't offer it up to her. *What if Rain was the one he could give it to?*

In the middle of troubled thoughts, the Holy Spirit of God stepped in and reminded Erin to cast her cares on the Lord. God's Spirit also commanded her to trust and not be afraid, because her life was ultimately in His hands. Moreover, she was encouraged to surrender all of her burdens to the One who loved her, knew her better than she knew herself, and had a wonderful plan for her life (Jeremiah 29:11).

It was difficult to cast her fears and insecurities on to her Heavenly Father. Images of Oliver with Rain for an entire weekend rattled Erin. Scenes of the two together kept playing in her head like a bad movie trailer. Whereas the struggle was very real, Erin was assured that the power of God in her life was even greater. So, the realization of *that* truth helped her to let go and to finally rest.

***

It was Tuesday night-the day after Judge Edward McGrath's funeral. Oliver and Rain had stepped out for a breath of fresh air and walked along the rocky shores of *Manor City Beach* in *Manor City, Rhode Island*. They were wearing proper winter attire-as it was brisk out. The fullness of the diamond moon hovering above affected the black waters and made currents shimmer like rolls of glittering stars.

Oliver had spent the past few days with Rain and her family in their upscale home overlooking the water. The house and backdrop were spectacular. Oliver wanted to revisit the area again on his own. Rain's family had treated him like royalty. Even if he'd told them repeatedly that he and Rain were just friends, Oliver could tell that Rain's family was hopeful of a lot more.

The family had been extremely kind and sweet. So, Oliver had done his best not to create any ripples in the water, while he remained there to support Rain in her hour of grief. Whereas Rain's family was sold on a future wedding between them, Oliver grasped that her family was a nonissue. Having spent the past few days with Rain, Oliver realized that *she* was the one who wanted to be more than friends. And yet, in her fragile state, he had no idea how to let her down gently.

"How are you doing?" Oliver crushed Rain in his arms in support, as they watched the dark waters crashing onto a myriad of rocks. He stared into her eyes pertained. "I know the past few days have been a total nightmare-"

Rain slipped her arms about Oliver's waist, and gazed meaningfully into his eyes. "The past few days *have* been a total nightmare. I can't believe Christmas is just a few days away." Her face warped in sadness. "I don't think Christmas will ever be the same for us again." Tears shone in her eyes. "I never expected to have to say goodbye to my dad at this point in life." She swallowed the chunk in her throat.

Oliver didn't speak. Rather, he stared down at her with sympathy and understanding.

"But the *one* thing that's kept me strong throughout this entire ordeal is you, Oliver," Rain's voice broke. "I can't even begin to express how much it's meant to me having you by my side through it all." Tears rolled down her cheeks, but Oliver gently brushed them away. "How are you so wonderful?" she marveled, shaking her head contrarily.

"Rain, trust me, I'm *not* that great. I haven't done anything that any friend would not have done. I'm just glad that I could take the time. *Time* is the one thing I haven't been able to afford of late."

"You temporarily set aside *all* of your responsibilities just to be there for me." Rain stared dotingly up at Oliver.

"Things at the office have been under control in my absence," Oliver countered. "Being here with you for the past few days *was* necessary."

"My sister Jenny is in love with you by the way," Rain said on a lighter note. "I apologize for her constant flirting." She smiled.

"Oh, that…," Oliver said with reddened cheeks.

Rain grasped his hands in hers. "I can't say that I blame her, Ollie." Rain eliminated the space between them and continued to stare hypnotically up at him. "I told Jenny she doesn't stand a chance, because you were *my* friend first," Rain admitted.

Oliver smiled uncertainly and tried not to react just then. "Rain, I've already told you that you don't have to worry. We're always going to be friends," he reassured.

"That's just it, Ollie," Rain's face warped in frustration, "I don't want to be *just* friends." She searched his eyes, holding both of his hands in hers. "If unexpectedly losing my father this week has taught me *anything*, it's that life is much too short not to try. It's much too short not to go after the things we want. Oliver, I *want* you," Rain disclosed with tears in her eyes.

"Rain…," Oliver began to say, feeling totally conflicted. As Rain had delineated all she'd learned in the past week after losing her dad, Oliver had had a few epiphanies of his own. Being away from home for the past few days had taught *him* that he was in love with Erin. There were no longer any questions or doubts. She had been on his mind incessantly, and he couldn't wait to see her and look into her eyes.

Rain pressed her finger up to Oliver's lips to silence him. She tiptoed, bridged her lips to his, and began touring every inch with warm kisses. "You don't have to say anything right now, Ollie," she said in between soft kisses.

Despite the fact that he didn't want to hurt Rain, Oliver pulled back. "Rain, we can't." He didn't have the heart to tell her that he was in love with someone else. "You're hurting over losing your dad, so it isn't wise to make any rash decisions," he justified, keeping his hands on her shoulders in both support and restraint.

"It may not be the best time, but I *know* that I'm going to feel this way about *you* a month from now-a year or even ten years down the line. When we ran into each other at the courthouse not too long ago, I thanked God. I told you that I believe everything happens for a reason."

"I'm a firm believer in that too. Maybe, that reason was for me to be here with you these past few days. It's difficult to tell, but it isn't the best time to sort through our feelings," Oliver evaded. He would tell Rain that his heart belonged to someone else just as soon as he could. However, just then, he did not have the heart to overtly reject her-as she was still in very delicate state. "We can revisit the matter at a later time," he said sagely, delving her eyes.

Rain nodded in agreement but slipped her arms about his waist once more. She buried her head in his chest and held on for dear life.

Oliver squeezed her supportively in his arms, tussling with consternations. It broke his heart to consider having to hurt Rain. However, nothing could stifle his excitement. For the *second* time in his life he was properly in love. He was also ready to admit that love had never felt so strong. He wasn't sure how Erin had managed to do it, but she had made him fall in love-deeper than he'd ever felt it before. There was a meme on *Pinterest* which went something along the lines of, "If a person can love the *wrong* person so strongly, how much more are they capable of loving the *right* one?"

Oliver could say that he finally had a handle on that truth. He and Erin had texted off and on for the past few days. The messages had been succinct-mostly about how Rain's family was holding up in their dark moment. He and Erin had not discussed work through the DA's officer out in Silver Water, neither had they discussed the party. Oliver admired Erin's discretion. In fact, there was very little he *didn't* admire about her. Her new relationship with Gray Andrews still concerned him, but Oliver had promised to stand on God's word. "There is no fear in love, but perfect love casts out fear…" (1John 4:18)

In the morning, he and Rain would be on a plane headed back to Georgia. And, in spite of the demands he was certain were waiting for him the moment he stepped back into the DA's office, Oliver didn't feel the least bit intimidated. It would all be worth it to look into Erin's eyes again, hear her voice and to be near her. Being close to the woman he loved trumped everything else as far as he was concerned.

Sometime later, Rain and Oliver came in from the chilly December night. They were spending time inside Rain's late father's study. Oliver had temporarily stepped away, but had left his phone behind. Rain had wanted Oliver to browse through the extensive collection of law books which had belonged to her dad. She had set aside a number of titles Oliver would appreciate for sure. Just then, Oliver's cell phone rang. The object was sitting close by on the hardwood table.

Rain traipsed diffidently over and saw Erin's name pop up as the caller. Her face creased in displeasure just then. Rain suspected that Oliver was hesitant to give her a chance, because Erin was standing in the way. Looking both ways, she hesitated a moment before answering the phone. "Hello," she announced sweetly over the line.

"Oh, I'm sorry, I thought…," Erin began to say, surprised that Rain had picked up the phone. She recognized Rain's voice right away.

"Oliver has stepped away for a moment. How are you, Erin?" Rain said *sounding* cordial.

"I'm good, Rain. Oliver told me about your dad. I'm deeply sorry for your loss," she said in earnest, but struggling with feelings of malaise. It bothered Erin that Rain had picked up Oliver's phone.

"Thank you so much. That's very kind of you. I can't even begin to tell you how much it means to me to have Oliver by my side during this sad time. I'm so touched that he took time out from his exacting schedule," she gloated. Rain inadvertently wanted to rub it in Erin's face that Oliver had made such a tremendous sacrifice for *her*.

"Yeah, it's just like Oliver. He's the kindest and most altruistic person I've ever known." Tears were stinging Erin's eyes.

"He *is* pretty wonderful, and I realize that it isn't hard to fall in love with him," Rain said flippantly. "He's really nice to everyone, but when it comes right down to the people he *loves*, he will not think twice about being supportive," she hammered.

Erin swallowed hard and fought back feelings of jealousy. "Oliver *is* one of a kind and a tough act to follow," she acceded. There it was again; her thoughts were racing. *Why was Rain trying to make conversation? Since they'd met, Rain hadn't really made a point of speaking to her.*

"Erin, I'm not sure what kind of friendship you and Oliver

have, but you know we go way back, right?" Rain said expressly. She loved Oliver, and she wasn't going to allow some career-challenged paralegal to get between them. "We'd dated in the past," she lied, "so actually, we're just picking up exactly where we left off years ago."

The strings of Erin's heart began to unwind just then, and the throbbing ache punctured a hole in the cavity. Tears shone in her eyes at that point. "That's really nice," she said thickly, "I'm really happy for the two of you. Oliver and I are just friends," she clarified in agony.

"Just so we're clear. It was so nice that my family got the chance to finally meet him. They're all totally in love with him-just like I am. Are *you* in love with *my* guy too, Erin?" Rain asked cunningly.

"Oliver and I are *friends*," Erin abdicated. Oliver had said those words to her not too long ago. *"My heart is in pieces, and I can't offer you the kind of relationship you're looking for...,"* his paraphrased word resonated just then-adding yet another stab wound to her already bleeding heart.

"I just wanted you to be the first to know that we may have an announcement soon enough. I would love to have you attend our wedding," Rain contrived.

"Will you tell Oliver that I called?' Erin said shortly. The last thing she wanted was for her nemesis to witness her falling apart.

"Sure, thing, dear. And, Erin...?"

"Yes...?"

"Thank you so much for extending your condolences."

"Sure. Give my best to your family."

"Of course," Rain stared suspiciously about the room.

After hanging up with Erin, she deleted the call altogether. She didn't want Oliver to see that Erin Brasfield had called him. It was the last night she and Oliver would be spending out on Rhode

Island with her family, and Rain wanted it to be just the two of them. Erin and all other women who had designs on Oliver Wright needed to back off. When it came to Oliver, Rain was ready to fight tooth and nail.

CHAPTER EIGHT

"Your Honor, the state is asking that these minors be charged as adults. On the night of November 5th of 2018, Bentley Scott and Damon Richmond brutally battered and shot the victim in a gang-related argument. They had no regard for human life and showed absolutely no mercy. For that reason, we're seeking the maximum sentence of 20 years to life-with parole eligibility after serving the full twenty-year sentence," David Reed, Assistant to the DA explained to the judge. He and Oliver were present at the sentencing of the two boys responsible for ending the life of 17-year-old Devon Gates who'd been beaten and shot to death last year.

"Your Honor, as we've noted from the outset of this trial, neither of the boys had any past felonious histories-just a few misdemeanors. We're asking for a total of five years in a state facility and five years of probation once they're released from prison," the defense argued. "It is our belief that they can be rehabilitated, and given time, reformed in order to reclaim their places back in society. We're asking that their age and non-felonious history be taken into account."

Oliver had been busy studying his notes and itemizing all of the evidence brought against the boys. Mrs. Anita Gates and her husband Warren were sitting in the congested courtroom that morning. Oliver had promised to see to it that justice was served in the way that they had hoped to see it enacted. Oliver's assistant David Reed had already delineated the facts. Nevertheless, Oliver knew no better way of making the family's wishes known aside from allowing Devon's mother to share her impact statement in the courtroom.

"Thank you, Counselors. Your arguments are duly noted," the judge told the defense attorneys. "Anything else from the state?" he directed towards Oliver and David.

"Your Honor, the Assistant to the DA has gone over the cold hard facts in respect to the heinous crime Bentley Scott and Damon Richmond committed on the night in question. There's very little left to argue in as far as their guilt and evident lack of remorse. At this time, if I may, I would like to invite Anita Gates, the victim's mother to say a few words," Oliver respectfully submitted.

"I will allow it," the judge acceded.

Oliver crossed over to the Gates and helped Mrs. Gates out of her seat. He gently guided her over to a podium in the front of the courtroom. "It's alright," he prodded, and affirmed that she should not be afraid. He also indicated that he would stand by her side.

"Thank you for allowing me to speak, You're Honor." Anita Gate's face warped in misery, and tears immediately began to fill her eyes. "It's difficult to express how I've felt ever since the night the police came to my door and told me that my son was murdered. As a mother, that is the last thing you want to hear. You invest your very heart and soul into raising a child. There are so many sacrifices made along the way. And yet, they don't seem like sacrifices at all, because there's nothing you wouldn't do to see your child grow up and have a bright future." Anita Gates began to tremble at that juncture.

Oliver pacifyingly rubbed her back and nodded in the affirmative that she should go on.

"Well, my son's future was taken away by these gang members. Devon will never get the chance to graduate from high school, go to college, get a good job, marry the love of his life, or to have any children," she spoke choppily, with a face warped in anguish.

"These boys have taken that away from him. Not only have they robbed my son of his life, but they've robbed a mother of her child, a father of his son, and a brother and sister of their brother. Devon's absence from our lives has left a void that will never be filled. Because we have faith in God, we know that only His healing hand can carry us through this maze of grief."

Tears were rolling down her cheeks, and Oliver fought back tears of his own, because he vicariously felt the devastation that losing her son had brought about.

"And, whereas my family and I don't believe in the death penalty, we *do* believe that retribution should be exacted for the despicable crime committed. And even if these boys showed absolutely no mercy to my son, I wouldn't want for them to spend their *entire* lives in prison." Anita looked over at the two young men sitting across the courtroom with their defense attorneys present.

"I would want for them to turn their lives around and ask for God's forgiveness and mercy. I would want for them to learn the value of human life-and to learn from these tragic set of circumstances. It is my prayer that they realize the unspeakable pain and grief they've caused. And with that knowledge, that they strive never to destroy the lives of anyone else in this way. It's been difficult to sleep, because there is a part of me as a mother who can't rest until *all* of my children are safe at home." She swallowed hard.

"I have to keep reminding myself that Devon is never coming home again. Still, even if I consciously understand that, my heart still won't allow me to rest. It is my prayer that given time, healing will take place-not only in the lives of the Gates family, but in the lives of all of the families impacted by this tragedy. Thank you for allowing me to speak, Your Honor."

Mrs. Gates broke down in tears, and Oliver collected her in his arms in consolation. "It's alright," he kept telling her, as he conveyed her back over to her family. "You spoke from your heart, and I'm sure that everything's going to work out." Oliver extended an encouraging smile.

Drifting back over to the podium, Oliver addressed the judge, "In this case, Your Honor, we are not seeking the death penalty, neither are we seeking life in prison without the possibility of parole for these young men. However, as you've just heard from the victim's mother, justice *has* to be enacted. Bentley Scott and Damon Richmond-though they are minors-should bear the weight and severity of their actions. In this case of first-degree murder, we're seeking 20 years to life in state prison," Oliver finalized.

"Your Honor, twenty years is excessive," the defense attorneys argued.

"I've heard both sides of this argument, and I am now ready to pronounce sentencing," Judge Vincent Gabriel said a few moments later. "Bentley Scott and Damon Richmond, what more can be said? Your blatant disregard for the law and for human life has been noted from the very outset of this trial. It would have been my ruling to sentence you to life in prison without the possibility of parole, because it would certainly level out the scale of justice.

"However, in this case, you should be grateful that the victim's family is willing to show the clemency neither of you showed when you murdered Devon Gates in cold blood. You've been found guilty of first degree murder and are hereby sentenced to twenty years to life. Parole eligibility will be determined at a later time. You will be immediately remanded to the state in order to begin service said sentence. You will both receive a credit of 135 days against said sentence...,"

Oliver and David both sighed in relief and hugged in the courtroom in celebration. In the background they could hear Devon's family celebrating as well. For Oliver, it had made his day that things had worked out in their favor. He whispered a prayer of thanks to God.

"DA Wright, thank you for helping us win such a tremendous victory today!" Anita Gates thanked Oliver outside of the courtroom, once court was in recess. Anita and her husband Warren's faces radiated both joy and relief. Oliver was alone by then, because David had gone on to represent the state in an arraignment hearing in another courtroom on the third floor of the courthouse.

Oliver smiled encouragingly. "Mrs. Gates, I'm just grateful to see justice prevail today. I'm also grateful that Devon's voice was heard. Thank you for speaking so eloquently on his behalf," Oliver extended kindly. "It took a great deal of courage to stand there, and to share from your heart." His eyes twinkled in affect.

"Yes, it did, sweetheart," Warren Gates told his wife. He secured his arm about her shoulders and pressed a kiss to her cheek. "DA Wright, I have to say that the people of Silver County are in very good hands," he uplifted.

"Well, it's my duty to serve this fine community to the best of my ability," Oliver deflected.

"And you do it so well," Warren Gates affirmed.

"You certainly do." Anita Gates threw her arms about Oliver's neck, and crushed him affectionately in her arms.

Oliver's eyes shone with tears as he hugged her back. "I'm just grateful that you and your family were able to find closure to this nightmare," Oliver told them in earnest.

"From the very beginning you took *our* grief and made it your *own*, DA Wright, and there just aren't enough words to thank you!" she acclaimed lovingly.

Oliver quietly took turns hugging the couple. He was completely stirred by their struggle, their grief and the victory they reveled in that morning. It meant a great deal to him whenever he fought and won justice for victimized families. It was the office he'd undertaken, and he would continue to fight to keep their community safe. For him it was always personal.

***

Soon after leaving the courthouse, Oliver was called in by the authorities on the crime scene of murder number six. Another young woman's body had been found in a house out on the outskirts of *Silver Ridge*. It seemed like the killer was making inroads closer to Silver City. The sheriff's office had been brought in, the coroners had already taken the body away, and forensics remained circumspectly combing through the crime scene.

"So, it's the same MO," Oliver told the authorities. "Twenty-five-year-old Linda Cross was brutally murdered and stabbed in excess of thirty times-just like the other five women."

"So, it seems. Apparently, we've been going up a dead end with the two men we suspected. So, what little progress we thought we were making has gone out the window. We really don't have anything to go on. I hope these murders don't become cold cases," FBI Agent Thomason told Oliver. "The DNA is what we're having trouble with."

"Look, we've got to find a way to stop this. As of today, my staff and I are going to prioritize working on this investigation. In fact, it's going to become our sole mission. Whatever it takes I want this dirt bag caught. We can't afford to lose another victim," Oliver railed, feeling frustrated and bordering helpless.

"We're doing all that we can to make that happen, DA Wright," Agent Thomason assured.

"Well, we're going to have to do better, because I refuse to allow Silver County to lose another young woman." Tears were in Oliver's eyes, as he took in all of the blood scattered throughout the victim's bedroom.

"God," Oliver prayed, "please show me what to do in this case. Help us figure out where to find the monster responsible for this." He inspected the crime scene in horror. "I depend on you in every area and aspect of my life, and there is nothing I can do on my own. I am crying out for help in this situation. Please, bring this individual to justice and stop the senseless murders."

Being brought into any crime scene was often overwhelming. There were times Oliver felt as if he wasn't cut out for it. Being in that milieu sickened him in every way possible, but it was paramount to work collaboratively with the authorities in exacting justice for the victims. Moreover, he had done everything in his power to comfort their families, who were left to pick up the broken pieces in the aftermath of such devastation.

***

Oliver gladly stood in at the arraignment of the three boys

implicated in the death of Noel Warner later that afternoon. Noel Warner had been shot close to a month ago out in *Silver Ridge*. He'd been walking home after attending a neighborhood party. His parents Roberta and Christopher Warner were both overjoyed, though shocked that the perpetrators had been apprehended. DNA evidence helped to piece the case together.

Each of the boys had committed other misdemeanors and had been brought in by police. Fingerprints and other DNA samples had highlighted their involvement in the murder. Oliver was encouraged because they were close to a conviction in the case. Oliver also anticipated a similar victory in bringing down the miscreant who was going around Silver County murdering unsuspecting young women.

It was after three in the afternoon when Oliver made it back to the DA's office. Thus far, it had been a long and difficult day, which had started in the early morning. He and Rain's flight had barely touched down on the tarmac out at Silver Water International Airport before Oliver was overtaken by a slew of critical matters. He'd known that it would have played out in this way the moment he got back from Rhode Island. And yet, Oliver hadn't anticipated not having a moment to come up for air.

There was so much on his mind in respect to public responsibilities. However, privately, he just wanted to find Erin and to say hello. He had not seen her since he'd gotten back from the trip. Oliver direly needed to talk to her, and to tell her that he'd fallen madly in love. Yet, he couldn't be sure, but he sensed something was wrong. He'd texted and had called Erin last night before leaving the island. However, her answers had been short and to the point.

Usually, even when discussing work, there was always some form of back and forth banter. However, Erin had sounded extremely impersonal, detached even. Oliver was confused, because being aloof was totally uncharacteristic of her. Thinking she was angry with him bothered Oliver a great deal, because he was *so* in love with her. Oliver had prayed for Gray Andrews to leave Erin alone. He hoped against hope that she hadn't seen Gray again.

Oliver's heart raced in anticipation over the thought of seeing Erin after four days. The thought of looking into her eyes again excited him to no end. Oliver felt lightheaded, as if he'd just stepped off of a roller coaster. Still, there was a sense of angst, because he was uncertain where Erin stood at that point in time. Regardless, Oliver was resolved to get over the hurdles, and to explore their special connection. Furthermore, he would stand on God's word not to fear. The love he felt for Erin was perfect, and he prayed that she felt the same.

Pulling into the parking lot of the office building, Oliver found a media circus. There had been times where the press lingered in the area for one reason or another, but this time around Oliver knew something was definitely up. Shying away from the cameras and evading the press himself, he found his way inside of the building.

Staff members met Oliver the moment he walked through the office doors. "Oliver, Mr. and Mrs. Kayden Bohm are here," they all announced in concert.

"I took the liberty to ask them to wait inside of your office," Betty, Oliver's receptionist told him.

"Okay…," Oliver said, head spinning. "Thanks, Betty," he told her. Oliver made his way through the crowded office. He was a few feet away from his office, when he was halted by Rain.

"There you are!" Rain gleefully announced. "I've been waiting for this moment all day."

"Hey, Rain," Oliver said affably. "I can't believe we were on a plane early this morning." He smiled, caringly searching her eyes. "How are you doing?" Rain and her family had suffered immensely in the past few days, and as a friend her wellbeing was essential.

Rain nodded. "I'm doing okay all things considered. I know you're probably tied up right now, but I have a little surprise for you in my office once you have a minute," Rain announced reticently, leaning into Oliver.

"Is that right?" Oliver said good-naturedly. "Well, then, I'm just going to have to make it a point to find out what this little surprise is all about later. But right now-"

"You don't even have to tell me. Kayden Bohm and his wife are here. That's what all of the fanfare's about. They seem like really nice people by the way," Rain uplifted.

"They *are* truly wonderful people," Oliver assented. "So, I will see you in a little while."

Rain wrapped her arms affectionately around Oliver and squeezed fondly. "I can't wait." She gently released him. "Bye."

"Bye, Rain," Oliver watched her walk away. The conflict returned. How on earth was he going to tell Rain that they couldn't be together-at least in the romantic sense? Oliver had to keep seeking God on the matter. There were so many loose ends, and only God could help him tie them up.

"Kay..., Kennedy!" Oliver celebrated the moment he stepped into his office.

Kayden immediately stood to his feet, beaming. "Well, if it isn't the DA of Silver County!" Kayden appraised with dignity.

Oliver chuckled, and extended his hand out in order to shake Kayden's hand. However, Kayden pulled him in for a rough hug, and patted him on the back. "It's so good to see you, Kay!" Oliver pulled away and stared into Kayden's twinkling blue eyes.

"It's great to see you again, my friend!" Kayden patted Oliver on the arm again.

"Hey there, Miss Kennedy," Oliver greeted, hunching down and pressing a kiss to her cheek.

"Hey, Ollie," Kennedy acclaimed, squeezing his hand affectionately. "I'm so glad we get to see you only four days before Christmas!"

"I'm so pumped that the two of you are here!" Oliver walked around to take his place behind his desk.

"I'm really feeling the vibe of this place," Kayden stared all around. "Love your office!"

"Thank you," Oliver said with cardinal cheeks. "To what do I owe the pleasure?" he asked skeptically.

"Ollie, Kay and I talked about the impact statement letter you wanted me to write for Taren," Kennedy said reticently. Discomfort veiled her sweet face to even bring up the matter.

Oliver shook his head in the negative, realizing just how difficult the subject was for Kennedy. "Kennedy, it's fine, you don't have to if you're not ready to," Oliver countered. "As you probably know, Taren will be sentenced next week. Mitch and I are hoping to sway the judge in her favor-"

"Ollie, Kennedy and I agreed that it's the right thing to do," Kayden interjected, eyes lowering urgently into Oliver's.

"Okay…," Oliver assented, encouraged by Kayden's words.

"It may not be the easiest thing, but we've decided that it's right to help Taren. She made a few mistakes, but she has paid dearly these past months," Kayden empathized.

"She was my best friend for a very long time-and she *was* a good friend. Something happened during that time, and Taren lost herself along the way." Tears gleamed in Kennedy's eyes. Her husband grasped her hand, and stared at her, affected. "Maybe," Kennedy went on to say, "we can help her to find herself again," her voice undulated.

Stirred beyond all comprehension, Oliver's eyes shone in affect. "Yeah, maybe we can," his voice was gravelly. "She's been really scared. This gesture, though indirect, will offer a tremendous source of encouragement." Oliver smiled openly at Kennedy. "In court this morning I was present when a mother shared her impact statement in an appeal for mercy for her son's murderers.

"I told the woman just how proud I was of her for making that appeal. It took a lot of courage. Well, I'm proud of you too, Kennedy. I *know* how much courage it's taken for you to come to this decision."

"I'm equally proud of her, Oliver," Kayden said, staring devotedly at his wife. "But I know my wife. She has too big a heart *not* to have been stirred by your request." Kayden winked at Kennedy and mouthed the words *I love you!*

Kennedy's face warped in sentimentality, as she mouthed the words back to her husband. She took a moment to remove a professional looking envelope from out of her pocketbook. "And, I am so proud of *you*, Oliver Wright," she said handing the letter over to him.

"And why is that?" Oliver said with a radiant smile, accepting the envelope.

"Because I don't think Silver County has ever had, nor will ever have a better District Attorney!" She winked at him.

"I agree one hundred percent with my wife," Kayden echoed.

"Kayden, Kennedy, stop…" Oliver's cheeks turned ruddy. "I can't thank *you* guys enough for doing this. It means even more to me because you decided to make the trip in person."

"Well, of course we made the trip in person. It *is* after all the most wonderful time of the year!" Kennedy said with a mischievous grin. "Ollie, will you excuse me for a minute?" she asked, standing to her feet.

Both men stood chivalrously to their feet in acknowledgement. "Not at all…" Oliver stared over at Kayden with a suspicious expression on his face. Kennedy crossed over to the door and let herself out.

"Don't look at me," Kayden told Oliver, "that woman has a mind of her own."

"Tell me about it," Oliver agreed.   He and Kayden talked for a few minutes. Oliver explained that he would possibly need them again in order to have a few documents notarized. Kayden reassured him that both he and Kennedy would cooperate in any way they could.

Kennedy diffidently stepped back into the room holding a sizable red gift bag. "This gift is from us, Ollie. Merry Christmas!" Kennedy said, handing the gift bag over to Oliver.

Tears were in Oliver's eyes as he drew Kennedy into his arms. "Thank you so much, but you really didn't need to."

"Oh, but we *wanted* to," Kayden said, totally overjoyed.

Oliver drew Kayden in for a hug as well and crushed the man in his arms. "Thanks, Kay." Pulling away, he gave his friend a quirky look. "So, you had no idea about this, huh?"

"Well…," Kayden began to say, chuckling, "maybe just a hint."

"I didn't get the chance to get anything for the two of you," Oliver admitted.

The couple guffawed in unison. Kayden slipped his arm around Kennedy's waist. "What else could *I* possibly need? I've got everything right here." He pressed a kiss to her cheek.

"Ollie, the boxed gift is for you to put under your tree. However, the other two, please use them wisely. I will tell you right now that *one* of the envelopes contains open-ended traveling tickets for a month-long vacation to any destination of your choice. Being the DA and all, you don't have to use up the entire month at once. You can use a week at a time," Kennedy instructed.

"Wow," Oliver said with tears shining in his eyes, "that is extremely generous of you," his voice sounded gravelly. However, he didn't get the chance to expound.

"And, the other sealed envelope is from *me*, Ollie," Kayden said more urgently. "Promise me something?" He searched Oliver's eyes in sincerity.

Overwhelmed, Oliver remained silent, humbled by their gesture. "Of course," he assented.

"Accept it in good faith from friends who truly love you!" Kayden's eyes gleamed in affect. "Merry Christmas!" Kayden proclaimed again.

He and Oliver hugged again and patted each other on the back. "I promise that I will. Merry Christmas to the two of you!" Oliver stated, stirred beyond words.

Moments later, still celebrating the Bohm's visit, Oliver walked the couple out to their limo. The press and media were waiting to pounce on all three for a statement of some kind, but Oliver managed to dodge them. Besides, he was certain that the hoopla would die down the moment Kennedy and Kayden left the locale.

Oliver stepped back into the office but stopped short-almost bumping into Erin. His heart immediately began hammering in his chest. For a spell he was frozen and totally entranced. "Hey there, stranger," he said over the top elated to see her. Oliver instinctively began leaning into to her, avid for a connection.

"Ollie, hello," Erin said shakily; surprised to see him, but completely captivated. She had not realized just how much she'd missed seeing him while he'd been away. Her heart thrashed in both celebration and excitement. It was always the same whenever Oliver was around. Erin had not yet learned to keep her strong feelings for him under wraps.

An automatic smile veiled her pretty face, but it was evanescent when she recounted the conversation with Rain the night before. Erin wanted to bolt, but didn't want to be cold or elusive to Oliver. "I didn't know you were back. I haven't seen you all day." Her eyes wandered in uncertainty and nervousness.

"It doesn't even feel as if *I've* gotten back yet, but I *have* been around since early this morning," Oliver explained, exploring her eyes. "Erin, I've missed you!" he said freely. Eliminating the space between them, he slipped his arms about her waist, and collected her into his arms. Squeezing her affectionately, he sighed reflectively, treasuring the moment he'd waited for.

"I've missed you too, Ollie," Erin muttered against his chest. At that moment it felt as if her heart was being ripped out of her chest. So, she brusquely pulled away, and patted Oliver's back in a detached manner. Tears were stinging her eyes, but she fought them back, staunchly holding his stare.

Oliver was forced to push away. His arms felt useless without Erin in them. Still, he tried to remain hopeful. "How are you doing?" he asked, pertained. It was clear that Erin was all set to go leave the office for one reason or another. However, Oliver didn't inquire about her impending departure just yet. He wanted to cherish the moment of finally being with her. "I'm so sorry about last week." He shook his head in denial about how things had played out. "We were supposed to get together at one point, and to…"

"Ollie, don't even worry about the party." Erin offered a sad smile.

"I wasn't worried about the *party*," Oliver clarified. "My only regret is that *we* didn't get the chance to work together."

"Oh…?" Erin's face changed, moved by his words. Regardless, she would not allow his words to affect her stance. She *had* to pull away. "About the party," she evaded, "everything's done. Whenever you have a moment, you should get into the meeting hall to get a look. It's all decked out. Even the stockings are done. Thanks for the cute things you picked up last week by the way."

"It was the very least I could do. Erin, you *are* amazing! I can't wait to see all you've accomplished!" Oliver's eyes sensitively searched hers. "*We* plan a party together, but *you* wind up doing all of the work," he emphasized. "I'm so sorry." Oliver's gape on Erin was reminiscent of a terminally ill person, who'd just stumbled upon the cure for his malady. His overwhelming feelings for her threatened to carry him away like a twister.

"Oliver, you've got nothing to be sorry about." Erin smiled faintly. "It was a lot of fun. I truly enjoyed doing it. Planning a

Christmas party isn't as important as say…, defending victimized families or conducting a murder investigation," she deflected, taking in his perfect face. Erin was totally enamored. *How on earth had Oliver gone away for a few days-only to return a hundred times more desirable? It wasn't fair that she couldn't make her heart stop wanting him.*

"Erin, I promise to make it up to you. This week did not go as planned. I hate that I didn't get the chance to work together. I *like* being a team." Oliver explored her eyes avidly. Everything inside of him screamed to touch her, take her in his arms, and tell her how he felt. However, he knew it was neither the time nor the place.

Erin smiled as tears formed in her eyes. "I guess we'll get a chance to work together again *one* of these days."

Oliver moved in even closer to Erin, eyes lowering touchily into hers. "Erin, is something wrong? You don't seem like yourself today. Is there anything you want to tell me?" Concern wrinkled his face.

"I'm fine, Ollie…really," Erin dodged. "I was just about to step out," she said elusively.

"Are you leaving for the day?" Oliver asked with a rending heart. Erin was being aloof again and he hated it. He hoped against hope that Gray Andrews had nothing to do with why she'd changed.

"Actually, I am," Erin said matter-of-factly. "I have a meeting with the law firm. There's still paperwork to get out of the way, and company protocol to discuss before I start working for them." Erin scrutinized every inch of Oliver. Her feelings were so potent she wanted to run away. Furthermore, the desire to feel his arms around her again was merciless.

Oliver's heart dipped to the floor in disappointment, as he processed Erin's impending departure from the DA's office. In fact, the party would be on Saturday-Christmas Eve, and that was only three days away. Soon after, Erin would no longer be a part of their team. He closed his eyes meditatively before speaking. "About that…? Erin, is there any way you see yourself staying on *here*?" His face strained in appeal.

"I don't think it's possible, Ollie. I've already told the law firm that I've accepted the job," Erin said with perfect aplomb, yet trembling on the inside.

"Oh… I was just hoping…" Oliver smiled sadly. "Well, I'm happy that you've already found a great position."

"Yeah, it's a pretty great firm," Erin affirmed, with a melancholic expression on her sweet face.

"Erin, you *know* you can talk to me if you need to...about anything," he offered.

Erin nodded and stared into his bronze eyes. "I know that, Ollie, but I'm fine," she said trying to sound convincing and smiling cursorily.

"There you are, Oliver…," Rain's voice drifted when she found Oliver engaged in conversation with Erin near the office's exit doors. "Oh, hello, Erin," she said frostily. Her eyes connected shiftily to Erin's just then with a venomous expression on her face.

"Hey, Rain," Oliver turned to acknowledge her. "I was just about to go and find you."

"Well, it's a good thing that I found *you* first," Rain said staring languorously up at him. "I have that surprise I told you about in my office," she reminded.

Erin stood there feeling totally inept. "Hi, Rain," she said casually. "Welcome back!"

"Thank you," Rain said, giving Erin the death stare again.

"I'm going to get going, Ollie. I've got to make that appointment I told you about," Erin redirected towards Oliver. "So, I guess I will see you later." Tears were pooling in Erin's eyes, remarking Rain's territorial exchanges with Oliver. Erin turned away and made a dash for the doors.

"Erin…," Oliver called out, but his voice trailed. It killed him to see the woman he loved disappear through the set of doors. Seeing Erin was something he'd anticipated for days, so things weren't supposed to play out in this way. Oliver knew something was very wrong, because she could barely look him in the eyes.

Noticing how distracted Oliver was, Rain quickly looped her arm through his. "Are you ready for your surprise?" She jarred him from sulking.

Oliver smiled and stared down at the young lady. "Sure," he said absently. Even as he and Rain walked back over to her office, the only thing pressed on Oliver's mind was Erin. He wanted to follow her. Where had the time gone? It had been almost two weeks since Erin had handed him that awful resignation letter. He could not have foreseen his feelings growing so exponentially for her.

Furthermore, he was ready to admit that he'd kept Erin at arm's length, because he'd been afraid of getting hurt. What happened with Kennedy had left such a lasting wound. Now that *he* was sure about his feelings for Erin, he was afraid that *she* no longer felt the same.

Oliver was crushed but tried to portray an upbeat façade when Rain opened up her office door and revealed the most elaborate picnic lunch. "Oh, my goodness!" he raved, sounding as optimistic as he could. "This is amazing!" He examined the picnic spread on the office carpeting. It was apparent that Rain had put in a lot of effort. "Thank you, Ms. Rain!" Oliver delighted.

"I know you probably haven't had a moment to yourself all day. So, I thought you might enjoy a little solitude before things get hectic again." Rain took the liberty to help Oliver off with his jacket. She cautiously hung the jacket on a hook to the side of her door. "Now, come with me, Mr. DA." She looped her arm through his again and guided him over to the picnic spread. She'd created an impressive arrangement!

Oliver was deeply moved by her gesture. "Rain, this is perfect." He set down on the floor. Luckily, the day was winding down, and his schedule was pretty much free for the moment. "How did you know that I haven't really had anything to eat?"

"Lucky guess," Rain said, taking her place across from Oliver on the blanket.

"Thank you," Oliver met her eyes in sincerity.

"No, I should thank *you*, Oliver Wright." Tears shone in Rain's eyes. "How can I ever thank you enough for being there for me and for my family these past few days?" Her eyes brushed sensitively over Oliver's features.

"Rain, you don't have to thank me. It's what friends do for each other," his voice broke.

"Speaking of which…" Rain inched in close to Oliver. She grasped his left hand in hers and stroked it fondly. Building up the courage to look into his eyes, she explored them avidly. "I meant what I said last night. I want to be with *you*, Ollie. Life is too short not to pursue the dreams and goals we have. We fool ourselves into thinking we have all the time in the world.

"So, we put things off, but we never really know." Rain beguilingly traced the lines in the palm of Oliver's hand. "You have no idea how happy I was to see you outside of the courthouse that morning. I said to myself, *Rain, this is your second chance. You didn't tell Oliver how you felt when you went to law school together. So, don't mess up this opportunity…*"

"Rain…," Oliver began, chagrined, with an ambiguous expression on his face.

"Oliver, you said it wasn't the right time for me to tell you how I feel, but you're wrong." Tears glistened in Rain's eyes. "What if, God forbids, anything should happen…" She hesitated for a moment before falling apart.

Oliver collected her in his arms. "Oh, Rain, I'm *so* sorry. Losing someone you love is devastating. The survived are left behind to pick up the pieces. I know your heart is broken," he consoled her. "I know you're scared. There's no guarantee that *any* of us will be here in the next minute-let alone the next day."

"That's why I want to tell you that I love you!" Rain pulled away, but gingerly draped her arms about Oliver's neck. She inched in closer, bridged her lips to his, and pressed kisses to every inch of his mouth.

Oliver's heart twisted in knots to have to pull away, because it was clear just how much Rain had come to care about him. Yet, he couldn't allow her to continue when he didn't feel the same way. Praying for wisdom, he cautiously edged away, still keeping a firm grasp on her shoulders. Oliver prodded Rain to look at him. "Rain, you *know* how much I care about you…"

Rain's face shrouded in dismay. "Oliver, I love you!" she said emphatically.

"Rain, we've been friends for a really long time." Oliver's face creased in jeopardy as he tried to find the words. "I value our relationship a great deal. I think you're awesome-"

"Please, don't say no, Ollie. All I'm asking is for a chance. We can take things as slowly as you want. I won't rush you," she said forlornly. "I know you were hurt before, but…"

"Rain, you know me well enough to know that I could *never* be anything but direct with you." Oliver sighed and rubbed supportively on her shoulders. "I think you're amazing, but I don't see a romantic future with us," he said in earnest, keenly searching her sad eyes.

"So, you can't see a romantic relationship right *now*, but that doesn't mean there can't be one in the future. Please, give me a chance, Ollie. I know God brought us back together for a reason."

"I'm *certain* that God *has* brought us back into each other's lives, but probably not for the reasons you might think." Oliver's face warped in commiseration seeing the distraught look on Rain's face.

"Are you in love with someone else?" Rain queried, breaking her own heart. Inwardly, she already knew the truth. She had been afraid to ask, but she sensed that Oliver was slipping from her grasp.

Oliver nodded in the affirmative. "Yes," he said plainly. His heart throbbed, because he was uncertain if Erin felt the same way about him. Something had definitely changed between them. He prayed that it wasn't too late to tell her that he'd fallen in love with her beyond all reason.

"I see..." Rain's head slumped.

"I'm truly sorry." Oliver cupped her chin and made her look at him. "The last thing I would ever want is to hurt you." Oliver hugged her in comfort. "You mean a great deal to me." Tears were in his eyes.

Rain began to sob into Oliver's chest. The reality of the matter was that Oliver loved someone else. She had poured out her entire heart to him, but he'd rejected her. Christmas was only four days away, and not only had she lost her father, but the man she loved had just admitted to loving someone else. Life had taken a turn for the worst, and Rain had no idea how to go about picking up the pieces. *Now what was she going to do?*

She had only taken the job working through the DA's office to be close to Oliver. Imagining seeing Oliver around the office, while feeling completely disconnected to him, seemed too harsh a sentence to bear. Then, there was the office Christmas party on Saturday. *How on earth was she going to attend, and pretend as if everything was peachy?*

As excruciating as it was, Oliver had to tell Rain the truth. He refused to string her along. Because Rain had gone through so much trouble to set up the picnic, Oliver fixed himself a plate, and promised to enjoy it later. "Rain," Oliver addressed, while standing in front of the office door, "I will call you later to check in, alright?" He cupped her chin and connected urgently to her eyes.

Rain nodded quiescently. "Alright..." Her red, sad eyes fastened to his.

"You will *always* be in my heart. I need for you to understand that. There's no need to feel weird or awkward about what just happened. I'm flattered beyond words that such a special young lady cares so much for me," his voice broke. "Zero weirdness, okay?" he tested. "I know that's a lot easier said than done," he assented.

"Leave it to *you* to break someone's heart with so much compassion that they can't be angry with you," Rain said, grieved.

"*Don't* be angry with me." Oliver pressed a kiss to her cheek. "I'll always be here for you if you need me." He cradled her face in his hand.

"I know." Rain forced a smile and threw her arms lovingly around him. "I'm blessed to have you as my friend."

"You can count on it." The two swayed lovingly in each other's arms.

Before Oliver left the DA's office on Wednesday evening, he went into the meeting hall in order to get a look. Beyond impressed, he perused how the expansive room had been transformed into a Christmas ballroom extravaganza. The entire backdrop was transposed by Christmas embellishments. Oliver appreciated the white and silver theme, the creative and elegant way in which Erin had set the stockings on the tree and in various corners of the room. He assessed that she'd outdone herself.

Oliver smiled reflectively, as he considered that Erin had singlehandedly done it all. She had worked around the clock in preparation for the party, and he was immensely proud of her. Furthermore, the staff seemed to have respected the boundaries. They had not used the meeting hall that week, as per Erin's instructions. The staff had occupied other conference rooms in the building but had been wise enough to leave Erin's handiwork alone.

"I'm so proud of you, Erin! You've done such an amazing job!" Oliver said quietly, taking in the ambiance. Erin had also included what they'd discussed in respect to a Nativity Scene. It was their intention to highlight the *true* reason for the season.

Luke 2:11, "For unto us a child is born, a Savior who is Christ the Lord." Those who worked through the DA's office needed to know that Christmas wasn't all about partying and gift-giving.

Neither was it about getting wasted, and even driving while intoxicated. Christmas was about God sending the only hope and light of the world to mankind-His son Jesus Christ.

Suddenly, Oliver was bursting at the seams to talk to Erin. She'd rushed away the moment he was finally able to connect to her. Her detachment bothered him a great deal. *Why had she been so standoffish? Had he done something wrong? Did she resent him for not helping out with the party?* It killed Oliver to consider that Erin was put out by anything he'd done. On instinct, he pulled his phone out to text her, but he didn't want to be all up in her face so soon.

Hopefully, they would see each other in the morning, but Oliver didn't know if he could wait that long. Things being what they were, it was quite possible that they would keep missing each other until the party. And, then she would be gone. Oliver resolved to make the most of every opportunity, because time was quickly running out.

***

Erin managed to make it home before seven in the evening. She'd just met with the gentlemen from the law firm she would soon start working for. They were a nice group and seemed eager to have her working through their office in the weeks ahead. Erin had fought herself on the matter but had concluded that leaving the DA's office was the right decision.

Crossing over to her bedroom, Erin peeled off of her work clothes. She then drifted over to her dresser drawer and pulled out comfortable stretch pants and a pale-yellow top. However, while holding the clothes in her hands, she toppled onto her bed, and broke down in tears. Why were things so complicated? She hadn't stopped crying since Rain had answered Oliver's phone out on Rhode Island.

Rain had emphasized that she and Oliver were picking up exactly where they'd left off. The woman had warned Erin to back off, because Oliver was *her* guy. Notwithstanding, Rain had alluded to possibly getting engaged. Erin wasn't the least bit surprised given their history. Oliver had told Erin that he wanted to be friends. Erin had believed that things were changing between them. However, it was clear that Oliver's heart was vested in Rain.

Oliver had sacrificed so much of his time to be with Rain. He'd gone to the hospital with her last week, even if Erin suspected that Rain had faked being sick just to spend time with him. Furthermore, Oliver had taken time away from his demanding schedule to be there for Rain and her family in their moment of grief. It wasn't fair for Erin to assume that Oliver would *not* have done the same for her, but her insecurities made it difficult to ascertain. Realizing that Oliver was totally out of her reach broke her heart.

"At least *now* I know that I can move on." She wiped the tears from off of her face. "There are no more guessing games. If Ollie wanted to be with you, he would have said so two weeks ago. He would have also done anything to make sure you keep your job through the DA's office," Erin rationalized, slipping on the tights and top. "But, he's told you time and time again that he wants to be *friends* and nothing more." She grimaced in misery.

"God, how on earth am I supposed to leave my job at the DA's office? How am I supposed to walk away from Ollie when I love him so much? Why am I going through this? It shouldn't be this hard to love someone. Still, if Oliver Wright isn't in your will for my life, please take away the love that I feel for him," Erin prayed. "Please help me to get over him. That's the only way that I can deal with walking away."

As Erin prayed, she received an impression from God's Spirit. Isaiah 41:10 "Fear not, for I am with you; be not dismayed, for I am your God. I will strengthen you, Yes, I will help you, I will uphold you with my righteous right hand." (NKJV)

"Thank you, Lord," Erin said with hands lifted up in praise. "I received those words." Her face warped in sadness again. "I could sure use your help in this situation."

Trying to pull herself together, Erin crossed out of her bedroom and ambled into the kitchen for a bite. She perused her kitchen cabinets, and also raided the refrigerator to see if there was anything worth making for dinner. She'd set her phone on the kitchen counter. Subconsciously, she kept checking for texts or calls from Oliver. Pragmatically, she grasped that Oliver was *Rain's* boyfriend. And yet, Erin couldn't help hoping that it wasn't the case.

"Erin, I would want for you to be the one. I would want you to be my person when I'm ready to open up my heart…" Oliver's words resonated, as she pulled out a box of spaghetti from the pantry. She had already settled on making pasta with Turkey meat. As she set the ingredients on the kitchen counter, the doorbell chimed. Startled, Erin froze for a moment. Anticipation set in. "Ollie," she said quietly with a hopeful smile.

Excited, Erin rushed out of the kitchen, and ran over to the front door. However, before opening it up, she checked her face and hair in the hallway mirror. The doorbell rang for the second time just before she opened it up. Erin's heart crashed to the floor, and she was shocked to see Gray standing at her door. "Gray," Erin said, sighing. "What are *you* doing here?" She set her hands on her hips and shook her head incredulous.

"Well, *gorgeous*, I'm here to take you out to dinner. Can't you tell from the way I'm dressed?" Gray showcased his proper date attire. "I don't just dress up like this for anyone you know."

"Gray," Erin began exasperated, "have you been following me around?" Her eyes narrowed in suspicion. "I want the truth." Erin did not want to invite him into her house.

"Okay, okay…," Gray acceded, holding both hands up in a halting manner. "I kind of looked for you on Facebook, and I was able to get an address." His face wrinkled in dread, expecting Erin to put him on blasts for making such a bold move.

"What am I going to do with you?" Erin asked, annoyed.

"You might want to say yes…?" Gray tested, smiling.

"Gray, you're going to drive me crazy. We talked about this the other day at lunch." Erin's eyes sparked in frustration.

Gray nodded with a sense of understanding. "I know what you told me, Erin. You told me that you're friends with someone, but it's complicated." His face wrinkled, pertained. "Listen, I already told you the truth. I haven't been able to stop thinking about you since the moment we met out at the *strip mall*. Unlike your *friend*, I *know* a good thing when I see. I'm not at all confused. Erin, please say you'll go out to dinner with me tonight?" Gray pleaded.

Erin sized Gray up in his butterscotch-colored designer dress suit. She assessed that he cleaned up pretty nicely. His good looks and charm weren't the issue. The issue was that he *wasn't* Oliver. Still, she couldn't help chuckling over Gray's antics. He'd gone to great lengths to ensure she'd have dinner with him. "Gray, you *can't* be this pushy when it comes to dating someone. You've got to give a girl the head's up." Erin examined her black stretch pants and pale-yellow top. "I'm hardly ready to go out with you."

Gray glanced at his obscenely expensive designer watch. "Could you be ready in say twenty minutes…?" he goaded.

"Gray…?" Erin began to say, but she stopped short and smiled. "I can't believe you."

"Erin, I *like* you. Your *friend* might be confused about wanting to be with you, but that's not me."

Erin sighed and shook her head nonsensically. Sadness loomed over her like overcast clouds, as she considered that Oliver was indeed just a *friend*. He'd made that more than clear. Besides, he'd found someone he could open up his heart to-and that was Rain. "Okay-you *will* wait outside for me as I get ready?" she delineated.

Gray held both hands up disarmingly. "If that's what you want, beautiful… I have no problem. My car is right there," Gray pointed over to his black Audi SUV which was parked in front of Erin's door, "I will be waiting for you in the car." He smiled expectantly.

"Gray, Gray, Gray...," Erin said shaking her head, but smiling. "I shouldn't be too long."

"Take your time," Gray encouraged.

"Now, you're going to have to excuse me...," Erin said, in process of pushing her front door closed.

"Of course," Gray acceded.

Erin shut and locked the front door. "Lord, what's going on with this guy? He's been following me around for the past few days. What does it mean?" Erin talked to the Lord, as she returned to the kitchen. She put all of the items she'd needed to cook dinner back in their proper place, and then crossed back over to her bedroom. She had to find something to wear. Despite the heartache she tussled with in respect to Oliver, Erin felt encouraged that someone *wanted* to take her out for dinner. Not knowing Gray very well, Erin prayed for God's wisdom, and his protection in getting to know the persistent stranger.

Erin picked out a stylish rust-colored dress, and high-heeled swanky leather boots. She rushed into the bathroom, washed her face and brushed her teeth. Taking a moment, she applied a light coating of facial powder, and smeared on rust-colored lipstick to match her ensemble. Slipping on her black knee-length leather coat, Erin was all set to step out with Gray. She tousled her hair once again in the hallway mirror, feet away from the front door. She let herself out, locked the door, and dismounted the front steps in order to meet Gray.

Gray was already standing outside of the passenger's side door of his car waiting to get the door for Erin. "Can you say *sizzling*?" Gray whistled. "You look amazing!" Gray secured her into the car.

"Thank you, Gray," Erin said as she strapped on her seatbelt. Being with anyone other than Oliver crushed Erin's heart. Although, the last thing Erin wanted was to stay at home drowning in self-pity. So, she took consolation in the fact that a charming, good-looking and successful man wanted to take her out. No one would *ever* come close to Oliver, in her assessment, but Erin assented to the fact that

Oliver had to love and want her *too*. Sadly, that just wasn't the case. So, she had to submit to the reality of the matter even if it was tearing her apart.

Oliver's heart bled as he watched Erin get into Grayson Andrew's car. He'd watched their interactions at the front door from a distance. He'd been on his way over to ask Erin out to dinner. It had been their ongoing joke that he'd owed her *two* proper dinners, because they'd ordered McDonald's a couple of times. Oliver had been positioned to turn into Erin's block, but had stalled at a corner, seeing Gray at her door properly dressed. It appeared the two had made plans.

Watching Erin step outside of her house looking incredibly beautiful for *someone else*, impaled Oliver's heart. Now, it was becoming clear why Erin's behavior had changed. As much as it killed Oliver to admit to it, his worst nightmare had come to pass. Erin was *into* someone else. Tears were in his eyes, and he felt completely helpless. It felt as if someone had just surgically removed his heart using plyers. "I messed up, Lord. I messed up," he groused, angry at himself.

"You're always making the same mistake, Ollie. Erin came to you in good faith and told you she cared, but you hesitated." Oliver rammed his fist against his steering wheel in frustration. "You did the same thing with Kennedy." He kept shaking his head in the negative. Oliver looked heavenward in utter dismay. "You shoulder the troubles of the world, while neglecting yourself." He sobbed.

"The only thing is that I *can't* lose Erin, Lord. I've never felt so strongly for anyone. I love her so much! I can't lose her. Please, Lord, give me the chance to get it right." Images of Erin getting close to Grayson overwhelmed Oliver with jealousy. He couldn't bear the thought of another man touching her, kissing her..."

At the height of Oliver's despair, he was reminded of what God had told him earlier on. (1 John 4:18) "There is no fear in love, but perfect love casts out fear..." Moreover, God reminded Oliver that he was to have faith, and to trust with all of his heart, even if the circumstances looked contrary. Oliver allowed the Spirit of God to mitigate his distress. Still, even as he began to pull away from the area, there were so many questions.

Not only had it been his intention to invite Erin out to dinner that night, but Oliver had wanted to ask her to be his date for the Christmas party. *Was it even worth it to ask at that point? Would Gray be her date on one of the very last occasions in which they would see each other? What would become of their friendship-if there was one left when it was all said and done?*

Concerned, Oliver put in a call to the local police precinct. He wasn't taking any chances when it came to Erin. *Who was Gray Andrews, and what did Erin really know about him?* Imagining Erin being alone with Gray to any capacity freaked him out. It was also disconcerting that Gray seemed to be following Erin's every move. "Hey, yeah, it's me. If it isn't too much trouble, can you have a few of your men keep an eye out for a black Audi SUV?" Oliver read off the license plate number.

"Everything's fine. I just want to make sure that the person's on the level. No, it seems that the gentleman is an acquaintance of a really good friend…," Oliver noted over the phone. He also indicated to the authorities that the automobile was currently out in *Silver Leaf Falls*. Knowing Erin was with Gray that night threatened Oliver's sanity. Regardless, he was concerned for her safety. Still, even if things were going awry, he kept reminding himself to stand on the word of God.

***

Sometime later, Oliver returned to his place. Inwardly, he felt broken and defeated. Just then, he caught a glimpse of his Christmas tree, which radiated with beauty and elegance. Oliver issued a sad smile recalling the special day he and Erin had shared not too long ago. He was also stirred by the number of presents amassed under the tree. Knowing that he wouldn't be traveling out to Michigan that year, his family had sent a gazillion gifts.

Oliver caught sight of the elaborate gift bag which Kennedy and Kayden had given him earlier on, as he hung up his coat in the foyer closet. Crossing back into the living room, he smiled reflectively, as he examined one of the gifts he'd gotten for Erin. They were diamond stud earrings. In addition, he'd gotten her perfume, and gift cards to her favorite mall outlets. Oliver had painstakingly chosen her presents, using the limited time he'd had in between court hearings.

Picking up the Bohm's gift bag, Oliver removed the bigger, gift-wrapped present and placed it underneath the tree. Floating over to the living room sofa, he sat down and examined the two small envelopes which had also been in the bag. Oliver explored. Just as Kennedy had said, one of the envelopes contained airline tickets to any destination of his choice, which could be redeemed at any time. He smiled quietly to consider their kindness and generosity. Ensuing, Oliver opened up the other envelope.

Oliver's mouth gaped, and he gasped his shock to see the check Kayden had tendered. *Was he reading the numbers correctly?* It read *two million dollars*. "What...?" Oliver flinched in utter amazement. "Kayden, you *didn't* really do this." Oliver kept shaking his head in skepticism. For a moment he was frozen, blankly staring at the check. "What on earth...?" Tears gleamed in his eyes. "I can't accept this..." Before completing that statement, Oliver read Kayden's handwritten note.

"I know you're probably thinking I can't accept this, but you'd better. If anyone deserves a little chunk of happiness in this world, it's you. You are out on the field day in and out to ensure our safety. I don't think the county has enough resources to reward your sacrifices. Please, accept this from your friends who truly love and appreciate you. P.S. I'd better not hear a peep out of you on the matter. Merry Christmas! And Happy New Year! From: your family, Kennedy and Kayden!"

Oliver cried. This time tears of joy were mingled with those of heartache. *Flabbergasted* was the only way to describe how he felt. He wasn't rich by any means, but he wanted for nothing. Money had never been very important to him, but suddenly he had two million dollars. In his sadness, God had given him a bit of encouragement. Oliver assessed that he had to find a way to be a blessing unto the community with this gift. Still, discovering such a windfall on that fateful night also gave him hope.

There were things he *wanted* to do which had very little to do with bettering the world. He smiled contemplatively to consider what he *really* wanted in life. Rain's words earlier that afternoon resonated, *'Life is much too short not to pursue the goals and dreams we want...'* Oliver deemed that his old friend was completely on the ball.

That night, Oliver resolved that he wasn't going to be the odd man out this time around. He refused to lose Erin to anyone-least of all to Gray Andrews. There was something about the man Oliver didn't trust. He was both a little too cool and *creepy*. He'd sought Erin out against her wishes and had continued to push his agenda. Therefore, Gray Andrews was someone he had to watch carefully.

But more importantly, Oliver was ready to tell Erin the truth. She needed to know that he loved her and couldn't see a life apart from her. Oliver had been guarded with his heart in the past, but not anymore. Coming out with both barrels blasting, he would fight for what he wanted most. And what Oliver wanted most was Erin. He wanted her all day and every day for the rest of their lives.

CHAPTER NINE

"You can put the wine and soda cases in the cafeteria fridge. The building custodian will escort you to the ground floor," Erin instructed the caterers on Friday afternoon.

"We should have the entrees ready by around five thirty tomorrow evening. Is that alright?" one of the gentlemen asked.

"Can you make it at six? The party starts at seven, and I don't want the entrees sitting for too long," Erin explained.

"We can definitely do six," the gentleman assured with a smile.

The catering staff drifted out of the expansive meeting hall. Erin scanned the room to see if she should make any last-minute changes, but everything looked perfect if she did say so herself. Furthermore, she was relieved that the event was coming together nicely. Erin went around fastening ornaments on the tree, propping Christmas stockings, and adding a dash here and there.

"Very impressive," Rain said, sauntering into the meeting hall.

Erin veered reflexively and saw Rain. Her heart immediately dipped down to her feet. It hurt Erin to see her. Rain had found a way into Oliver's heart, and she'd failed to. "Thank you," Erin said, forcing a smile.

"You've really done an awesome job with the place! The hard work you put into this venture really shows," Rain uplifted, gravitating closer-eliminating the gap between Erin and herself.

"Well, it was a labor of love," Erin said, wringing her hands together nervously. "I really enjoyed working on this project."

"I know that I'm fairly new around here, but I would have gladly helped." Rain issued a curious smile, as she explored Erin's eyes.

"Oh, that's awfully nice of you. If I had known you were interested in helping, I would not have hesitated to ask. I guess when I get started on a project, I throw myself into it. Thanks for offering," she added with an uneasy smile. Erin kept her distance, frozen and guarded, because Rain was totally untrustworthy. Erin bit her bottom lip nervous and leery of the woman.

"Erin, I'm sorry about the other night." Rain edged closer. "I could have handled the matter a little bit better," she feigned remorse. Inwardly, Rain seethed with angry and jealous feelings. Without a doubt, Erin Brasfield was the woman Oliver had confessed to loving. Oliver had let Rain down gently. However, Rain had no intention of making things easy for Erin-handing him over on a silver platter.

"I don't know what you mean," Erin said coyly, guarded.

"I meant when you called Oliver the other day, and I answered," she reminded, with a cunning smile.

"Oh, that…?" Erin tried to keep a temperate smile on her face. There was no doubt that Rain had an angle. "No worries." She feigned lightheartedness. "You didn't do anything wrong," Erin baited to see what Rain would say.

"Oh, so you *don't* mind that Oliver and I are seeing each other?" Rain asked calculatingly; knowing that nothing could be further from the truth. Even now, she was hopeful that she could possibly have a chance with Oliver if she divided and conquered.

Erin's heart twisted in knots, and her throat felt scratchy, after hearing Rain say that she and Oliver were indeed a couple. The realization was tearing her apart. Tears gleamed in her eyes, but Erin had to keep a stiff upper lip, and pretend to be totally unaffected. "Not at all… I *did* say that Oliver and I were just friends."

"Yes, you did say that. Since you and Oliver are such *great* friends, it can't be easy for *you* that we're dating. I mean, Oliver and I just recently reconnected." Rain had a smug and cunning expression on her face. "I can't believe how easy it's been just to pick up exactly where we left off. Being with Ollie again has been absolutely amazing!" she raved. "I understand how someone *could* become jealous when a close *friend* reestablishes a connection with someone else."

"I see where you're coming from," Erin granted, "but that isn't who I am at all. If Oliver is happy, then I'm happy," her voice undulated, and she smiled until her face hurt. "I would never want to hold him back in any way." She wanted to run away. *How on earth was this happening?*

"That's good to know. As long as there are no hard feelings between us," Rain said, standing only inches away from Erin at that point.

"Not at all, I'm *happy* for you and for Oliver," Erin said as her heart rent in half. "He deserves to be happy," she uplifted.

"So, it doesn't bother you that he's asked me to be his date for the party tomorrow night?" Rain's eyes lowered shrewdly into Erin's eyes.

Upon hearing that question, Erin's heart crashed to the floor. There was a bleeding cavity left in its place which pulsed in indescribable pain. The matter was cruel. She had hoped that Oliver would have asked *her* to the party. After all, it had been their project to begin with. Erin couldn't see Oliver asking Rain to the event. She assessed it to be totally uncharacteristic of him. "Oliver asked *you* to be his date?" Erin asked, warily. Tears pricked her eyes, but she fought them back.

"Yes, he asked me while we were out on Rhode Island. He *did* tell me that the two of you had planned the party together. When I asked if he wouldn't rather go with *you*, he said you wouldn't mind if he and I went together, because the two of you are just friends," Rain lied.

Erin kept shaking her head in denial, trying to process all she'd just heard. She couldn't imagine Oliver being so dismissive of her feelings. "Right… We are *friends*. I hope the two of you have a wonderful time tomorrow night," Erin said with a wavering voice, trying not to fall apart.

"Just wanted to give you the head's up that Ollie is *my* date tomorrow night," Rain added insult to injury.

"Thanks. How thoughtful of you!" Erin said caustically. "But, I'm fine."

"I'm assuming that *you* have a date for the party?" Rain pried.

"Oh, my goodness," Erin evaded, "thank you for reminding me. There are a few last-minute details I forgot to go over with the caterers. Thanks for stopping in, Rain, but I've got to catch them before they leave." Erin ditched Rain and made a dash for the meeting hall doors. "Would you be kind enough to shut the doors on your way out?" Erin asked just before she scuttled away.

"Of course," Rain said, swerving towards the set of doors, catching a glimpse of Erin, who was already halfway down the hall. "It's not that easy, my dear. I'm not going to roll over and play dead, while you walk off into the sunset with *my* guy," she jeered.

Her break was almost over, but Erin needed a bit of air. She drifted out to the parking lot, found her SUV and hopped in. She trembled, and tried to push back the tears, to no avail. They rolled down her cheeks unrestrained. Erin clutched her heart and surrendered to bawling. *How on earth was this happening?* She'd prayed, cried, fasted, and had waited for God to move in her relationship with Oliver.

Had Oliver *truly* disregarded her feelings, and asked Rain to be his date to the Christmas party? It didn't seem to make any sense. Erin was finding it difficult to pull herself together, and definitely needed a moment. Gray had taken her out last night, and they'd had a decent time. Gray was handsome, charming, successful and funny. However, there was something missing, and Erin couldn't fathom giving her heart to anyone else but to Oliver.

It didn't seem to matter one way or another. She couldn't remain on this emotional roller coaster. She had to find a way to get Oliver out of her heart once and for all. It then dawned on her that choosing to leave her job through the DA's office was probably for the best. It would mean less facetime with Oliver Wright, who'd made it clear that they would always be just *good friends*.

Oliver had been away from the office in the early morning. Erin had seen him briefly when he'd returned. However, it wasn't long before other responsibilities had pulled him away again. Erin kept reminding herself that Wednesday December 28th would be her last day working there. Then, it would be all over. She would no longer have to work in close proximity with Oliver Wright. *"You will never have Oliver. He will always be just beyond your reach,"* Anika's words resonated just then-adding acid to Erin's already bleeding heart.

It went against her better judgement, but Erin decided to be proactive at that moment. She pulled her phone out of her pocketbook and deliberated for a moment. Although conflicted, she autodialed Gray's number. "Hey, it's me," she said into the phone with a muffled tone of voice.

"Hey, there, gorgeous," Gray celebrated. "How are you?"

"I'm fine, Gray. How are you doing?"

"I'm wonderful. I was so happy I got to have dinner together last night. You looked amazing!" he complimented.

"Thanks, Gray. I had a nice time at dinner too," Erin said ironically, forcing a smile through the tears. There was something on the inside admonishing her *not* to entertain Gray, but Rain's and Anika's words resonated, along with Oliver affirmation of their platonic stance. Erin had to find a way to anesthetize the agony.

The truth was that she wasn't altogether comfortable with Gray. He was the perfect *date*, but she questioned whether or not he was husband material. And as a Christian woman, she wasn't looking to date. She was searching for someone who could potentially be her husband. And as handsome, suave, charming and smooth as Gray was, Erin knew that he didn't fit the bill.

"Oh, it was my pleasure."

"Gray, what are you doing tomorrow night?" Erin found herself asking, flinching.

"Isn't your office party tomorrow night?" Gray quizzed in

anticipation.

"It *is*. So, would you like to be my…?"

"You're asking me to be your *date* to the party?" Gray filled in, ecstatic.

"Yeah, I guess. Would you be my date to the party, Gray?" Erin vocalized, going against all she believed. She had looked forward to spending as much time with Oliver at the party as possible, but things being what they were, it just wasn't mean to be.

"Erin Brasfield, I would *love* to be your date for the party!" Gray declared, on cloud nine.

"Great! So, it starts at seven."

"I will be by your place to pick you up at around six. I know you're the party planner, so you would probably need to get there earlier than everyone else."

"Right… Thanks, Gray." Erin resigned. She refused to show up to the party alone, when Oliver would be bringing Rain as *his* date.

"Again, you don't have to thank me. Erin, you've just made my day!"

Erin laughed lightly over Gray's celebration and told him she had to go back into the office. As she hopped out of the car, and trekked back into the building, Erin was remind of Isaiah 54:17, "No weapon formed against you shall prosper, and every tongue which rises against you in judgement you shall condemn. This is the heritage of the servants of the Lord, and their righteousness is from me," Says the Lord." (NKJV)

***

"Grayson Andrews checks out. He's the head investor and Liaison for *Silver Dollar Bank* out here in Silver Water and nationally. With the exception of a DUI when he was about twenty, he's clean as a whistle," Detective Rogan told Oliver over the phone on Friday afternoon. Oliver had just gotten back from a parole board hearing, about two hours away from town.

"Are you sure you ran the name in *our* database?" Oliver grasped, totally frustrated. He pulled into his parking space in the lot of the office building.

"Grayson Bennett Andrews is his full name, and yep, I checked out his profile. No priors."

"Okay, thanks, Ben," Oliver said, simultaneously shutting down his cellphone, and hopping off of his SUV. Oliver couldn't shake the feeling that something was off about Gray. Granted, Oliver understood the entitlement of being rich. People with means often felt authorized to get whatever they wanted. And, in this case, Gray wanted Erin. However, Gray wasn't going to win her heart-not if Oliver could help it. Oliver was ready to go to war for Erin if it came to that.

All of his life he had been odd man out whenever the dust settled. However, this time around he couldn't risk losing. Erin meant far too much to him. Oliver smiled as he traipsed the lobby of the building, and saw the festive décor, and the Christmas tree - dazzling enough to give the one out in Rockefeller Center in New York City a run for its money. His heart inundated with pride as he considered that Erin was the mastermind behind such an incredible undertaking.

On that notable afternoon, Oliver was ready to show Erin that he meant business. He would start by properly asking her to be his date for the Christmas party. Then, there were other surprises he had in mind for the woman-who'd not only managed to mend his broken heart-but had stolen it. Oliver was met by members of his staff the moment he stepped back into the general office area.

"Ollie, I need for you to look over the Abbey motion. It has to be delivered to the courthouse by next Tuesday," Jason, Deputy to the Assistant DA, reminded Oliver. "As you well know next week's going to be a little hectic."

"Sure, of course," Oliver reassured. "You can rest it on my

desk," he told Jason.

"Judge Hendricks dismissed Lauren Miller's case. Got the call earlier on," David announced.

"DA Wright, in the Morgan case, the defense is doing all he can to have your bail recommendation overturned, so please call the judge at your earliest convenience," Betty, Oliver's receptionist informed.

"Don't worry, Betty, I will take care of it," Oliver reassured.

And on it went... It was always that way whenever Oliver had been out of the office for the day. He was beginning to get used to the bustle, but at the moment there was only one thing on his mind. It was almost four, and if he didn't take a moment, he wouldn't get to connect to Erin at all. Oliver managed to make it through the maze of public responsibilities. He would handle the details just as soon as he found Erin. There was a smile of anticipation pasted to his face, as he crossed over to Erin's office.

However, he was only a few feet away when Jeannette Meeks halted him. "Oh, Oliver, in case you were looking for Erin, she's gone for the day."

Oliver made an instinctive turn to address the young attorney. "She's gone for the day?" His face wrinkled in both jeopardy and disappointment.

"Yeah, there were a few last-minute details she needed to handle for the party tomorrow night," Jeannette informed. "Glad you're back, Ollie. We really miss you around here when you're gone." Jeannette smiled.

"Thanks, Jeannette," Oliver said, feeling totally displaced. He turned and lingered there for a moment staring at Erin's office door. He couldn't believe he'd just missed her. Even if they hadn't spoken since yesterday afternoon, he'd assumed that she'd be around. Oliver sighed in disillusionment, wandered away from the area, and crossed back over to his own office.

The moment he settled in, before even examining the

paperwork, notes, letters and post-it's on his desk, he pulled out his cell in order to text Erin. It wasn't the way he'd hoped to ask her to escort him to the party tomorrow night, but he didn't want to put in the request too late, as Grayson Andrews was standing in the wings waiting to pounce.

Oliver deliberated for a moment trying to find the right words. As he did, there was a light rap on his office door. "Yep," he called out-inviting the party in. Oliver watched the door open slowly. "Rain...?" he said, startled. Oliver set his phone down, and examined his old law school friend, both pertained and amazed.

"Hey, Ollie," Rain said reticently, standing in the doorway. "I thought I heard you come back. Are you terribly busy now?" Her face strained in ambiguity.

"Of course I am, but come in...," he invited graciously-poised to hear her out.

Rain slipped inside of the office diffidently and set down in the armchair across from Oliver's. "How are you?" she asked staring reservedly into his eyes.

"I'm fine. How are you?" Oliver's face creased in involvement. "Again, I apologize for yesterday..."

"Why? You didn't do anything wrong," Rain countered.

"Still, I'm sorry if I made you feel uncomfortable in any way."

"Oliver, we've been friends for a very long time, so it's *all* good. You are the best person I've ever known, and that's not going to change just because... Well, it's okay."

"Thanks for saying that, Rain. Your friendship means a great deal to me." Oliver gave her a pleasant smile.

"Speaking of *friendship*, I'd like to attend your first Christmas bash as the DA of the districts of Silver Water," she stated properly with a canny smile.

"That's great. It's *your* party too, so you're welcome to

attend," Oliver encouraged.

"I would love to, but I really don't want to attend alone." Rain's face twisted in uneasiness. "So, I'm asking if you'd be my date for the party-as *friends* of course," she clarified.

Oliver's face frowned in conflict. "Rain, I'm flattered, but I had already planned on-"

"I know that you and Erin are great friends, so before I even came in here, I asked *her* if it was okay."

"Oh, really...?" Oliver's brows furrowed, and he immediately snapped to attention. Jeopardy masked his handsome face, and his heart thrashed in his chest.

"Erin told me it was okay for me to ask you, because she *already* has a date," Rain contrived with her fingers crossed.

"Oh...? Is that right?" Oliver asked with a gravelly voice. "Are you sure she said she'd be going with someone else?" Oliver tested, crushed.

Rain smiled. "I believe that's what she said," she told Oliver-trying not to renege on her lies. Rain hoped against hope that Oliver would say yes right then and there. If he called or texted Erin, there was a chance that she'd be caught in her web of lies.

Oliver tried not to wear his heart on his sleeve just then, keeping a temperate smile on his face. "So, can I get back to you a little later about the party?" he asked cordially. He wanted to ask Erin for himself if she planned on attending the party with someone else. The party had been their *thing*-even if Erin had singlehandedly thrown it together. He'd assumed that they would have attended together. Oliver couldn't imagine Erin bringing Gray Andrews as *her* date.

"Sure," Rain said with a clever smile, standing to her feet. "Sorry to have bothered you. I know how busy you are," she said meekly.

"You're never a bother, Rain, "Oliver said flashing one of his friendly smiles. "I will call you later."

"It would mean a lot to me." Rain inched towards the office door but turned and gave Oliver a well-meaning look.

"See you later," Oliver said, watching her go through the door.

He pushed back in his armchair and tried not to react. He needed to speak to Erin first to see what she had to say. However, Oliver grappled with the idea. *What if she'd already promised Gray that they'd attend the party together? What if Erin just wasn't that into him anymore? What if he'd lost her for good?* Erin had changed with him, and Oliver wasn't sure why that was. *What had he done wrong?* The question needled him.

He couldn't imagine Erin being angry with him for any of the choices he'd made of late. Perhaps, she just wanted to move forward with someone she was certain wanted to be with her. Oliver wanted to make her understand that *he* was the one she needed to open up her heart to. He picked up the phone decisively in order to text her. However, at that very instant, he received a text. It startled him because it was from Erin.

"Hey, Ollie, sorry I missed you at the office today. I know you were out of town most of the day up at Greensville Correctional. I had hoped that we would have been able to touch base before the party, but I guess it just wasn't meant to be. You should know that everything's done. I'm glad we got the chance to make tentative plans a couple of weeks ago. Even if things haven't gone according to our plans, I think you'll be happy with the way everything has turned out.

"Because I was uncertain of what your plans were for tomorrow night, you don't have to worry about going to the party together. Gray has offered to escort me. Things have been a little complicated for us lately, so I didn't want to assume that you and I were going together. I also didn't want to hold you back in the event you had other options. Hope to talk to you soon, Ollie. Bye."

"Why are you doing this, Erin?" Oliver's voice broke. "I *only* wanted to go with you. Why on earth would you think that I would ever want to go with anyone else?" he questioned in jeopardy. "God, how did things get so off course? Two weeks ago, Erin and I had the most amazing day together. Since then, things have gotten increasingly more complicated. Jesus, I need your help. Please, don't let it be too late for me to tell her how I feel. I can't stand that this Gray guy is in her life." Oliver brushed his fingers through his thick wavy head of hair in turmoil. Conflicted, he still needed to return Erin's text. Moreover, he *had* to find a way to respond without sounding like a jealous and possessive ogre.

Oliver had already made up his mind and knew exactly what he wanted. In fact, he'd already tentatively made plans for Erin and himself on Christmas day. Hopefully, he'd get the chance to see her on Christmas day. Oliver hated that Gray Andrews was standing in the way. And yet, he understood that being possessive and overbearing just wasn't the way to go. The only way to win the heart of the woman he loved was to let her know that she had *his* and holding it together while the storm passed.

"I guess apologizing up and down for not being there for the past couple of weeks sounds a bit trite. But I am truly sorry, Erin. I had looked forward to helping you with the details of the party every step of the way. I had also looked forward to throwing fries in your face, LOL, as we worked together in the late afternoon whenever we found a moment.

"I am extremely proud of the work you've done. I am amazed every time I step into the office building. What you've accomplished in the past couple of weeks is nothing short of remarkable! Although, I'd be less than truthful if I said that I wasn't a little disappointed that I won't be the one escorting you to our first *Christmas party through the DA's office. I am however looking forward to seeing you there. Talk to you soon... Ollie."*

Oliver hoped that Erin would read into his heart through the returned text message. He couldn't outright tell her *not* to go with Gray, but he *could* express disappointment over her choice. Even if he wouldn't play the role of the jealous boyfriend, Oliver had already made up his mind to aggressively pursue the matter, because Erin was so worth it. He'd never felt so strongly for anyone. Oliver shook his head marveling over how much he'd come to love her.

He had operated under the misconception that he'd been

incapable of loving anyone more than he'd loved Kennedy, but God had proven him wrong. God had promised him a love incomparable to anything he'd ever known, and Oliver believed wholeheartedly that God had made good on His word. Erin was his miracle from God in the aftermath of a shattered heart, and he would do everything in his power to fight for this amazing otherworldly love.

***

The monster made his way to the back of his spacious home on Friday night. Drifting over to the giant bin in the shed, he perused his collection. There had been layers of bloody clothing which he'd kept in that bin, souvenirs from the murders. Moreover, he'd garnered locks of hair from all six of the women he'd killed so far. From time to time, he liked going into the shack to admire his handiwork. After having left the bar after work, he'd driven over to Silver Commons Adjacent. There was a young woman whom he'd had his eye on for the past week.

The svelte blonde had caught his eye the moment he'd seen her coming out of a beauty salon in that area. His target was beautiful young women who lived alone. The monster had evaluated that this woman would be a perfect addition to his growing collection. If everything went according to plan, she would be victim number seven on his hit list. So, after a few more days of studying her routine, he would have her exactly where he wanted. At some point she would invite him into her home, and then it was game on.

For as long as he could remember, beautiful women had looked down on him. He'd been the lanky, nerdy kid who wore glasses. Not only had beautiful women ridiculed him in the past, but they'd always turned down his advances. Now, he was getting the last laugh. It had taken years, but he now looked like their dream prince. Not only was he good-looking, but he had the wealth and charm needed to seduce them. Furthermore, he'd bulked up tremendously since his high school and early college days and had found *killer* contact lenses.

Holding all of the cards at that point, it was time to make the women pay for mocking and rejecting him. The monster stepped into his spacious and lavish bedroom and stripped off his designer clothes. Before long, he crossed over to the adjoining bathroom and stepped into the shower stall. Turning the water on, he allowed it to run warm. Lathering up, he hoped to wash away the *grime* of being exposed to the elements all day.

It felt good to get clean. And in some tainted reality he was washing away his sins. However, he was neither repentant nor remorseful. To the contrary, he was looking forward to his next conquest. It thrilled him to no end to bait his victims with his charisma. And once he had them exactly where he wanted them, he made them pay for snubbing him and guys who were just like him.

Before long, the demon was situated in his living room, eating Thai takeout food. Turning on the news, he was over the top happy to see and hear stories in respect to his body of work. They were calling him *Silver County's Serial Killer.* "Wow, I can't believe I'm famous. That's me. Ooh… I'm like the boogeyman of *Silver County.*" He thrust his head back and allowed a ripple of laughter to issue from the hollow of his throat. He shook his head in irony. "Go figure… Who would have thunk it…?"

Before long, his phone was ringing. The killer recognized the number right away. It was the woman he was currently dating. He'd already decided to date this woman for a while as a cover. Regardless, if *she* messed up in any way, or if he got tired of her, he would silence her for good- whichever came first. "Hey there, sweet girl, how are you? I was just thinking about you…" He stretched out on the sofa, as he philandered with his next potential victim.

***

Erin had to sit under the dryer at the beauty salon late Saturday morning. Her hair stylist had just rinsed perm out of her hair and had set her hair in giant hair rollers. Now, she was waiting for her hair to dry. Erin had gotten up with the sun that Christmas

Eve, and had spoken to her parents, her brother Darryl and her sister Laurie to wish them a Merry Christmas. She had already sent gifts for her family who lived in upstate New York. They, in turn, had sent her gifts via post.

Her family had decided to come out to Silver Water at the turn of the New Year. Because she'd given the DA's office her two-week notice and had planned their Christmas party, Erin had forfeited taking a trip out to New York to visit with her family. While sitting under the dryer, Erin still felt needled about asking Gray to be her date for the party. Fiddling with the phone in her hand, she pulled up Oliver's text message from yesterday afternoon. Pouring over every word, Erin felt conflicted. It was obvious she and Oliver had gotten their signals crossed.

In light of what Oliver had texted, it was obvious that he had wanted to be her date for the party. So, Erin concluded that Rain had lied about Oliver asking *her*. Erin felt foolish for taking the bait. She'd made a snap decision, and had asked Gray to be her date, playing right into Rain's hands. Furthermore, she felt the conviction of God's Spirit censuring her for making such a rash decision. Erin realized too late that she should have waited to speak to Oliver before listening to anything Rain had to say. Erin felt out of sorts, because God had dealt with her for not trusting Him enough in her circumstances.

Notwithstanding, the greatest reproach Erin received from her Heavenly Father was from 2 Corinthians 6:14 (KJV): "Do not be unequally yoked together with unbelievers: for what fellowship hath righteousness with unrighteousness: and what communion hath light with darkness?" The message came in loud and clear that Gray *wasn't* in the will of God for her life, because he was a nonbeliever. Gray had spoken extensively about his faith and had attested to believing in Jesus. He'd also shared testimonies with her in respect to his faith. However, God, who could see into the hearts of men (and women), had revealed that Gray wasn't right for her.

Erin felt conflicted to say the least. She'd already asked Gray to be her date for the Christmas party. The last thing she wanted was to jerk him around. So, her plan was to play it cool at the party. After the party she would tell him she didn't see a future between them. Prayerfully, Gray would honor her request.

"Erin, I'm ready for you," Velma, Erin's hair stylist said, shutting off the hair dryer, and guiding Erin over to the styling chair. "You weren't too uncomfortable under there, were you?" the older Spanish woman asked.

Erin guffawed. "Not at all, Velma. Sitting under the hot dryer for close to an hour didn't faze me in the least." She winked, after sitting down in the huge chair.

"You know what you want to do with your hair, Mama? You want flat-iron bangs, curls, or a French roll?"

In spite of the disappointment Erin tussled with because Oliver wasn't her date for the party, she tried to perk up. At least she would get to see and be near him later on. "I want the top part upswept in a roll, but I want the rest of my hair out in curls," Erin explained, gesturing with her hands in the mirror.

"I *got* you, Mama. I know exactly what you want," Velma said, with an understanding nod.

"I know you do. I want it the way you fixed it for the fundraising dinner that time…," she reminded Velma.

"Oh, yes. That was some of my best work," Velma raved, and immediately started tousling Erin's full head of hair.

Erin fiddled with her phone, as Velma worked on her hair. She grappled with the idea of calling Gray and canceling their date altogether. Then, she would call Oliver and apologize for being so presumptuous. Erin missed him so much it caused physical pain. In the past week they'd only connected once. They'd seen each other briefly on Wednesday when Oliver had returned from Rhode Island. She wished they could spend *quality* time together without all of the interruptions.

While toying with her phone, Erin's mouth gaped in shock. The texting notification bell had just gone off, and the text was from Oliver. She was trembling as she anticipated reading his message. The party was only a few hours away, so she was a bit apprehensive about what he had to say. Erin wished that Oliver was texting to tell her that Rain couldn't attend the party. Granting, Erin realized that this was wishful thinking on her part.

Taking a deep breath, Erin finally accessed Oliver's text. *"Hey, stranger, how's it going? I just wanted to connect to you today so that I could properly ask what you're doing on Christmas day. So, what are you doing on Christmas day, Miss Erin? (Oliver included a smiley face emoji)."* Erin's face lit up in expectation over Oliver's initial invite, but she kept reading.

"I didn't want to assume that you didn't have plans with family and friends, but I'm taking a chance to invite you over to breakfast at my place in the early morning. That is if you have no other prior commitments."

Erin's jaw dropped in amazement, and tears shone in her eyes. She couldn't believe what she'd just read, and how openly Oliver had expressed his desire.

"Somebody's getting *really happy* about reading a text message," Velma razzed on Erin. "He must be someone special." She winked as she straightened Erin's hair with the flat-iron.

Erin's cheeks turned florid. "Velma, you *really* need to focus on my hair," she teased.

"Uh-huh," Velma playfully rose to the occasion, "now I *know* he's special."

Erin ignored her and kept reading. *"Even if we're not escorting each other to the party this evening, I am looking forward to seeing you. Gray is really lucky to be going with you. He'd better treat you like royalty tonight. That's what I would have done if you'd allowed me to take you. In any event, please save at least one dance for me?"*

"I want to save them all for you, Ollie," Erin said quietly. She tried not to cry right then and there. "He's super special, Velma," she acceded, catching Velma's eye.

"You look so happy when you talk about him. I hope he's the

one, Mama. I know how long you've been waiting and praying for the right one. God is good and He's faithful!"

"Yes, He is," Erin's voice broke.

Happiness bubbled up on the inside. Her joy was just as heightened as the pain she'd felt after Rain had told her she and Oliver were an item. Erin felt tremendously blessed and favored if Oliver wanted to spend Christmas morning with her. She wondered where *Rain* fit into the equation, but immediately dismissed the thought. It didn't really matter. Erin would trust God to fulfill His plan and purpose for her life.

Over-the-moon happy, Erin estimated that not even Rain McGrath could rain on her parade. Erin cheerfully and excitedly text Oliver back, affirming that she would love nothing more than to have breakfast with him on Christmas morning. She thanked him for the invite and expressed how disappointed *she* was that they weren't escorting each other to the party. Moreover, Erin added that she would definitely save a dance just for him.

"You've just made my day, Stranger." Oliver included a wink emoji. *"I'm looking forward to seeing you later,"* he texted back.

***

Erin had a few errands to run in the area after leaving the hair salon. With the top portion of her hair upswept, her lengthy hair bounced healthily over her shoulders and back. Erin was proud of the work her old friend and hair-stylist Velma had done with her hair. It was close to four when she pulled into the driveway of her house.

The crisp December air gusted, as she stepped out of the automobile. She had a few items in the trunk of the car. Quickly retrieving them, Erin hastily made her way up the stairs, trying to sheath her wispy curls from the puffs of wind.

Turning the key in the lock, Erin let herself into the house. She sighed feeling totally relieved to be at home. Erin felt nice and toasty being home. There were also warm and fuzzy feelings on the inside, because of her exchanges with Oliver. She still couldn't believe he'd invited her over to his place for breakfast on Christmas day.

Erin had been praying for a breakthrough with Oliver for some time. Tears were in her eyes, as she lifted up her hands in praise to God. God had surprised her in the best way. Just yesterday she had been crying sad tears, but today she was crying tears of joy. Suddenly, she couldn't wait to lock eyes with Oliver at the party.

If only there was a way she could have made both *Gray and Rain* disappear. She wanted tonight to be about Oliver and herself. Erin wished she could make the entire world go away. In spite of how encouraged she felt by Oliver's invitation to breakfast, Erin still struggled with uncertainty, because of the way things had played out in the past. Nevertheless, it was hard not to be excited about finally getting some one on one time with Oliver

Crossing over to the bedroom, Erin rested some of her purchases on the bed. She drifted over to her full-length mirror and admired how pretty her hair had come out. Taking a quick peek at her phone, it was almost twenty after four. So, she needed to shower and groom for when Gray swung by to pick her up.

Slipping on her favorite turquoise blue terrycloth robe, Erin was just about to begin applying hair removal lotion to her legs, when the doorbell rang. "Really…?" she questioned, annoyed. Her doorbell always seemed to ring at the most inopportune moments. "Lord, I hope that's not Gray. It isn't even five yet," she complained.

Tightening the belt around her robe, Erin wandered over to the front door. The doorbell rang yet again before she got the chance to get it. "I'm here," she said opening up the door. Her mouth gaped in shock when she saw the messenger, holding the most extravagant arrangement of baby's breath roses.

"Are you Erin Brasfield?" the young, thin Caucasian kid with dark hair asked.

Overwhelmed, Erin nodded. "I *am*."

"Well, these are for you," he told her gladly, handing the bouquet over to Erin.

"Thank you," Erin said taking the arrangement out of his hands.

"Merry Christmas," he heralded.

"Merry Christmas to you," Erin said, adrift and surprised. She signed for the delivery, then pushed the front door closed pressing her back up against it. Then, she cut across over into the kitchen, and set the huge arrangement on the counter. Prayerfully, she picked up the little green card wedged in the red pitchfork which had her name on it.

"Erin, I can't thank you enough for all of your hard work, and the sacrifices you've made in order to make this event possible. The DA's office will probably never look this good again, and it's all thanks to you. I wanted to let you know that I don't take anything you've done lightly. I wish that I had been in the trenches right alongside you while planning this party. You're making us all look good. I am unabashedly proud and grateful to know you, Erin Emily! Regards, Oliver."

"Oh, Ollie," Erin whispered with tears in her eyes, taking in the fragrant bed of roses. There were three dozen to be exact. "God, I can't believe this," Erin marveled. "What does this mean? Can it be that you're finally answering my prayers?" She sighed, deeply stirred by Oliver's gesture. She had thought for sure that the flowers were from Gray. He was the type who loved showcasing grandiose gestures.

Erin admired the exquisite arrangement and decided to take it over to her bedroom instead. She wanted to be able to look at the flowers while she got dressed. Furthermore, she wanted to see them once she got home from the party. And then, if God willed, she wanted to contemplate the flowers when she woke up on Christmas morning. Erin was virtually floating on a cloud as she got ready for the party. Her heart fluttered in excitement, there were butterflies in her stomach, and her legs felt wobbly in anticipation of seeing Oliver later.

It was a few minutes before six when Erin stood back and inspected herself in the full-length mirror in her bedroom. She was wearing a short-sleeved, V-neck, sequined-form-fitting wine-colored dress and looked absolutely amazing in it-if she did say so herself. With her hair done up, with curls cascading over her shoulders and back, she was pleased with the results. Her heart inundated with love for Oliver. It felt odd to be waiting on *Gray* to pick her up for the party.

The only person Erin wanted to see at that moment was Oliver. She was more in love with him than ever. Hence, she wasn't looking forward to seeing Rain on his arm. However, Erin would take heart, because she would have him all to herself tomorrow morning. The thought of being alone with Oliver for just a little while deluged her heart in excitement. Having *Real* face time and sharing more than just a word or two had evaded them for the past two weeks.

It was three minutes past six p.m. when Gray shot Erin a quick text telling her that he was outside. Still on a virtual cloud, Erin glided over to the front door. She was still on a high because of everything she and Oliver had shared throughout the day. Erin was euphoric, and nothing-not even having to spend the night with Gray-would bring her spirits down.

Expectantly, she opened up the front door. "Good evening, Gray," she said pleasantly. Gray looked amazing in dark jeans, a red shirt, and matching tie. His dark hair shimmered and had been stylishly tweaked to accentuate his handsome face. Erin assessed that Gray knew how to rock the casual yet sleek look. In his red shirt and red designer tie, he was modeling men's Christmas party attire to the nines.

"How *are* you this gorgeous?" Gray raved, taking in every inch of Erin. "You're taking my breath away right now, Ms. Erin Brasfield!" Gray shook his head and grunted gutturally. "I can't wait for everyone to see the most beautiful woman on my arm tonight!" he praised.

"Thanks, Gray," Erin said reticently. Her cheeks turned scarlet, because he was laying it on thick.

"Are we ready to wow them?" Gray asked quirkily, scrutinizing his date.

"We're all set," Erin said with waning enthusiasm. She locked the front door, then turned and looped her arm through Gray's. In a chivalrous manner, he escorted her down the steps, and helped her into his car.

Gray hopped into the driver's seat but found it difficult to keep his eyes off of Erin. "Wow!" he said staring sidelong at her. "Am I *really* this lucky?" His face radiated joy and dignity.

"Gray, you are so dramatic." Erin shook her head comically.

"Well, lady, you bring it out of me." He kept ogling.

At a red light ahead, Erin noticed he was still gawking. "You should really keep your eyes on the road," she teased.

"Believe me, I'm trying, Erin. I really am…"

Erin laughed and shook her head humorously. Nevertheless, she knew that she had to sever ties with Gray that night. There was just no easy way to tell him that she didn't see a future there. Luckily, she and Gray had only gone out a few times. They had not even yet engaged in a proper kiss. Regardless, the Lord had made it clear that Gray wasn't in His will for her life. Perhaps, Erin considered, she'd invite Gray to Deliverance Tabernacle. Having to close the door with Gray made Erin feel uncomfortable, but it had to be done.

Gray seemed like a very nice guy, and Erin couldn't imagine he'd take it personally if they stopped dating. Regardless, it was what *had* to happen if things were to ever pan out with Ollie. Being with Oliver was what Erin wanted more than anything else. The thought melted her heart, made it race and flutter all at once. As she and Gray drove over to the party, the only thing on Erin's mind was seeing Oliver again and locking eyes. She was completely and unabashedly in love.

CHAPTER TEN

"Would you do me the honor of dancing the next number?" Oliver's voice was throaty, as he came up behind Erin. Erin had been at the buffet table fixing a plate.

"Ollie?" Erin said, turning back, startled. She set the plate down on the table. "Hi," she said excitedly delving his eyes. Her heart began hammering the moment their eyes met. "I've been hoping to have a moment with you all night, but your date hasn't let you out of her sight-not once," Erin said, trying not to wear her heart on her sleeve.

She couldn't help contemplating how amazing Oliver looked in dark jeans, a formal rust-colored shirt and matching tie. His skin appeared more malleable than cream, and his freshly cut and shaped hair outlined his winsome face. Erin's legs felt as if they would give way, just because he was near her again. That he smelled heavenly also didn't mitigate her struggle.

Oliver laughed lightly over Erin's comment. "I know…sorry about that. I've been meaning to connect, but Rain has been a little bit territorial. She's very possessive of our friendship," he acquiesced.

"So, I gather, but you do have *other* friends," Erin said softly-totally swept away.

"Don't I know it? I have some of the best friends in the world," he said transported. Oliver was all smiles, as he admired just how incredible Erin looked in her burgundy sequined dress. The bodice hugged her in all of the right places, outlining her tiny waist and curvy hips. It was taking a moment for him to remember how to breathe. "I didn't want to be rude-pulling you away from *your* date. It's kind of hard *not* to notice how Gray has been following you around all night," Oliver pointed out, trying not to sound too jealous.

"*I'm* sorry, Ollie." Erin sighed. "Gray *has* been shadowing me all night." She laughed lightly, searching Oliver's eyes. "I didn't get the chance to say thank you for the roses! They're absolutely breathtaking!" Erin said stirred, as she stared yearningly into Oliver's face.

"Are you kidding me? Erin, I can't thank *you* enough. This party is a total success!" Oliver gestured to his surroundings. Everyone who worked through the DA's office had come out. They were dressed to the nines-totally filled with holiday cheer and expectation.

There was laughter, dancing and celebration all around, as Christmas music hummed in the background. It was perfect. What Oliver liked the most was that he'd finally gotten a moment alone Erin. "I would have bought out the entire flower shop to show you how much all of this means to me. I can't believe you took the ideas we tentatively planned that night and turned it into all of *this*-far exceeding each and every detail."

Erin was overjoyed and totally touched by Oliver's compliment. "You're giving me way too much credit. I had the *best* time planning this event." Erin searched his eyes. "My only regret is that *we* didn't get the chance to work together. I was really looking forward to hanging out with you."

"I feel the same way. We were going to rock this event together, but..."

"Duty called *every* time," Erin filled in.

"That's one way of putting it." Oliver explored her eyes intuitively. "But I promise that if we ever do plan an event together again, I *will* find a way to get it done." His heart thudded in his chest as he moved in closer to Erin. Oliver was totally awestruck, staring at her as if she was an oasis, and he'd been trapped out in the hot dry desert for quite some time. "Did I tell you how incredible you look tonight?"

"No, you didn't," Erin said reticently, shying away from his intent stare.

"Well, you look *incredible* tonight!" Oliver gaped mercilessly, taking in every inch of her.

"Thank you," Erin said meekly, edging in closer to Oliver, as magnets of opposite charges often did. "You look pretty dapper yourself," she remarked in a reserved manner, enraptured. In that moment the entire world had gone away. For all intents and purposes, they were the only two people in that expansive hall full of partygoers.

"Thank you. It's weird, because I actually dressed *down* tonight, since I'm usually wearing business attire," Oliver said with reddened cheeks, uncertain as to why he was suddenly bashful around Erin.

"Both looks work *equally* well for you," Erin voice trailed, as they gravitated closer.

"That's a very sweet thing to say." Oliver gazed devotedly into Erin's eyes, completely hypnotized. "You're so beautiful!" he said throatily, reaching for her hand.

Erin's heart thrashed, inundated with love for Oliver, as her eyes gently brushed over his comely face. It was the first time he'd ever told her she was beautiful-at least in that way. "Thank you so much!" Her heart missed a beat, as she savored the sensation of his strong gentle hand enveloping hers.

"You're welcome," Oliver said, enrapt. In a tender way he began guiding her over to a clear spot out on the dancefloor. "Will you dance with me now?" he said, pulling Erin into his arms, securing a gentle yet firm grasp about her waist.

"I've been waiting for this moment all night." Erin stared up at Oliver, completely captivated. She gingerly brought her hands up to his strong shoulders. In a subtle way, she draped her arms about his neck and clasped her hands together. The two swayed in tune to an instrumental version of *"I'll Be Home for Christmas,"* while staring fondly and fascinatingly into each other's eyes.

"I'm sorry about the misunderstanding," Erin said, breathless, looking up into Oliver's eyes.

"What misunderstanding, *honey*?" Oliver said thickly, as he pressed in more intimately. At that moment, all of the near misses which had kept them apart for the past couple of weeks faded into oblivion. Holding Erin in his arms as they danced had dispelled the struggle.

"I wasn't sure if you wanted to attend the party with me," Erin's voice undulated, as she leaned into Oliver's chest.

"Erin," Oliver inched back enough to establish eye contact, "you're the *only* person I would have wanted to be with tonight." His eyes fondly searched hers, as he fastened his hold on her waist. "This was *our* project, remember?"

"I didn't want to make trouble for you and Rain," Erin confessed, grimacing in uncertainty, and looking away from Oliver's intent stare.

"Erin, what do you mean make trouble for me and Rain?" His face creased in jeopardy. "Look at me," he prodded gently. "Rain and I are *friends*-nothing more."

Erin's face veiled in surprise. "I thought the two of you were-"

"No...," Oliver affirmed, shaking his head in the negative. "Whatever gave you that idea?" he tested, devotedly caressing Erin's face with his eyes.

Erin pursed her lips as if she wanted to explain, but desisted. It was Christmas Eve, and Oliver was Rain's date. So, she didn't want to make any waves by telling Oliver that his old law school friend had probably lied to the both of them. "I'm sorry. I should have asked *you* to be my date."

"Yeah, you *really* should have." Oliver smiled hopefully and gave Erin a playful wink. "Can I tell you something?" He leaned in, whispering in her ear with a racing heart.

"Anything...," Erin said delicately.

"I would have wanted to dance *every* number with you tonight." Oliver closed his eyes meditatively, as his cheeks brushed the sides of Erin's cheek and her fragrant hair.

"Me too, Ollie," Erin said softly, hugging him more intimately. For Erin the moment felt surreal. She had only dreamed about being this close to Oliver.

"Is that so?" Oliver pulled back and stared yearningly at Erin. "About our breakfast rendezvous, I will swing by your place at around eight tomorrow morning," he said gruffly. "There's no *misunderstanding* in that. In the morning I want *you* all to myself-no Gray or Rain…," his voice wavered, as he delicately took in every inch of her.

Erin smiled hopefully. "That's what I want too, Ollie. I can't wait. So, you'd better not be late," she vamped.

"Yes, Ma'am, you're *not* bossy at all," he razzed, folding her closer to his heart. Oliver moved to the sound of music, with Erin secure in his arms in a world all their own.

"Nope, I'm *not* the slightest bit bossy." Erin allowed her fingers to rake through Oliver's torturous, wavy hair. "You made my day by inviting me to breakfast tomorrow morning," she said softly pressed up to his chest.

Oliver was lost in the moment, totally beguiled. His face grazed Erin's, and his mouth inched in closely to her ear. "You really made *mine* by saying yes."

Erin got chills hearing Oliver's mellow voice so close to her ear, and she was virtually melting in his arms.

Oliver pulled back and just admired her. Smiling, he began leaning in with his eyes affixed to her candy lips. Erin had the kind of lips that made it impossible not to want to kiss her. Compelled to explore, he was thirsty for a long and satisfying drink.

"There you are, Ollie," Rain said, finding Oliver and Erin together, after returning from the ladies room.

Rain's voice shattered the serenity Oliver and Erin had been locked into. Oliver and Erin instinctively pulled away but continued to stare dotingly at each other.

"Hey," Oliver told Rain, with an uneasy smile. Her sudden

intrusion was frustrating, but he didn't want to be rude. "Erin promised me one dance tonight, and I was just collecting," he told Rain, with his eyes affixed devotedly to Erin. Oliver sensed that Erin was perturbed by Rain's sudden emergence.

"Is that so? How are *you* doing tonight, Erin?" Rain asked with a fake smile glued on her face. "This is an awesome party by the way," she uplifted, trying to *play nice* for Oliver's benefit. Inwardly, she seethed and resented Erin.

"I'm doing just fine, Rain," Erin obliged. "Thank you." Erin stared all around at the festivities. Her coworkers were having the best time! "Actually, things turned out even better than I expected!"

"I'm totally impressed," Oliver said, feeling cold and withdrawn. He longed to feel Erin in his arms again. The desire to feel close to her was unyielding.

"Yes, Erin did an awesome job. I *did* tell her that I would have loved to be a part of things," Rain said-doing all she could to show Oliver that she was a team player. In a possessive manner, she looped her arms through his.

"That *would* have been fantastic," Oliver granted, finally looking at Rain. However, his gape instantly reverted back to admiring the love of his life. There was so much he wanted to tell her-so much he needed to make her understand.

"Maybe, next time, Rain," Erin said in a detached manner, feeling alienated outside of Oliver's arms.

"Maybe, next time what…?" Gray suddenly happened on the scene and took his place right beside Erin. He slipped his arm about her waist and stared fondly at her. "Sorry, I took so long. I had an important phone call." He smiled down at Erin and connected furtively to her eyes. "I shut off my phone, and I promise it won't happen again."

"Don't worry about it, Gray," Erin said, staring uneasily into his eyes. Her gaze regressed back over to Oliver, and their eyes fastened ruefully. Their eyes communicated the intense yet furtive dialogue of wanting to be together.

"Erin was just encouraging me to help out with the party-planning next year," Rain inserted, picking up on the electric currents sparking between Oliver and Erin.

"That would be great, but I have to say how proud I am of *this* young lady." Gray's arm tightened around Erin's waist.

Oliver shot Gray a menacing look. It bothered him that the man kept touching Erin so familiarly. Oliver seldom got hot under the collar, but just then, he felt the need to introduce Gray's face to his fist. He had to remain prayerful so that he wouldn't lose his cool.

"Gray," Erin's cheeks turned cardinal, "you're embarrassing me."

"Well, you *are* pretty awesome!" he uplifted.

Just then, Mariah Carey's version of *Miss You Most at Christmas Time* came on. "Oh, Ollie, I love this song. Come and dance with me," Rain propositioned, staring devotedly up at him.

Oliver smiled uneasily. "Of course," he told Rain, staring wistfully over at Erin. Grudgingly, he took Rain's hand, and guided her over to the dancefloor. Oliver's eyes remained affixed to Erin the entire time. From a distance, he heard Gray asking Erin to dance with him as well.

Before long, Erin was wrapped in Gray's arms, and they were swaying quietly and exclusively to the music. Oliver felt as if his and Erin's perfect moment had been violated. For a little while he'd experienced the heaven of having Erin in his arms. Even as he danced with Rain, Oliver couldn't help staring over at Erin. Intermittently, their eyes clasped yearningly. He hated having to share her with anyone else that night. However, he would count down the hours, minutes and the seconds until they could be together in the morning. The party was totally perfect. The only setback was that he wasn't with the woman he loved.

It was almost midnight when Gray secured Erin inside of his

SUV. From the passenger's side window, Erin caught Oliver's eye as he helped Rain into his car. Erin held her hand up as a farewell gesture. They stared achingly at each other, as Oliver held his hand up and said goodbye as well.

The party had been amazing, but Erin had only gotten to connect to Oliver once. Being in Oliver's arms for that little span of time only confirmed that she was head-over-heels in love. And, for the first time in their history, Erin was encouraged that *maybe* Oliver felt the same way. Conceptualizing that Oliver might care just as much overwhelmed Erin with unspeakable joy.

"Did you have a good time tonight?" Gray asked, pulling out of the building lot.

"Did you say something, Gray?" Erin asked distracted, watching Oliver's SUV pull out of the lot.

Gray gave Erin a rattled sidelong look. It was beginning to become clear that Erin was *into* Silver County's new District Attorney. From the outset, he'd tried not to allow that to get under his skin, but it was truly beginning to. He smiled temperately and asked again, "I just asked if you had a good time."

"Oh," Erin said, snapping to attention, "I did. Thank you again for agreeing to come with me."

"Yeah, sure. I had a blast!" Gray pulled into the local highway. "And, I mean it. You throw a mean party, young lady! Have you ever thought about doing it professionally?" he asked, evadingly. Gray didn't want to focus on Erin's relationship with Oliver Wright, because it bothered him.

"Oh," Erin laughed lightly, "I've never thought about that. I mean, it's just *one* party. I can't really base an entire career in party-planning, because *one* event turned out well," she deflected.

"Well, all it takes is *one* event to get anyone started, and you totally killed it tonight," Gray said staring out into the open road.

Inwardly, Erin felt conflicted. She was struggling to find the words to come clean with Gray. There was no future between them.

The last thing she wanted was to hurt him, but Erin couldn't see herself stringing him along until after the holidays. It hardly seemed fair. Even if it was
Christmas-a terrible time to crush anyone's heart-she had to find a way to let him down gently.

They were about ten minutes away from her place out in *Silver Leaf Falls* when Erin tried to veer the subject to what needed to be said. "Gray, there's something I have to tell you." She began fiddling nervously with her fingers, but made her eyes connect to his at a stop light.

"Alright," Gray assented, frowning. "Are you alright?"

"I'm fine, Gray." Erin's eyes connected furtively to his. "You know that I like you a great deal, right?" Her face warped in uneasiness.

"I would hope so, because I like *you* a lot, Erin."

"Here's the thing." Erin's face wrinkled, pertained. "As much as I like you, I don't see a future with us." Her heart ached in her chest upon saying those words.

"Oh…?" Gray questioned, silent for a moment.

"Gray, we talked about my faith, and how God is the one guiding me through every decision. Moreover, you *know* how I feel about dating just to be dating. If I date someone it has to be with the end goal of marriage," she disclosed. Tears were gleaming in her eyes, because Gray had gotten super quiet. "I'm sorry," Erin's voice broke, as Gray pulled into her driveway.

"I see…" Gray's face was sullen. "I really wasn't expecting this-least of all today," he said straightforwardly.

"Erin's face twisted in remorse. "I didn't think it was fair to keep you guessing, Gray. Would it have made a difference if I'd waited until after New Year's?"

"No, you're absolutely right. If you're not feeling it…"

"It's not that I'm not feeling it. I just know that we're *not* meant to be together," Erin said truthfully.

Gray nodded, staring at Erin with an understanding expression. "So, this sudden change of heart has *nothing* to do with the fact that you have feelings for Oliver Wright?" he asked directly.

Erin flinched, but rose graciously to the occasion. "It probably has *everything* to do with that," she admitted.

"Okay, I get it," Gray acquiesced. He sighed with a sense of frustration. "I'm not happy about this, Erin, but I *can't* be angry with you." He smiled. "You are a class act, and an amazing woman!"

"Thanks, Gray," Erin's voice undulated, as her eyes linked to his.

"You're welcome, beautiful! I hope Oliver Wright knows how lucky he is." He winked at her.

Erin didn't say a word. Rather, she just smiled reflectively.

Gray stepped out of the automobile in order to get the door for Erin.

Erin took Gray's hand and allowed him to help her out of the car. They quietly made their way up the steps. However, Gray held on to Erin's hand, reluctant to let go. He pulled her closer to himself and pressed his lips to hers. "At least I got to do that just once," he said, exploring her eyes.

Taken aback and feeling a little out of sorts, Erin smiled. "Goodnight and Merry Christmas, Gray!" she declared.

"Does that mean I can't call you from time to time?" Gray tested, finally releasing his hold on her hand.

Erin smiled. "Of course, you can call me if you need to, but I'm *definitely* inviting you to church."

"Will I meet someone as good as you at your church?" Gray teased.

"Probably someone better," Erin uplifted.

I seriously doubt that, but thanks for encouraging me," Gray said. He explored her eyes once more before hesitantly turning away.

Erin watched Gray hop into his SUV, and slowly pull out of her driveway. She then stepped into the house and locked the front door. Telling Gray that they didn't have a future together was a lot harder than she'd expected. Nevertheless, Erin was grateful to have been able to sever ties-just as God had asked her to. Shaking off feelings of guilt, she relived being in Oliver's arms while they'd danced. The exchanges between them had been intense. Erin could still hear Oliver's resonant voice in her ear, telling her how he'd wished they'd danced every number together.

Captivated, Erin floated into her bedroom in order to change for bed. She slipped on her toasty Christmas jammies. The print on her PJ's were of presents, Christmas Trees and teddy bears. Erin was on a high, but got down on her knees in order to express gratitude to God for the work He was doing between her and Oliver.

Erin prayed that nothing would stand between Oliver and herself. As she waited in the presence of her Heavenly Father, she was reminded of Isaiah 14:27, "For the LORD of hosts hath purposed, and who will annul it? And his hand *is* stretched out, and who will turn it back?" (NKJV)

Slipping into bed sometime later, Erin mulled over those words. She was confident in the knowledge that nothing and no one had the power to overturn God's will and His purpose. It was Christmas morning! Erin was so excited about seeing Oliver in just a few hours, she could hardly quiet her mind long enough to sleep. Still, she prayed for God's peace, and before long she managed to drift off to sleep. However, Oliver was the star in every single dream she had on Christmas morning in the very wee hours.

***

"Thank you so much for being my date tonight, Ollie. I had a wonderful time!" Rain told Oliver. He'd just walked her to her door. She was staring dreamily up at him. In his dark jeans and rust-colored shirt, he looked swelteringly hot. Rain liked to see Oliver dressed in business suits, but every once in a while, it was nice to know that he could genuinely rock *any* look, and still be the most gorgeous man she'd ever laid eyes on.

"You're welcome! I had a great time," Oliver said in earnest.

"You made the party wonderful for me, Ollie!" Rain attested. Wrapping her arms around Oliver, she drew him in for a lasting hug.

Oliver laughed lightly. Hugging Rain back, they swayed in a gentle embrace. "Merry Christmas, my dear friend!" he said, pulling back to connect to her eyes.

"Merry Christmas, Ollie," Rain said quietly, losing herself in his honey eyes.

"Well," Oliver pulled away unobtrusively, "I have a little something for you." His coffee skin turned ruddy, and there was a twinkle in his eye.

"Oh...?" Rain questioned, surprised. She was surprised that Oliver wanted to offer up a gift at that time. She had thought that he'd come over later, and that they would exchange gifts then. Rain was having a get together with friends, some of her guests had known her and Oliver since law school.

Oliver pulled out the festive red envelope he'd kept concealed behind him, as they'd walked up to her apartment door. "Merry Christmas," he said again, extending the envelope to Rain. "I hope you like it." His face furrowed in uncertainty.

"I'm *sure* I will," Rain affirmed. "Ollie, I thought you were coming by my place later-you know for the luncheon?"

Oliver frowned. "Rain, I'm sorry. You *do* remember that I said that I wouldn't be available at all tomorrow," he stated directly. "I'm so sorry I won't be able to make the luncheon."

"Oh...?" Rain assessed, disappointed. "I must have

misunderstood what you told me that day. But Janet and Raj are coming. They were so excited to hear that you would be here," Rain argued, totally bummed out.

"Please, tell them I said hello and Merry Christmas. I promise to do a raincheck with them, but tomorrow doesn't work for me."

"What about later on in the evening? You can come over. Maybe we can go see the new superhero action movie that came out on Friday?" Rain enticed.

However, Oliver held his ground with an irresistible smile. "I wish I could, Rain, but no. In fact, a lot is riding on how things play out tomorrow. I will call you just as soon as I can. We can plan something for another time. So, I'm afraid this is goodnight. Merry Christmas again!" Oliver heralded.

Rain couldn't even conceal her disappointment, as Oliver began to turn away. "Ollie, hold on a minute," she said, halting him.

Oliver stood out in the hallway and waited while Rain went inside of her apartment. Moments later, she returned holding a large gift bag containing a pretty sizable gift. Her pretty face veiled in frowns, but she forced herself to sound optimistic. "This is for you. I thought we'd get to hang out later, but..." Rain's expression was that of disillusionment.

Oliver gasped to catch his breath in shock. "You really shouldn't have." He marveled as he examined the huge gift box, meticulously and professionally wrapped in glossy red and gold gift-wrapping paper. "This is beautiful!" Tears gleamed in his eyes. "Thank you so much!" He hunched down and pressed a kiss to Rain's cheek. Pulling away, he gave her an endearing smile. "I really appreciate it!"

Rain guffawed but couldn't bring herself to smile. It seemed she had lost Oliver for good. There was no doubt in her mind that Oliver's plans more than likely included Erin Brasfield. Rain had seen the intense exchanges between Oliver and Erin at the party. Their connection was magnetic. "I really hope you like it," Rain told Oliver, trying to keep her voice from wavering, even if she was falling apart.

"I'm sure I will. I'll call you," Oliver said, before turning away. He held his hand up, gesturing goodbye. Rain did the same. Ensuing, he turned away and strode over to the elevator.

***

Later, when Oliver got to his complex, he walked down the hallway to Lilly's. Gingerly, he slid a Christmas card underneath her door. The card had within it a gift card to a very popular day spa. Oliver thought she should have something nice. Lilly had been aloof and out of sorts the last time they'd seen each other. Oliver knew that Lilly had gone through a lot, even if she'd recently finalized her divorce. Moreover, her only daughter who lived in Ohio couldn't make it out to *Silver Water* for Christmas.

Oliver veered and began to head away from Lilly's place. However, to his surprise, Lilly's pleasant voice halted him, "Oliver, wait a minute."

Oliver made a sudden turn and smiled timidly at Lilly. "It's late, so I really didn't think you'd be up. I'm so sorry if I woke you." His face strained apologetically, as he floated back over to Lilly's door.

Lilly's expression was sappy and tears shone in her eyes. "*You're* apologizing to *me* for leaving a Christmas card at my door?" She smiled openly, threw her arms around Oliver and hugged him affectionately. "Thank you so much. You are too wonderful for words!" She pulled away and admired him.

Oliver's cheeks were flushed, and he guffawed in deflection. "Lilly, it's not that big a deal. I just wanted you to wish you a Merry Christmas!" Oliver hunched down and pressed a kiss to her cheek.

"Merry Christmas to you, Oliver!" Lilly declared with a face warped in sentimentality. "Thanks for being such a great friend!"

Oliver's face wrinkled in concern. "I just want for you to be alright. I know you've been having a tough time lately." His eyes searched hers, pertained. "Things will get better...I promise." He offered her a genuine smile.

"I think they already have. You're a *great* DA, Oliver Wright," Lilly praised. "But you're an even *better* man."

I'm okay...I guess," Oliver said with florid cheeks. "Didn't mean to wake you up after midnight, but Merry Christmas, Lil!" he emphasized.

"Oliver, wait-" Lilly told him with a matter-of-fact expression on her face. "I've got something for you too."

"Wow, okay... I wasn't expecting anything....," Oliver began to say.

"Well, that's what *surprises* are all about. Wait here." Lilly gestured that he not move.

"I'm not moving." Oliver smiled musingly-nonplused that Lilly had thought to get him a gift.

"So, this is for you!" Lilly breezed back over to the front door and handed Oliver a very elaborate gift bag.

"Aw, Lil, you really shouldn't have," Oliver said stirred.

"Oh, yes I should have. You're amazing, and you deserve everything great," she praised.

"That's very sweet of you to say." Oliver humbly accepted her gift. "Thank you so much!"

"Are you having friends and family over later?" Lilly asked.

With a curious expression on his face, Oliver admitted, "Not exactly, but I *do* have plans."

"Well, I hope they're wonderful." Lilly frowned for a moment. "Can I say something?"

"Of course," Oliver encouraged.

"That girl you were leaving the building with on the morning we bumped into each other…?"

"Okay… What about her?" Oliver's face creased in concern.

"Well, she *isn't* right for you. Now, the *other* young lady who helped you with the tree a couple of weeks ago…," Lilly inferred with a widening grin.

Oliver smiled and shook his head nonplused. "Alright… What about *her*?"

Lilly nodded quiescently. "She's the one!" Lilly said straightforwardly.

Oliver's face turned cardinal, as he contemplated that Lilly was on to something. In his heart of hearts, he knew that Erin *was* the one. She was the woman he'd waited for all of his life. "Okay, I will take that under advisement," Oliver said with a quiet smile.

"You *really* should." Lilly laughed and got Oliver to laugh as well.

"Goodnight, Lilly and Merry Christmas again," Oliver said tactfully.

"Merry Christmas, Oliver," Lilly said, as Oliver turned away. She meditatively examined the card in her hand-knowing that Oliver had probably slipped something pretty special on the inside. Oliver was the embodiment of kindness and generosity, and Lilly loved him for it.

It had just turned 1 a.m. when Oliver finally jumped into bed. He set his alarm clock for 6 a.m., because he wanted to get breakfast going for Erin. Everything had to be perfect for their Christmas breakfast rendezvous. It was difficult to keep his mind off of her and kept belaboring all of the wonderful interactions they'd shared at the party. He couldn't wait to see her in just a few hours, stare into her jewel eyes, and to tell her just how much she'd come to mean to him. Holding Erin in his arms and being able to kiss her for the first time, was the stuff dreams were made of. So, for a few fleeting hours until they could be together, Oliver remained in a world of reverie dreaming about Erin.

***

"Good morning, *Stranger*, and Merry Christmas!" Oliver greeted the moment Erin opened up her front door on Christmas morning. He was on top of the world-beaming, and totally excited to be staring into Erin's beautiful face again. Oliver took a moment to scrutinize how amazing Erin looked in her jeans, a stylish red sweater, which covered her small waist and curvy hips.

Erin had a black halter top underneath, because the sweater was off the shoulder. Her stylish short, black coat was partially unzipped, so Oliver admired her flawless skin. It was as malleable as a butterscotch pudding. Notwithstanding, Erin's lengthy hair bounced in curls over her shoulders and back. Oliver was totally enrapt and adrift, as he examined the rare beauty facing him.

"Good morning and Merry Christmas, Ollie!" Erin said. "You're right on time I see," she razzed.

"Well, I had to be, because someone kind of threatened me last night," Oliver joked feeling satiated just standing on Erin's front steps.

"Really...?" Erin bantered, placing her hand on her chin in introspection. "I wonder who on earth would *ever* threaten *you*?"

"Let's just say that I didn't want to rock the boat with this young lady." Oliver winked playfully.

"Oh, she sounds mean," Erin teased, laughing. Taking a moment to size up how gorgeous Oliver looked in his cream-colored sweater, dark jeans, Timberland boots and a stylish butterscotch colored coat, Erin assessed how much she loved his style. Those earthy colors did something to his caramel skin and honey eyes-short of taking her breath away. Oliver's clothes always looked as if they'd been selected straight from a men's fashion catalog.

"She *is* a little dangerous," Oliver said trying not to laugh. However, when he and Erin's eyes fastened, they both burst into laughter.

"So, is that what you think of *me*?" Erin set her hands on Oliver's shoulders, and brushed over them caringly. Touching him so familiarly felt like paradise.

Oliver was still laughing. However, he was taken aback by Erin's sudden display of affection. She rested her hands gently on his shoulders. "The truth is that I think she's pretty wonderful." His eyes connected expectantly to hers.

Erin issued a quiet smile, as she searched Oliver's eyes and caressed his shoulders. "She thinks you're pretty wonderful too, and she should *not* have threatened you." She stared fondly at him.

"It's alright, because I forgive her," Oliver rose playfully to the occasion. For a moment he stood there totally bedazzled, overpowered by Erin's tender touch. "So, are you all set to have breakfast with me?" Oliver asked, breaking through the intensity. He was cheerful, and virtually floating on a cloud.

"I'm all set," she said reticently staring sensitively into Oliver's eyes. Erin's arms fell away from Oliver's shoulders.

However, Oliver grasped her right hand, brought it up to his lips and pressed a kiss to it. "Then, let's get you nice and fed, *Stranger*."

"Ollie...?" Erin said as he led her over to his SUV

"Erin...?" Oliver razzed as he secured her inside of the car.

"I'm so glad to be with you today," Erin's voice wavered, as her shimmering eyes fused to his once he took his place behind the wheel.

Oliver issued a quiet and timid smile. Oliver's eyes shone in affect, seeing the glimmer in Erin's eyes. "I'm glad to be with *you*," he emphasized, totally transported.

"I can't believe I get to spend more than just two minutes with you. It's been close to impossible to see you these past couple of weeks," Erin relayed, as Oliver drove away from the house. It had been a little over two weeks since she'd smiled so much. Every time she and Oliver locked eyes, it was overwhelming.

"Yeah, I know. I apologize for that. I hate to admit that you were right," Oliver told Erin at a stop light.

"What was I right about, Ollie?" Erin asked, curious.

"Well, you *did* say that we would probably get to spend a little time together *after* the Christmas party."

"I did say that, huh?" Erin's face crinkled in irony. "And you listened to me?"

"I always listen to everything you say," Oliver announced. He'd just slipped into the expressway. It was early enough on Christmas morning not to be bombarded by traffic.

"You do?" Erin asked, surprised. "Why?"

"Because you're wise. I also think you're smart, and that you have the best intuition of anyone I've ever known." Oliver turned to smile over at her.

"Aren't you sweet? Thanks for saying that, Ollie," Erin gushed.

"Here we go again with the *sappy*. Now, Miss Erin, we've already talked about that. Is this what I'm to expect this morning?" Oliver quipped.

Erin feigned a surprised expression. "Ollie, *you* started it. You do this to me all the time. You'll say something totally uplifting." She gestured as Oliver laughed. "And then, when I start to get all sentimental, you zap me."

Oliver couldn't help laughing. "I would never *zap* you," he teased, chuckling.

"You *zap* me all the time," Erin said. Realizing just how silly she sounded, she burst into laughter as well. She tried to keep a serious expression on her face while staring over at Oliver, but couldn't.

"Okay, so I'm a *zapper* now?" Oliver badgered. He winked and shook his head nonsensically.

"You're a total zapper," Erin said giggling. "You have a PHD in the field."

"I graduated at the top of my class," Oliver joshed.

"And with honors...," Erin heckled as they drove over to his place.

There was an underlying sense of contentment just being together. For Oliver and Erin, it didn't matter whether they were on a drive, putting up a Christmas tree or planning a party. Being together was all that mattered. That Christmas morning the two exchanged furtive looks and quiet smiles. They were both aware that something had changed between them, and they were excited to unfold the next chapter in their story.

***

"I beat you over to the elevator, so that means you get to open *my* presents first," Erin announced, brushing her shoulder against Oliver's once on the elevator.

Oliver grasped Erin's hand, and playfully collected her in his arms. Keeping his right arm around her waist, he gently restrained her as he stared into her eyes. "Do you really think you won fair and square?" he asked, magnetized.

"Yes, I won fair and square," Erin quipped, surprised by Oliver's sudden move, and overwhelmed by his loving touch. Her heart was racing and trouncing all once, and her stomach lunged as if she'd just dipped down while on a roller coaster.

"So, you really don't think it was cheating that you ran ahead of me the moment we got out of the car?" Oliver teased, encircling Erin in his arms, completely absorbed.

"No, it wasn't cheating," Erin's words trailed as she inched up closer to Oliver. "It's not my fault that you're a slowpoke, but you should definitely open up my presents first…" Erin was swept away, and the moment felt surreal.

"So, should we open up our presents *before* or *after* breakfast?" Oliver asked breathily-totally gripped, with his eyes affixed to Erin's candy mouth. "Since, after all, *you're* making up the rules…" Oliver leaned in to kiss her, but the elevator doors opened just then, revealing a few people who lived on his floor. Oliver and Erin gave each other curious looks, and instinctively pulled away.

"Merry Christmas," the building tenants said.

Both Oliver and Erin muttered the same before stepping off of the elevator. Erin kept a hold on Oliver's hand, as they made their way over to his apartment. Oliver kept staring down at her protectively, relishing the feel of her hand on him. "So, here we are, Miss Erin!" Oliver announced, after opening up the front door.

"The tree looks even prettier than I remembered," Erin acclaimed, staring at the tree and marveling. "Look at all those gifts!" She turned and found Oliver standing close behind her. "It's so beautiful, Ollie!" Erin looked up at him, grinning.

"It's breathtaking!" he said adrift, compelled by everything Erin. "Even more than that *tree you* brighten up every corner of this place," Oliver said with a gravelly tone.

"I love being here!" Erin met his eyes expectantly.

"I love *having* you here!" Oliver affirmed. There was so much he wanted to say, but he wanted to share his heart at the right moment. "So, come with me…," he introduced, taking Erin's hand in his. "I have breakfast all set up for us."

"Oh, in that case, lead the way, Mr. DA." Erin squeezed his hand in hers and smiled up into his eyes.

Oliver led Erin over to the kitchen where he'd set up an elaborate breakfast spread. Oliver had taken time and had cooked omelets, pancakes, French toast, crepes. Moreover, he had fresh fruit, toast, coffee and juice. Erin marveled as she stood in the doorway. "Did you do all of this?" She turned to face him.

"Pretty much," Oliver said, taking in how pretty she looked against the backdrop. Up until that very moment he had not fully grasped just how much he'd missed her.

Tears gleamed in Erin's eyes. She instinctively threw her arms around Oliver and squeezed him lovingly. "How could you be so wonderful?" She crushed him in her arms and didn't let go for a moment. "This is incredible," she muttered.

Oliver had gulped because Erin had knocked the wind out of him. Laughing, he slipped his arms around her waist, and held on just as potently. "I wanted to make Christmas Day special for you," he said, throatily, squeezing her devotedly.

"Ollie, this is perfect," Erin pulled away enough to stare into his eyes. "I guess when you invite a girl over for breakfast, you're not playing around."

Oliver laughed and sensitively explored her eyes. "Well, this isn't for any ordinary girl. She's *very* special," his voice broke. "So, everything had to be perfect." He smiled sentimentally into her eyes.

Erin's face warped in nostalgia, as she inched up and pressed a kiss to Oliver's cheek. She wanted to *really* kiss him, but didn't want to be the one to initiate it. She sensed that Oliver probably wanted to kiss her too, but he was holding back for one reason or another. However, Erin decided to wait until all of the roadblocks were gone, because it would be so worth it when it finally did happen. "Thank you so much."

"You are very welcome!" Oliver smiled warmly at Erin. He didn't realize how difficult it would be to hold off kissing her. But until they talked things out, he couldn't let her know that he was madly in love. Gently pulling away, he grasped her hand in his. "So, come on, *Stranger*, let's get some breakfast into you," he said leading her over to the quaint kitchen table.

"Everything looks so good! Where do I even start?" Erin delighted as she perused all of the wonderful fixings on the counter. "I've got to have some of the crepe with icing." Erin began to put items on her plate.

Oliver stood back, quietly contemplating how happy Erin was. At that moment it dawned on him how much he enjoyed putting a smile on her face. It was something he wanted to do every single day.

"Ollie, aren't you going to join me?" Erin asked, overwhelmed by the way Oliver was staring at her.

"Of course, I am," Oliver told her, still totally fascinated by the rare beauty standing in his kitchen.

"Well then, come on…" Erin grasped his arm, and had him pick out the things he wanted. She figured that at the very least she could fix him a plate.

"Alright, *bossy*, I will have everything you've set on *your* plate." Oliver shook his head amused by Erin's excitement. He'd gotten up pretty early to create the Christmas feast just for her, and he was totally stirred that she was impressed by his gesture.

"Thanks, Ollie. I love all of this!" Erin emphasized, as he pulled out a chair for her at the kitchen table.

"It means so much to me that you do." Oliver took his place across from her at the table, and just watched her. Sporadically, Erin had to keep reminding him to eat, because he couldn't take his eyes off of her. Every time their eyes locked, it established just how much he needed Erin in his life. And, that morning Oliver determined to let Erin know how much she'd come to mean to him.

It was after nine a.m. when Oliver and Erin drifted back over to the living room. By then, the sun was peering through the living room curtains, and filtering through the expansive room. She and Oliver were sitting on the plush carpeting across from each other, crisscross-applesauce style near the majestic Christmas tree. It was just like the last time they'd been together. The faux logs in Oliver's synthetic fireplace were radiating, toasting the air around them. Notwithstanding, Oliver had Christmas music playing in the background.

Both kept the gifts they'd gotten for each other close by. The couple momentarily basked in the joy of being alone together again. Erin stared devotedly over at Oliver-totally overwhelmed to be so close to him. "Breakfast was wonderful, Ollie! Thank you so much!" She smiled into his eyes.

"I'm glad you enjoyed it." Oliver grew pensive. Inwardly, he was struggling to find the right words to share his heart.

"So, are we ready to open up gifts?" Erin asked in order to overcome the intensity in the air. She could feel something weighing heavily on Oliver's heart. There was a lot *she* wanted to say, but she would wait for the proper segue.

"I'm totally ready to open up gifts." Oliver nodded in agreement. "So, since you beat me over to the elevator," he winked, "I guess *you* should be the one to start." Oliver kept staring meditatively over at Erin-taking in every inch of her in utter fascination.

"Yay," Erin cheered like a little girl. "So, okay," she searched Oliver's eyes wonderingly, "this is the first one." She handed a beautifully packaged gift box over to Oliver. The present was wrapped in white and gold paper and a gold ribbon.

"For *me*, *Stranger*?" he teased, exploring her beautiful face.

"For you…," she assured.

"Alright…" Oliver gingerly undid the wrapping paper. Opening up the white gift box underneath, revealed a stylish designer burgundy colored sweater. It appeared to be very expensive! His face lit up as his eyes connected to Erin's. "This is gorgeous and just the right size!" he praised, pulling the sweater out of the box.

"Do you like it? When I saw it at the department store, I *knew* I had to get it for you," Erin cheered.

"Are you kidding me? I love it. Thank you!" Oliver reached over and pressed a kiss to Erin's cheek.

"I'm so glad you like it. I can't wait to see you in it." Her entire face lit up. "Now, open up the others," Erin goaded.

"Okay, Miss bossy." Oliver winked. He then ventured into the two smaller gift boxes. Erin had gotten him a very pricy and trendy men's cologne and cufflinks. Oliver was over the top excited about her gift choices. As he sat there and watched her celebrate every time he opened up a present, it endeared her all the more to him. "Erin, I love everything you've gotten for me!" Oliver was stirred, and his eyes gleamed in affect. "Everything's perfect."

"Well, the gentleman is *very* special, so I had to choose only the very best," Erin uplifted with tears shining in her eyes.

"Oh, Erin…" Oliver grasped her hands in his, brought them to his mouth and covered them in kisses.

"Ollie…," Erin said, breathless and overwhelmed by his fond kisses. She sighed in bewilderment, because Oliver wouldn't let go of her hands.

"So…," Oliver deliberated, trying to weigh his words. His heart thudded in his chest as he kept a firm grasp on Erin's hands. He kept stroking them caringly and covering them in kisses.

Confused and totally mesmerized, Erin remained silent. She was befuddled as she examined Oliver. "Is everything alright, Ollie?" she finally asked in a hushed tone.

Oliver nodded. "Everything is just wonderful!" He smiled sentimentally. "*So* much has happened in the past couple of weeks. I've been longing to share the ins and outs of *everything* with you," Oliver began to say, exploring Erin's eyes. "It has killed me to be pulled away from you for one reason or another these past couple of weeks."

Erin's chest rose and fell dramatically, and her breathing was suddenly labored. Her heart kept skipping a beat as Oliver caressed her hands. She gulped nervously, doing all she could not to interrupt him.

"I've wanted to share all of my courtroom victories with you. I wanted to tell you that things are beginning to look up for Taren, because Kennedy decided to write that impact letter after all. I also wanted to tell you that she and Kayden gifted me with two million dollars…"

Erin's eyes widened in shock, and she nodded quiescently. "That's wonderful, Ollie! I'm so happy for you!" she cheered.

"It *is* pretty wonderful." Oliver smiled into her eyes. "Erin, I've been meaning to tell you just how much I hate driving over to Greensville Correctional to attend parole board hearings. Then, there's this serial murder case which has me going in circles. I feel so burdened at times that it's difficult to sleep," he admitted.

"Ollie, you can always talk to me," Erin reassured, vicariously feeling his pain.

"I know that, Erin. The truth is that I *want* to talk to you *all* the time." Tears were in Oliver's eyes. "What I'm trying to say is that it has taken some time, but I realize just how much I need you," his voice broke.

Erin's face wrinkled in mawkishness, and her mouth gaped in shock. "Ollie…," she whispered, heartened. "I need you too."

Oliver brought her hands up to his lips once again and kissed every inch. "Erin, there's more," Oliver disclosed with a face wrinkled in involvement.

"What is it, Ollie?" Erin searched his face and eyes expectantly.

Suddenly bounding to his feet, Oliver extended his hand out to Erin. Placing her dainty hand in his, he guided her up to her feet. With a firm grasp on her hands once again, he explored her eyes sensitively. "I'm so sorry, honey."

"Why are you sorry, Ollie?" Erin's voice undulated.

"I'm so sorry that I pushed you away. You didn't deserve to be treated that way. When things fell apart with Kennedy, *you're* the one who kept me from losing it. I'm *so* sorry." He kept shaking his head in regret.

Erin gently reclaimed her hands, and gingerly draped her arms about Oliver's neck. Crushing him to herself, she ploughed her finger through his soft thick hair. "You have nothing to be sorry about."

"Yes, I do," Oliver refuted, inching away to connect to her eyes. "I didn't realize just how scared I was after I lost Kennedy. I was terrified of having my heart broken again, and I hurt *you*." His arms encircled Erin's waist as he tenderly examined her. "Look at me," he gently prodded.

Erin looked up and met Oliver's sad eyes with uncertainty. "I know you've been scared. You were devastated after what happened. I understand that," she granted.

"Well, I'm not scared anymore." Oliver shook his head contrarily. "Erin, I love you!" he finally said, with tears escaping the corners of his eyes.

Erin gasped in shock, totally nonplused. "What...?"

"I love you!" Oliver said again. Propping his heard to hers, he covered her face in tender kisses, while avidly searching for her lips. Finding her lips, Oliver teased the corners of her mouth, until she surrendered to his embrace. Ravenous, he traced the outlines of her mouth, avidly extracting honey from its source. Erin responded just as ardently to his kiss.

For Erin, the experience felt out of body. She had prayed and had fasted for this moment. Oliver had just told her that he loved her. She was wrapped securely in his arms and tasting his candy mouth. The reality far exceeded any of her dreams and brought tears to her eyes. Erin had known that it would have been this way if Oliver ever kissed her. Everything about him was addictive, his touch, his caress and his scintillating kiss. "I love you too, Ollie," Erin

whispered in between fluttery kisses. She cradled his face in her
hands and raked her fingers softly through his hair.

"I love you, and I want to be with you," Oliver declared. "I'm
so sorry for hurting you." He kissed away all of her tears. "You
mean the world to me!" he stated emphatically.

"I want to be with *you*." Erin crushed him in her arms.
Pulling away, she caressed his face, and searched his eyes. "You
don't have to be sorry. Everything happened the way it was
supposed to." Fresh tears shone in her eyes. "I've prayed and cried
for this moment. I love you so much!"

Oliver held Erin acquisitively, swaying her body in a gentle
rhythm. "I love you more, babe!" He covered her in kisses and
nestled closely. "I've wanted to tell you that for the past couple of
weeks," he admitted throatily.

Erin couldn't stop crying and trembling, because she was
completely overwhelmed. Her face warped in brokenness,
incredulous, as she searched Oliver's face. "Is this *really* happening
right now?"

Oliver laughed, and pressed kisses all over her face. "If for
some reason we're *both* dreaming, I never want to wake up. I'm so
sorry that it took so long for me to come to my senses." He pressed
his lips to hers in wispy kisses-smiling through tears of his own.

"It's alright, Ollie. I would have never given up, because
you're so worth it."

"*You're* worth it, baby." He pressed a kiss to her forehead
and smiled. Keeping his arms enfolded about Erin's waist, Oliver
pulled away enough to look into her eyes. Utterly enthralled, his
face relayed the joy welling up on the inside. "I knew that I was in
trouble two weeks ago after spending the day together," he
confessed. Oliver's hand brushed rhythmically on the sides of Erin's
waist.

Erin was all aglow in Oliver's arms, and she savored their
closeness. At any moment she kept expecting someone to rouse her
from reverie. "I was doing all I could to pull away after the talk we

had in your office a couple of weeks ago. And yet, when I saw you that Saturday afternoon... Well, staying away from *you* is easier said than done, Oliver Wright," Erin disclosed.

"I'm so glad you offered to help me with the tree. The truth is that if you hadn't, I wouldn't have cared." Oliver cradled Erin in his arms and stared fondly at her. Exploring her eyes, he went on to explain. "When you handed in your letter of resignation, it really hit home. I didn't know how much that would hurt. It made me realize just how much I would miss you.

"It bothered me that we'd stopped talking and texting. So, telling me you were leaving the DA's office was a total nightmare for me." Oliver's face bridged to Erin's again. "It felt like I was losing my best friend," he said hoarsely and pressed a kiss up to her nose. "Nothing mattered if I couldn't do it with you. So, when I saw you at the office on that Saturday afternoon, I knew that God was answering the cry of my heart," Oliver admitted.

"I was so scared, Ollie," Erin admitted. "I didn't want my feelings for you to keep growing, but it was a losing battle. I was afraid that you'd *never* feel the same way about *me*."

"Well, you don't have to be afraid about anything, Erin Emily." Tears were in Oliver's eyes again, as he covetously pulled her to himself. "I love you more than anything in the world!" Cradling her face in his hands, he emphasized, "*More than anything.*"

"Oh, Ollie..." Erin surrendered to his arms and wrapped her arms about his neck. For a moment, neither spoke, but swayed in tender cadences in each other's arms.

When they finally pulled away, Oliver still kept a firm grasp on Erin's hands.

"I thought *I* was the sappy one," she said laughing through the tears.

"I guess you caught me at a rare moment." Oliver laughed but held on.

"Uh-huh-whatever you say, Mr. DA," Erin quipped. *"I'm* going to have to zap *you."* She smiled into his eyes.

"Oh no, *please* don't zap me." Oliver chuckled.

There was a quirky expression on Erin's face. "Okay, I might not zap you today, but…"

"Well, before you consider firing up the laser, can we open up *my* presents now?" Oliver teased.

Erin's smile was uncontainable. "What laser?" she heckled. "I will gladly open up *my* presents now, Fine Sir," she joshed.

"I *thought* you'd say that." Oliver winked, guiding her closer to the Christmas tree. "So, close your eyes," he encouraged.

"They're closed," Erin said in anticipation.

"So, this is your first present," Oliver announced. "You can open up your eyes now."

Erin opened up her eyes and smiled excitedly when Oliver tendered a small wrapped gift. Their eyes connected with so much love and promise. "Ollie, what is this?"

"Well, there's only one way to find out." Oliver watched Erin undo the giftwrapping paper on the present. Admiration and dignity inundated his heart watching her. She was so beautiful to him, and he quietly celebrated the fact that she loved him.

Erin's mouth gaped in shock when she saw the black velvet jewelry box. "Ollie…" She stared at him in skepticism when she opened it up and saw the diamond earrings. Her face warped in sentimentality. "They're beautiful!" She cradled his face in her hands and pressed a honey kiss to his mouth. "I love it! I love you!" Tears were in her eyes.

However, Oliver pulled her in for a few more kisses. "I love you too, baby. You're my heart," he reminded her. "So, don't fire up the zapping laser yet. There are a few more things I wanted for you to have today," his voice broke.

"I have *everything* I've ever wanted right in front of me." Erin kissed him again. "I get to kiss you and be close to you. What more can a girl ask for?"

"You deserve the world, baby, and I want to give it to you." They nestled.

"Oh, Ollie…"

Oliver gently pushed away. "There's more," he goaded. He hunched down and retrieved a small gift bag containing Erin's perfume. What she didn't know was that he'd had a fragrance designed just for her. Fittingly, he called it *Stranger-Erin's Song.*

"Oliver Wright, what is this?" Erin examined the thirty-two ounce bottle of perfume. "I've never seen this one before. Oh, my goodness!" she celebrated. "Ollie, you didn't…" She stared at him marveling.

"It's your *own* fragrance, *Stranger*," he quipped. "I worked with a few specialists in creating it just for you."

Erin excitedly removed the hourglass-shaped bottle from the box. She removed the cap off of the spray nozzle, and released the sweet, spicy and floral fragrance into the air. "Oh, my goodness, it's wonderful!" Erin sprayed the insides of her wrists and rubbed them both to the sides of her neck.

"Mm…," Oliver relished, hugging her to himself. "It suits you, my beautiful queen!"

"I love it, Ollie!" Erin inhaled the lovely scent Oliver had created just for her.

"You smell like a dream!" Oliver was ecstatic. "Okay, so that's enough of that," he said with a mischievous smile. "There's a lot more, but I'm going to have to rush the process along." Oliver glanced at his watch.

"Ollie, I don't think I can handle anything else," Erin complained.

"Oh, but you're going to *have* to indulge me. Do you trust

me?" Oliver's eyes lowered weightily into hers.

"You *know* I do," Erin said shakily, uncertain as to why Oliver had just asked that question.

"So, if you look in *that* gift bag over there," Oliver pointed to an eclectic green and gold colored gift bag, "there's a gift card to all of your favorite shopping outlets."

"Now, *that's* romantic-telling a girl what her gift is before she opens it."

"I happen to think that it's *very* romantic." Oliver sweetly bridged his lips to hers. "Do you trust me?" he asked again with an undulating voice.

"Of course I do, Ollie." Erin's face wrinkled in concern.

"Okay, so *this* present is the last of them." Oliver hunched down and picked up a tiny silver gift box from underneath the tree. However, he didn't hand it over to Erin. Rather, he removed a small forest-green velvet jewelry box from inside.

Erin's jaw dropped, her eyes widened, and her mouth gaped seeing the jewelry box in his hand. Erin set her hands over her mouth in utter shock. "Oliver, what...?"

Oliver genuflected to one knee, opening up the jewelry box uncovering a clear Princess Cut 20 carat diamond engagement ring. Smiling through the tears in his eyes, Oliver humbly inquired, "Erin Emily Brasfield, will you marry me?"

Erin's mouth was still covered in astonishment. Tears meandered down her cheeks, and she was trembling. Nonplused, she shook her head contrarily. "Oliver Wright, what are you doing?" she was finally able to verbalize.

"I'm asking if you will marry me, *Stranger*. Do I *have* to remain in this position all day?" Oliver quipped. "Now what do you say?"

Erin pulled him up from off of his knees and wrapped her arms lovingly around him. She began to cry unrestrained, as she held on portentously. "I love you so much, Ollie! I love you."

Oliver laughed, and swayed her gently in his embrace. "I love you too, baby! I love you more than life itself."

Erin pulled away cradling his head in her hands, still in tears and trembling. "I want to marry you more than anything else in the world!" she affirmed.

"Okay, so you *had* to leave me hanging…," Oliver jested.

"Shut up," Erin heckled.

"Make me," Oliver said huskily, pulling her in close again. His lips connected hungrily to hers, and he took his time kissing every inch of her mouth. In between butterfly kisses, he kept reminding her of how much he loved and cared.

"So, are you ready to go home and pack? It's just after ten, and I figure we can make it over to the private jet at about half past noon-*Georgia* time," Oliver said as they snuggled.

"Oliver Wright, what are you talking about?" Shock and uncertainty veiled Erin's sweet face. She pulled back to stare incredulously over at her fiancé.

"I'd like to get married as soon as possible, if that's alright with you," he stated decisively. "Did you think I proposed *today*, because I wanted to get married months down the line?" he questioned.

"You want for us to get married *today*?" Erin's face creased in incredulity.

"That is if you don't have any other plans. Please say you don't…"

"Oliver," Erin guffawed, "I don't even have a dress."

"Do you trust me?" Oliver asked again urgently.

Erin nodded in the affirmative. "With my life…"

"So, here's the plan. We're going on a little trip just you and me. Time is very limited for us. We only have until Wednesday to return to the mayhem of the DA's office. So, I wanted to make the most of our three-day break by spending it together." Oliver removed the ring from its box and slipped it gently on Erin's finger." Tears shone in his eyes parallel to Erin's upon doing so. "It looks so perfect on your finger."

"*You're* perfect," Erin uplifted, fighting back sentimental tears.

"I guess you didn't understand what I tried to explain before. Erin, I want to share the ins and outs of *every* day with you. Being without you these past two weeks has been sheer torture. I don't *ever* want to be away from you. I want to wake up to you every morning, and I want to come home to you every night."

"Ollie," Erin questioned bewildered, "are you sure?"

"I've never been surer of *anything* in my life. We've known each other for a while now, and we've only grown closer in the past year. Sometimes, you just know." He searched her eyes portentously. "You should know that I experienced withdrawal symptoms after I said goodnight to you on that Saturday. We'd spent the entire day together, and I couldn't breathe when you were gone. You should also know that last night, I wanted to beat Gray Andrews to a pulp," he admitted.

Laughing, Erin shook her head humorously. "Oh, Ollie, *you* wanted to beat up Gray?" she questioned.

"To a *pulp*," Oliver emphasized, comically.

"I'm so sorry about that whole thing with Gray. I really didn't plan it."

"I know you didn't. What can I say? Gray has great taste, but he can't have you, because you're *mine*. Promise that you'll be mine forever and always, Erin Emily?" Oliver's face frowned in jeopardy.

"When does our flight leave?" Erin asked, wrapping her arms around Oliver and holding on for dear life. "You've made my dreams come true," she whispered into his chest. "I love you so much!"

"Love doesn't even begin to cover it for me. Baby, I want to take care of you for the rest of our lives." Oliver planted kisses all over Erin's face. The two smiled into each other's eyes with a sense of expectation and adventure.

"So, how long do you think it will take for you to pack a bag?" Oliver asked after they cleaned up from breakfast, and the clutter around opening up gifts near the tree.

"Not long." Erin stared admiringly over at her fiancé and examined the ring on her finger. "But you didn't tell me where we're going."

Oliver had just gotten Erin's coat, but he came up behind her, slipping his arms about her waist from the behind. "It's a surprise," he said hoarsely. He then helped her on with her coat and turned her around to face himself. Gazing lovingly down at her, Oliver zipped up her coat. "Do you trust me?" he asked once again, searching her eyes.

"You *know* I do." Erin cradled the side of his face and pressed her lips repeatedly to his. "Where *you* go, I will follow."

"That's good to know, because I'm *never* letting you go."

CHAPTER ELEVEN

On the private jet Oliver had retained, it took less than three hours to get to Aspen, Colorado. Erin and Oliver enjoyed a peaceful and halcyon flight. They cuddled and fell asleep in each other's arms, because both been up with the sun back out in Silver Water.

Erin was like a little girl when they got into their car rental. Oliver had rented a capable 4x4 to handle the mountainous, and snowy terrain over to their private lodge. The two held hands taking in the gorgeous scenery of purple mountains with white icing covering the peaks. The sun blazed vigorously in the vista pouring over the majestic mountains like melted caramel. "Ollie, this is beautiful!" Erin took in the snowy backdrop. "This is what Christmas *should* look like!"

"Yeah, we're cheated of feet of snow yearly living out in Silver Water." Oliver met her eyes for a moment and smiled. He then lovingly squeezed her hand in his.

"But I love living out in Silver Water!" Erin said timidly meeting his eyes. "It's where I met the man I'm going to marry," she affirmed, elated.

"Is that so?" Oliver bantered.

"I hear Silver County's DA is really *hot*." Her cheeks turned scarlet.

"Well, *I* heard that there's this gorgeous and amazing woman who works through that office that he's absolutely crazy about."

"Does she know?" Erin rose playfully to the occasion.

"Yeah, he told her…today in fact." Oliver pressed a kiss to Erin's hand.

"She's very lucky."

"I think he's the lucky one." Their eyes met again at a red light.

"It's only 12:15 p.m. out here."

"Yeah, I knew that. There's a two-hour difference."

"You couldn't have planned it more perfectly."

"I *know* what I want." He winked. "Speaking of which, as soon I unload the truck, I'm going to bring you over to *Audrina's Wedding House*, where they're going to get you all ready for…" Oliver's cheeks turned cardinal.

"Ollie, you planned all of this? What if I'd said *no* today?" Erin quipped.

"I would probably be here all by my lonesome, but I hoped and prayed."

"I would have said *yes* even if we only had *today* to spend together," Erin said sappily. "I love you!"

"I love you, baby!"

"What about *you*, Ollie? Where will you be while I'm at *Audrina's*?" Erin asked.

"I will be nearby picking up a tux and making sure our pastor will meet us at the lodge by five."

"Do we have witnesses?" Erin tested.

"I've already taken care of all of the intricacies. The wedding officiate will provide our wedding license and certificates."

"I'm impressed to no end, Mr. Oliver Baron Wright. You've left no stone unturned."

"You'd better believe that I wasn't taking any chances when it comes to you," Oliver said more critically.

***

Erin and Oliver settled into their private lodge in the heart of *Crested Butte*, which said to be Colorado's last great skiing town. The area was landmark and historic. Their private suite included a family room, kitchen, spacious master bedroom, a Hot tub and Jacuzzi. However, before they left their private lodge, they took a moment to explore the deck area outside of their bedroom, which overlooked the picturesque violet mountains. "Ollie, this is perfect," Erin praised, while taking in the scenery. "You've paid such close attention to every detail." She turned to face him, but found herself caught up in his arms.

Oliver crushed her in his arms and kissed every contour of her face. "I had to." He pulled away to examined her. "I wanted this day to be very special. It isn't every day that I get to marry my *stranger*." Moved beyond words, Oliver tightened his arms about Erin's waist.

"I keep thinking that any minute someone's going to wake me up." Erin stared dreamily into Oliver's eyes. "I want to stay in this dream with you forever." She cradled his face in her hands, reached up and pressed kisses to his mouth.

"You don't have to worry about waking up, because I'm *never* letting go," Oliver said in between honey kisses. "Erin," he admitted tearing up, "I didn't think I could have this with anyone. I was always the odd man out, but I made up my mind that things would be different this time." He kept shaking his head in the negative. "There was way too much at stake. I wasn't about to lose you." He buried his head in her silken bed of hair.

"I would never hurt you, Ollie." Erin swayed tenderly in their embrace. "You never have to worry about being odd man out with *me*. You will always be my first choice," she affirmed. Pressing kisses to his cheek.

"You will always be my *only* choice," Oliver stressed, pulling away to connect to her eyes. "Are we ready to do this?" He stared lovingly into her eyes.

"I've been ready for a while now." Erin winked.

"Sorry to have kept you waiting." Oliver hunched down and bridged his mouth to hers.

"That's alright. All is forgiven today," Erin said in between kisses.

"Thank you for forgiving me," Oliver said, touring her mouth with sugar kisses.

"Anytime…"

"So, I will see you in just a little while," Oliver told Erin just before he left *Audrina's Wedding House*. "I love the ring you picked out for me by the way," he complimented, devotedly searching her eyes.

"I thought it looked good on your finger too, Ollie," Erin agreed. She suddenly frowned as their eyes locked. "Ollie, I know it's only a few hours, but I don't want you to go," she complained, slipping her arms about his waist.

"It will fly by like nothing, baby. I promise." Oliver hunched down and coated Erin's lips with confectionary kisses.

"I just want you with me all the time." Erin lavished tender kisses all over his face.

"Do you see what I mean? It's difficult to breathe even for a minute when we're apart. But, we're strong enough to handle it," he inspired. "At the end of this wonderful Christmas day, we'll never have to be apart again." His eyes glistened affectively.

Erin nodded and kissed him again. "I love you so much!"

"Oh, babe, I adore you!" he emphasized. "Will you meet me at the altar at five?" he said thickly.

"Just try and stop me." Erin held on to Oliver's hand as he inched away.

Hesitant to leave, Oliver pulled her in for one last kiss. "I can't wait to make you my wife. I love you, baby!" His face warped sentimentally as he said goodbye. Oliver walked away backward, before making himself go through the revolving doors of the bridal shop.

Erin stared ruefully at him through the glass doors. She felt totally disconnected as she watched him jump into their Jeep rental. There was a sense that this dream would evanesce. She kept expecting to wake up in her room at any given time. Erin couldn't bear the thought that none of it was real. The concept was much too cruel.

It didn't make any sense to be this ridiculously happy, and in love with the most wonderful guy in the world. There was a sense that she didn't deserve such a blessing. At that moment, the Spirit of God placed an impression in Erin's spirit.

"This is the moment you've been praying and waiting on. Why would an answered prayer ever be a dream? If you ask anything in my name, I hear, and I answer. Furthermore, Erin, I am gifting you with such a wonderful man of God, because you refused to compromise. When Anika tried to tempt you to go about getting the desire of your heart through treachery and witchcraft, you ran to me. You showed me your heart full of love for my child. It's a love worthy of him, and I have placed a love in his heart worthy of you. So, bask in my blessing and my glory on your wedding day."

Erin allowed a hopeful smile to curve over her lips. Tears of joy were in her eyes, she lifted up her hands in praise to God. She couldn't believe that this was actually happening. She was about to marry Oliver Wright-something she'd never thought would happen. She was head-over-heels in love with him, and he loved her just as fervently. It was all too much to bear.

However, Erin realized that she needed to seize the moment when Audrina Taylor came out to get her. "We're already working on dress alterations, but are you ready for hair and makeup?" Audrina asked. She was a kind woman with a huge head of red hair and a grand personality to match.

"I'm more than ready. Let's go!" Erin affirmed, allowing Audrina to guide her to the hair and makeup room.

"You're going to look amazing, sugar. With that tiny waist

and those curvy hips, you're going to rock that dress," Audrina said taking hold of Erin's hand excitedly in hers.

"Thanks, Audrina," Erin said realizing that this was *really* happening.

"And, about your *fiancé*…?" Audrina brought up.

"Yes…?" Erin asked frazzled.

"He's absolutely *beautiful*! You are one lucky girl!"

Erin's eyes shone in affect, as she met Audrina's eyes. "He is absolutely amazing in every way. I'm not just lucky, Audrina, I'm *blessed*!"

"You sure are, sugar."   Audrina squeezed Erin affectionately.

***

"Mitch…," Oliver announced hugging his friend and law colleague. "You made it! I can't believe you're here," Oliver celebrated.

Mitch patted Oliver's back fraternally and chuckled. "I told you I would show up, and here I am." Mitch pulled away. Opening up his arms, he put himself on display. "You clean up nicely, Ollie," he said with a keen smile.

"You don't look half bad yourself," Oliver returned, beaming. He and Mitch had been good friends for a few years. They'd known each other through the court circuit. However, they'd reconnected when Taren had invited Mitch to come out to *Deliverance Tabernacle*. "I'm so glad you were in the area." Oliver nodded affably, walking through the small church. Mitch would witness Erin and Oliver's wedding.

"I guess it worked out. I had no idea what your plans were

when you called the other day." Mitch shook his head in the negative. He looked every bit the part of the best man in his designer tux. With his milk chocolate skin, button brown eyes, Idris Elba had nothing on the young attorney. "Ollie, I can't tell you enough how happy I am for you. Erin is a great girl!"

"Thanks, Mitch! I'm totally smitten," Oliver admitted overjoyed.

"Well, you deserve to be happy. I knew you were in love with Erin. I could tell on the occasions that I came by your office."

"How on earth did *you* know when *I* didn't even know?" Oliver asked, incredulous.

"Well, it was in your eyes every time she was around. The way you looked at that girl... Man! I kept saying to myself that my buddy's totally in trouble. And I guess I was right, because here you are standing at the altar today. I'm impressed, Ollie. You literally whisked Erin away for a secret wedding rendezvous."

"I'm just glad she decided take me up on my offer."

"Are you kidding? Erin's over the moon in love with you. She has been ever since she started attending *Deliverance*."

Oliver smiled contemplatively to consider those words. It warmed his heart to know that Erin was genuinely the woman God had chosen for him. There were no questions or doubts. He was crazy in love with her, and this time around, the object of his affection loved him back. That realization overwhelmed him with love for Erin and gratitude to God.

"I can't wait to stand in for *you*, Mitch," Oliver uplifted. Even if it was a sore subject. No one knew how things were going to play out for Taren. Would she be sentenced to a year or two in prison, or would she be granted probation? Oliver knew how deeply Mitch loved Taren, and he would continue praying in faith for a favorable outcome.

"Yeah, well, *that* remains to be seen." Sadness masked Mitch's handsome face. "Let's just focus on *you* today." Mitch placed his arm about Oliver's neck and squeezed affectionately. "You make a dapper groom, buddy!" Mitch inspired.

"Thanks, Mitch-and thanks for showing up for me today."

"That's what friends are for," Mitch enlivened.

Sometime later, Pastor Paul Evans told Oliver and Mitch that the ceremony would be starting shortly. Before long, Oliver was standing at the altar, with Mitch to his right-hand side. Pastor Evans and some of the members of his clergy were standing by as well.

The small rustic chapel was embellished with flowers everywhere, and a very impressive wedding arch. There were just about ten people in attendance. The pastor's wife Marjorie would be another witness to the ceremony. However, Mitch was Oliver's main witness and closest friend. Still, it really didn't matter how many people were in attendance. In Oliver's heart and mind, nothing and no one else existed except for Erin and himself.

Oliver quietly anticipated seeing his bride-to-be come through the set of doors within the sanctuary. And right before the wedding march began to strain in the air, his heart anxiously thudded in his chest. Moments later, Oliver saw Erin emerge from the set of doors in her wedding gown. "*Wow!*" he said instinctively, because he was totally breathless.

Tears immediately filled his eyes, as he inspected just how resplendent she looked in the simple white silk gown. The dress hugged Erin's curves and accentuated her tiny waist. The elegant gown was short-sleeved, had a very modest plunging neckline. There was a stylish oval opening in the back, and sheer white buttons along the waistline. Erin's lengthy hair had been highlighted in shades of auburn, honey, maize and amber. The curls tumbled graciously over her shoulders and back, and her face looked positively flawless. Their eyes fastened as they shared loving smiles.

Oliver was completely hypnotized, as his eyes locked to his fiancée's.

Mitch smiled and rubbed supportively on Oliver's arm.

"*Wow*!" Oliver whispered again, dazed and awestruck. In his heart he kept praying and thanking God for giving him this moment. He blinked back tears, as he considered that this was the first time someone loved him back, and it was his God-chosen wife. Bemused, he humbly worshiped God for answered prayer. His heart raced in eagerness as Erin neared the altar.

Erin had to try to keep a stiff upper lip when she saw Oliver standing at the altar. She was completely rapt to see her prince. She'd seen Oliver more than a few dozen times. Each and every time he'd taken her breath away. However, seeing him in his designer navy tux, with navy and royal blue accents, made her legs feel wobbly.

In fact, she was so captivated she was afraid she was going to trip and fall over her new diamond encrusted and pearl heels. She couldn't believe she was a bride. Notwithstanding, she wasn't just *any* bride, but she was about to become the proper bride of Oliver Baron Wright, District Attorney of Silver County. He was the man she'd dreamed about marrying since moving out to Silver Water.

As a very high-profile attorney, Erin had *heard* about and had seen Oliver on social media. So, when Anika had informed her that Oliver Wright attended Deliverance Tabernacle, Erin had made it a point to visit the church. She wound up falling head over heels upon first sight. Almost immediately, she had made up her mind to leave *Touch of God's Spirit Church*, and had started attending Deliverance Tab. Now, this dream man was about to become her husband. Erin couldn't hold back the tears and kept shaking her head in doubt. Her eyes fastened to Oliver's. There was a compelling expression on his face which left her totally captivated.

Erin tried to measure her breathing by inhaling and exhaling as she walked up to the altar. She handed her bouquet over to Marjorie Evans, the pastor's wife. From that point on, she and Oliver were locked into a private world. The two stared hopelessly into each other's eyes sharing furtive messages and smiles. Oliver instinctively grasped Erin's hands in his, focusing on her as if she were the sole person on the planet. "You're absolutely stunning," he said throatily, shaking his head amazed. "You've taken my breath away."

"Can you tell how shaky I am right now? You're *so* handsome," Erin said softly, taking in every inch of the man she loved. Her heart began to hammer in a way it never had before- and that was saying a lot. There was always a similar reaction whenever Oliver was in close proximity. However, this time around, Erin's heart sank to her feet. Furthermore, the butterflies in the hollow of her stomach made her feel woozy and tremulous.

"I love you!" Oliver mouthed just before the pastor began to speak.

"I love you too," Erin said softly, enchanted.

Mitch examined Erin and Oliver's exchanges with extreme gratification. The love emanating from between the two was almost tangible. So, he was overjoyed that someone as wonderful as his buddy Oliver had found such a precious gift. Mitch said a prayer for the couple just before Pastor Evans began to speak.

"On this Christmas day, I pledge myself to you, Erin Emily. I promise to take care of you and to love you through the difficult times. I vow to stand by your side and support you, even if everyone else should turn away. I will cherish every moment we share until the Lord calls me home. You can lean on and depend on me, and I promise to be your biggest fan and advocate.

"This gift of love given to us by God is something that I will *never* take for granted. There will never be a day where you'll have to wonder how I feel about you. Every precious day we have together, I will show in a million different ways that you're everything to me. You can be sure of this one thing. There isn't anyone who will ever love you more!" Oliver shared those words after citing the traditional vows with Pastor Evans.

Erin was in tears after hearing Oliver share his heart. Shakily, she tried to speak, but it took a moment to get her bearings. Oliver stared devotedly into her eyes and squeezed her hands in support. So, she found the strength to speak. "Oliver Baron, the first time I saw you I knew that you were special-unlike *anyone* I'd ever met before. Because I thought you were *so* amazing, I was intimidated, and too afraid to even talk to you.

"However, your kindness and warmth put me right at ease from the moment we were introduced at church. I wasn't sure what to expect, but I've since discovered that you are the truest and most genuine person in the world. There isn't anyone who doesn't benefit from your kindness and generosity. You pour out your entire soul into championing all that is right and just in this world."

Oliver's eyes shone in affect, as Erin poured out her heart. To say he was moved was a total understatement. It was the first time he was hearing how she truly felt. Totally floored and humbled, he found it difficult not to cry.

Overwhelmed, Erin went on to define, "I love you because of your character, your integrity, your tender heart and magnanimity of spirit. You embody all that is good in this world. And," her cheeks turned scarlet, "you're wrapped in the most beautiful package," Erin delighted.

Oliver laughed through the tears forming in his eyes. "You're my queen!" he declared.

"Oliver Baron Wright, I'm so in love with you! On this Christmas day I can't stop praising and thanking God for blessing me with the desire of my heart. I will forever be your biggest fan and cheerleader. Standing staunchly by your side, I will be an avid crusader for all of your worthy causes. You will always be my safe place to fall, and I promise to show you every day just how much you mean to me. I vow to honor and to protect this precious gift given to us by God." Erin stared lovingly into Oliver's eyes as she made her declaration of unremitting love.

"Erin and Oliver today you solemnly pledge to love, cherish, honor and to protect each other forever. The bible teaches that what God has joined together let no man put asunder (Matthew 19:6 Mark 10:9). That means that you, Erin and you, Oliver are that three-fold cord spoken of in the book of Ecclesiastes (4:12). A woman draws her life from man then gives it back again. Fiercely protect your marriage covenant, and God will continue to bless your union," Pastor Evans affirmed. Then, looking from Erin to Oliver with a radiant smile he attested, "We'll have the exchanging of rings at this time."

Oliver was eager to take Erin's hand in his. Gingerly, he slipped on the gold and diamond band-adding to her engagement ring. He smiled devotedly into her eyes, swept away and ecstatic.

Erin delicately grasped Oliver's hand in hers, and slid the gold, diamond encrusted wedding band on his finger. She stared up into her husband's eyes with so much love and dignity stirring on the inside. Their shimmering eyes clasped sentimentally, as they awaited Pastor Evan's cue.

"By the power vested in me by the state of Colorado, I now pronounced you, husband and wife!" Pastor Evans declared with both hands up in the air. "Oliver," he lowered into Oliver's eyes, "you may kiss your bride!"

Entranced and ecstatic, Oliver adroitly drew Erin into his arms, and pressed a soft kiss to her mouth. "I love you, baby!"

"I love *you*," Erin said, smiling deliriously, in between sweet kisses.

"We did it, babe! We're married! I can't believe you're mine," Oliver proclaimed, face propped to his wife's in celebration, while the bystanders clapped and cheered along with them.

"Yes, we did. Ollie," Erin realized, "you're my husband!"

"Yes, babe, I know. That's exactly what I *wanted* to be." His lips amalgamated with Erin's again.

"I'm so happy!" Erin's face warped mawkishly. "I know, I know... You're going to tell me that I'm being sappy again."

"That's okay." Oliver crushed her to himself lovingly. "We're allowed to score high on the sappy meter today." He pressed a kiss to her forehead.

"Ollie, Erin, congratulations!" Mitch drew the newlyweds into his arms, as soon as he had a moment.

"Mitch, I can't believe you're here," Erin marveled, shaking her head incredulous. Oliver was standing close to her side. "Did Ollie let you in on his little plan, and *force* you to come out here?" Erin gave Mitch a quirky yet suspicious look.

Mitch hugged her. "Believe it or not he didn't even tell *me* what he was doing. And he didn't *force* me to come out here. It's an honor for me to witness such a beautiful wedding ceremony," Mitch delighted. "You make a stunning bride!" He pulled away and admired Erin.

"Doesn't she?" Oliver slipped his arm possessively around his wife's waist and stared devotedly at her. "You've taken my breath away, babe!" Oliver pressed a kiss to her cheek.

"Hey, Ollie, take it easy and save some of that for later," Mitch badgered.

"I will try but it isn't easy," Oliver said, catching Erin's eye. He was still having a difficult time wrapping his head around the fact that they were now married.

"Don't worry, Mitch, my *hubby's* the perfect gentleman," Erin stated with pride. "I can't believe I get to say that I have a hubby," she delighted.

Oliver laughed. Shaking his head amused, he hugged her closer to himself. "I can't believe that *I'm* a hubby," he countered playfully. He and Erin exchanged a sweet kiss just then.

"The two of you are already and old married couple," Mitch quipped. "And as corny as the two of you are, I *am* so jealous right now," he teased.

"Aw, Mitch, it's only a matter of time," Erin uplifted.

Oliver reached over, patted Mitch on the arm, and gave him a knowing look.

"Are you ready to get the paperwork out of the way?" Marjorie Evans drifted over to ask the couple.

Both Erin and Oliver nodded in agreement and exchanged

excited looks. "We're ready."

"Mitch, can you hang out for a bit? My wife and I are going to have cake and champagne just next door." Oliver's face fused with joy. "Did I just say my *wife*...?"

"*Yes*, you did. I'm truly happy for you, Ollie! You're a standup guy and great friend! I hope you and Erin have many happy and blessed years together!" Mitch said in earnest with a warm smile.

"Thanks, Mitch," Oliver said, beaming. He kept looking across the room at Erin, who was engaged in conversation with the pastor's wife.

"Of course, ... Are you kidding me? I can't miss having champagne with my best buddy and his new wife." Mitch winked. Oliver grabbed him fraternally by the neck and squeezed. "Come on then, let's get this paperwork out of the way." Oliver conveyed Mitch over to the table just to the side of the pulpit where they had to sign the official documents.

For Oliver the moment felt surreal. There was a new level of dignity as he signed the papers with a wedding band on his finger. It meant that he belonged to someone, and that someone belonged to him. It was all he could do to keep from falling apart, but Erin understood and helped him to hold it together. On that fateful and extremely eventful Christmas day of 2019, their score on the sap-o-meter was a *tilt*, but neither of them cared because both were deliriously happy.

***

Later, back at the lodge Erin and Oliver dressed for bed. Shortly after the reception, they'd taken a drive through the historical town for pictures and videos with the videographer Oliver had hired. Mitch had hung around as well to take a few shots with the newlyweds. Erin and Oliver had ventured into the picturesque village ensuing and had taken a number of pictures using their phones.

Tentatively, they'd made plans to go skiing in the morning. There was a lift service only feet away from the lodge. Besides, having located a number of boutiques, specialty shops and restaurants, the couple couldn't wait to explore the cozy town before returning to Georgia on Wednesday morning.

Oliver had just finished changing and had on a silk wine-colored pair of PJs. They were the *sexiest* thing he had in sleepwear. Usually, he was very modest, but it was his and Erin's wedding night, and he wanted to *look* the part. He couldn't ever remember feeling so happy and content! It had been the best day of his life, and he hoped Erin felt the same way.

Erin slipped out of the adjourning bathroom reticently. She was wearing a pink satin Teddy. Her face appeared fresh and natural. She'd brushed out her lengthy hair, which bounced healthily over her shoulders and back. To Oliver, she was even more beautiful than earlier on-and that was saying a lot. His heart inundated with love and admiration. "Hey there," he said huskily, gaping devotedly at her.

"Hey," Erin said with an irrepressible smile on her face. "You look so good!" She sized Oliver up in his burgundy silk PJ's. Her heart raced, and the butterflies returned to the hollow of her stomach with a vengeance. Erin couldn't believe that this incredibly gorgeous and kind man was *her* husband. She glided over to where Oliver was standing.

"Thank you, baby," Oliver said, pulling her gently into his arms. His face bridged caringly to hers. "So, how are you doing?" he asked throatily.

"I'm in heaven," Erin admitted, still totally enthralled. She had been under the impression that she would have stopped swooning because Oliver was now her husband. However, it seemed that her condition had only worsened. Being in his arms was sheer paradise.

"We've had a pretty eventful day. Are you alright?" Oliver pulled back to connect to her eyes, clasping his arms firmly around her waist.

"I'm great," Erin cheered. "You've made me so happy, Ollie!" she said emotionally with tears shining in her eyes. "I can't believe this day. It has been the most amazing experience of my entire life!" Her face warped sensitively, and tears escaped the corners of her eyes. "I love you so much!"

"Oh, don't cry..." Oliver crushed her to himself and kissed her tears away. "I wanted you to know that you mean *everything* to me." His eyes lowered pivotally into hers. "I didn't want to waste another day holding on to the past, denying that I'm shamelessly in love with you, Erin Emily. I've lost so much in life, but you're the *one* thing I couldn't afford to lose. So, I thank you for taking this chance with me." Oliver smiled wistfully. "You really didn't have to."

"Are you kidding me?" Erin shook her head in skepticism. "For me, this was the chance of a lifetime. Ollie," Erin cradled his face in her hands, "if you had asked me to go to Mars with you today... Guess what? We would be on a spaceship headed over there right now." She reached up and coated his honey-dripped mouth with tender kisses.

"*Oh*, the idea of going away to Mars with you and *never* coming back," Oliver said, sighing and nestling closely to Erin. "I loved exchanging vows with you today, *Mrs. Wright*."

"I loved exchanging vows with *you*, *Mr. Wright*," Erin told him. "Ollie, speaking of love, we've got to go back to that antique shop tomorrow," Erin introduced.

"I saw the way your eyes lit up when we swung by. There were antiques dancing in them," Oliver joked, holding Erin dotingly, and massaging her waist and back.

"And *I* saw the look on *your* face when we passed by the old bookstore. There were books dancing in *yours*," Erin teased, staring at her husband as if he were the ninth wonder of the world.

"Ah, you *do* know me so well," Oliver assented, chuckling.

"'There's something about old books that really get to me,'" Erin spoofed, trying to sound just like Oliver.

"I can't believe you just did that." Oliver shook his head nonsensically. "So, you *have* been paying attention-I guess a little bit too much," he said amusingly.

"'Just give me my *Kindle* on a rainy day,'" Oliver imitated Erin, making a silly face.

"Okay, *touché*, Counselor," Erin granted. "You got me on that one."

"Do I?" Oliver hunched down and began to bait her lips, cautiously administering special attention to every contour. "I want to know everything there is to know about you, baby," his voice broke. "I want to see you when you wake up in the morning in a horrible mood. I want to see tears shining in your eyes after you've watched a sad movie. I want to know when you're happy, stressed, scared…," Oliver interpreted.

"I want to explore everything there is to know about you too, Ollie. You *are*-and *always* will be the most fascinating man I've ever met," Erin said in between butterfly kisses.

"You're just saying that because you married me," Oliver quipped, probing her eyes.

"You, Oliver Baron Wright, my husband, fascinate me to no end," Erin vamped, and squeezed him affectionately.

"Thank you, my love. So…, what do you want to do now?" His brows furrowed in mischief.

Erin blushed and her eyes shied away from staring at him. "Ollie, are you teasing me?"

"Would I *ever* tease you?" he asked farcically tightening his grasp about her waist.

"*Yes,* you would," Erin heckled reticently looking into his eyes.

"Hey," Oliver said seriously, "it's been a long day, and we don't have to…"

"You don't want to?" Erin asked surprised.

"Oh, Erin Wright, do we *even have* to go there?" Oliver stared at her totally nonplused.

The expression on his face made Erin laugh. "Okay, so I'm guessing that you *do* want to."

"Being with *you* in that way for the first time is something so sacred to me. You didn't know you were getting married this morning. So, I don't want to rush into anything else." Oliver cradled Erin's face in his hand and gazed softly into her eyes. "We have our entire lives to be together. I just wanted you to know that there's no pressure. We can take our time developing that part of our relationship," he explained temperately. "Don't you agree?" Oliver's face was masked in uncertainty. The last thing he wanted was to rush that part of their relationship.

Erin was floored by Oliver's words, and she kept shaking her head in disbelief. "I agree, Ollie," she acceded. "I want to be with you more than anything, but it doesn't necessarily *have* to happen on our wedding night."

Oliver smiled into her eyes and rubbed affectionately on her arms. "We've had quite a day, Mrs. Wright, so I'm guessing you're just as tired as I am," Oliver presumed.

"It *has* been a long day, but it's the best day of my entire life." Erin pressed her lips to his. "Let's go to bed." She took Oliver's hand in her.

"I thought you'd never ask." Oliver helped pull back the covers. They slipped into their comfortable, cozy king-sized bed, and cuddled up in each other's arms.

"So, I'm guessing you're not going to leave your poor husband all alone in that den of thieves called the DA's office?" Oliver asked hopefully.

"I've already signed the paperwork for the new law firm...," Erin jested.

"Really...?" Oliver questioned incredulous.

Erin laughed and secured Oliver's arms about her waist. "Just kidding… I would never leave my poor husband all alone in that den of thieves," she bantered. "What I want is to remain as close to him as I possibly can," she delineated.

Oliver sighed in relief. "You really had me going for a moment there, babe."

"So, you're not going to get tired of seeing me at home and around the office?" Erin questioned.

Oliver pressed kisses to her cheek. "My guess is that the DA's office will probably be the only time we get to spend any real time together," he said facetiously, laughing.

Erin giggled. "Oh, my goodness! You're probably right about that. So, I *have* to keep my job there."

"For the record, baby, I don't think I will *ever* get enough face time with my beautiful wife." Oliver squeezed her more endearingly.

"I feel the same way, Ollie," Erin reciprocated. "So, what are we going to tell everyone in the office on Wednesday? They're going to see the rings on our fingers and blast us for not telling them we were getting married."

"Our work colleagues are lovely, but we don't owe them any explanations. We did something for ourselves for once, and I am so happy that we did." Oliver's face wrinkled in the shadows. "There is no way we could have had a big wedding back at home. There's too much happening in Silver County right now." Oliver created affectionate circular patterns on Erin's arm, and her head was pressed up to his chest.

"Especially with a suspected serial killer on the loose," Erin agreed.

"And I didn't want anything or anyone to stop us from living *our* lives, and from grabbing this little chunk of happiness," Oliver explained. "*Stranger*, I do want for us to have a big wedding, once things are a little bit more settled."

"You do?" Erin asked, excited.

"Of course I do, baby. We didn't get to properly celebrate with our families and friends. Today was for *us*, but a few months down the road, it will be for our loved ones," Oliver said wisely. "I want to give you the kind of wedding you've always dreamed about."

"We can plan it for early June-right after your birthday," Erin contrived.
Oliver chuckled, tickled by his wife's enthusiasm. "We can do whatever you want. And this time it's a *party* that we're definitely going to work on *together*." He kissed her.

"I'm so excited, Ollie. So, we can tell our work family that we are planning on having a big wedding. So, they might be just a little bit less mad at us. Of course, there's *one* person who's going to be mad any way you look at it." Erin's face frowned in jeopardy, as something came to mind.

"Who might *that* be, Mrs. Wright?" Oliver was curious.

"Ollie, there's something I have to tell you," Erin brought up.

"What is it, baby?" Oliver asked, disconcerted.

"You should know a few things about your friend Rain," Erin disclosed.

"What's wrong, honey? Did something happen with Rain?" Oliver instinctively held Erin closer to himself.

"You should know why I was a little distant on the day you got back from Rhode Island."

Erin told Oliver about Rain answering his phone, while they were out on Rhode Island visiting with her family. Erin also detailed how Rain had lied, telling her how they'd dated in the past, and how they were a couple. Moreover, Erin explained to her husband how Rain had lied on Friday afternoon in purporting that *he'd* asked to be her date for the Christmas party.

Oliver was both irked and disappointed hearing about the

tricks Rain had pulled in the past couple of weeks. Something else also occurred to him. "Rain lied to *me*. She said that she'd asked *you* whether or not it was alright for me to be her date." Oliver kept shaking his head in total skepticism. He felt betrayed by someone he considered a good friend. However, he was more peeved than hurt by the circumstances. "Rain and I definitely have to talk once we get back," he settled.

"Don't be angry, Ollie," Erin tried to talk him down. "Believe me, I know what it's like to want someone so much that you're willing to compromise your core beliefs just to have them." Erin pressed in closer to Oliver's chest.

"You do?" Oliver softened, pressing kisses to her face.

"Yes, I do. I've made poor choices in the past because of the way I feel about you," she admitted. "It hurt so badly when I loved you so much, and you had eyes for someone else."

"Oh, baby…" Oliver's heart broke as he caressed her. "Hindsight is 20/20. I wish I had had the wisdom to know what was best for me. I'm so sorry for hurting you that way."

"Things had to happen the way they did, Ollie. Otherwise, we would not have matured in the areas we needed to in order to be good for each other. I was sassy and had attitude around Kennedy. I even pulled you away from her a few times," Erin confessed. "So, I get Rain's motivation for being duplicitous."

Oliver chortled. "Oh, honey, thank you for coming clean." He covered his wife in loving kisses. "Now I know that you were willing to fight for me, even back then."

"Like *you* were willing to beat up Gray for *me*?" Erin pressed kisses up to his nose.

"I would have pulverized him," Oliver said only half-joking. "I would fight lions, tigers and bears for you, Mrs. Wright."

"Oh, my!" Erin teased. Laughter resonated in the air.

"Do you want to know something else, Ollie?"

"What, my love?"

"I also don't think anything was wrong with Rain that night you took her to the hospital," she disclosed.

"That…, I kind of figured out on my own," Oliver said, laughing.

"You knew?"

"I had some idea."

"And you went with her anyway?"

"What was I supposed to say, baby? Rain, I know you're *not* really having any abdominal issues. You're a liar, and I'm *not* going to the hospital with you," Oliver heckled. Even *he* had to laugh when he finished saying that.

Erin couldn't help snickering. "Sure, that's *exactly* what you should have told her. " The couple laughed uproariously.

"Come here," Oliver said gutturally, shifting on the bed with Erin in his arms. This time he and Erin were spooning. Oliver held her possessively, pressed kisses into her silken bed of hair, and spoke resonantly into her ear. "You are too much."

"Well, I have to keep up with the DA of Silver County," Erin ragged, caressing Oliver's stalwart arms which encircled her waist. "Are you happy we're spending the night like this?" her voice tinkled like festive bells.

"Erin, *happy* doesn't even begin to cover how I feel right now. More than happy I'm content, because it doesn't really matter what we do. I am on cloud nine just having you close to me. Whether we're skiing or falling asleep in each other's arms, I'm equally satisfied." Oliver pressed devoted kisses to the side of her face and cradled her even more securely.

"Oh, Ollie, I love you so much!"

"I love you even more, *Stranger*."

"Are you tired of talking yet?" Erin goaded.

"You will know when I am," Oliver teased.

"Well, in that case, I can't wait to see some of the old pieces down at the antique store tomorrow. I just love anything vintage," Erin began to say.

Oliver's arms went limps from about her waist, and he feigned very loud snoring.

"Ollie…," Erin said, pretending to be hurt. "Really…?"

"Just kidding," Oliver joked. His arms tightened around her waist again, and he playfully manipulated her to face himself. With their faces pressed up close, he encouraged, "I would love to pick up an old pocket watch for my dad. Maybe, we can find one of those over there."

"I was thinking about shopping for those old-fashioned broaches for my mom. She loves to style out in scarves of all kinds…"

"Oh, that's nice. I want to know more about your parents," Oliver insisted.

The newlyweds stayed up until well past midnight on their wedding night and talked about everything under the sun. When they were too sleepy to say another word, they cradled protectively in each other's arms, and delighted in the safety and refuge of their new relationship. For Oliver, being able to have *pillow talk* with his new wife was the most gratifying experience in the world. He'd battled loneliness for such a very long time.

And yet, for Erin, it thrilled her to no end to have married the man of her dreams. The security of knowing that she was deeply love and cherished filled her heart with hope and gratitude. Finding a safe harbor in Oliver's arms dispelled all of her past fears and insecurities. With Oliver, she felt loved and wanted, and that meant everything to her.

CHAPTER TWELVE

Oliver and Erin were thoroughly enjoying their brief honeymoon getaway out in Aspen. On Monday morning, they went up on ski lifts, and had enjoyed the majestic scenery. Later, the newlyweds had taken in the sights of the historical town of Crest Butte and its landmarks. And as planned, on Tuesday morning, the two got a chance to shop, and had found some cute items at the antique store. Erin found a number of jeweled-encrusted broaches for her mom, but Oliver didn't have much luck in finding a vintage pocket watch. Undaunted, he refused to give up, and was determined to find one by any means necessary.

"Did *you* have a good time today, baby?" Oliver asked as he and Erin returned to the lodge on Tuesday in the late evening.

"I had the best time!" Erin stated, as they returned to their bedroom. They'd spent almost the entire day out. They'd just had dinner at a very quaint little restaurant which had come highly recommended by the locals. "I absolutely adore this town, Ollie! With its snow-capped, picturesque mountains and its tiny houses, it is positively storybook!" Erin commended, taking off her winter gear.

"I agree, baby, it is very pretty out here," Oliver said, totally hypnotized watching his wife, while peeling off all of his winter layers. "I'm really going to hate leaving in the morning," he said, setting his coat inside of the closet, and simultaneously pulling Erin into his arms. Oliver's face bridged to hers. "I just want to stay in this moment with you forever." He sighed.

"I know just what you mean, Ollie. I wish we could make the entire world disappear for a little while. The past few days have been sheer heaven," Erin said softly with her face pressed up to her husband's. "We *can* pretend for a while," Erin heartened.

Oliver smiled and covered her face in kisses. "I like pretending with you, but we really don't need to. This is *real*, and I promise you a honeymoon every single day of our lives, whether we're out in Aspen, Silver Water or anywhere else." Oliver pressed a sweet kiss to her nose.

"You *are* my honeymoon forever and always," Erin whispered fondly, totally entranced.

"Is that so, my love?" Oliver said huskily, magnetized once again. "Did you still want to see that movie down at the old theater?" he tested, baiting the corners of Erin's mouth.

"No, I want to stay in with my husband tonight," Erin's voice was wispy. Cradling Oliver's head in her hands, she reached up, pressed her mouth to his, and thirstily extracted sweet cane from its source.

Covetously, Oliver's mouth coated Erin's, and he kneaded every corner with tenderness. "You want to stay in tonight?" his voice was croaky in between hungry kisses. "Are you sure?" he confirmed

"Uh-huh," Erin said as she lost himself in Oliver's embrace. "All I want is to be close to you." Erin draped her arms about Oliver's neck, and raked her fingers through his thick hair in loving cadences.

"I just can't get close enough to you right now." Oliver quietly guided his wife over to their bed, while gazing fondly into her eyes. He was utterly swept away, uncertain was to why he was trembling with every touch. Erin caressed his face, hair and neck delicately. "Are you scared, honey?" he asked, concerned.

Erin shook her head in the negative before pulling Oliver closer. "Not in the least. I feel safe, secure and loved in your arms," she affirmed.

"That's because you *are* all those things with *me*." Oliver tenderly scooped her up from off of the floor, and quiescently laid her on their *marriage bed.* With a great deal of love and gentleness, he touched, kissed and caressed his wife, as Erin surrendered to his embrace. Oliver could feel that he was loved by his wife. It was in the way she held, touched and kissed him.

Not only was he overwhelmed by desire, but by the magnitude of love emanating between them. Tears were in Oliver's eyes to consider how deeply he loved Erin. They were on the same page, and she loved him just as profoundly. His love was indeed requited, and it was wonderful to be able to express his heart to his wife in a brand-new language.

Erin had only dreamed about being with Oliver in this way. And, so for her, the moment felt surreal. She had always known that Oliver's hands on her body would be utopia, but their newly found intimacy far exceeded any dream she could have had. Oliver's love was a world of enchantment, and she wanted to lose herself in the safe harbor of his arms forever. It didn't even seem possible to be so completely loved and wanted. There it was again- the dream factor. Erin kept expecting to wake up from the most beatific dream. Even if it was a reverie, while it lasted, she knew what it felt like to be properly loved and cherished by the man of her dreams.

Two truly became one that last night out in Aspen. Erin and Oliver broke out of the confines of their past relationship and embraced a new level of depth and devotion. Poetry and motion were reintroduced, as the two explored unchartered territory. It was a place they'd always wanted to visit, but neither wanted to leave that night. So, for a fleeting moment the newlyweds drifted into a realm of unrestrained love, desire and romance in a way they'd never known before.

***

Oliver and Erin held hands on the plane headed back for Georgia early Wednesday morning. The two were totally rapt in each other, but solemn to be leaving their paradise behind. Erin rested her head on Oliver's shoulder, as he kept his arms protectively around her waist. The couple was being jolted from the heaven they'd experienced and were going back to the *real* world. The demands of the DA's office would be thrust upon them once more.

Erin was worried for her husband. Oliver was always being pulled away, and had ceaseless responsibilities as the DA. She prayed for the strength, and for the grace to be understanding, as he spent hours on end fulfilling his role to their community.

Oliver tried not to think about the mountain of work stacked on his desk at the office back home. Staying in the moment with his wife was paramount. It was sad saying goodbye to their little respite out in Aspen. It had been such a wonderful whirlwind. They'd slipped into nirvana for a few days. "Why so glum?" he asked Erin, breaching the silence.

Erin looked up into Oliver's eyes with a face warped in sadness. "Is it that obvious that I don't want to go home today?"

Oliver's face bridged to hers, grimacing in discontent as well. "I don't want to go back so soon either." He toured her face in kisses. "I wish we could have stayed a little longer out in Aspen, but there will be other sneak getaways." His brows furrowed in mischief.

"Really…?" Erin asked, surprised. "Ollie, I want to go everywhere with you!"

"I want to take you everywhere," he affirmed. "I promise to surprise you with these little impromptu trips quite often."

"And *I* can surprise you with a few of my own." Waggishness veiled Erin's face.

"Oh…," Oliver said alluringly, "I can't wait." His lips fused to hers. "How do you like married life so far, Mrs. Wright?" he dallied.

"I'm the happiest woman in the world, and it's only day four."

"I guess we'll just have to wait until you spend a few nights over at the apartment. After I snore loud enough, and steal the covers every night, you might be filing a complaint of irreconcilable differences." He winked playfully.

"Never… I don't care if you sleepwalk, while snoring and taking away the covers-"

"Which will in all likeliness happen," Oliver humored. "So, you were warned."

"Nothing about being with you scares me." Shadows momentarily danced on her features.

"What's wrong, baby?" Oliver instantly picked up on her mood change.

"I'm just worried about your work, especially with the serial murder investigation," she admitted. "Before, you were doing your thing in the courtroom. That was dangerous enough, but…"

"Sweetheart, you don't have to worry about me-or *us*. We're one unit now, and God's got us. It's going to be alright…I promise. I *know* that the murderer will be brought to justice. I don't claim to have all of the answers, but I trust in the One who does. He's the One guiding us every step of the way," Oliver reassured, searching her eyes. "We're okay." He pressed a kiss to her forehead.

"So, here we go…back to the grind," Erin reminded, as they nuzzled.

"The grind is going to be so much more tolerable, because my wife will be standing by my side." Oliver's face lit up. "And I get to go home to her every night." He squeezed Erin lovingly. "I love you so much! Did I tell you how much I love you today?"

"You might have told me a couple of dozen times this morning, but feel free to keep telling me, because that *never* gets old. I love you too, Ollie!" Erin brought his hand up to her lips and covered it in kisses.

Oliver smiled into her eyes, so content and overjoyed he was floored. "You make me happy, you know that?"

"Ditto," Erin said searching his amber eyes.

"That's what we have to focus on today as we return to the Lion's Den," Oliver said good-naturedly.

Erin nodded in agreement. "So, I'm just going to swing by the house and pack a few things," Erin reminded.

"I don't want you doing too much packing and lifting-not until the weekend," Oliver advised. "Also, we don't need to stay over at the apartment tonight. We *could* spend it over at your place," Oliver tested. "Whatever you want is fine by me."

"I feel the same way, but I'd rather be over at your place," Erin admitted.

"Is there a reason for that, my love?" Oliver asked, curious.

"Well, some of our best memories so far have been there, and I want to keep making them with you."

"Okay…," he acquiesced. "I truly believe that we can make awesome memories anywhere."

"I believe that too, but I also like being over at your place."

Oliver laughed. "It's ideal for us to find a place together just as soon as things are a bit more settled. It won't be *my* place or *your* house, but a place that we pick out together. This is a fresh start for us, baby," Oliver explained.

"Ollie," Erin's heart melted, "is it any wonder why I'm so in love with you?" Erin linked her mouth to his. For a while their kiss scintillated and welded like liquid fire. At least for a few fleeing moments they could enjoy the solitude of their private love realm and escape the cold reality of the life beyond it.

***

The entire DA's office was up in arms, as a result of the latest on social media. Their beloved DA and the beautiful paralegal who worked alongside him, had gotten married. Apparently, the couple had posted pictures on their Instagram, taken out in Aspen, Colorado on Christmas day, shortly after they'd tied the knot.

The staff down at the DA's office was over the top excited for Erin and Oliver. Of course, they were hurt for being left out of the loop. Because they loved both Erin and Oliver so much, they would have wanted to be included in the celebration. Their secret nuptials had taken everyone by surprise. No one had been was aware of the blossoming romance between them.

Some of the members of the DA staff had suspected that the two had feelings for each other. However, no one knew just how deep those feelings ran. Oliver and Erin had managed to keep their romance a secret for quite some time. Regardless, everyone was thrilled to hear that Oliver Wright had found his silver lining. In their assessment, he could not have found a better life partner.

The couple would be coming in to work together for the first time that morning. So, the staff had already set up a special brunch for the pair. It was important that the newlyweds knew just how much they were loved and supported. Although, members of the staff were also ready to chew them out for going away and excluding everyone from the ceremony. Regardless, they understood that it was because of the public nature of Oliver's work that the two had opted for privacy.

As everyone bustled about in preparation to receive the newlyweds, Rain remained in her office distraught and in tears. She couldn't believe what had occurred. Oliver had taken Erin away on Christmas day, and had secretly married her. Rain felt like a total fool. She had tried to reach Oliver since they'd parted ways early Christmas morning. And now she understood why Oliver had been totally indisposed all weekend long.

The realization that Oliver had put a ring on Erin's finger, had flown her on a private jet, and had secretly married her, was tearing Rain apart. Up until that weekend she'd thought she'd had the upper hand. Rain perceived that she'd had Erin believing that Oliver was *her* guy. Now, Rain realized just what a fool *both* of them had made of her. She had thought that she could have controlled the outcome of the circumstances. However, Oliver and Erin had made the ultimate move, and she'd lost the war.

As she mulled over the defeat of losing Oliver forever, a light rap came on her door. Rain instantly brushed the tears away from her eyes, and poised herself at her desk before calling out, "Come in."

"Hey, Rain," David popped his head through her door, "we've got fresh muffins. We've got cake too, but we're waiting on the newlyweds to break that out along with the sparkling cider." He winked impishly.

"Oh," Rain forced a smile, "that sounds great. Maybe, I'll come out in a little while."

"Are you sure?" David asked trying to tempt her.

"Yeah, I'm pretty sure," Rain said. The elastic smile stretched over her face until it hurt.

"Suit yourself. There are plenty of goodies out there. You know how fast it all goes around here, so I wouldn't stay in here too long. Go figure… Who would have thought we would be celebrating Oliver and Erin's wedding just days before the New Year?" David shook his head in irony.

"Yeah…, go figure," Rain said caustically, doubting David picked up on her sarcasm.

"Alright, see you in a bit," David said, still euphoric.

"Sure," Rain said with aplomb.   The painted-on smile reemerged until David closed her office door.

Soon after, she buried her head in her hands and cried unrestrained. Before long, there was another knock to the door. Rain's face twisted in annoyance, and she stared at the door as if it were an enemy. Trying her best to compose herself, she called out, "Come in."

"I'm really not hungry right now, David," Rain said before even seeing who was standing beyond it. However, when she looked up, David wasn't the one standing there. "What…?" Rain questioned, surprised to see Grayson Andrews at her door. She pushed out of her armchair and drifted over to connect to him. "May I help you, Gray?" she asked with a face creased in puzzlement.

"Hey, how are you?" Gray offered a faint smile. "Can I come in for a minute?" he asked with an affected expression on his face.

Not bothering to say one word, Rain gestured for him to come in. She then shut the office door closed. Turning to face Gray with a cagey expression on her face, she crossed her arms over her chest.

"What is it?" she asked peeved.

"Is it true, I mean what I heard on the news this morning?" Gray's face contorted in bewilderment.

"You mean that Erin and Oliver got married over the weekend?" Rain explored, bitingly.

Gray nodded affirmatively.

"Yeah, it's true. Can't you tell from the festivities? The entire office is throwing them a special brunch or something." Rain guffawed in total skepticism and looked down at the plush carpeting beneath her feet.

"Man… I can't believe it," Gray admitted. "But, I guess it shouldn't come as a surprise to either of us. It was obvious that they were in love from their interactions at the party."

"Right…," Rain said irritated. She glared over at Gray. "Sorry, Erin isn't here-if that's why you came over here this morning. As we've both established, she's *married* now."

Gray's eyes lowered into Rain's eyes, and he edged in closer to her. "I didn't come here looking for Erin. I came to check in on you." Gray eliminated the space between them.

"What…? I don't understand," Rain said confused. Tears of frustration gathered in her eyes. "I'm fine. You don't have to check up on me." She shot Gray a chary look.

"I make my own decisions, and you're right. I don't *have* to do anything, Rain. Still, just like I noticed how much *Erin* was into Oliver on Saturday night, I noticed the same about *you*. Your heart's got to be broken right now. I liked Erin, and what happened stings, but I sense that you *love* Oliver," Gray evaluated. Cupping her chin, he gazed caringly into her eyes. "I *know* how much that's got to hurt." Gray sensitively gazed into her eyes.

Rain's tear-filled eyes connected intuitively to Gray's, and she surrendered to weeping. Perhaps, it was his kindness and understanding that made her feel confident enough to pour out her heart. Rain surrendered to Gray's arms and allowed herself to grieve over losing Oliver.

Gray comfortingly held Rain in his arms-internalizing her heartbreak. He'd taken a chance to come out there to let her know that he felt for her. It had only been a few days ago since they'd been on dates with Erin and Oliver.

And whereas Erin had told *him* the truth early Christmas morning, and had let him down gently, he was certain that Rain hadn't seen this coming. "It's okay. It's going to be alright. I know, sweetheart," Gray consoled. "Just let it go. You will get through this. In fact, we both will, and we will be stronger for it. You'll see." He crushed Rain caringly in his arms, and tenderly cradled her head in his hands as she bawled.

***

The tenor inside of the courtroom was such a contrast from the celebration back over at the DA's office. Oliver was sitting inside of the courtroom with Mitch and Taren. Having just said goodbye to Erin, Oliver assented to how difficult it was being apart. Yet and still, he had to temporarily stifle his new role as a husband and shoulder the responsibilities of the DA's office. At the very core of those responsibilities was to be present for Taren on the morning of her sentencing.

"You're going to be alright, honey," Mitch encouraged Taren, squeezing her hand in support. "We've done everything we could, and now the matter is in God's hands."

"I just wish that this was over already," Taren said with a face strained in jeopardy. "All of this waiting is…"

"I know, Taren. It won't be long now. You took responsibility for your actions, and sought help," Mitch heartened in sympathy. "Remember, whatever happens *I'm* not going anywhere."

Taren nodded and tried to find comfort in Mitch's words. However, her heart whipped in angst as she awaited sentencing.

Oliver's heart went out to Mitch. Sitting on Mitch's left-hand side, Oliver rubbed on his arms reassuringly. He sensed just how nervous and stressed Mitch was. It was also clear that Mitch was putting up a good front for Taren's sake. The truth was that they had no idea how things were about to play out. Finally, the verdict would be read for the felony Taren had committed last spring.

Taren assaulted Kennedy at her home and held her at gunpoint. The confrontation was deescalated by the authorities, with Kayden Bohm's help. Kayden had talked Taren down from doing something reckless. Taren had voluntarily submitted to psychiatric care and was hospitalized for a few months after the incident.

Ensuing, she'd been arraigned, and had pleaded guilty to aggravated kidnapping, assault, home invasion, and endangering the lives of others by threatening to use a firearm. The charges carried a combined sentence of ten years. Taren continued outpatient care through the psychiatric hospital, while awaiting sentencing.

Taren had been evaluated by psychologists, who maintained that she was coherent enough for sentencing. At first, it was argued that she had suffered from some form of a psychotic break at the time, but those notions were never substantiated. Still, because she had no prior criminal record, Oliver and Mitch were hopeful of a marginal sentence.

Two years of probation rather than facing jail time was what they were advocating. Kayden was in the courtroom that morning, minus Kennedy. Oliver knew that anything having to do with Taren was a sore subject for Kennedy. So, he wasn't surprised that Kennedy had decided not to show up.

"Oliver, I'm really scared. What if the judge decides to make an example of me?" Taren told Oliver, with a face wrenched in turmoil and fear.

Oliver stared reassuringly into her eyes. "We talked about this. I doubt that the judge will hand out an unfair sentence. And whatever happens, we can always appeal the case."

"Taren, listen to me," Mitch compelled, "we've got to play it cool right now. God's will be done." His eyes lowered urgently into hers.

"I'm sorry that I'm such a mess this morning." Taren took deep breaths in order to calm the jitters.

"It will be fine," Oliver reassured giving Taren a well-meaning look.

Before long, Judge Gabriel Baldwin took his place at the bench. "Good morning!" he addressed everyone inside of the courtroom.

Everyone was asked to stand to their feet, and court was officially in session.

There were a number of matters discussed in respect to Taren's case-most of which had already been covered. However, the judge wanted to get an idea of Taren's emotional state.

"Your honor, I just wanted to take a moment to express to everyone I hurt how deeply sorry I am for making such a huge mistake," Taren stated. "They say that hindsight is 20/20. At this point, I can see how I allowed my emotions to get the better of me. I became unrecognizable." Tears were in her eyes. "I know that it probably sounds trite and even cliché, but if I *could* take it all back I *would* in a heartbeat.

"I lost myself in the process, and I wound up losing some of the dearest people on earth to me." Taren's eyes drifted across the courtroom and caught Kayden's. "I've hurt some pretty amazing people, and I've paid a very high price for my poor choices. I know that I probably don't deserve a second chance, but I am asking for the opportunity to turn my life around," Taren petitioned.

Regardless of the outcome, Oliver was staunchly proud of Taren and her appeal. There was no doubt in his mind that she was genuine in her remorse. She had pleaded guilty to the charges brought against her and had submitted to psychiatric care. Oliver prayed that Judge Baldwin would see things his way.

Prior to the reading of the sentence, Kayden was asked to come up to the podium, and say a few words as a stand-in for Kennedy. Oliver wasn't too concerned that Kayden would say anything amiss. Yet and still, his chest tightened in angst as he waited to hear Kayden speak. As expected, Kayden was extremely kind and forgiving of Taren's mistakes. He expressed the same generosity of spirit which Kennedy had in her impact statement letter.

"I've taken all statements into consideration this morning. Does the state have anything more to extend at this time?" Judge Baldwin asked.

"No, your honor," Both Oliver and Mitch said in concert.

"So, there is no reason to prolong sentencing," Judge Baldwin delineated. He then looked over at Taren. However, he didn't address her right away. Judge Baldwin expressed gratitude for everyone who worked on the case. Then, he commended Taren for her earnest display of remorse. That said, he asked Taren to stand to her feet.

Oliver took measured breaths in order to quiet his racing thoughts. The matter was in God's hands. He and Mitch exchanged knowing looks just before the verdict and sentencing was pronounced.

"Taren Amelia Cook, you pleaded guilty to aggravated kidnapping, assault, home invasion, and endangering the lives of others by threatening to use a firearm. You *have* taken responsibility for your actions in past months and have subsequently sought counseling. That said, the crimes committed are of a very serious nature. Although, I have taken into account the impact statements from the victim and her family. You are hereby sentenced to serve one year at the Silver Water Correctional Facility, and subsequently one year's probation."

Taren's heart dipped to the floor, and she grimaced in incredulity and regret.

Oliver and Mitch exchanged befuddled looks. Tears shone in Mitch's eyes, as he listened to Judge Baldwin read off all of the conditions of Taren's sentence.

Even if the judge showed leniency, Oliver had hoped for a less rigorous sentence. It killed him that Taren was going to have to serve one year in prison. And Oliver knew that it was killing Mitch. Mitch appeared stunned, as he strove to process the information. The love of his life would indeed have to serve time behind bars.

With a broken heart, Oliver watched Mitch and Taren hug. The two clung to each other, as the officers of the court were waiting in the wings to take Taren away. Taren would be detained in county jail until she could be transferred to Silver Water Correctional.

"It's okay, baby. It's alright. I promise. I will get started on an appeal just as soon as possible," Mitch reassured, holding Taren acquisitively in his arms.

"I'm so scared, Mitch. I didn't think this was going to happen."

"I know, sugar, I know… It's okay. Things could have been much worse," Mitch upheld. He pulled away in order to look into her eyes. "You're not alone in this. We're going to be working every step of the way to get you out of there." He pressed a kiss to her forehead. "I love you!"

"I love you too, Mitch!" Taren's face warped in anguish.

Oliver stood steadfastly by Mitch's side, as the officers of the court came to claim Taren. There was very little he could say to his buddy. However, he kept a firm hand on Mitch's shoulder and squeezed in support. They'd done everything humanly possible. Things had not gone exactly as they'd hoped, but they weren't giving up.

Oliver was leaving the courthouse when Kayden caught up with him. Oliver had just said goodbye to Mitch. He and Mitch had resolved to strategize an appeal for Taren's sentence. Seeing Kayden standing in front of his limo outside brought an instant smile to Oliver's face. Oliver dismounted the courthouse steps and made quick strides to connect to Kayden. "Kayden!" Oliver heralded.

"Hey, Ollie!" Kayden greeted affably. The two hugged, and

Kayden patted Oliver on the back.

"I can't thank you enough for being here this morning. It meant a lot to Mitch and to Taren," Oliver said pulling away to establish eye contact.

Kayden guffawed and nodded quiescently. "I *know* Taren had it rough during that time, but I never *truly* thought that she intended to hurt Kennedy. Taren herself probably can't believe that things got so carried away," Kayden articulated sympathetically.

"Yeah, I know she's sorry. Judge Baldwin could have sentenced her to the max, but didn't. Mitch and I wouldn't have wanted her to face any jail time, but…" Oliver's words trailed.

Kayden stared at Oliver musingly. "You and Mitch did the very best you could. I *am* very grateful that Taren's sentence wasn't more stringent in light of the circumstances," Kayden admitted. "Kennedy and I had hoped that she'd be given probation, but all things considered…" Kayden stopped short. "Great work, Ollie!" he praised and patted Oliver's arm.

"Thanks, Kay. Again, Mitch and I couldn't have done this without you *or* Kennedy. Please, send her my regards!" Oliver offered a genuine smile. "Also, tell her I totally understand why she couldn't be here today."

"I will." Kayden smiled curiously at Oliver. "From what I understand, congratulations are in order!" Kayden introduced, staring at the ring on Oliver's finger.

Oliver's face turned crimson. "Yeah, well," he said timidly, "thank you."

"Kenney and I are over-the-moon happy for you!" Kayden said in earnest.

"And, thank you for the early wedding gift," Oliver said cryptically, with a knowing look on his face.

"You're most welcome, my friend! I'm just glad that you didn't argue with me."

Oliver smiled curiously. "Believe me, I thought about it."

"You don't have to tell me. I know. Listen, Kennedy and I are having a New Year's Eve party. It would mean a lot to us if you and your beautiful new *wife* would attend!" Kayden extended a proper invitation. "Kennedy and I want the very best of *everything* for you and Erin,"

"Thank you, Kay. That means more to me than you even know!" Oliver endeared. "So, let me talk it over with my wife, and I will get back to you," Oliver said, pleasantly surprised. "By the way, will the two of you be attending service on New Year's Day?" Oliver asked. Kayden and Kennedy had found a church-one closer to the town of *Glistening Pines*, however they did occasionally show up at *Deliverance Tab*.

"Yes, *absolutely*, we plan on attending! Kenney misses the services at Deliverance when we can't attend for one reason or another. It's a fantastic church, and Pastor Timmins is awesome!"

Oliver nodded. "It's a pretty great place to worship, and Pastor Timmins *is* the best. I don't think he's going to be too happy that Erin and I *didn't* share our plans," Oliver considered, frowning.

Kayden laughed lightly. "He's just going to have to get over it."

"He'll forgive us, because Erin and I *do* plan to have a full-on ceremony. That is the plan once certain matters are resolved-namely some of the DA's ongoing investigations."

"No doubt, Ollie. I'm confident that the DA's office will be prosecuting that *serial monster* sooner than you know," Kayden attested.

"From your lips to God's ear." Oliver nodded in agreement.

"And once that's out of the way, Kennedy and I better be at the very top of your list for the wedding." Kayden's brows furrowed farcically.

"Absolutely... You and Kennedy are always at the very top of all of our *lists*," Oliver declared.

"Now, that's what I like to hear."

"It's the truth. Kay, tell Kennedy thank you again."

Kayden assented. "Absolutely…" He and Oliver hugged again. "Take care of yourself, Ollie."

"You take care as well, Kay."

"Give my best to your wife."

"I will…only if you promise to do the same."

Oliver watched Kayden take his place inside of the limo. He stood out in front of the courthouse and waved as the automobile rolled away. Oliver then drifted out to the parking lot in order to find his SUV. Hopping into the vehicle, he took his phone off of silent mode, and noticed that his wife had called several times. Without hesitation he called her back. "Hey, baby, how are you?"

"Ollie!" Erin cheered. "I'm good. I was *finally* able to get into my office just a little while ago. Everyone around here had a gazillion questions about our secret wedding," she explained. "I miss you so much!" she told him right off.

"I miss you too, my love! I had no idea it would be this bad."

"What, sweetie?"

"I didn't think it would be so hard being away from you," Oliver's voice was gravelly.

"It's pretty hard when *you're* not near *me*, but I'm trying to be strong."

"I'm so proud of my strong girl," Oliver uplifted.

"She's proud of you too. How was court?" Erin asked.

"Things didn't go *terribly* wrong, but they didn't work out in the way Mitch and I had hoped."

"Taren *is* facing jail time?" Erin's face creased in turmoil, and her heart rent in half.

"Yeah, she's going to have to serve a year through the correctional facility out here, plus one year of probation," Oliver explained, sighing.

"I'm so sorry, Ollie," Erin's voice wavered. "I know how hard you and Mitch worked so that wouldn't happen. I'm so sorry, baby."

"I am too, but it's alright. In light of the charges brought against her, Taren was looking at a decade."

Erin commiserated while sitting at her desk. "That's right, sweetie. So, all things considered it's a total *victory* for you and for Mitch. I would not have wanted for Taren to spend *any* time in prison, but things being what they are, there was always that possibility."

"Sure, I get that, baby," Oliver assented.

"Ollie, with everything else on your plate, please don't get bogged down with guilt over today's sentencing," Erin said, concerned. "Promise me?" she urged.

"I won't allow myself to be bogged down by guilt," Oliver avowed. "Right now, I just want to be with you," he evaded. "I want your lips on mine, and I want to feel your fingers brushing through my hair."

"Are you getting fresh over the phone with me, Mr. DA?" Erin razzed.

"Guilty as charged," Oliver rose playfully to the occasion.

"Well, in that case, can you hurry back?" Erin's voice was velvety soft.

"I'm on my way, baby," Oliver said gutturally. "I'm going to take my beautiful wife out of the office-maybe we can take a stroll through the park."

"I'd like that. I love you, Ollie! Be safe," Erin reminded endearingly.

"I love you more, and I will see you in a little while."

All smiles, Oliver shut down his phone. It was difficult to wrap his head around how much his life had changed in less than a week. He took a moment to lift up the name of the Lord for blessing him with the desire of his heart. For some time, he'd closed himself off to the possibility of love. What he had not taken into account was that *Erin Emily Wright* would have torn down all of his walls. Oliver loved her beyond all reason and logic.

***

"Thank you for going out with me this afternoon, baby," Oliver said, holding Erin acquisitively in his arms outside of her office. Their faces bridged lovingly.

"I can't believe I get to be close to you every day," Erin delighted, reaching up and pressing her lips to his. "Taking that little stroll through the park was another little getaway for us." She beamed.

"Uh-huh," Oliver said, entranced. "So, we *don't* have to be out in Aspen to vacation." Oliver covered her face in kisses. "Every time I look into your eyes I'm already in paradise."

"Oh, Ollie…," Erin staid, stirred.

"What's that noise I'm hearing?" Oliver pulled back playfully, with one arm encircling his wife's waist, cupping his right ear. "Is that the sap-o-meter?" he teased.

Erin poked him in the ribs. "Well, your scores are *always* just as high as mine," she disputed, gazing lovingly into his eyes.

"Alright… I'll give you that one. Still, you just got an A, and I might have like an A-" Oliver smiled down at Erin, clasping both arms possessively around her waist.

"Liar," Erin teased, "I'm giving you an A+…" Erin's voice trailed, as she and Rain locked eyes down the hallway. Erin's face immediately changed, twisting in remorse.

Oliver turned around to see what had made his wife's face change so drastically. "Rain," Oliver acknowledged, surprised to see her standing down the hall. Rain was staring ruefully over at him and his new wife.

Lingering only for a moment, Rain glared, then turned away.

"I'm so sorry, Ollie," Erin said, grieved that Rain had been privy to their affectionate exchanges.

"Well, I'm *not*. I'm the happiest I've ever been, and I need to tell her that." Oliver's eyes lowered sensitively into Erin's.

Erin nodded compliantly. "I trust that you will find a way to set things right with Rain."

"And *that's* the reason why I love you so much! In spite of all of the tricks Rain has pulled on you…on us, you're still kindhearted." Oliver smiled.

"I learn from the very best." Erin inched up and planted a kiss to her husband's lips. "Go on…," she encouraged, knowing that Oliver wanted to set the record straight with his old friend. "I will see you later."

"Promise…?" Oliver asked, transported.

"I promise," Erin said.

Oliver hesitantly pulled away and began to distance himself. However, he was walking away backward. Yearningly, he held his hand up to say goodbye.

"Call me later, Ollie," Erin told him just before he turned away.

"Will do, baby," Oliver reassured, veering back to look at his wife.

Erin sighed as she stepped into her office. It was nice to have gotten a little bit of fresh air with her husband. They hadn't bought lunch, because there was plenty of food around. The DA's office had been celebrating their private wedding all that day. Erin couldn't believe the accolade. Being in the public eye, Erin hadn't expected anything else. It was only a matter of time before *everyone* knew that she and Oliver were now husband and wife.

As she settled back at her desk and continued to work on a number of law documents, Erin whispered a prayer for Oliver's friendship with Rain. Moreover, she prayed that Rain would come into a relationship with Jesus Christ. Erin evaluated that Rain needed God more than anything else. Still, she knew for sure that Oliver would be kind to Rain, because Oliver didn't know how to be anything but. For that reason and many others, Erin was absolutely crazy about him. As she typed away on the keyboard, the wedding ring and band intermittently caught her eye. Each time the facets of the diamond sparkled on her finger, her heart inundated with joy and great dignity.

"Rain," Oliver called out while standing in front of her office door.

"Yes...?" Rain reluctantly answered, hearing Oliver's voice. She was doing all she could not to be angry at him, but it was a real challenge.

"Can we talk?" Oliver asked through the door in diffidence.

"Sure," Rain said in a detached manner. Her heart thudded in her chest in expectation. She wasn't sure how she was going to react when she saw his face and looked into his eyes.

Oliver deliberately opened up the office door and stepped inside. Seeing the gold band on his ring finger confirmed Rain's worst nightmare. However, Rain was determined to be strong. Gray stopping in to see her earlier on had offered hope and strength.

"Hey," Oliver said, inching in closer to Rain's desk. She was standing in front of it. "How are you?" he asked, with a guilt-ridden expression on his face.

Rain shrugged with her arms crossed over her chest. "I've

been better." She urged herself to look into Oliver's honey eyes. Once again, he took her breath away. So, Rain grasped that getting over him was going to be a process.

"Look, I'm really sorry that I didn't expound on my plans this past weekend," Oliver expressed in earnest. He placed his hand gently on Rain's shoulder and stared contritely into her eyes.

"You owe me no explanations, Oliver Wright-and you certainly owe me no apologies," Rain asserted, shying away from his addictive touch.

"Yes, I *do* owe you an apology, Rain. I'm sorry if my decision has caused you pain. You know how much I care about you, and I would never want to deliberately-"

"Ollie, I'm okay," Rain said shortly. "I'm *happy* for you and for Erin. You *did* tell me that you loved someone else." Her face seared in hurt, even if she was trying to conceal it.

"I *did* tell you that there was someone else. Still, Rain, I'm sorry that I didn't tell you that I wanted to marry Erin. Things have been so complicated for me...for us. We both took advantage of the little window of time we had a few days ago. We didn't know when we'd get the opportunity again." Tears shone in Oliver's eyes. "I realize that I should have given you the head's up, and I'm *truly* sorry."

"Don't...," Rain held her hand up haltingly, but suddenly broke down in tears.

Oliver collected her into his arms. "I should have told you, and I'm sorry. Please, forgive me." Oliver blinked back tears, as he searched Rain's tear-filled eyes. "Please...," He frowned in regret.

"Ollie," Rain shoved away, and hit him playfully on the shoulder, "you *really* should have said something." She stared reproachfully at him, but began to soften. "How can I *ever* truly stay mad at you? You're the best person I know...on the planet," she uplifted, laughing through the tears.

"I'm no saint, Rain. Trust me..." Oliver's brows furrowed in impishness. "But, I *am* truly sorry that I hurt you." His eyes lowered urgently into hers. "Do you forgive me?" he tested.

"Of course, I do."

"Are we okay? I mean, I would totally understand if you didn't want to be here. I could refer you to another office," he mitigated.

Rain wiped the tears away from her eyes and offered Oliver a sincere smile. "I just need a little time to sort things out. In a month or so, I will let you know if I want to stay on working through this office."

Oliver acquiesced understandingly. "Of course, … You take your time. I understand that things are a little uncomfortable right now. Rain, you need to know that I care about you. I hope that we can continue to be friends," he inspirited.

Rain offered a faint smile. "Friends till the end, Ollie." She draped her arms about his neck and squeezed affectionately. Pulling away, she told him, "I hope Erin Brasfield-"

"Wright," Oliver quickly corrected.

"Alright then, I hope Erin *Wright* realizes just how lucky she is." She gazed wonderingly into his eyes.

Oliver smiled temperately. "*I'm* the one who's lucky to have *her*," he assented, being fiercely proud.

Rain nodded quiescently. "I'm happy that you found your person, Ollie," she said courageously.

"And you will too," Oliver encouraged. "Speaking of which, I hope you decide to come out to Deliverance Tab one of these Sundays. The *person* we all need is Jesus Christ," he pronounced.

Rain issued a quiet smile. "I just might take you up on that…and I might also bring a friend…"

"Oh, a friend... Do tell…?" Oliver quipped.

"Nope," Rain jested, "that remains to be seen."

Oliver held both hands up disarmingly. "That's more than fair."

Rain thought about asking Gray to come out to service with her. His initiative to check in on her earlier on had taken her by surprise. She had no idea what a decent a guy he truly was. The times Rain had seen him with Erin, he had seemed like a player. However, Rain had seen a different side to him. It also didn't hurt that Gray was easy on the eyes and wildly successful. So, despite having been bulldozed by Oliver's secret wedding, Rain was hopeful of a new friendship with Gray.

"Thanks for taking the time, Ollie," Rain said, alleviated.

"Of course," Oliver explored her eyes. "Will I see you later? I just wanted to make sure you're okay." His face strained in concern.

"Don't worry, Ollie, I'm *not* going anywhere without saying goodbye."

Oliver smiled earnestly. "That's good to know." He turned and headed for the door. Oliver opened it up and stepped out into the hallway.

Rain stood in the doorway and called out, "Ollie…?"

"Yep," Oliver veered in order to reconnect to her.

"Congratulations!"

Oliver smiled pleasantly. "Thank you. That really means a lot." He winked, turned and continued down the hallway.

CHAPTER THIRTEEN

"No, it looks perfect right there, Ollie," Erin told Oliver on Saturday morning. Oliver was in process of adding a small storage shelf to the adjourning bathroom in their bedroom. He wanted to create extra space for all of Erin's toiletries. "And it doesn't clutter up the room."

"Sure you don't want it a little closer to the mirror, baby?" Oliver asked, as he supported the shelf with both hands.

Erin frowned in uncertainty as she examined the possibilities. "You might have a point, sweetie. Maybe, just a little bit closer to the mirror." Erin smiled, and folded her hands with a sense of dignity. The moment felt surreal. With every little adjustment made to Oliver's place, Erin was feeling more at home. "Thank you for doing this for me, Ollie," she said amiably, doting on him.

"You're welcome, my love!" Oliver winked at her. Using the drill, he finished adjusting the bolts and screws to support the shelf. "Did you want this painted, or do you like it off white?" he asked, testing the shelf's sturdiness.

"It's fine just the way it is for now," Erin said, admiring how pretty it looked. It seemed to fit right into that little corner. In that respect she felt the same way. In a week's time hers and Oliver's lives had drastically changed. Oddly, as complicated as both of their lives had been prior to getting married, they were a perfect fit. "Yay, it looks perfect, Ollie!" she cheered.

"You know what's perfect?" Oliver set his work tools aside, took Erin's hand in his, and gently guided her into his arms. Clasping his arms about her waist, he stared devotedly into her eyes. "*You* Mrs. Erin Emily Wright are perfect!"

Erin gazed lovingly into her husband's eyes. Caressing his face and brushing her fingers through his hair, she declared, "My husband's pretty perfect too." Standing on her tiptoes, she pressed her lips repeatedly to his. "We got a lot done so far today, sweetie. Everything's coming together nicely."

"I didn't want you stressing too much about moving in. It's a process," Oliver told her. "I want you to feel totally at home. So, whatever you want to change…" His face bridged to hers. "*Are* you at home here?" his voice was croaky.

"*You are* my home, Ollie. I love being here with you. As long as we're together I'm happy!" Erin closed her eyes meditatively, as Oliver covered her face in kisses.

"Aw, baby, you're killing me," Oliver said, affected.

"I think I'd be happy living on Venus with you."

"*Maybe*, we can book a flight." He winked playfully. "Are we ready to ring in the New Year, baby?" Oliver asked. "I can't believe we've just celebrated our first Christmas, and *now* by God's grace this is our first New Year's Eve together," he marveled.

"I know," Erin smiled nostalgically, "it's been such a whirlwind."

"But so worth it. There is only *one* thing that I would change," Oliver introduced, eyes lowering affectionately into hers.

"And what's that, sweetie?"

"I wish that I had come to my senses and married you sooner."

Erin smiled up into his eyes. "I wish that too, but everything happens when it's supposed to." She cradled his face in her hands and kissed him again. "By the way, what time is the party tonight?"

"Kayden said around eight or so. Are you *sure* you want to go?" he tested.

"Why *wouldn't* I want to go to the Bohm's New Year's Eve party?"

"Well, since it's *our* first New Year's Eve together I was hoping…?" Mischief colored Oliver's face.

"Oh… You wanted it to be just us, huh?" Erin asked, shaking

her head nonsensically.

"Well, it's all up to you, baby. We have a few hours until the party, and we can show up *fashionably* late." Impishness veiled Erin's sweet face.

"Hmm," Oliver considered, "you *do* have a point, Mrs. Wright."

"You're such a mess," Erin said farcically. "As soon as we're done cleaning up, we can start *our* own little celebration."

"Oh, I think I like the sound of that," Oliver said. Bending, he took the time to cover Erin's mouth with his-fondly kneading every corner. "Are you happy?" he asked in between butterfly kisses.

"I'm happier than I've ever been." Tears shone in her eyes. "I love you so much!"

"Oh, baby, *happy* doesn't even begin to cover it! I've been amazed every second we've spent together this past week! I didn't think that there was this kind of happiness for *me*," his voice broke. Oliver planted loving kisses all over her face. "I love you more than anything, Erin Wright! There isn't anything I wouldn't do for you."

"Oh, Ollie," Erin said, moved, "You're my heart!"

Oliver's mouth fused to Erin's, and his lips brushed over hers rapaciously.

"Ollie, I thought we were going to clean up first," Erin said, being virtually ingested by her husband.

"We *are*, babe, but we're just taking a little break," Oliver said gutturally, totally enraptured.

"You're so bad," Erin teased, as Oliver guided her over to their bedroom.

"Uh-huh," Oliver murmured, taking Erin into his arms, and consuming her with love and tenderness.

***

"No worries. I'm glad you called me in," Oliver told authorities down at the police precinct. The body of another young woman had been discovered out in Silver Commons. Tanya Macintosh-only twenty-five years old-had been brutally stabbed inside of her apartment. This time around the killer had carelessly left behind DNA evidence. Skin, blood and saliva were a factor, and footprints for a specific brand of boot. With every step, it seemed investigators were getting closer to discovering who the perpetrator was.

"Have you narrowed down possible suspects through the database?" Oliver asked. It was New Year's Eve, and he had not expected to have yet another murder on his hands. The killer had remained dormant for a while, but now he was back in business.

"We're getting closer, Ollie. Hopefully, we can figure this out sooner than later. This has gone too far. That bastard can't hurt one more person in this county."

"*One* murder is one too many," Oliver contended. "So, we know that he is sticking close to the Silver Commons area?" Oliver examined, along with the authorities and investigators.

"We don't know that for sure, Ollie. It seems as if this miscreant is moving into some of the neighboring towns."

"I want that perp stopped as soon as possible," Oliver said irate. "We're not doing this again. I'm not coming out to another crime scene. That's unacceptable."

"We've already started narrowing down a few suspects, so it won't be too much longer," Detective Patterson told Oliver.

"Please contact me the moment you have something," Oliver exacted, miffed. It was almost seven in the evening. He and Erin had already told Kennedy and Kayden they'd show up for their New Year's Eve party. However, after learning of Tanya Macintosh's murder, Oliver was sick at heart. He felt personally responsible, because another murder had taken place under his jurisdiction as the DA.

"We will absolutely contact you the moment we know anything, DA Wright."

"Please…," Oliver appealed.

Oliver needed to leave the precinct just as soon as possible. He had to swing by Erin's house out in *Silver Leaf Falls*. Prior to being called in by the authorities, he and Erin had been over at her place packing up a few more of her belongings. "God, please help me. I hate this," Oliver complained, cradling his head in his own hands, once he hopped into his car.

"I can't do this without you, Jesus. Please help me, Lord. Help Silver County find the demon who keeps claiming the lives of these young women." Oliver sighed, allowing God's Spirit to bring about calmness and peace. Before long, he was pulling away from the area. It was New Year's Eve, but he hardly felt like celebrating. What Oliver wanted at that moment was to hold Erin in his arms, and to stare into her cinnamon eyes.

Oliver was close to the expressway when his phone rang again. He immediately recognized the number as from one of the detectives. Without hesitation, he pulled over to the shoulder of the road. "Wright here," he said anxiously.

"Ollie, based on DNA evidence, we've narrowed down the assailant. We had the name wrong in our database. His name is Killian Danes. He works for *Silver Wind Plumbing* out in *Silver Wind*. He's been with that company for the past ten years. He doesn't have an extensive criminal history, but was diagnosed with mental illness in his late teens."

"Wow! Okay… How can we get our hands on him?" Oliver's heart whisked anxiously.

"A man matching his description, and with the license plate number registered to his car was seen about ten minutes ago out in *Silver Leaf Falls*. He was parked on Rayburn Street for a while," the detective told Oliver.

Oliver gasped in shock, and his heart immediately began to hammer in his chest. "Did you just say Rayburn Street?"

"Yes. Are you familiar with the area?"

"Listen, you need to get over there just as soon as possible. That's where my wife's house is." Oliver tossed his phone to the side and ripped back onto the expressway. He was a man on a mission. The implication that this monster was on the block where Erin's house was located, freaked Oliver out. He couldn't stop shaking as he rushed out to *Silver Leaf Falls*.

"Lord, I'm sure Erin's fine, but please watch over her." Tears of frustration and uncertainty gathered in his eyes. "God, I'm sure my wife is just fine. Jesus, I trust you. I know you've got her. She's okay…," he kept repeating as if trying to memorize a script of some sort. All the while his heart thrashed in apprehension and dread. If anything happened to Erin, Oliver knew there would be no coming back from it. However, he was trying to convince himself not to panic. Psalms 34:7 (NKJV). "The angel of the Lord encamps all around those who fear him, and delivers them." That passage of scripture resonated for Oliver, as he burned rubber on the highway headed over to Erin's.

***

Erin had just finished packing up clothes, and a few personal items to bring back over to Oliver's place. Intermittently, she checked the living room window to see if Oliver was there. They were running behind schedule in as far as getting ready for the Bohm's New Year's Eve party. Remembering that she'd forgotten her curling iron, Erin crossed back over to the bathroom in order to retrieve it. As she did, the doorbell rang. "Ollie," Erin said excited, smiling.

Erin took a moment to shut off all of the house lights, and hurriedly crossed over to the front door. Anxious, she opened it up, but there was no one there. Bewildered, she stepped out of the house and drifted out onto the front porch. Not seeing Oliver's SUV out in the driveway, she called out his name, confused. "Ollie…?" Scanning the area, there didn't seem to be any indication that anyone was around. "Alright then…," she muttered, and headed back over to the front door.

However, at that very moment, someone came up behind her. Erin felt strong hands pressed to her mouth, and loud breathing resonated in her ear. Terrified, her heart thrashed inside of her chest, and she began to quaver like a wet leaf in a thunderstorm.

"How are you doing tonight, Pretty lady?" the intruder's throaty and raspy voice grated in Erin's ear.

Panicked, Erin instinctively began shoving away, kicking and fighting for her freedom. However, the vise grip hold of the stranger was more restricting than that of an Anaconda. Horrorstricken, tears brimmed over Erin's eyelids and effortlessly rolled down her cheeks.

"Listen, we're *not* doing this tonight. You're not going to fight me, because that will only make things worse. You're going to be a good girl. You and I are going to quietly step back inside of this lovely home of yours," he placated threateningly. With his body pressed up to Erin's back, constraining her, he brought out a knife, and pressed it up to Erin's neck. She shivered from the chill of the blade touching her skin. "Are we clear? Do we understand each other?" he disparaged.

Quivering, Erin nodded quiescently. She was terrified to go into the house. Without equivocation, she knew that this man was the serial killer who'd claimed the lives of a number of women in Silver County. Moreover, he had targeted her as his next victim. Inwardly, Erin prayed and made supplications to God for help. Paralyzed by fear of being dragged back into the house, Erin did all she could not to give in to despair.

Tears were in her eyes as she staunchly tried to resist the offender. The man handled her as if she were a piece of Styrofoam. Cautiously removing his hand from off of Erin's mouth, he immediately set duct tape over her lips. Holding her in position, he used his free hand to bind her wrists with the tape as well.

"Now, we're going to play a little game-you and me. I think I've saved the best one for last," he salaciously assessed, staring provocatively at Erin. "I might have to indulge in a little chocolate for dessert before I put it *away*," he said cryptically.

Erin flinched in dread, as she assessed the hooded man. It

was now that she could see that he was Caucasian. Still, it was too dark to truly see his face. The moment felt like an out of body experience. How on earth could this be happening? Erin kept thinking about Oliver. They'd just gotten married and were starting a life together. *Was this the way her life would end?*

She and Oliver had barely been married for a week, and it was New Year's Eve of 2019. Would she live to see 2020? *"Jesus, please help me,"* Erin prayed as the assailant forcefully began to drag her through the house. She was also reminded of passages from scripture, "Call upon me in the day of trouble; I will deliver you, and you shall glorify me (Psalms 50:15).

2 Chronicles 20:9, "If disaster comes upon us-sword, judgment, pestilence, or famine-we will stand before this temple and in your presence (for your name is in this temple), and cry out to you in our affliction, and you will hear and save (NKJV)." She was also reminded of Isaiah 46:4 "… Even to your old age, I am He, and even to gray hair I will carry you! I have made, and I will bear; even I will carry, and will deliver you."

Erin's thoughts were racing, but she was still trying to hold on to the word of God. If God had brought Isaiah 46:4 to mind, there was a reason. God had promised to care for and deliver her until the hairs on her head were gray. So, at that moment, she determined to fight back, using her legs and her bound arms to shove the demon away.

"Now, I wouldn't do that if I were you, little lady. I already told you what will happen if you resist," the assailant's voice was brusque, as he squeezed Erin in his malevolently strong arms, crushing her. "We can do this the easy way or the hard way," he intimidated. "One more stunt from you, and I will slit your throat from ear to ear. Do you understand?" he bellowed.

Erin nodded in compliance with tears streaming down her cheeks. She decided to stop moving, because the aggressor pressed the knife up to her throat again. She grimaced in trepidation and distress as the point of the knife made contact with her neck.

"I *thought* that would get your attention," he said. "You *are* beautiful!" He ogled and began unbuttoning Erin's cardigan.

Erin closed her eyes in despair, because she knew what would follow. Inwardly, she felt totally disconnected from the experience. However, in the tangible realm, she couldn't deny what was happening. Just then, she assessed the perpetrator. He was about 6 feet tall and had a muscular build. In as far as his features. She couldn't see his eyes very well, but he had a square chin, thin pointy nose, thin lips and markings on his neck-perhaps a tattoo of some sort. It was all Erin could decipher in the shadows.

The fiend was impatient at that point, and shoved Erin onto the bed. Erin had shut off the lights prior to getting the door, because she'd thought Oliver had finally come out to get her. So, she lay on the bed in the obscurity, trembling, petrified and in tears. She anticipated God's intervention in one way or another. God had always helped her and had always come through.

Furthermore, God had just blessed her with the husband of her dreams, so Erin couldn't see Him taking it away so soon. The thought of never seeing Oliver or her family again tormented her. She closed her eyes in misery, as this rogue hovered over her. His presence lingering over her added another layer of darkness to the already tenebrous room.

Oliver inconspicuously skulked inside of Erin's house. All of the lights were off, so he continued to slink through the dark as quietly as he could. The police were already on their way. Oliver knew Erin was in trouble, because he had heard scuffling. Notwithstanding, Erin had set her packed bags to the side of the front door, but she was nowhere to be found. Tears were in his eyes, but he blinked them back, refusing to give in to despair. Nothing was going to happen to his wife-not on his watch. Oliver assessed that even if *he* didn't make it that day, he would die knowing that Erin was safe.

Creeping to the side of Erin's opened bedroom door, Oliver peered in and caught sight of the miscreant. The reprobate had his wife pinned on the bed. At that moment, Oliver snapped. Crazed and undaunted, he charged into the bedroom at lightning speed.

Letting out an angry wail, he lunged into the man. Oliver disable the degenerate, tossing the sizable knife to a corner of the room. Taking the killer by the neck, he tossed him to the floor like a sack of potatoes.

Seeing red, he began throwing punches. "So, you want to go around killing unsuspecting women." Oliver pounded the goon. "You've taken away so much from so many people. But you made a huge mistake by coming here tonight. Touching my wife was a big mistake." Oliver's face twisted in rage, and his eyes were red in paroxysm. "You put *your* hands on *my* wife."

Erin watched how powerless the man was under Oliver's affront. She managed to roll off the bed without falling onto the floor and scurried over to stand behind her husband. Oliver had the killer on the floor, pinned with his foot on the man's throat. "You *dared* touch *my* wife," he reproached, outraged. "I could kill *you* right here, since you find pleasure in killing women. Snapping your neck would be too easy. You're a coward!" Oliver accused. "You put your hands on my wife…," Oliver kept shaking his head in the negative. "That was the mistake you made tonight."

"Oliver, step away from him," one of the officers who just happened on the scene instructed. "We'll take it from here."

Oliver stared down at the culprit in disdain. The fact that this killer had touched Erin had left him outraged.

"It's alright, Oliver," the officer said again, as police infiltrated the room.

Erin's face twisted in remorse to see Oliver so shaken. Her eyes connected to his, communicating that he allow the police to handle the rest. Seeing Erin's face drew Oliver back from the brink, and he instinctively rushed over to her. "Oh, baby… I thought I lost you." He crushed Erin in his arms. Oliver gingerly removed the tape off of her mouth and from off her bound hands.

"Ollie," Erin cried into his chest, as he held her securely. "I didn't think I'd ever see you again." Erin sobbed, as Oliver held her securely in his arms.

"I'm right here, babe. I'm right here," Oliver reassured. Cradling her head in his hands, he examined her, pertained. "Are you alright?" he confirmed.

Erin nodded, and swallowed hard. "I'm fine now that you're here. You're so brave. I can't believe you just rushed him that way," Erin said, marveling.

"I would *never* let anyone hurt you. I'd sooner die, baby." Tears rolled down Oliver's cheeks. "I'm so sorry…so sorry, honey." His face warped penitently. "I should have gotten here sooner."

"No, Ollie, it isn't your fault. You had no way of knowing this was going to happen," Erin said with a wavering voice, still trembling. "I've never been happier to see anyone in my entire life!" She surrendered to her husband's arms.

"Did he hurt you?" Oliver quizzed, holding Erin protectively in his arms.

"I'm okay," Erin said shakily.

The two watched the police take the man into custody. Before they dragged the fiend out of the bedroom, they removed the hoodie from his head, revealing his curly brown hair. The man was indeed identified as Killian Danes, the serial murderer. "His name is Killian Danes," Oliver told Erin. "He's the serial killer."

Erin nodded. "I knew who he was the moment he put his hands on me outside. Oh, Ollie, I was so scared." Erin began quivering again, and her eye deluged with tears.

"I know, baby." Oliver held her protectively in his arms and cried along with her. "I wish that had gotten here sooner. You're alright. I promise you're going to be okay." Oliver looked heavenward, and praised God that things had not turned out worse. He also thanked God for answered prayer. After having hurt so many women and families, the heinous felon would finally be off the streets.

Oliver couldn't stop thanking God for sparing his wife. "Do you *know* what broken looks like, baby?" he asked, cradling Erin's face in his hands, and brushing away her tears. *"Broken is* me without you." His face linked to hers, and they remained locked in the moment.

--

Oliver and Erin held each other supportively, as they watched the authorities lead Killian Danes away. Erin was still shaken up by what had just occurred. Oliver had promised an official statement, and to go over the technicalities of the case as soon as he could. In the days ahead he would launch a campaign to push for the prosecution Killian Danes to the maximum extent of the law.

However, just then, Erin was his top priority. He needed to take her home to ensure her safety. Kennedy and Kayden had texted him individually about the party, but Oliver resolved to return their messages just as soon as he got a moment. There were only a few hours remaining in 2019.

"Are you ready to go home, baby?" Oliver asked staring at Erin in concern. His heart twisted in knots imagining what she'd just gone through. Oliver would have wanted to spare her from it, but life seldom worked that way. That night, he realized just how powerless he was as a *man*. However, whenever human strength failed, that was when the omnipotent power of God factored in.

"Take me home, Ollie," Erin said softly. As she and Oliver dismounted the steps, she looked back at the house. The ordeal she'd just endured hardly seemed real. Now, more than ever, she understood why God had led her to stay over at Oliver's place shortly after they'd gotten married. She would never be comfortable in that house again. It also occurred to Erin that if she and Oliver hadn't gotten married, the serial killer would have found her all alone, and would have probably succeeded in his ploy.

Marrying Oliver a week ago had altered her destiny. So, marrying him had proven to be the best decision she'd ever made for a number of reasons. However traumatized she'd been by the experience, Erin realized that God had spared her life. God had also given her a chance to ring in the New Year with her incredible husband. As Oliver conveyed them away from *Silver Leaf Falls*, Erin held his hand without saying a word. It felt good just to have him close to her. Still too victimized to say very much, she silently worshipped God in her heart, and clung to her husband for dear life.

***

In spite of the ordeal which had occurred on New Year's Eve, Erin and Oliver still managed to make it to the brief New Year's Day service at *Deliverance Tabernacle*. Pastor Timmins had kept the service only one hour long. However, Erin and Oliver got the chance to catch up with some of the members of their church family. Kayden and Kennedy had been there that morning. The couple had expressed their concern and profound regret over what Erin had suffered the night before. It had been all over the news how the DA of Silver County had singlehandedly subdued the serial killer who'd sent shockwaves throughout Silver County.

"Ollie and Erin," Pastor Timmins acclaimed, catching up to the couple in the church lobby after service. Placing his hand affectionately around their waists, he affirmed, "You *know* that I will never consider the two of you as *good and married* until *I* perform the ceremony!" His bright smile transported the entire lobby.

Erin and Oliver laughed in concert.

Erin took hold of the pastor's hand, and encouraged, "Don't worry, Pastor Timmins. Oliver and I have decided to hold a *proper* wedding in the spring. Isn't that right, babe?" Erin's affectionate gaze rested on her husband.

"That's absolutely right," Oliver uplifted. "And we would *love* nothing more than for you to officiate the ceremony," Oliver told Pastor Timmins, as he slipped his arms possessively around Erin's waist.

"Wow! Okay then, I can't even stay mad at you. I *am* looking forward to officiating your *official* wedding." Pastor Timmins winked. "Let me just say how proud I am of both of you. The two of you are such an example, and I admire your steadfastness in the faith. And I might add, look how God has honored your faithfulness!"

"Thanks, Pastor Tee," both Erin and Oliver said in unison.

"So, you *will* keep me posted about wedding plans?" Paul Timmins's brows furrowed in inquisitiveness.

"Of course, … It would mean the world to us to have *your* official seal. Then, Erin and I will be *good and married*," Oliver razzed on the pastor and issued a playful wink.

"That's right," Pastor Timmins said humorously, making the couple laugh.

"Pastor Tee, we will definitely keep you posted. But, Ollie and I haven't really gone over the details yet." Erin looked up fondly at Oliver. "But we're hopeful that it will be pretty special." Her eyes shone in affect.

"There's no doubt in my mind that it will be, because the two of you *are* pretty special," Pastor Timmins affirmed.

"Thank you so much for saying that," the couple expressed kindly. Both hugged Pastor Timmins again, and wished him all the best for the New Year.

That morning, the pair had stopped to chat with virtually everyone at the church. Their church family had a gazillion questions about their secret getaway wedding. Even if it felt a bit awkward to keep retelling their story, the newlyweds gladly shared their testimony.

"Are you hungry, baby?" Oliver asked, holding Erin's hand in his, as they headed out to the church parking lot. It was late morning by then, and they were about to leave. "Do you feel like going out to *Steam and Grill*?" Oliver queried, unsure whether or not Erin just wanted to go home. "Babe…?" Oliver asked, but realized Erin was a bit distracted.

Erin froze in her steps, seeing Anika standing next to her car only feet away. There was a befuddled expression on Anika's face. "Huh?" Erin redirected towards Oliver.

"I was asking if you wanted to go for a bite, but I think you might need a moment to catch up with Anika," Oliver presumed, following Erin's gaze. "I'll go get the car," Oliver said decidedly. Oliver stared warily over at Anika. Erin and Anika had been besties for a long time, and he was aware of their falling out. In his heart he hoped that they could have a fresh start on the first day of 2020. Pressing a quick kiss to Erin's cheek, he cautiously drifted away. Oliver kept looking back to make sure Erin was okay.

Erin had already been through the wringer. So, she was reluctant to give Anika another chance to crush her heart. She and Anika had had a run in at the *Dollar Dream* convenience store a few weeks ago, and Anika had nothing positive to say.

Erin dreaded yet another verbal tongue-lashing from her ex-bestie. However, there was something on the inside driving her to connect to Anika. Erin felt extremely confident in her new status as Oliver Wright's wife. It was something that Anika had said would never happen. She had mocked and berated Erin to no end.

Erin issued a quiet but prideful smile, as she sashayed over to Anika. The closer she drew to where Anika was standing, the wider Anika's eyes and mouth gaped. "Good morning, Anika!" Erin said pleasantly, standing a few feet away.

"Morning, Erin," Anika said plainly. There was a look of utter defeat on Anika's face-almost as if she was *sorry* to see Erin.

"My *husband* and I wanted to wish you a Happy New Year!" Erin announced with dignity. "Ollie should be right back. He just went to get the car," Erin said gratifyingly.

Anika's face twisted in discontent. "I didn't think you could pull it off," she admitted.

"Pull *what* off, Anika?" Erin tested, wanting to hear the words come out of Anika's mouth.

"You *snagged* Ollie," Anika said, incredulous.

"For the record, Anika, Ollie hasn't been snagged. *God* gave us a very special miracle! *God* was so faithful in answering our *prayers*."

Anika's face turned white as a blank sheet of paper. "I really didn't think it was going to happen." She kept shaking her head contrarily.

"Well, it *has* happened," Erin reveled, flashing the 20 plus carat diamond on her finger. "And you know what the best part is?" she added.

"Why don't you tell me?" Anika said defiantly, with her arms crossed over her chest.

"The best part is that it's a blessing from God. The bible teaches that the blessing of the Lord makes a person rich, and there's no sorrow or regret attached to it (Proverbs 10:22). Taking favors from the devil by engaging in witchcraft... Guess what, Anika? There's *plenty* of sorrow there. God promised that he was going to work things out with Ollie. There were moments where *I* doubted, because the circumstances seemed so impossible. But, I'd rather place my entire life in God's hands, and to trust His wisdom than to try to manipulate circumstances on my own."

Anika's face soured as she stared into Erin's eyes. She pursed her lips to speak, but didn't know quite what to say. The relationship with her boyfriend Donovan had just gone south. She had initially employed witchcraft and divination to get the attention of the entrepreneur and potential millionaire. Donovan had broken her heart and had found someone else. Anika was still dealing with the backlash of her poor choices.

"So, to answer the question you asked that day a few weeks ago at the convenience store... Trusting in God's wisdom, his love and in his provision *worked* out just *fine* for me. I don't know where *your* life is at right now, Anika. What I *do* know is if you continue to dabble in the occult, while attending church, you're only going to curse your own blessings. You can't walk with Jesus Christ, but leave your window opened for the devil every night. You've got to make a choice. You can't straddle the fence when it comes to salvation, and where your eternity is concerned," Erin shared wisely.

Anika remained totally speechless. She felt like a fool. She had made so many mistakes, and now some of her past choices were catching up to her. She had hoped for a proposal at Christmas from Donovan. However, instead of proposing, Donovan had kicked her to the curb.

Even more embarrassing was the way in which she'd tried to shame Erin. And now, Erin was married to the DA of Silver County. Anika felt ashamed, because she had predicted that Erin's efforts at winning Oliver Wright's heart would have failed. Moreover, she had deemed that trust in God through Christ just wasn't enough. However, her former bestie had proven that God's ways were much higher.

Erin waited for Anika to speak, but the words never came. A surly and rueful expression veiled Anika's pretty face. "Think about what I said, Anika. We were close at one time, and I would hate to see you forfeit everything over things of no value. Satan shows loyalty to no one. If he *does* give you something that you want, you can rest assured that he will take away a hundred other things. Just ask Taren Cook. I'm sure you've heard that she was sentenced to a year in prison. She was also convinced that witchcraft was the answer. Just think about it."

At that moment, Oliver rolled up in his SUV. "Are you all set, baby?" he asked Erin. "Happy New Year, Anika!" he told Anika with a cordial smile.

"Happy New Year, Oliver," Anika said cursorily, with a taut expression on her face. She gave Erin a look of disdain and rolled her eyes. Inwardly, she felt conflicted. There was a part of her that realized that Erin was right. However, at that moment, her pride refused to allow her to give Erin the satisfaction.

"Well, take care of yourself, Anika," Erin said graciously. "I'm praying for you always. I hope you decide to make the right decision. Otherwise, expect to crash and burn. Satan takes no prisoners." Her eyes were critical as they speared into Anika's.

"Bye, Erin," Anika muttered, uneasily.

Oliver had already stepped out of the automobile in order to secure his wife inside. He offered Anika a faint smile before walking around to take his place behind the wheel.

Erin felt as if she'd already said too much. So, remorse veiled her sweet face as she continued to gape at Anika through the car window. She had not intended to impugn or demean her former bestie. However, Erin couldn't say that she didn't feel in some way vindicated, because Anika had dared to say that Oliver would always be just beyond her reach.

Erin delighted in God's specialty in delivering into the hands of his children the things others often said were out of their reach. So, even if she wasn't purposefully reveling in this victory, it was hard not to. God had exceeded her fondest dream by blessing her with Oliver. Erin smiled musingly seeing the expression on Anika's face, as she and Oliver pulled out of the parking lot.

The look on Anika's face was classic. Still, regardless of the happiness she felt because of all God had done in her life, Erin resolved to pray for Anika. She would continue to pray for Anika to get right with God. The truth was that Erin wanted for everyone to experience the special love God had blessed her and Oliver with.

***

"Ladies and gentleman, please help me to welcome the Governor Elect of the commonwealth of Georgia, Oliver Baron Wright!" Congressman Fields, who was affiliated with the Republican Party, gladly announced at Oliver's inauguration.

Outrageous applause and celebration resonated all through the expansive open square in *Silver Gate Main*. Erin sat in the first row along with other dignitaries, holding hers and Oliver's little girl Olivia in her arms. It had been three years since she and Oliver had married, and Olivia Emily was their first child. Erin was in tears watching her gorgeous husband take his place on the stage.

She was so proud of Oliver she could burst. However, she composed herself long enough to listen to his inaugural speech.

Oliver had everyone spellbound as he expounded on state pride, economic surpluses, education, affordable, and accessible medical health coverage for everyone in the state of Georgia. Kennedy Proctor-Bohm and her husband Kayden Bohm were sitting close by as well. Each had one of the twins, Kayden Jr. and Kent Dexter in their laps. From the looks on their faces, Erin sensed that they were just as proud of Oliver as she was.

It was nice whenever Olivia spent time with the twins. It was still hard for Erin to believe just how close she and Oliver had gotten to Kennedy and Kayden. Despite their past histories, Kennedy and Kayden were their closest friends. Erin marveled as she considered God's orchestration in all of their lives.

As she sat there within earshot of her husband's eloquent speech, Erin realized that there wasn't one thing she would have wanted to change. Olivia had finally stopped fidgeting in Erin's arms, and was down for a nap. She and Oliver had gotten Olivia up quite early that morning, so Erin wasn't at all surprised that Olivia was down.

"I am honored that you have chosen me as your governor! The state of Georgia is like no other! Some of the towns in this commonwealth may not be the most notable locations on the map. However, the state of Georgia is rich in history, culture, dignity, pride," Oliver went on to say.

"We value fellowship, camaraderie, and strive to protect the family at its core. In fact, family is our number one priority. And as your governor, I will steadfastly adhere to those principles and core beliefs. With bipartisan support, we will continue to strive for excellence, and to be that little star which shines so brightly on the map. Thank you so much for your standing behind my vision. Thank you for your votes and support." Oliver's eyes glinted in affect, as sunlight filtered through the open square. "Thank you… Thank you very much," Oliver expressed gratefully, as he took in his vast audience.

This was the moment dreams were made of! Oliver couldn't stop praising God for how far he'd come. It was only by God's favor and grace that he was now the new governor of Georgia. And yet, in the middle of the celebration, he took a moment to connect to the eyes of his beautiful wife Erin. Oliver's heart melted to see Erin holding their baby daughter Olivia.

Smiling mawkishly, his eyes fastened to hers, and he mouthed the words *"I love you!"*

Erin folded her hands together, totally stirred and gratified. Her eyes were luminous with sentimental tears, as she quietly reciprocated her husband's sentiment. *"I love you too, Ollie. I always will."*

Caught up in the ostentation and festivity, Oliver was totally euphoric. However, his excitement wasn't for the obvious reason. Even more satisfying than the promotion he'd been granted, and above his material successes, he'd found an inestimable treasure. It was *true love*- a gift given by his creator God. Oliver delighted in this victory. Nevertheless, he was humbled by the love of his beautiful wife and their adorable little girl. They were a family, and that was the accomplishment he cherished most.

THE END

Other titles from Higher Ground Books & Media:

Wise Up to Rise Up by Rebecca Benston

A Path to Shalom by Steen Burke

For His Eyes Only by John Salmon, Ph.D.

Of Love and Witches by Marjorie Joseph

32 Days with Christ's Passion by Mark Etter

Saved by a Mystery by Deborah Randall

Out of Darkness by Stephen Bowman

Breaking the Cycle by Willie Deeanjlo White

The Bottom of This by Tramaine Hannah

Chronicles of a Spiritual Journey by Stephen Shepherd

The Real Prison Diaries by Judy Frisby

My Name is Sam…And Heaven is Still Shining Through
by Joe Siccardi

Add these titles to your collection today!

http://www.highergroundbooksandmedia.com

Do you have a story to tell?

Higher Ground Books & Media is an independent Christian-based publisher specializing in stories of triumph! Our purpose is to empower, inspire, and educate through the sharing of personal experiences.

Please visit our website for our submission guidelines.

http://www.highergroundbooksandmedia.com